Also by Chris Manby

Flatmates
Second Prize
Deep Heat
Lizzie Jordan's Secret Life
Running Away from Richard
Getting Personal
Seven Sunny Days
Girl Meets Ape
Ready or Not?
The Matchbreaker

About the author

Chris Manby is editor/contributor to the *Girls' Night In* anthologies, which have so far raised more than £1,000,000 for humanitarian organisations War Child and No Strings, and topped book charts all over the world. Raised in Gloucester, Chris now lives in London.

CHRIS MANBY

Marrying for Money

HODDER

Copyright © 2007 by Chris Manby

First published in Great Britain in 2007 by Hodder & Stoughton
A division of Hodder Headline

This Hodder paperback edition 2007

The right of Chris Manby to be identified as the Author
of the Work has been asserted by her in accordance with
the Copyright, Designs and Patents Act 1988.

A Hodder paperback

5

A CIP catalogue record for this title is available from the British Library

ISBN 978 0 340 83885 3

Typeset in Plantin Light by Hewer Text UK Ltd, Edinburgh
Printed in Great Britain by Clays Ltd, St Ives plc

Hodder Headline's policy is to use papers that are natural, renewable
and recyclable products and made from wood grown in sustainable forests.
The logging and manufacturing processes are expected to conform
to the environmental regulations of the country of origin.

Hodder & Stoughton Ltd
A division of Hodder Headline
338 Euston Road
London NW1 3BH

For Sophie and Felix Hamilton, with much love.

ACKNOWLEDGEMENTS

With thanks to: the usual suspects. Send an SAE to the author c/o Hodder & Stoughton for the full, appropriately gushing, love-filled list.

PROLOGUE

May, Royal Park Hotel, London

What is the correct etiquette when the three-month-old Maltese terrier you've just picked up from Harrods' pet department poops in the middle of the carpet in a smart London hotel room? Do you:

a) *Use one of your numerous shopping bags to poop-scoop the offending deposit, then attempt to freshen up the remaining stain on the shagpile using the swanky hotel shower gel as a carpet shampoo?*

b) *Call Housekeeping, full of embarrassment and contrition, apologize profusely and offer a hundred pounds in cash to whoever has to clear the mess up?*

c) *Go shopping, leaving the dog mess exactly where you found it, with the subtle addition of a one-pound coin on a Post-it note, as a tip for the maid, right beside it?*

Alas, Marcella Hunter chose the latter route. She tapped her new puppy Choate on the nose – 'Naughty boy, Choate!' – tucked him into her crocodile-skin Hermès Birkin handbag and headed for Harvey Nicks as planned. Nothing was going to interrupt her busy shopping schedule.

Half an hour later, the hotel maid, unable to see over the enormous pile of bed linen she was carrying, put her foot right in the dog mess. That was bad enough – she was wearing open-toed sandals at the time – but it was the pound coin which really got to her. And the accompanying Post-it note, which said, '*Clean this up*'. Not '*Clean this up, please*', nor '*Clean this up, thank you*'. Just '*Clean this up*'.

It was the rudeness of the dog's owner which prompted the maid to take action. She took a teaspoon from the abandoned breakfast tray, used it to pick up the most solid part of the turd and slipped it into the toe of one of Marcella Hunter's brand-new red satin Manolos.

I

June, Little Elbow, the Hamptons

Four weeks later, Marcella Hunter had almost forgotten about her ruined Manolos (she'd pretty much forgotten about the dog as well. He was still languishing in a boarding kennel somewhere near Heathrow, awaiting the inoculations that would allow him to fly). Marcella hadn't really been that fond of the shoes. She'd bought them on a whim. They were a good half-size too small and so pointy her toes hurt if she so much as looked at them. But the red satin sling-backs were the 'it' shoe of the season and she simply had to have them.

Marcella Hunter lived her entire life in search of the latest 'it' thing. 'It' shoes, 'it' bags. The 'it' dog. If she'd devoted the same energy to finding a new species of flower or lizard as she did to keeping up with fashion she might have won a Nobel prize.

As it was, it was quite possible that Marcella might never have worn the Manolos again, but the idea that someone had taken the decision for her was just too much. She marched straight to the hotel reception, wriggling puppy still tucked under one arm, and smacked down the violated shoe on the chest-high desk, right in front of the manager and an elderly American couple visiting London to celebrate their golden wedding anniversary.

'I want to know who did this!' Marcella demanded loudly. 'Who put this shit in my sling-back?'

The golden-wedding couple recoiled in horror and said they would check into the Dorchester.

The maid on duty, when confronted, claimed that the dog must have relieved itself directly into the shoe. This turd, the maid insisted, was a different turd entirely from the one Marcella had so kindly drawn her attention to with the Post-it note (and which the maid had, of course, carefully cleared up). Marcella merely narrowed her eyes at that explanation and reminded the manager that she was a regular customer who spent more than a month's worth of the maid's wages on room service every time she visited London on one of her shopping weekends. She demanded the girl's resignation and it was duly given. Along with the cost of the shoes, of course. All six hundred pounds of it, which was pretty much exactly what the maid earned in four weeks. In all probability, the affected shoe could have been cleaned, but together with its pristine twin it was left in a wastepaper bin when Marcella flew back to New York. First class. And without the dog.

A month later, on a pretty June evening at her beach house in Little Elbow, a tiny hamlet situated on the coastal road between East Hampton and Montauk, Marcella slipped on the pair of shoes she'd actually bought on that ill-timed trip to Harvey Nichols with her puppy in her handbag. These newer shoes were much more comfortable than the red Manolos. They were 1920s in style: silver satin, beautifully beaded, with a low Louis heel and a strap across the instep to hold them firmly in place while dancing. Absolutely perfect for the theme of Marcella's birthday party, which was, as befitted the venue with its fabulous ocean view, 'The Great Gatsby'.

Marcella smoothed down the silver flapper dress she had specially commissioned to match the shoes and admired the sharp dark-brown bobbed wig that covered her straight blonde hair. She kicked up a heel in a parody of the Charleston to see her fringed hem jiggle. Perfect. She might have been on her way to meet F. Scott Fitzgerald himself.

Outside, Marcella's staff flitted around the garden putting the finishing touches to the party scene. The housekeeper, the gardener and the pool boy had swapped their casual clothes for cool, crisp whites. The band had arrived – a five-piece jazz ensemble flown in especially from Louisiana. They were tuning up their instruments in the newly constructed poolside gazebo that would act as a bandstand.

On the other side of the pool, a barbecue had been lit. The caterers were taking Saran Wrap off the canapés. Three hundred crystal champagne flutes were polished and waiting to be filled with vintage bubbly for the first toast of the evening. Which would be to Marcella, of course.

Marcella was determined that her twenty-seventh birthday party would be the perfect start to another perfect summer. Even the weather was cooperating – it was the warmest June evening in years. This would be the party that everybody talked about. (At least until the beginning of September, when Marcella's annual Labor Day party would mark the official end of the season.) Everyone who was anyone in Little Elbow and its surrounding towns had been invited. There would be heirs and spares and self-made billionaires. The crème de la crème of East Coast society. The very best fancy-dress shop in New York announced that it had hired out all its flapper dresses within half an hour of Marcella sending out her 'save the date' e-mail. The evening would be spectacular. And Marcella would be the belle of it all.

* * *

Marcella Hunter was used to being the centre of attention. She was the richest girl in town. In fact, she was probably the richest girl in the county. If the average upper-class gal was born with a silver spoon in her mouth, Marcella got the whole golden shovel.

She was sole heiress to a family fortune made in the lumber business. Wood chips and pulp. After that unglamorous start, a series of clever investments meant that by the time Marcella's trust fund matured, it would have been hard for the most careless shopaholic in the United States of America to spend the Hunter fortune as quickly as it continued to grow. Marcella did her best, of course. She started by having the house in Little Elbow remodelled at enormous expense, with Italian marble floors, antique French furniture and wood panelling in the dining room made from some of the world's most endangered trees.

Marcella made much of the fact that her family had lived in Little Elbow for almost 150 years. She talked particularly proudly about her paternal grandfather, the visionary wood-chip magnate Edgar Hunter, who landscaped the beautiful gardens that swept down to the sea. Edgar Hunter had a keen interest in horticulture and the land – he planted the wind-break of arbor vitae himself, placing each sapling in the ground with infinite care. As Marcella stressed to anyone who would listen, Edgar Hunter wasn't afraid to get his hands dirty and work alongside his staff.

Now Marcella summoned her almost legal housekeeper, Anjelica, with the little silver bell on her dressing table.

'Necklace,' she barked when Anjelica arrived seconds later.

Anjelica dutifully fastened the diamond necklace around Marcella's neck, taking care not to touch her mistress's skin as she did so. Marcella didn't thank her. It didn't even cross her mind. She was too busy examining her choice of accessories for the evening.

The necklace had belonged to her maternal grandmother. It was a wedding gift, which passed to Marcella when her grandmother fell off a diving board into an empty swimming pool after one too many gin fizzes. She had been wearing the necklace at the time. But the tragic history of Marcella's diamonds was forgotten now. All that mattered was that the brilliant white stones complemented the silver dress perfectly.

As Anjelica hovered and awaited further instructions, Marcella pulled on a pair of pale silver silk gloves and topped them off with two more enormous ice-white sparklers – one was a cocktail ring that had belonged to her unfortunate grandmother, the other her own late mother's engagement ring (coincidentally, her mother had also died in a pool. A full one this time . . .). Marcella picked up a cigarette holder and the look was complete. She glanced over at Anjelica to see the approval in the girl's dark eyes, then dismissed her with a flick of her hand.

Outside, the valets – two of the pool boy's cousins – parked the first of a dozen top-of-the-range Mercedes that would arrive over the next couple of hours. (The cousins claimed to have great experience of driving luxury cars. 'Lexus, BMW, we drive anything.' Marcella didn't realize their experience was of the 'grand theft auto' kind.)

Moments later, Marcella heard a holler of 'Par-taaaaaayyyyy!' as the Mendelsohn brothers staggered into the marble-floored hallway, carrying the brown-paper-bagged bottles they had been swigging from en route.

'No, but you can suck my dick,' cried Jonathan Mendelsohn, educated at the best schools in the USA and heir to a fortune made in religious publishing, when Anjelica asked whether she could relieve him of his coat.

The festivities had begun.

2

The Grosvenor sisters – Charity and Grace – had no need for valet parking, coming as they were from the house just next door. Unlike most of the guests, who had been preparing for this special evening for the best part of a month, the sisters cobbled together their costumes in something of a hurry. Their invitation to the party had arrived just a day before. As had Charity and Grace. This was their first ever summer in the Hamptons.

The sisters were renting the old place known as the Rose House – a beautiful colonial-style residence right on the beach. The Rose House had never been rented out before. In fact, until that year it had been pretty much uninhabitable for as long as anybody could remember – abandoned and boarded shut like a tenement.

Summer after summer, rich Manhattanites holidaying in the chi-chi beach town of Little Elbow did their best to find out who owned the place and whether they might take an offer. But no offer was ever accepted. The house stayed in the hands of heaven only knew who (no one – not even a gardener – had been seen there since the 1970s) and year on year, it fell a little further into disrepair. A few more tiles fell from the roof. The white paint on the clapboard peeled and flaked beneath the hot summer sun and harsh winter frost. The brambles in the garden grew a little higher until eventually the place started to look more like Sleeping Beauty's palace during the hundred-year snooze than a 'magnificent example of the colonial style', as the local real estate agents might have put it if they only had the chance.

The house became an eyesore. A total wreck. More offensively to the Wall Streeters with second homes in the town, it was also a shocking waste of money. The Rose House had direct beach access, for goodness' sake! That kind of feature was worth a *bomb*. So, when the contractors arrived one sunny morning and took down the boards, it was the talk of the town.

First the plantation shutters were opened to let light into rooms that had been dark for decades. A truck arrived to take away the old sanitary ware and the ancient furniture that had been crumbling away in the dark (a local antique dealer actually wept when he saw so many Arts and Crafts masterpieces reduced to sticks on a bonfire). The broken and missing roof tiles were painstakingly replaced. The peeling paint on the outside of the house was burned away and replaced with a coat of pristine white. Eventually curtains were hung at the windows. A new red-painted mailbox appeared at the gate on to the street.

The garden was the final part of the Rose House estate to undergo a transformation. It looked like a job for ten men. Twenty men, even. With flame-throwers. But like a prince hacking his way through the enchanted forest to find his sleeping bride, it was a single gardener who cut down the weeds and replanted the roses that had given the house its name. Roses fit for any fairy-tale princess.

With the house restored to its former glory, everyone waited eagerly for the return of the mysterious family who owned it. But within days of the lone gardener planting the beautiful flowers that lined the path to the door, the local real-estate agent announced that the house had been put up for rent and found some tenants within the hour. Before anyone else even had a chance to get a snoop around!

The Grosvenor sisters of London would be arriving in June.

'The Grosvenor sisters of London?' said Marcella, when she heard. 'Should I know them?'

'Almost certainly,' said her friend and house guest Simon McDonnough (third son of the Clan Chief McDonnough), from Scotland.

Simon was one of those ultra-smart Scotsmen without a trace of a Scottish accent. Marcella met him at a Burns Night party in a Manhattan loft and adopted him immediately. He seemed well worth adopting. His family had owned half the Highlands. He had three different tartans: hunting, fishing and dancing, or something like that.

'Do you know them?' Marcella persisted. 'These Grosvenor girls?'

'The name rings a bell,' Simon said casually. He didn't look up from his book.

'Hmmm.'

There was nothing that discomfited Marcella more than not knowing someone worth knowing. And if Simon McDonnough knew of these girls, then they must be worth knowing. Simon often reminded her that before he relocated to the United States to try his luck as a documentary director, he had moved in the very best of British circles. In fact he was one of London's 'most invited' bachelors, according to some glossy monthly that had an annual 'eligibles' party (the Princes William and Harry were also on the list, but alas, Simon hadn't kept a copy).

'Yes,' said Simon firmly. 'Now I think about it, I'm sure I've met them before.'

But he wouldn't elaborate. And Marcella's surreptitious Google search threw up nothing useful at all. No pictures. No profiles. Nothing.

They must be important, though, Marcella decided, or at least very rich, if they could afford to take a rental next door to her own place. Two years before, the house on the other side of the Hunter estate had been rented out between May and the end of September for close on fifty thousand dollars a month, without staff. Little Elbow was a very exclusive town.

Thank goodness, thought Marcella, these new London girls would be right on her doorstep and thank goodness she would be throwing the first party of the year. It wouldn't do for some other local hostess to get to know them first. Marcella arranged for a basket of fruit and flowers to be delivered to the Rose House the moment the girls arrived. Tucked in next to a perfectly ripe pineapple was one of her beautiful silver-edged party invitations. It was a lovely gift, so Marcella was more than a little put out that they didn't rush right over to thank her.

In fact, the sisters made themselves known to no one in the twenty-four hours before Marcella's party, though rumours abounded. They were terribly wealthy. They were both very beautiful, said the mailman, who glimpsed them on his rounds. The younger sister had worked as a fashion model in Milan. The older sister had dated Jude Law. Linda Deuble, the real-estate agent, thought they might be directly related to the Queen . . .

'The American embassy in London is in a square named after one of their ancestors,' she said authoritatively.

Marcella couldn't wait to meet them. If they were related to the royal family, then she was damn well going to make sure they got her invited to a garden party next time she was in London. If not lunch with Liz herself. And if the older sister had really dated Jude Law, then so much the better. Hopefully she and the movie star were still on speaking terms. It was just a matter of time before Jude was single again and in need of introductions.

It was all very exciting. In the mysterious girls next door, Marcella saw her entrée to a fabulous new world of British glitterati. She imagined polo with the Princes. Premieres in Leicester Square . . . Not that she would let the sisters know she was in the least bit interested in their connections, of course. She was going to play it very cool. The key to infiltrating their glamorous world was that they see her as their social equal. Which she was, make no mistake about that. Marcella counted the Hilton sisters – Paris and Nicky – as friends.

'OK, then,' she admitted when pushed. 'Acquaintances.'

'What are you plotting?' asked Simon McDonnough, noticing the far-away look in his hostess's eyes.

'World domination,' Marcella half joked.

3

By nine o'clock the birthday party was in full swing. The take-up rate for Marcella's invitations was in the region of ninety-nine per cent (it would have been a hundred but a cyclone kept a few private jets stuck in Palm Beach). The band was playing. People weren't dancing but they were definitely swaying. Actually, the Mendelsohn brothers *were* dancing. Either that or *fitting*, Marcella observed as they pogoed dangerously close to the pool. The champagne was almost finished. The lethal fruit punch had already claimed the first of its victims. Marcella fully expected that some of the cars handed over to the valet parkers would still be in her driveway the following afternoon.

Marcella drifted about her guests gathering compliments. Some of them were really getting into the spirit of things, talking as if it were 1925.

'That dress is just *divine*.'

'Your hair! So *delightful*. Have you really had it cut and dyed?'

Marcella smiled and gave her new bob a bounce.

'You look fabulous as a brunette.'

'Perhaps I'll have it done for real if I decide I'm having more fun,' Marcella laughed, using the 'tinkling laugh' she had decided upon to complement her outfit.

Simon even went so far as to sing three verses of 'The Way You Look Tonight' in Marcella's honour. Excruciating.

Everybody looked wonderful. A Great Gatsby theme always ensured elegance (this was the third time Marcella had thrown a Gatsby bash since remodelling the house). Even the guys who complained about having to wear ties scrubbed up when they realized that every man looks better in a tuxedo. Jamie Iley was looking particularly great, thought Marcella. She caught his eye across the corner of the Olympic-sized swimming pool. Perhaps he would be the lucky boy who got to stay in Marcella's Moroccan-themed bedroom that night.

Perhaps it was time to begin the dancing properly. Marcella started to head towards him with the intention of leading her target on to the floor for a smooch.

'Marcella.' A hand on her elbow brought her to a halt.

'Oh. Choate.'

Marcella turned to greet the man after whom her dog had been named with far less enthusiasm than she reserved for his fluffy namesake. The real Choate Fitzgerald, heir to Fitzgerald Lumber, Hunter Lumber's biggest rival, was anything but fluffy. A rather stiff man with his short blond hair combed flat against his head, he looked, unlike most of the other guests, as though he really had just teleported in from the 1920s. So many of the others got the clothes right but kept their hair and make-up true to the twenty-first century, rather spoiling the overall effect.

Choate smiled a little sheepishly, as though he knew he had interrupted a manhunt. For her part, Marcella wasn't trying terribly hard to disguise the fact that she had been on her way somewhere else and was frankly irritated by this delay.

'Happy birthday,' said Choate.

'Thank you,' said Marcella.

'I brought you a gift.'

'Oh, thank you!' Marcella's face was momentarily transformed as Choate pulled a necklace-sized package from his jacket pocket. It was carefully wrapped and tied with a ribbon. Marcella discarded the ribbon and tore off the blue paper with unseemly haste.

'What can it be?' she asked playfully. 'Choate, have you been to Harry Winston, you naughty man?'

Choate blushed. He hadn't been to Harry Winston.

The box contained a circuit-testing device.

'When you told me that the lights in the pool house kept going out for no good reason, I thought what you need is one of these,' he explained.

'Well, thank you. It's very thoughtful.'

Marcella placed the circuit tester on the nearest table with a barely concealed sigh.

'I'll pick it up later. Right now, I've got to . . .' She gesticulated in the general direction of her other guests and waited for Choate to excuse himself. He didn't. Damn.

'How are you?' he asked.

'I'm fine,' said Marcella.

'You look . . . er, you look beautiful tonight.'

'Thank you. Thank you for coming along.'

Marcella was already turning back towards Jamie Iley.

'I was wondering if perhaps, later, we might . . .'

'Choate, I'm the hostess. I'm going to be *really* busy all evening,' Marcella replied, without waiting to hear what they 'might' do. Knowing Choate, he was probably going to suggest they try out the circuit tester. A circuit tester! *Puh-leese!* What kind of birthday present was *that*?

'Just a few minutes of your time,' Choate said plaintively.

Marcella pretended not to hear his plea. 'You know plenty of people here, don't you, Choate? Look, there's Eddy Kitsantonis.' She pointed him in the direction of the sec-ond-most boring man in the place. 'Help yourself to punch!'

she concluded. It was an invitation that was meant as a dismissal. She might as well have shouted, 'Get lost!'

Choate retreated, his expression as hangdog as the puppy's when Marcella left it in quarantine without so much as a squeaky toy. But Marcella didn't care. She quickly reoriented herself in search of Jamie Iley. Only to catch him putting his arm around Shereen Petersen.

'Damn,' Marcella muttered. Choate had ruined her chances. His timing had always been bad. But she wasn't going to turn back to him and get stuck making small talk about stock options or, even worse, DIY, so she made a beeline for Stephanie Blank, the potato-chip heiress, instead. Stephanie was a bitch on a stick but at least she always had gossip. Choate, on the other hand, thought gossip was pointless and cruel. What a bore.

'Where are those English girls?' was the first thing Stephanie – Marcella's best 'frenemy' – asked.

'They've been invited,' Marcella replied. 'I'm sure they'll be along any minute.'

'Good. Because God knows we need some new blood around here. Is it just me or is this party *deadly* dull? I don't think I have been this bored since that Republican benefit at the Planetarium.'

Marcella stiffened. The Republican Party benefit at the Planetarium was pretty hard to beat on the dullness scale. No hot waiters. No vodka luge. Nothing.

'Oh God, Marcella. I'm sorry. That sounded *so rude*. For a moment there I completely forgot it was *your* birthday! I mean, I'm sure you've done your best.' Stephanie smiled. Marcella smiled back. Neither girls' eyes crinkled at the edges. These were the smiles of two cats squaring up in an alley.

'Where's the Brit pussy?' asked Bradley, the last Mendelsohn brother standing, as he lurched on by.

'They've been invited,' Marcella said again through clenched teeth.

When she was asked for the tenth time what had happened to the Brit chicks, Marcella decided she wasn't happy about it at all. Somehow, people seemed to have forgotten that Marcella always had a party at the beginning of June and that the reason for the party was to celebrate *her birthday*. Not to welcome the English girls to town. Yet people were talking about them as though they were the guests of honour. And by leaving it so late to make their appearance, the Grosvenor sisters were acting as though they *were* the guests of honour!

'I expect they'll be along any moment,' said Marcella brightly. Again.

They arrived at exactly the same time as the birthday cake.

The grand entrance wasn't deliberate. Grace and Charity Grosvenor simply happened to walk out through the French doors that led from the conservatory into the garden just as the band went quiet. A spotlight was focused upon Marcella, specially positioned to highlight her fabulous heirloom jewellery to best effect. She was beaming at her guests, waiting for complete quiet, unaware that two girls in 1940s-style dresses had just stepped into view behind her and that suddenly her four-tier birthday cake wasn't the focus of anyone's interest but hers.

'I think we got the period wrong,' said one of the sisters, in a small voice that was nonetheless picked up by Marcella's microphone and boomed to the entire garden. 'Was Great Gatsby set in the nineteen twenties?'

A roar of friendly laughter greeted her mistake.

After that, Marcella had no choice but to introduce the late arrivals to the cream of Little Elbow and welcome them on the whole town's behalf.

'Well, here they are, ladies and gentlemen,' she said. 'The glorious Grosvenor girls.'

4

'How lovely to meet you at last,' said Marcella, when her speech was over (she had to cut it short) and everyone was back on the hunt for free booze and barbecue ribs (totally against Marcella's current diet principles but an essential for the male guests). 'I was beginning to think that perhaps you hadn't moved in yet. Did you get my flowers?'

'Oh yes,' said the older one.

'And the fruit? I'm so sorry,' Marcella added smoothly. 'I should have brought the basket round myself. It was *totally* remiss of me to have a gift delivered straight from the store. It's just that I've been so busy preparing for my party . . .'

'Oh no. We should have . . . thank you. We ought to have come over right away. We've been a bit jet-lagged.'

'Transatlantic travel is *so* much harder on the body now that Concorde is out of action,' Marcella commiserated. 'I'm Marcella Hunter. But then you already know that. Seeing as how this is my birthday party and you arrived in the middle of my speech.'

'We're so sorry about that. Happy birthday. I'm Charity Grosvenor,' said the older girl.

'And I'm Grace,' said the younger one. The prettier one, Marcella noted at once.

Charity Grosvenor was passably good looking, Marcella thought. About Marcella's age. She had a good figure and nicely highlighted hair that complemented her lightly tanned skin. But Grace Grosvenor was stunning. She had the ice-queen beauty of a Hitchcock blonde. She could have been a supermodel. Except that she didn't have the outsized lollipop head and wrap-around eyes so many of the top models have in real life. Marcella was immediately on the lookout for Grace's fatal flaw. A lisp or a limp, perhaps. Either would do.

'Charity and Grace,' Marcella mused. 'How unusual. How biblical. So how long are you staying here in Little Elbow?' she asked.

'The whole summer.'

'Really? Whyever do you want to spend the summer in this boring old town?' Marcella rolled her eyes theatrically. 'I thought that everyone stayed in London until the beginning of August at least. You're missing so much of the season over there. Wimbledon. All the balls.'

'Tennis balls?' asked Grace.

Marcella smiled weakly. An inability to tell jokes. Perhaps that was Grace's Achilles heel.

'But we're here at your party instead,' Charity interrupted. 'Makes a nice change from doing the boring old season back home. Ascot, Wimbledon, the Serpentine Galley party . . . yawn, yawn, yawn. Same old, same old, every year.'

'I know *exactly* what you mean,' said Marcella.

'I must say everyone has made an effort this evening,' said Charity.

'They certainly have.'

'And your dress is particularly beautiful.'

'How kind of you to notice.' Marcella beamed. 'I had it specially commissioned to go with my shoes.'

'It's lovely,' said Charity. 'We feel such idiots, dressed like this.'

'Oh, but you look *great*,' said Marcella, larding the emphasis on the last word. 'And you're so *late* that almost everyone is too hammered to notice you're dressed in completely the wrong style. Besides, you're only twenty years out. Perhaps F. Scott Fitzgerald isn't quite the international literary force we Americans like to think he is. Good job because I was about to bore everyone rigid with a little reading from his work when you arrived. It's a tradition. I do it every year when I'm welcoming people to my birthday party.'

'I'm really sorry we walked in right in the middle of your speech,' said Charity for about the fifth time in as many minutes.

'Oh, that is quite OK,' said Marcella. 'Let me introduce you to some people.' She linked her arms through the sisters' so that she had one on either side. 'Everyone worth knowing is right here on my lawn.'

Marcella walked the girls around the garden, stopping by each group of people and reeling off hundreds of names, though she never let the sisters remain anywhere long enough to actually have a conversation. It was pretty clear to anyone watching what was going on. It wasn't just about being a good hostess. Marcella was marking her territory, making it known to her other guests that these new glamorous English girls were to be her friends first and foremost. She had appointed herself gatekeeper to the social scene of Little Elbow and she would decide who got the chance to chat. At least for that night.

And what a lovely night it was. Truly idyllic. The blazing heat of the day had subsided to a gentle, caressing warmth, softened by a sea breeze that lifted the scent of the garden flowers into the air and stirred it around like a magical mist that intoxicated as well as any champagne cocktail. Meanwhile, the dying light of the sun cast a delicate soft-focus glow that made the old look young and everyone look beautiful.

And of course, the house itself – a sprawling two-storey Palladian that was turning from icing sugar white to candy love-heart pink as the sun set – was very impressive.

'It's like a dream,' said Grace when Marcella had them pause at the top of a sloping lawn to get the best view of the garden that led gracefully down to the sand. 'Your garden looks wonderful. And I love the music.'

'Having the band flown in cost me twenty-five thousand dollars but I'd say it makes the party,' said Marcella. 'You've got to have good music. And compared to the cost of the caterers!' Marcella rolled her eyes. 'Come on. A view's a view. You need to meet some more folk.'

Back in the thick of the action, Marcella glowed as she pointed out more major players and gave their potted biographies.

'Stephanie Blank,' she whispered. 'Potato-chip heiress. Spent half last year in rehab in Arizona. Prescription pills and bulimia. I shouldn't be telling you that but, hey, it's a totally open secret.

'Jamie Iley. New money. Father made a fortune in tele-coms. Now he *should* be in rehab. He lives on pills and booze. Shereen Petersen. I don't know where she came from but she's a first-class bitch.'

Though she wasn't within hearing distance of Marcella's comment, Shereen suddenly looked up. Marcella flashed an enormous smile at the girl who had usurped her in Jamie's affections. Shereen gave her a wave in return. 'Watch that girl,' Marcella hissed to the sisters. 'She will stab you in the back as soon as look at you. Never a kind word to say about anyone.'

'Really?' said Charity. 'That's not nice.'

'Mendelsohn brothers.' Marcella waved in the direction of a pair of well-shod feet sticking out from beneath a tablecloth.

'Everyone should know Johnnie and Brad. Jonathan is the one under the table. Can't hold his drink. It's a family trait. Bradley is the one with his face on his plate. Can't hold his drink either . . . Anjelica.' Marcella summoned her housekeeper. 'Would you make sure that Bradley Mendelsohn doesn't actually inhale any food?' She turned back to the sisters. 'I do not want to have an air ambulance landing on my lawn this year. Took *for-ever* for the grass to grow back . . .

'That girl in the corner, crying into a tablecloth, is Jonathan Mendelsohn's ex-girlfriend, Darleesa Cahuenga. Claims she was a Victoria's Secret model but I've never seen her in the catalogue. And those aren't her real breasts.'

The sisters goggled.

'It's completely obvious. Emily Barham had hers done by the same surgeon.' Marcella pointed out a woman dressed in green. 'See how they're almost identical. Good job they got their noses done by different people. They might have ended up looking like twins!' She laughed her tinkling laugh.

'Sarah Rabin, in the pink dress, used to be quite a pretty girl. Had botox. Took her nephews to the theme park the same afternoon. Teacup ride moved the stuff all over her face and she looked like Deputy Dawg for three months.' Sarah looked in Marcella's direction. 'Hey, Sarah. Looking lovely tonight . . .'

'Why thank you, Marcella!' Sarah called back.

'Shame about the jowls,' Marcella half whispered to her new best friends.

'Oh, there's Titchy Henderson,' Marcella carried on. 'Hardly "titchy" these days. When she came off the booze, she went straight on to the chocolate. She was on the booze because her fiancé ran off with a gardener. A male gardener,' Marcella added in a whisper. 'Such a shame. How on earth do you come back from that?'

'I don't know,' Charity admitted.

'It's not even as though he was the first fiancé she mislaid. Oh, that's quite funny. Mi*slaid*. You didn't hear it from me, but basically the reason fiancé number one broke up with her is that she wasn't a patch on a certain other girl in the sack.'

The sisters looked at Marcella quizzically.

'Oh, whatever must you think? You're looking at me like *I'm* the boyfriend-stealer.'

'Oh no, we . . .' Charity began.

'Well, it's hardly stealing if you leave them unattended, is it?' Marcella winked. She spotted another character in need of elaboration.

'Chelsy Cialdini, with the feather in her hair, used to have the nickname "Half and Half".'

'Half and half?' asked Grace.

'Like the creamer. On account of her being born with a vagina *and* a penis. She had the penis taken off in eighth grade. That was back in California. Her family brought her to New York to start over. But you can't really escape your past these days, can you? Not now there's the Internet.'

'Poor girl.'

'Poor half-girl!' Marcella tittered. 'With a jawline like that, she might have been better hanging on to the dick. Especially if she's interested in Ralph Sacks,' Marcella continued, indicating the man at Chelsy's side. 'Really, there isn't a closet big enough. Gay, gay, gay, gay, gay . . .' Marcella pointed out five other random guys in quick succession. 'FYI.'

'Thank you,' said Charity.

'You know,' Marcella said suddenly, 'you girls are going to *love* it here. Everyone is so friendly and warm to one another. Everyone looks out for everyone else. There's no nasty gossiping or sniping behind people's backs and . . . Oh, I didn't know Jenny Nixon was going to come. I would have thought she would be too ashamed to show her face after that scandal with the purse at Hermès . . .' Marcella gave the girl in question a friendly wave. 'Now, what was I saying? Oh, yes. You are going to love it here. It's the nicest town in the USA. People are just so lovely.' She froze. 'Oh, my God. Not again. Ladies, will you excuse me? I'm avoiding Choate Fitzgerald. He's America's most boring man.'

And with that, she flounced away, leaving the Grosvenor girls to make their own introductions.

5

It wasn't until three o'clock the following afternoon that the last of Marcella's party guests finally left. Bradley Mendelsohn was the very last one to go. He had spent the night under the decking by the pool house and was discovered only when one of the gardener's dogs chased a rabbit under there and pulled the billionaire-in-waiting out.

Marcella was glad to see the back of Bradley (which was covered, Lord only knew how, in vomit) and to have the house to herself once more. Well, almost to herself. As Marcella was fixing herself some breakfast/early supper (or rather, waiting for Anjelica to fix her some breakfast/early supper), her one official house guest stepped into the sunroom, yawning ostentatiously. Simon McDonnough still wasn't dressed. Instead he was wearing just the paisley-print silk dressing gown he claimed had been given to his grandfather by the Duchess of Devonshire. As he sat down, it fell open to reveal a hairy thigh.

'Not this early in the day, please,' said Marcella.

Simon pulled the fabric back over his legs. Not that they were such bad legs.

Simon McDonnough was very happy that his national dress included a skirt. He was a very handsome man. There was a hint of Clark Gable to his look at the moment, accentuated by the thin moustache he had been sporting for a couple of weeks in preparation for Marcella's party.

Now that the party was over, Simon no longer needed his moustache but he had decided to keep it anyway. It was, as one party guest had put it, quite *louche*, and louche was a word Simon approved of. It could be applied to most areas of his life.

'I'm in a vile mood,' Marcella warned him now.

'So am I. Why on earth did you let me drink so much?'

'Because you're unstoppable.'

'That's true,' Simon mused, a little pleased with himself. Unstoppable was unstoppable, even if it was only in the matter of inebriation. Almost as good as louche. 'But why are you in a vile mood, my American princess? Didn't you have fun at your party? I thought it was an absolute triumph.'

'I *was* having a wonderful time. Until *they* arrived.'

Simon knew at once whom she meant by 'they'.

'Can you believe they interrupted my speech? How wrong is *that*?'

'Oh, I don't think they meant to upstage you. I imagine they were pretty embarrassed, having dressed from the wrong period.'

'So they should be! That's another thing. What kind of morons don't know that *The Great Gatsby* was set in the 1920s? They did it deliberately to make themselves stand out more!'

'I'm sure the thought never crossed their minds,' said Simon, marvelling once again at how little girls need to do to secure each other's disapprobation. 'Anyway, what does it matter? You looked beautiful in that silver dress. You were the belle of the ball.'

'Hmmmph,' said Marcella.

She hadn't felt like the belle of the ball by the end of it. She had slept alone. Jamie Iley had gone home with Shereen

Petersen (that was them off her Labor Day guest list) and the Mendelsohn brothers had been covered in vomit when they made their separate consecutive overtures. A very disappointing result. Surely the birthday girl deserved a little action? But Marcella didn't tell Simon any of that. Instead she said, 'Anyway, I've invited them to dinner.'

'Who?'

'The Grosvenor sisters, of course.'

'But I thought you'd decided you didn't like them.'

'I don't. But Stephanie Blank has invited them to her house on Thursday, so we're having them here on Wednesday.'

Simon shook his head and smiled.

Over tea in the Grosvenor household, Charity and Grace were also reliving the party. Specifically, they were reliving Grace's half-hour-long turn about the dance floor with Choate Fitzgerald.

Choate was already making a beeline for Marcella and her new friends when Marcella ran away. What could he do except pretend he had been aiming for the sisters? Grace felt extremely sorry for the chap, though it quickly became clear that Marcella was right. He wasn't exactly full of social grace.

'I don't do small talk,' was his opening gambit, as he sprayed the girls with crumbs from a canapé he hadn't quite finished.

'But I bet you can dance,' said Grace.

She was correct to surmise that he could, sort of, dance. And oddly, he could also make small talk while dancing. After a fashion.

'Though all he ever talked about was money!' Grace complained.

'That's because he's got so much,' said Charity. 'I imagine it's quite preoccupying to be so very blessed.'

'Everybody here has so much. And they're not afraid to show it. Can you believe someone would have valet parking for a house party?' said Grace. 'And a five-piece band and ice sculptures as big as people *and* a champagne fountain! It's not even as though it was a wedding!'

Charity laughed at her little sister's theatrical dismay.

'This town is completely unbelievable,' Grace continued. 'I mean, on the surface it looks like Hicksville – the post office is in someone's front room, for heaven's sake – but I haven't seen that many serious cars in one place since we watched Princess Diana's funeral go down the Mall. And the jewellery! I'm sure most of those diamonds were real.'

'What did I tell you?'

'It's definitely not Littlehampton,' Grace mused.

'Thank God.' Charity shuddered.

'Did you spot any millionaires you could marry?' Grace smiled.

'Give me a couple of days.'

'And what did you think of her?' Grace asked suddenly. 'Marcella Hunter?'

'She's a bitch on wheels.'

'You're telling me. Was there a single person at that party she actually liked? I don't know why she bothered to throw a party for so many people she hates . . .'

'Unless she intended to punish them with the canapés,' said Charity.

Both sisters pulled faces of distaste as they remembered the food. Pretentious was the only possible adjective.

'I can't believe we ended up next door to her. Are you sure she's the same girl?'

Charity nodded. 'Must be.'

'Do you think she recognized you?'

'No. But even if she did, I don't suppose for one moment she remembers where we met.'

'Do you think we made a good impression?' Grace asked.

'Better than the one I made on the gardener,' said Charity.

6

Two days earlier

The Grosvenor sisters arrived in Little Elbow by train. Smart Manhattanites either drove or took the Jitney out to the Hamptons, but Charity was reluctant to try to navigate her way out of the city in a hire car (her sister refused full stop) and Grace always got travel sick on coaches, which is all the Jitney turned out to be.

'How disappointing. It sounded like it would be pulled by horses,' said Grace.

So they took the Long Island Rail Road from Penn Station instead, changed at a place called Jamaica, which was nothing like its namesake, and endured a fairly dull three-hour ride to East Hampton, where they were met by the real-estate agent, Linda Deuble, who had offered to drive them the last five miles.

Linda Deuble was exactly as Charity had imagined her on the basis of their few brief transatlantic telephone conversations. She had the kind of bright blonde ultra-coiffeured hair you could bounce coins off. Her coral-coloured lipstick was perfect (if unflattering). She was wearing an immaculate suit, in pale taupe linen. The jacket was neatly buttoned, even though by the time the sisters arrived around lunchtime it was getting uncomfortably hot.

'We're just so happy to have you here!' Linda trilled as the girls stepped off the train.

'A real Stepford Wife,' Grace mouthed to Charity as Linda clipped ahead of them to the car, moving twice as fast as they could in the heat despite the fact that she was dragging both their cases.

'Come on, come on,' she shouted back at them. 'I'm taking you the scenic route.'

Really all the routes around this part of Long Island were scenic. The road between East Hampton and Little Elbow was picture-postcard pretty. It was lined with tall trees shading the sort of beautiful houses that warrant a six-page spread in *Architectural Digest*. From time to time, the girls glimpsed the coast. And it was a fabulous day on which to first see this particular coast. The clear blue sky reflected in the water made the sea look almost tropical. On the horizon, a hundred white sails fluttered like cabbage white butterflies on the wing as sailing enthusiasts made the most of the gentle wind. It was the kind of day that makes you believe the United States really is God's own country. Blessed in every way. Linda Deuble commented to that very effect.

The journey to the Rose House would take the girls right through the centre of Little Elbow.

'Everyone knows everyone here,' said Linda as she slowed her car down.

It wouldn't be hard, Charity decided. The sign at the start of the town announced a population of less than a thousand. Fewer than the number of pupils at her secondary school.

'I'll give you the tour,' said Linda.

Though it was just three hours away from the Big Apple, Little Elbow could not have been more different from

Manhattan. It was like a film set. Not that Manhattan doesn't feel like a film set when you first visit. But this was the set for an entirely different movie. A romantic comedy rather than a thriller. Something starring a hero who starts out shy and taciturn but ultimately proves himself to be strong and thoughtful and sexy as hell . . .

The dinky houses that lined the main road through Little Elbow were painted candy colours and surrounded by gardens as neat as game boards. Charity wondered whether there was a prescribed height for hedges. The natives too looked as though a Hollywood wardrobe mistress had dressed them. There was something faintly 1950s about the way everybody was attired, Charity observed. The edginess of Manhattan's high fashion had definitely not made it this far.

Several locals waved at the car as Linda Deuble drove on by.

'I hope you're bringing those girls to the Bible brunch!' called one lady as Linda paused at the traffic lights.

Grace and Charity shared a look. You could live in London for twenty years and never know your neighbours. Ten minutes in Little Elbow and they'd had their first invitation.

'This is a very social place,' said Linda. 'And to take up all the invitations you're going to be getting, you'll want to look your best. There's Mimi's salon.' She pointed out a shopfront shrouded in net curtains. 'Best place to get your nails done. And,' she lowered her voice, 'best place to hear what's really going on behind closed doors. Be warned,' she added. 'Very thin walls at Mimi's. I found out I was getting a divorce over a pedicure . . . Can you imagine *that*?' Linda swivelled to grin at her passengers.

They couldn't.

'I'm over it,' Linda assured them as the salon receded into the distance. 'Oh, look, the Blank family has painted their mailbox green. You'll like Stephanie. Their daughter. I'd say she's about your age. As is Marcella Hunter. Who lives in that house. On her own.'

Linda waved her hand at a pair of enormous wrought-iron gates that looked as though they had been built with the express purpose of keeping out peasants. On the other side they glimpsed a manicured garden, flanking a huge white house. Charity and Grace could only imagine what this Marcella Hunter's life must be like. A girl their age living alone in that mansion? Did people really have that much money?

'And here we are. At last . . .'

They were even more shocked to find they would be living right next door.

7

'The Rose House,' Linda announced as she turned her beige Lexus into the very next gravelled drive.

This was a long drive. It was another minute or so before they got close enough to see the house. When they did, Grace was speechless. She just turned to her sister and squeezed her hand.

'Whaddya think?' Linda wanted to know.

'It's . . . it's . . .' began Charity. 'It's just beautiful. Just like the pictures.'

'Of course. Linda Deuble always represents her properties accurately.'

Linda smiled indulgently as the sisters climbed out of the car and just gazed at their new home. It was as though she were making a gift of the house to them herself. After a moment, she pressed a set of keys into each of their hands.

'I have to tell you, girls, you're the envy of quite a few people around these parts. The Rose House has not been lived in for a very long time.'

'Why not?' asked Grace.

'There was some kind of scandal to do with the family who own it. Tax evasion. Probably. Divorce. Or murder. Or divorce *and* murder. Nobody knows.'

Charity and Grace didn't care how the house had come to be empty. They simply couldn't believe their luck that it had fallen into their hands. They continued to look up at the white building – too delightedly stunned to say anything much.

'But there'll be no murder or divorce for you young ladies,' said Linda. 'I hope you'll be very happy here.'

Charity assured her they would do their very best.

How could they *not* be happy in this house?

It's not just people you can feel an instant attraction to. Charity felt at once that the two-storey building in front of her had a good vibe. Even the set of the windows and front door gave the impression of a smiling face. The pediments above the uppermost windows were like eyebrows raised in recognition and greeting. 'Welcome,' the house seemed to be saying with every brick, slate and pane of glass.

'I used to dream of a house like this,' Linda continued, as she pushed open the front door. 'But that's just a fantasy since I got screwed over in the divorce. Heigh-ho. Shall we go inside?'

The interior of the house more than lived up to the façade. As Linda gave them the guided tour, Charity and Grace had to keep themselves from laughing out loud at the fabulousness of it all.

'There is a bathroom for each of the seven bedrooms and one extra for luck,' Linda explained.

'Just in case raging diarrhoea strikes a dinner party of eight guests at once?' Charity whispered to Grace.

In addition to the bedrooms and the bathrooms Linda mentioned, there were six other rooms. There was a 'lounge room' and a 'den' and a 'sitting room' and a 'dining room'. The kitchen was big enough to cater for a party of twenty. There were two ovens for expressly that purpose and two dishwashers also, of course.

The utility room was bigger than the average London kitchen. In fact, thought Grace, the washing machine was bigger than the average London kitchen.

Upstairs, as downstairs, every room was beautifully decorated and furnished. The walls were dotted with tasteful
paintings, mostly, Grace noticed at once, of roses. It became
clear that each of the bedrooms was themed around the
colour of a rose blossom. Yellow, white, pink, deep rose
red. Roses everywhere.

'So that's it,' said Linda, when they found themselves back
downstairs again. 'Except for the garden.'

And with that she opened the French windows from the
sitting room on to a garden straight from the pages of a
coffee-table book. Not a leaf out of place. The glittering
ocean as a backdrop. This time, Charity really did laugh out
loud.

It was the most beautiful garden the girls had ever seen
outside of the stately-home estates they had visited on school
trips. A luscious lawn rolled down towards the sea. The lawn
was skirted by formal flower beds. In the very middle was a
knot-garden of roses. Most were still in bud but in a few weeks
it would be spectacular.

'So you like it?' Linda asked unnecessarily.

'Linda,' said Charity, 'I think I'm in love.'

It took a long time to persuade Linda Deuble to leave that
afternoon. Eventually she had to go back to her office to deal
with a fax machine crisis. Her assistant had caused a paper
jam while trying to fax a nineteen-page memo to Linda's
divorce attorney.

'I'll see you girls soon,' Linda called as she left.

'Not if we see her first,' mouthed Charity to Grace.

They couldn't wait to close the door on her. With Linda
gone, they could really explore the house.

'This bathroom has a steam cabinet!' Charity exclaimed.

'What on earth is an In-sink-erator?' Grace asked as they inspected the kitchen.

The sisters chose their bedrooms. At least, they chose the two bedrooms they were going to use first. Grace picked the 'pink room'. Charity settled on yellow, which had always been her favourite colour. They unpacked their cases in their respective 'dressing rooms'. They bounced upon the beds that were furnished with mattresses as thick as in the tale of the princess and the pea.

'I am a real princess!' said Grace, belly-flopping into the six pillows piled against her headboard.

'Just so long as you remember to act like one,' said Charity when Grace surfaced.

'From this moment on,' Grace promised, 'I'll be such a princess, you can call me Your Royal Highness.'

'I don't think we should go *that* far.'

'No. I'm good at being royal. Look.' Grace gave her sister a regal wave.

Charity curtsied. The sisters shook hands.

'And what do you do?' Grace asked without moving her lips.

'By George, I think she's got it,' said Charity.

8

A couple of hours later, Grace was finally overcome by jet lag and took to her new bed for a nap. Charity was much less sleepy. She was too excited for that. This summer in the Hamptons was the result of a great deal of planning on her part and she wasn't going to let a single moment go to waste.

Having tested just about every appliance in the house, she set about exploring the garden.

At the bottom of the rose-edged lawn was a neat picket fence with a tiny gate that led directly on to the beach. On the other side of the fence, a strip of tall rough grass gave way to soft clean sand the exact colour of demerara sugar. And it was deserted. There was no sign of any other people. There weren't even any footprints except those left by a flock of tiny birds that strutted along the waterline and ran rather than flew away from the breakers, like children daring each other to paddle. They were sandpipers, she would later discover.

Charity stepped out on to the sand and bent down to let a handful run through her fingers. She found tiny shells in there. But no broken glass. No plastic. No cigarette butts. Perfect.

The beach was so empty it might as well have been private. Charity turned and looked back towards the house. The steep slope of the lawn meant that she couldn't see the Rose House from where she was standing. She couldn't see their new neighbours' houses either. Careful landscaping had ensured as much privacy as possible for each of the multi-million-dollar homes on Low Tide Lane. She wondered what they would be like, the neighbours? Would they become friends? The basket of fruit from Marcella Hunter had been a nice surprise.

As she wondered about the weeks ahead and the new relationships they might bring, Charity walked right to the water's edge. The tiny seabirds skittered away. She flipped off her sandals and let the wet sand seep between her toes. She filled her lungs with ozone and let the sea breeze speckle her warm face with salt.

The idea of a swim was tempting. The day had been hot and felt hotter still, having been spent for the most part in trains and in cars. Charity considered going back to the house to change into her bikini. But then she thought better of it. Who was there to mind if she was wearing a bikini or not?

A moment later, Charity was out of her sundress and in the water, wearing nothing but her knickers. She ran in until the water was thigh high then belly-flopped into the next big wave. The chill made her gasp, but at the same time the cold was perfect. Exhilarating. She laughed out loud as she flipped on to her back and performed a few untidy strokes. Then she floated for a while with the sun on her face, watching gulls wheel lazily in the sky, which was blue like old denim worn soft as silk.

Just forty-eight hours before, Charity and Grace had closed the door on their flat and rushed out to the waiting taxi through horizontal rain. London had been its usual summer grey for weeks on end. A promised heatwave hadn't materialized, though curiously the hosepipe bans were already in place and all the public parks were yellow. Heathrow had been the usual overcrowded nightmare full of fractious travellers bemoaning tightened security and out-rageous coffee prices. The flight to JFK had been long and bumpy. The aeroplane food smelt poisonous and tasted worse. Now here they were in the Hamptons on the most beautiful day imaginable. London seemed a lifetime away.

Charity knew in that moment that she had made the right decision in opting to leave the United Kingdom and bring Grace along with her. They were going to make a success of this chance to be in paradise. This would be the summer when everything changed.

Charity splashed about in the ocean for another five minutes or so before deciding to go back to the house. The water was too cold to loll about for any longer. She didn't have a warm towel to wrap herself in when she emerged, after all. The plan was to run straight up to the house and try out her new steam room. An excellent idea.

Charity waded out of the water, grabbed up her dress and, without putting it on, started jogging, naked but for a pair of white cotton knickers gone see-through, up the lawn. Up the lawn and right into the Rose House's resident gardener . . .

Grace watched it all from her bedroom window. The look of horror on Charity's face as she realized she no longer had a clear run to the house. The look of horror on the gardener's face as he realized that a semi-naked woman was bearing down upon him at high speed. The sheer dismay on both their faces as they found themselves practically engaged in a dance as they attempted to step around each other and somehow always ended up stepping in the same direction.

'I'm turning away!' the gardener shouted, as he stood still and theatrically covered his eyes.

But his belated chivalry was a hopeless gesture. Just as he

found the presence of mind to cover his eyes, Charity tripped over a metal sprinkler and took him down with her into the grass like a rugby player.

'Ooof.' He made a winded sound.

'Ow!' said Charity.

They lay on the grass for a moment, just taking in the nightmare of it all. Eventually, one of them would have to move but neither wanted to be the first.

In the end it was Charity who took the initiative. She sat up and folded her arms across her breasts.

'I'm Charity Grosvenor,' she said primly, offering the gardener her right hand without actually unfolding her arms.

The gardener struggled into a vaguely upright position. 'Ryan Oldman,' he said, shaking Charity's hand by the fingers.

Charity smiled at him brightly. As brightly as she could manage, considering she was half naked and had just stubbed her toe rather badly.

'I was just setting the sprinklers,' he explained. 'I do it every evening about this time. If you do it too early then the water just evaporates. And when I'd done that I spotted you out there in the sea so I thought I should wait around on the lawn and say "hi" since we're going to be seeing a fair bit of each other. But I didn't realize you were . . . that you were . . . Hell, you probably don't want to hear any of this right now, do you?'

'I'm a little bit cold from swimming,' said Charity with incongruous politeness. 'Perhaps we should try to introduce ourselves properly tomorrow?' she suggested.

Ryan agreed. 'You're absolutely right. I don't know what I was thinking. Till tomorrow.' He jumped up, tipped his baseball cap at her and set off at high speed. 'Jeez, I . . .' he muttered as he went.

*   *   *

Two days later, the memory of her collision with Ryan still brought a blush to Charity's cheeks.

'Somehow it wouldn't have been so bad if he had been unattractive.' She sighed.

'I know what you mean. He's definitely the best-looking gardener I've ever seen,' said Grace.

Grace was right. Like everyone they'd seen in Little Elbow so far, Ryan the gardener looked as though a model agent had chosen him for the job. His baseball cap had been shading a gob-smackingly handsome face. His blond hair was sun bleached almost white at the tips. His skin was a warm nut brown. His arms, in their rolled-up sleeves, sported the type of muscles that make a girl want to swoon just so she can feel what it's like to be caught up in them.

'Nice eyes too,' said Grace.

'I wasn't looking at his eyes,' said Charity.

'I don't suppose he was looking at your eyes either!' Grace snorted with delight.

'Why did he have to be so gorgeous? Less a horny-handed son of toil than just plain horny! I'll have to spend the rest of the summer avoiding him.'

'Going to be difficult,' Grace reminded her. Ryan the gardener lived in the grounds.

'What a fantastic way to get to know the neighbours,' Charity sighed into her tea.

9

Marcella Hunter was certainly determined to get to know her new neighbours properly. As she had mentioned to Simon, the very day after her birthday party, she sent a card to the Grosvenor sisters inviting them to supper.

Charity was delighted when the thick cream-coloured envelope inscribed with perfect penmanship landed on the doorstep. It had been delivered by hand. Though not Marcella's own hand, of course. Anjelica had scuttled round on a brief break in cleaning up after the birthday party. Who would have believed that so few guests could produce so much vomit?

'We've been invited to dinner next door,' Charity told her sister. 'To properly welcome us to the neighbourhood.'

'By that Marcella girl?'

'Perhaps she isn't as bad as we thought.'

'It's a really nice gesture,' Grace agreed.

But there was nothing nice about it. Marcella wasn't so much being neighbourly as military, like a general, trying to get the measure of a potential enemy. When she first heard that the Rose House had been let, Marcella had very much liked the idea of living next door to a couple of English girls with connections. She did not, however, like the idea of living next door to a couple of extremely attractive English girls who seemed intent on making connections with the people Marcella had hitherto regarded as her own. Where was the reciprocity? In their tour of the party, neither girl had mentioned the Queen or Jude Law once.

And to make matters worse, the Grosvenors had accepted an invitation from Stephanie Blank! As anybody who cared to study the social structure of Little Elbow soon came to realize, there were just two hostesses of real note in the town: Marcella Hunter and Stephanie Blank. And if you were going to get tight with one then you would definitely not be tight with the other.

Marcella almost growled as she imagined Stephanie Blank usurping her position by the Grosvenor sisters' side at Jude Law's next birthday party. If they indeed knew him at all.

'I need to find out exactly what those Grosvenor girls are about,' she told Simon once the girls had responded to her invitation in the positive. 'So you have to be at this dinner too. I want you to smoke them out. Find out who they know back in London.'

'Uh-huh.' Simon shrugged from behind a copy of the *New Yorker*.

Marcella threw legendary dinner parties. The ambiance, the company, the food . . . Particularly the food. She was renowned for her cuisine. Or rather, for the cuisine prepared by the best chef on the peninsula. Marcella had an account with Paul Bustan, who had once cooked at the White House. But Mr Bustan just happened to be catering for a ruby wedding anniversary party on the night that Marcella wanted to throw her special 'welcome to Little Elbow' dinner for the Grosvenor sisters.

'What do you mean, he's busy?' Marcella barked at his assistant. 'I've got to have him.'

Marcella offered him twice his usual rate. Three times. Four and the promise of a hundred-guest buffet to come. And the happy ruby-wedding couple was left trying to find a replacement chef for their anniversary supper with just twenty-four hours to go.

The guest list for the welcome party was relatively short for a dinner at the Hunter house. The grand French table in the panelled dining room could seat twenty, but that night there would be just twelve. There should have been twenty but half Marcella's most wanted were already booked up for the evening. Some pesky Democrat event. Which surprised Marcella because she thought that all rich people were Republicans. As a result it took Marcella three hours to gather together six girls and five boys. By that point she was getting desperate. So desperate that she had to consider calling Choate Fitzgerald.

Simon was disparaging.

'What do you want to invite Choate for? He's the world's most boring man.'

'I have uneven numbers if I don't,' Marcella snapped.

Simon sighed. 'Hopefully he'll be busy.'

'Choate won't be busy,' Marcella predicted. 'In any case, he'd leave his own mother's funeral to take up an invitation from me.'

'Of course,' said Simon. 'And what did he get you for your birthday again?'

'A circuit tester,' said Marcella. Simon rolled his eyes. 'But you have to understand that practical is Choate Fitzgerald's romantic. It's the way Choate shows he cares.'

Simon made puking motions. Marcella couldn't help thinking he was right. Choate wouldn't add anything to the party other than body heat. But eleven was such an ugly number. So she went ahead and called Little Elbow's dullest man. And she was correct. He wasn't busy. Marcella had her dozen.

*   *   *

One person who wasn't very excited about this impromptu dinner party was Anjelica.

Anjelica Solorzano was Marcella's live-in housekeeper. Wednesday nights were supposed to be her night off. As it was, she hadn't had any time off at all for the past couple of weeks. Preparing for Marcella's extravagant birthday party had taken priority over Anjelica's need to have a moment to relax or even to wash her own smalls. Even when there wasn't a party to plan for, looking after the Hunter residence was a job for more than one woman, but Marcella was surprisingly stingy when it came to hiring help.

Still, Anjelica didn't want to rock the boat by refusing to don that stupid white apron for another night. Not when she was so close to getting what she really wanted: something that mattered much more than the chance to slump down in front of the TV. Marcella had promised she would arrange a meeting for Anjelica with an immigration lawyer.

'Can he really help me?'

'This man could get Saddam Hussein a tourist visa,' Marcella boasted. 'He'll get you a green card no problem.'

As yet, however, the date for the meeting had not been set. But Marcella promised it was at the top of her 'to do' list. 'Right at the top, I swear.' She promised again when she told Anjelica that her services would be required that Wednesday night.

'I know it's your night off,' said Marcella sweetly. As sweetly as she ever did. 'But you're going to need time off during the day some time soon to go and see that lawyer.'

'Have you made the meeting, Miss Hunter?' Anjelica asked excitedly.

'I will . . . Right after the dinner party. You know, entertaining takes up so much of my energy.' She put her hand to her forehead to emphasize just how very tired she was. 'Now I need you to go to the store and buy these items.'

Anjelica took the list and nodded meekly. Though inside she was boiling like a vat of the sodding refried beans Marcella's house guest Simon was forever getting her to cook.

'Just like your momma used to make back in Mexico, eh?' he joked every time.

'Oh, yes, Mr Macdonald,' Anjelica replied, getting his name wrong quite deliberately. 'Stick a haggis up your arse, you ignorant pig,' was what she wanted to say.

Anjelica wasn't destined to be a housekeeper for ever. She knew that much. As she scrubbed and polished the marble floors and endangered walls of the Hunter house, Anjelica was busy making plans totally beyond the comprehension of a woman like Marcella. Anjelica hadn't come to the States to clean floors so she could send home fifty dollars a week for the rest of her life. She had come to the States for an education. The minute she got that green card, Anjelica would leave Marcella to clean her own bloody house. She would get herself a proper job, one that paid the minimum wage, at least, and start saving for her college degree.

Marcella would have laughed to hear Anjelica's plans.

'She doesn't even speak proper English!'

That wasn't exactly true. Anjelica didn't speak English, or rather what Marcella would have called 'proper English', around her employer, because she didn't want to. There were, however, some people she enjoyed practising her English on very much.

IO

Wednesday night. Seven o'clock. The doorbell rang. Anjelica broke off from shelling peas for Paul Bustan's famous 'petit pois cappuccino' to examine the face of the caller on the CCTV. The first guest of the evening.

It was Choate Fitzgerald. Of course it was. Choate was pathologically punctual. As a result he often found himself waiting half an hour for everyone else to arrive. Sometimes, as was the case that evening, he was even ready before his host or hostess. He belonged to an era before mobile phones when people actually bothered to stick to agreed arrangements rather than taking 'seven o'clock' as the time at which he was supposed to call up and say, 'I'm on my way. Stuck in traffic.'

Seeing Choate there on the CCTV screen, Anjelica automatically smoothed her hands over her soft brown hair and straightened up her skirt. Choate looked so handsome in his navy blue blazer and chinos. He was wearing a shirt and the green and yellow striped tie of the Harbor Club. As Anjelica watched, Choate obviously thought better of his outfit and took the tie off.

That's much better, Anjelica thought. She liked him a little bit casual. If he would only let his hair grow a little longer too.

She was just touching a finger to Choate's face on the CCTV screen when he rang the doorbell again. She snapped to attention and dashed out into the hall.

*   *   *

'Mr Choate.'

She acted as though she were surprised to find him there.

'Anjelica.' He nodded.

She liked the way he pronounced her name. Properly, with a soft 'j'. 'An-hel-lica'. He was the only American she'd met so far who did so.

He handed her his raincoat. There was very little need for a raincoat from June through September but Choate always liked to be prepared. Anjelica accepted the coat with a little bob.

'How have you been?' he asked her.

'I have been very well, thank you.'

'Good. Good.'

'I have been reading Twain's *Innocents Abroad* like you suggested, Mr Choate.'

'Oh, that's good. Good.' He seemed distracted.

'You were right. It is very funny.'

'Mmm-hmm,' he said. But he was looking past her down the corridor. Anjelica was disappointed. Ordinarily, she could engage him on the subject of reading for at least a couple of minutes. 'Are the other guests here?' he asked.

'No, you're the first,' Anjelica told him. Perhaps if he knew he was the first, he would relax a little. Have a chat.

'Where should I wait?' he asked.

'You can wait through here.'

She showed him into the main reception room.

Choate eschewed the comfortable seats for a high-backed chair. As he always did. He'd once explained that it was because he had trouble with his lower back and needed the support. Anjelica hoped he wasn't in pain right then. She would have liked to help him if he was.

'Can I get something for you?' she asked.

'Oh, er, a glass of water. Please. If it's not too much trouble.'

'No trouble at all,' she said. And meant it. She returned with a glass in record quick time.

'Thank you.'

Anjelica hovered. And eventually she was rewarded with another sentence.

'I nearly forgot,' said Choate. 'I have something for you. It's in the pocket of my raincoat. Don't let me leave here without handing it over.'

Anjelica's mouth fell open. 'For me?'

'Well, you said it was . . .'

They were interrupted by the doorbell – the Grosvenor sisters had arrived – and a simultaneous scream of pure anguish from the top of the stairs.

'Let them in and then come straight up here!' Marcella hissed down to Anjelica through the banisters.

Marcella was in a state.

'Are you OK, Miss Hunter?' Anjelica asked. 'I heard you scream. Did you hurt yourself?'

It was much more serious than that.

'I can't choose an outfit!' said Marcella.

'What are they wearing?' she asked when Anjelica came into her bedroom.

'I don't know. Dresses?'

'For goodness' sake. Be more observant! This is important. Go back downstairs and find out. Properly.'

When Anjelica came back upstairs again, Marcella had laid out three dresses on the bed.

'Choose the one which is better than the dress that Grace is wearing.'

'Which one is Grace?' Anjelica asked. 'The pretty one?'

'Yes, the pretty one.' Marcella sighed.

Anjelica pointed at a little red number by Michael Kors.
'Are you sure?' asked Marcella.
Anjelica said that she was.
'Hmmmm.' Marcella wore the beige Donna Karan instead.

Once she was convinced that she was suitably attired, Marcella finally graced her guests with her presence. It was a full
half-hour after the appointed time. Simon was already downstairs. He gave her the obligatory wolf whistle. But that didn't
count. He had to. He was staying in her house. Still, Marcella
was satisfied that she had chosen well. The Donna Karan
whispered sophistication and class. Charity was in a bog-
standard LBD. Could have been from Banana Republic.
Grace was in blue. Very 2004. Confident that she was the
best-dressed woman in the house, Marcella felt much more
magnanimous.

'Welcome to my humble home,' she said, opening her arms
to encompass all present.

Charity smiled into her glass. Marcella's house was called
Hunter Cottage and the sisters had quickly learned that the
word 'cottage' in the Hamptons refers to a house with at least
eight bedrooms.

'Thank you so much for coming to my impromptu dinner,'
Marcella continued.

In the kitchen, the chef was red faced as he put the finishing
touches to fifteen thousand dollars' worth of soufflé.

The remaining guests drifted in over the next hour. If Choate
was pathologically punctual, then Robin Madden, the final
guest to arrive, was the Marc Jacobs of fashionable lateness.
He didn't apologize.

'The money markets don't close just because I have a
dinner to go to,' he said instead. 'How are you?' He slapped

Simon on the back. 'Ready to conquer Hollywood? Or still trying to find your *muse?*'

Simon winced. He'd meant it nastily. That much was obvious to everyone present.

With Robin Madden there at last, the party proceeded to the dining room. The chef, disgusted that his guests had not been ready to eat his perfect soufflé the moment it came out of the oven, had actually left in a rage fifteen minutes earlier, leaving Anjelica to save the day on an hourly rate roughly point one per cent of his fee. But in the dining room, Marcella's guests had no idea of the drama unfolding in the kitchen. While Anjelica struggled to rescue the soufflés, Marcella continued to act the consummate hostess. Utterly unruffled.

'Shall we sit anywhere?' Grace asked.

'Oh no,' said Marcella. 'The seating plan has been very carefully worked out.'

Charity found herself seated between Robin Madden and Simon McDonnough.

Charity had hated Simon McDonnough on sight. Seeing him for the very first time at Marcella's Gatsby-themed birthday party, she had thought that perhaps he looked like a dishonourable sort of man simply because he was dressed as one, with his slicked-back hair and pencilled-in moustache. Now, however, she realized that the moustache wasn't false and he habitually dressed like a wealthy playboy from the 1920s. Still, at least he had manners.

When Marcella announced that dinner was served, Simon pulled Charity's chair out for her before Robin Madden could get anywhere near. Then he gave her a courtly bow and slipped into his own seat.

'Well,' he said. 'You're the lady on my left so that means I have to talk to you first. Sorry, Grace.'

'That's OK,' said Grace.

'I'm sure Choate has plenty of great jokes to tell you.' Simon turned back to Charity and rolled his eyes to let her know that he was being sarcastic about Choate's potential as a stand-up. But Charity was pretty sure that Grace had got the better end of the arrangement. Meanwhile, Robin was observing the social niceties and talking to the girl on his left. The one who'd taken her newly Botoxed face on the teacup ride. Sarah Something, if Charity remembered correctly.

'You know,' said Simon, 'since I saw you at Marcella's party, I've been wondering if we've met before. Tell me all about you.'

The grilling had begun.

11

'I'm sure I know you,' said Simon.

'I don't think so,' said Charity.

'No,' he said. 'You look familiar. Definitely.'

Charity shook her head again. 'I would stake my life on it. We haven't met before.'

'But we must have been at the same parties,' Simon insisted. 'London just isn't that big.'

'It has a population of more than seven million,' Charity pointed out.

Simon wasn't to be put off. 'Where have you been living?'

'In Kensington,' said Charity at once.

'West or South?'

'South.'

Simon nodded his approval.

'And you?' Charity asked automatically.

'Near-by,' said Simon.

He paused to break the top of his soufflé. It smelled delicious. Anjelica's rescue mission had been a great success.

'I love soufflés,' said Charity. 'But they're very difficult to make. Do you cook?' she asked, hoping to change the subject.

'Do you know the Forbes Hamiltons?' Simon asked in response.

'I don't.'

'The Grieve family?'

'No.'

'The Yorks?'

'Uh-uh.'

'The Corbetts?'

Charity shook her head.

'The Shropshire Corbetts?' Simon clarified.

'I'm afraid not.'

'How strange. I don't know how it's possible that we've both been in London all these years and don't have any people in common.'

'You've only mentioned four or five sets of people,' said Charity.

'That's true. Adam and Caroline Featherstonehaugh?' Simon suggested, as though he'd had a eureka moment.

'No,' said Charity. 'You've struck out again.' A thin smile spread across her lips as Simon threw a few more names in her direction.

'Everybody knows Minky and Pongo!' he exclaimed when she denied knowing the final couple in his barrage of monikers.

'Minky and Pongo'? Were they people or rabbits? Charity wondered. Whoever they were, Charity had never knowingly been in the same room.

But when Simon said that 'everybody knows Minky and Pongo', Charity knew that what he really meant was, everybody of a certain socio-economic bracket knows everybody else in the same little box. Are you in the same box as Minky and Pongo? Or out?

This habit of trying to find people in common was a peculiarly British one, thought Charity, and one that really got on her nerves. It wasn't about finding common ground, something to talk about, it was all about determining whether the person you were talking to was 'PLU', 'People Like Us'.

It was just a way of working out how much money someone had in the bank without asking them outright for their post-code, then dashing upstairs to look up their address on www.houseprices.co.uk.

Charity had looked forward to three months without having to have such conversations. In the United States, she had hoped, people were judged more on their personal talents and attributes than their breeding or connections. Charity definitely didn't want to be judged by the company she had kept in the past or by what her father had done for a living. Sod's Law that her new neighbour's house guest was exactly the kind of class-obsessed Brit she had been trying to escape.

'Where on earth have you been spending your evenings?' Simon asked in exasperation. It seemed to be upsetting him, this inability to pigeonhole the sisters. But he was determined. Just as Charity had expected he would be from the moment he opened his mouth and she, much as she hated to admit it, pigeonholed him as a toff. 'Where did you go to school?' he asked at last. 'Where did you go to school?' was a variation on the 'D' you know who I mean by . . .' name game.

Charity decided to throw him a bone.

'Well, Grace and I haven't always been in London,' she said at last.

Simon leaned forward eagerly to hear the Grosvenor sisters' story.

'Grace and I were born in Kensington,' Charity began. 'But we left England shortly after Grace's fifth birthday. Our father's job took him all over the world and together with our mother, we followed him around from place like the Family von Trapp. But without the great singing voices.'

Simon laughed politely.

'We had to have new passports every couple of years for all

the stamps and visas we collected. Namibia, Dubai. Saudi Arabia . . .'

'But you must have had to go back to the UK to go to school?' said Simon simply.

'No, we boarded at a school overseas,' Charity told him. 'I don't suppose you know it.'

'Try me.'

'Our Lady's School for Girls in Pondicherry,' said Charity.

'Pondicherry?'

Charity nodded. 'Pondicherry,' she repeated neatly. From the look on Simon's face she would have bet that he wasn't entirely sure where Pondicherry was.

'Our father worked all over the Middle East and Asia but he was mostly based in India,' she said to help him out.

'And you went to school there?'

'That's right. To start with, we were too young for it to matter where we went to school. In fact, our mother taught us at home for several years. But later, when Mummy started to get out of her depth on the home-schooling front, she decided she didn't want to send us all the way back to London for our education. You see, she herself had been sent to boarding school in England while her parents were in Africa. She didn't see them for months on end. Sometimes she even had to spend the holidays at school. Hated every minute of it.'

'I can imagine,' said Simon. For just a second, he looked as though he had been ambushed by a slightly uncomfortable memory of his own school days.

Charity carried on. 'She didn't want that for us, so she found us places as weekly boarders at an Indian school instead. A Catholic school, actually. Run by nuns from the same convent as Mother Teresa. It was an unconventional decision but a good one, I believe. The education was equally as good as any English school. And both Grace and I can cook a mean curry.'

That latter comment was entirely true. And it wasn't just curry. Grace in particular was surprisingly talented when it came to making poppadoms. She could make them as delicate as lace. Something to do with having naturally cold hands.

'Anyway, we were in Pondicherry until the mid-nineties, when Dad's company recalled him to London. By that time, I didn't want to leave. I love India.'

'But you came back.'

'Yes. We had to. Mum was ill by then, you see.'

'Nothing serious, I hope,' said Simon.

'Lung cancer,' said Charity lightly.

Simon looked appropriately dismayed.

'She was a lifelong smoker,' Charity explained. 'Thirty to forty a day from the age of sixteen. And those Indian cigarettes just weren't filtered like the ones in the UK. Anyway, we came back to London and she started chemotherapy and radiotherapy at once. It didn't work, but she was tough, our mum, and she carried on for several years after her diagnosis. We nursed her at home, Grace and I, while Dad continued to travel for work. That's why we weren't much on the party scene for a while.'

Simon looked suitably chastened, for having been so hell-bent on working out where the girls socialized, when clearly they'd had much more pressing concerns.

'But these last few years we've tried to make up for it. Since Mum died.'

'And how about your father? He must miss you, both of you being out here?'

'Oh no. He's dead too,' said Charity simply.

Simon nodded sympathetically. 'Not the big C as well?'

'I'd rather not go into any detail.'

'Of course.'

'So there you have it. Our complete life story. Grace and I are just two poor orphans from Kensington by way of India.' Charity laughed. 'I'm having a last holiday before I go to university. I'm a mature student.'

'You don't look so mature to me,' Simon smarmed.

'And Grace is taking a break from her career in public relations to find herself. It's been particularly difficult for her. All this bereavement.'

'I understand.'

'I'm hoping that she'll find something to distract her here in Little Elbow. Or someone.'

Charity glanced at her sister, who was mid-gesture, fork in the air. She looked away quickly to make sure Simon didn't follow her gaze. How many times had Charity told Grace not to wave her cutlery to make a point?

'Well, that's just about all there is to know,' she said. 'And where were you at school?' With that question, she batted the ball back into Simon's court. She was gratified when Simon muttered the name of somewhere she hadn't heard of, leaving them one for one.

'It's quite small,' he admitted. 'A Catholic boys' school.'

'Oh.'

Simon paused for a moment, then he asked, 'Are you Catholic? Do you know the Bruce-Gardynes of Arbroath?'

'I don't,' said Charity.

'What about Colin Webster?'

'Never heard of him.'

'We could go on like this all night,' said Simon.

'Yes,' said Charity. 'If we're really unlucky.'

Across the table, Grace was on the receiving end of an altogether less combative set of questions.

'Are you enjoying your stay here?' Choate asked.

'So far,' she said. 'The Hamptons are lovely. Little Elbow is beautiful.'

You're beautiful too, thought Choate. Then he blushed as though he had accidentally said his thoughts out loud.

Grace Grosvenor was the reason for Choate Fitzgerald's unusual distractedness that evening. When Marcella told him that she wanted him to help properly welcome the Grosvenor sisters to Little Elbow, Choate had felt something akin to nausea at the prospect. He often felt something akin to nausea at the prospect of social occasions, but this time he quickly decided it was for reasons other than the fact that he hated making small talk and lived in fear of breaking wind at table.

Grace was just as lovely as Choate remembered. More lovely, in fact. Now that he had a chance to look at her properly (while they had been dancing, he had been too busy trying not to step on her feet), he saw that she had sky-blue eyes, not unlike his mother's. Her pink cheeks were soft and luminous, as though someone had pressed dusty rose petals against them. Her nose tilted up at the end, in the manner that so many plastic surgeons tried and failed to emulate. Her soft yellow hair made Choate's fingers itch for want of touching it.

Choate didn't care where Grace had been to school or what crowd she ran with back in London. He was much more intent on impressing her into liking him back than checking her credentials.

Unfortunately, when Choate tried to be impressive, he more often than not ended up sounding pompous. He was, as he had announced at Marcella's birthday party, uncomfortable with small talk and thus inevitably tried to move the conversation into waters where he felt safer. The money markets, for example. Or international trade and industry. For light relief he would talk about great American literature. With the opacity of a university lecturer who needs to give the impression that there's something complicated about a certain book so that he can keep his job . . . When the people Choate talked to started to glaze over, it was as often with panic as boredom. Choate gave the impression that he was a very cerebral man indeed.

Still, an hour into the dinner party, Grace had yet to yawn openly and Choate allowed himself to think that perhaps she thought he was quite interesting. He hoped she did. He thought she was fascinating. If she hadn't yawned by the time the entrées were cleared away, Choate decided, he was going to ask her on a date.

12

Grace rubbed her eyes and stretched her arms above her head.

'That,' said Charity, 'was one of the nastiest evenings I have ever spent in my life. That man – Simon McDonnough – is such a slimeball. Sitting next to him was like being at a job interview. Where did you grow up? What did your father do? Where did you go to school?'

'Perhaps he's not very good at making small talk.'

'Oh no, he's very good at it. But those questions weren't about finding common interests. They were about measuring our net worth. He knew it and I knew it.'

'And what do you think he measured it at?'

'I made quite sure he was left guessing,' Charity snarled. 'How about you?'

'I had an OK time,' said Grace.

'Every time I looked up you were yawning,' said Charity.

'I think I must still be a bit jet-lagged.'

'You can't still have jet lag. We've been here for almost a week.'

'Oh well. Do you think anyone else noticed?'

'I imagine Choate Fitzgerald might have done. He had an unrestricted view of your tonsils for most of the night.'

'Oh no. I hope he doesn't think it's because he was boring me.'

'Was he boring you?'

'A bit,' Grace admitted.

'I think he likes you, though,' said Charity.

'Really?' Grace sniffed.

The girls were sitting on the veranda at the back of the Rose House. There was a swinging love chair out there, just like in *The Waltons*. They were cradling camomile tea – just as they would be after a night out back home. Except that they were thousands of miles away from London.

Grace looked out over the dark ocean – a sea of ink between America and England. She swallowed hard and Charity, knowing exactly what was on Grace's mind as she gazed eastwards, reached across and squeezed her little sister's hand.

'It will get easier,' Charity promised.

'I know,' said Grace. 'I just wish it would get easier more quickly.'

'Distractions might help,' Charity suggested. 'Like a date with Choate Fitzgerald.'

'I might have known you would bring it back to that,' said Grace.

'I thought that was why you came with me. To find yourself a new man.'

'I came with you to clear my head!' said Grace precisely.

'Well, when it does clear you'll want a rich husband.'

'And, don't tell me, Choate Fitzgerald is the one.'

'He's the ultimate catch,' said Charity. 'Don't laugh, Grace. He *really* is. Choate Fitzgerald of Fitzgerald Lumber. You could be Mrs Woodchip USA.'

'Stop teasing me,' said Grace. 'Or I'll go home.'

'You don't want to do that.'

'No,' said Grace. 'You're right. I don't want to do that. Though I didn't expect to be sitting here with you in the Hamptons, this is a good place to be.'

'Well, here's hoping we get to stay here after the end of the summer. I don't see why it shouldn't happen. I think we're fitting in rather well.'

'So? Where do they fit in?' Marcella asked.

'Everything seems to check out,' said Simon.

'Where are they from?'

'London via Pondicherry.'

Marcella's brow wrinkled. 'Where?'

'Pondicherry. In India,' said Simon with a touch of impatience.

'India? That doesn't sound right. Who lives in India?'

'Billions of people,' said Simon.

'*Ha ha ha.* But not English girls who can afford to rent a six-bedroom house in the Hamptons.'

Simon shrugged.

'It just doesn't sound right to me. I need to know more about those girls,' Marcella continued.

'Sure.' Simon yawned.

'We should check *Tatler.*'

'What?'

'Well, if they're anybody at all, they should at least have made an appearance in the Bystander pages at the back of *Tatler*, right? Let's do it now.'

'Where on earth are we going to find a copy of *Tatler* at this time of night?'

Marcella knew exactly where.

The sumptuous library at the back of the Hunter house had been installed in the 1950s by Marcella's grandfather Edgar. He had a passion for reading and the wood-panelled library was his pride and joy. It was modelled on the reading room of an Oxford college he had visited while in Britain on his way home from the Second World War. He had been impressed by the serenity, the history and the class of the place. It took another ten years before he could afford to build his own exact replica in Little Elbow. But that gave him plenty of time to think about how he would stock it.

Marcella's grandfather was responsible for the extensive collection of English and American classics, all bound in matching red leather, which covered the west-facing wall. Thirty years later, Marcella's own father had added a similarly extensive array of quality contemporary literature – again in red bindings. The old man approved of his son's choices.

In the three years since the house had become her primary residence, Marcella too had made her contribution to the expanding library. Like her father and grandfather before her, Marcella had bound her offerings in expensive red leather with titles gilded and embossed. She felt her own little surge of pride as she watched Anjelica slot the handsome books into place . . . Three years' worth of issues of *Tatler, Harpers and Queen* and *Country Life*. It was the perfect twenty-first-century archive of the crème de London's crème.

'My God,' Simon breathed when Marcella pointed out her collection of glossies.

'I also have five years' worth of *In Style* at the binders right now,' she told him. 'I knew my magazines would come in handy one day,' she added, pleased as Punch with her foresight.

She sent Simon up a library ladder to fetch the *Tatlers* down. He carried them to the red-leather-topped table where Marcella's grandfather had signed so many important and lucrative contracts before he retired to play golf in Florida, and where Marcella wrote cheques in settlement of her credit account at Barneys. Marcella settled herself in the leather swivel chair. Simon perched on the corner of the desk.

'If they're anyone they are going to be in here.'

She began to speed-read the back pages.

'Is that the older one?' asked Simon from time to time, drawing Marcella's attention to a variety of gently highlighted brunettes with their faces half turned from the camera. There were a number of pretty close matches. For the younger Grosvenor sister too. It seemed that every London girl worth knowing these days got her hair done in the same place.

'That looks like the end of the younger one's nose,' said Marcella in a moment of desperation. 'That could be her ear.'

But ultimately, there was no sign of the Grosvenor sisters in three years' worth of *Tatler*. Or *Harpers and Queen*. Or *Country Life*.

'I knew it,' said Marcella. 'Not a single picture.'

'Perhaps they just shun publicity,' said Simon.

'Rubbish. Even people who shoot paparazzi they find outside their own homes are happy to appear in Bystander,' said Marcella. 'It's an institution. The only explanation is that they just weren't at any of the parties. Which leads on to the question, why weren't they at any of the parties?'

'They're not party people?'

'Of course they're party people. They came to my party. Goddammit.'

Marcella's gaze drifted around the library as she wondered how to continue her research. 'A-ha!' Her eyes lighted on one of the many red-covered books and a rare smile stretched her mouth. 'Why on earth didn't we look in here first?'

She sent Simon up the library ladder again and intoned, as though she were pronouncing a death sentence, 'Fetch Debrett's.'

*   *   *

There were several editions of *Debrett's Peerage and Baronet-age* in the Hunter family library. Her grandfather had been the first to purchase a copy. It was the one subscription that Marcella had kept up. Simon visibly strained as he hefted the latest three-thousand-page tome from its place.

'No sign of them,' he quickly confirmed, flipping straight to the Gs and putting the book back on the shelf immediately he had seen there were no Grosvenor sisters of Pondicherry to be found there.

'How can you know? You took twenty seconds.'

'I looked under G. They're not there.'

'Well, you can't just look for them under G. Bring it down here. Perhaps their father isn't the important one. What was their mother's maiden name?'

'I don't know.'

'You were supposed to be getting all the important information over dinner.'

'Hang on. Perhaps Charity did say something. Smyth? With a "y" perhaps?' Simon plucked a name out of the air.

'Then look under that name.'

'Nothing there either,' said Simon, slapping the book shut again seconds later. 'That's conclusive, then. They're officially unimportant.'

'But if they're not important, who are they?' Marcella wouldn't give up. 'They must be wealthy. How can they possibly have afforded to rent the house next door otherwise? We need to do some more investigation. We've got to see inside their house. See what kind of furniture they have.'

'What if the house was rented furnished?' Simon asked as he climbed back down to ground level.

'Well, they're bound to have family photographs or something like that. There's got to be some clue as to where their money comes from. Letters from the bank about their trust funds. That kind of thing.'

'Marcella, could you explain to me exactly why any of this matters?'

'Simon!' Marcella was surprised. 'I would have thought that you of all people would know *exactly* why it matters. Little Elbow is an exclusive town full of people who have a right to be here, bestowed upon them by generations of good breeding. These girls could be anybody. They could be journalists! It happens. What about that Johnson and Johnson kid who stitched up Ivanka Trump and Georgina Bloomberg with his "documentary"? Those Grosvenor girls are probably working for the BBC. They don't even look like sisters, if you ask me.'

'No,' Simon disagreed. 'They do. They've got different-coloured hair but their mannerisms . . .'

Marcella interrupted him. 'I can't relax until I know *exactly* who they are. We're going to get ourselves invited to dinner next door. Whoever they are, they can't be so ill bred that they don't realize they have a reciprocal arrangement to honour. I'll go round tomorrow morning with some cookies and damn well sit on the doorstep until one of them invites me in.'

'They're English,' Simon reminded her. 'It takes a while for the English to open up enough to allow people into their homes.'

'But we are in America,' said Marcella emphatically. 'And when in America . . .'

Simon climbed the library ladder and Marcella handed the magazines up to him.

'Why don't you get Debrett's down again,' she asked him. 'You know, I've never seen your entry in there. It would be fun to see one of my dearest friend's names in there in black and white. It makes me feel quite proud to know a real McDonnough.'

Simon raced down the ladder and scooted it away on its rails as far as it would go.

'Oh, don't be silly. It's so embarrassing. Besides, it's terribly bad manners for a real aristocrat to draw attention to his ancestry. Even if it is in the company of friends.'

Marcella pouted.

'In any case, it's much too late. I need my beauty sleep.'

Marcella glanced at her watch. 'You're right. I'll have to be impressed by your antecedents some other day.'

Simon followed Marcella out of the library, locking the door behind them and pocketing the key.

13

Two hours after the last of Marcella's guests had bid her goodnight, Anjelica was still hard at work cleaning up. It had taken two hours to make enough space in the kitchen for the dirty crockery. Paul Bustan, the chef, had used almost every pan in the house before he left. And because they were all copper pans, they could not go in the dishwasher.

Now Anjelica walked around the dining table with a dustbin liner, tossing into it the dead candles and other detritus. She was exhausted after her impromptu stint as chef, but there was no question of leaving the washing up until the following morning. Marcella would expect the kitchen to be spotless when she came downstairs for breakfast (which Anjelica was expected to cook, of course). The work was never ending. Still, Anjelica managed a smile as she picked up Choate's name card and tucked it into her pocket. She smiled again as she remembered how much warmer he had been towards her at the end of the evening when she helped him into his coat and he handed her the parcel he had asked her to remind him of – the parcel that now waited for her in her room.

Anjelica finished tidying up at almost four o'clock in the morning. She made sure the house was secured and crept into her bedroom (she was forbidden to wear her shoes in her room, since Marcella, whose room was below, claimed she could hear a pin drop. Above her own snoring? Anjelica doubted it. But all the same, she crept into her room.) And felt her heart swell with warmth when she saw the simple brown-paper package secured with four neat little pieces of sticky tape. Anjelica's name was written on the front in familiar no-nonsense handwriting.

'Happy birthday,' Choate had muttered as he handed the parcel over while Marcella wasn't looking.

He had remembered. Apart from the usual card from her mother – which had arrived a week early – Anjelica hadn't expected anything to mark the day. Marcella certainly didn't remember. Or chose not to, when she was scheduling her dinner party. But Choate had remembered her birthday. If every other man in America had sent Anjelica diamonds, it wouldn't have meant as much to her as this package did.

Inside was a hardback copy of *The Adventures of Huckleberry Finn*.

'Next on your reading list' said the note tucked inside.

Anjelica noticed at once that it wasn't a new book, but she didn't mind that. She actually liked second-hand books better. She enjoyed the sense of connection it gave her with the people who had read the book before. This time she didn't have to wonder too long who had read this copy of Huck Finn first. Inside the flyleaf, in handwriting that wasn't much different from the way he still wrote, Choate had signed his name: 'Choate Fitzgerald, aged ten and a half'.

Anjelica's heart did a tap dance.

This meant something, didn't it? He could have ordered a new copy of the book from Amazon, but instead he had chosen to give her the book he himself had been given as a child. His own book. A treasure that he might have kept for his own future children!

Anjelica read the brief note Choate had written on the front of the package ten or twenty times, as though it were a love letter. Holding Choate's book was like holding his hands as far as she was concerned. Eventually, Anjelica put the book under her pillow and settled down for the sweetest of dreams.

14

Perhaps Grace was right about the persistent effects of jet lag. The morning after Marcella's dinner party, Charity found herself wide awake at half past five in the morning – ten o'clock London time. Though it wasn't unusual for her to be awake at such an early hour back in London, rarely did she feel quite so good for it.

In the pink room next door, Grace was still sound asleep. It would have shocked most of the men who fell for Grace's ethereal charms to know just how loudly she could snore. Her bedroom door was ajar and almost vibrating with the force of her snorts. Charity pulled the door shut and peace was restored.

Having made herself some coffee, Charity walked out on to the veranda to admire the day. At this time of the morning, the whole world was pastel coloured. The sky was baby blue and pale lemon yellow at the horizon where the sun was creeping upwards through the haze. The tide was high, but the sea was flat and calm. The waves whispered softly like the breath of someone sleeping (though not the way Grace slept, Charity thought with a smile).

She found herself drawn down to the sand. It was, as usual, completely deserted. Not even a dog-walker. Just a couple of gulls and those other little birds, the sandpipers, still playing grandmother's footsteps with the water. Charity wondered where they slept. Or whether, indeed, they slept at all. Perhaps they spent the whole night strutting up and down the sand, just ahead of the waves.

She had yet to see a single other person on the beach. It seemed that most of her neighbours preferred to stay by their pools. One of the guests at Marcella's dinner party had expressed outright disgust at the idea that anyone would actually swim in the sea. What a waste. It didn't seem quite right to Charity that anyone could own a beach and not use it. In fact, the beach was very much public property, but apart from the Rose House, all the other residences with shorefront boundaries had extended their garden fences as far as possible on to the sand, to discourage day-trippers from getting too close. Signs announced that trespassers would be met with an 'armed response'. Draconian parking laws at the town's tiny beachfront parking lot also helped to keep the beach empty outside the hours of nine till five.

Ah well. Charity had to admit that she appreciated the peace as she strolled along the sand with her coffee mug still in her hand. It definitely beat popping into Starbucks before heading for work.

Turning back to the house, Charity spotted Ryan the gardener.

After that embarrassing first meeting, the promised formal introduction had not materialized. In fact, Charity guessed that Ryan had deliberately stayed out of the way. It was quite something to recover from. As Grace pointed out, most girls let a man buy them a couple of drinks before they pressed their naked bodies against him. Charity felt a blush flood her body at the thought.

But Ryan and Charity couldn't avoid each other for ever. A garden the size of that which surrounded the Rose House required constant attention. Not to mention the fact that Ryan actually lived in the grounds. Charity could see the back door of the guest house from her bedroom window. She heard him going in and out. So, anticipating that they would be seeing a great deal more of each other whether they wanted to or not, she made the decision to break through the embarrassment barrier right there and then.

'Ryan!' she called when he was within earshot.

He looked up and smiled.

So far, so good. At least he hadn't pretended not to hear her or run away.

Charity strode the last few steps to the garden gate boldly, hoping that her confident bearing would completely drive from Ryan's mind the fact that he had last seen her looking like a contestant in a wet T-shirt contest. Without a T-shirt. That morning, she was wearing some baggy thing that almost reached to her knees.

'Shall we start again?' she asked, sticking out her hand. 'Charity Grosvenor.'

Ryan wiped his hand clean on his jeans and they shook on it. 'Ryan Oldman. Pleased to meet you.'

'Properly.'

'Properly,' Ryan agreed.

'Trouble with the sprinklers?' Charity asked gaily.

'Yep,' said Ryan. 'I guess this one is finished.'

They both looked at the sprinkler head Ryan was holding. Charity realized at once that it was the one she had tripped over; the very sprinkler head that had thrown her into Ryan's arms. Half naked and dripping wet. Of course, she couldn't help replaying the whole scene in her head after that. She hoped in vain that Ryan was just thinking about how to fix his watering system. She caught his eye briefly. He quickly looked back to the sprinkler. He was definitely thinking about her boobs.

'Do you work here alone?' Charity asked to break the silence.

Ryan nodded.

'There's a lot of work for one person.'

'There certainly is.'

'The garden is beautiful,' said Charity. 'I'm not quite sure what I expected from a garden right next to the sea. I suppose I didn't expect it to be quite so pretty. I thought it would be wilder.'

'It's still pretty wild in places,' said Ryan, jerking his head towards the area behind the guest house, which was still firmly in Mother Nature's grip.

'Wow. Yes,' said Charity.

They lapsed into silence again. Ryan turned the sprinkler head over and over in his hand. Charity thought about the big wet patch she had left on the front of his shirt when they had crashed into one another. He was wearing another checked shirt that morning. Blue this time. Charity counted the fastened buttons from the waist up, until she came to an open button and a glimpse of chest hair. She'd felt that chest when they were pressed up together. The more she tried not to think about it, the more clearly she remembered.

'Well, I . . .' She felt red to the roots of her hair. 'I should be . . .' She gestured towards the house.

'Would you like me to show you around the garden?' Ryan interpreted. Badly.

'Why not?'

Having a tour of the garden was a far better way to repair relations with Ryan than standing in the middle of the lawn making awkward small talk. It gave them a purpose. It wasn't long before Charity was able to convince herself that Ryan wasn't thinking about her boobs any more. He was too absorbed in showing off his handiwork. As they strolled around the perimeter of the house, he named each and every tree as though they were old friends. There were several that Charity had never heard of.

'I'm impressed by your memory,' she said as he trotted out a string of Latin.

'Just don't ask me to remember anything but the names of trees and flowers,' he warned her.

'What's that one called?'

She started him off again.

As Ryan talked, Charity had the perfect opportunity to properly study the good looks that Grace had already inventoried while spying on him from the bedroom window. She guessed that he was about her age. Late twenties. He hadn't shaved that morning, but he was obviously the kind of guy who had to shave every day. Charity liked that.

He had his sleeves rolled up again. The hair on his forearms was bleached blond. His hands were large. They looked capable. Hard-working hands. But his nails were well shaped and, surprisingly, very clean. Perhaps that was just because the working day had hardly started.

'Do you have those in the UK?'

'What?'

Charity realized that she hadn't exactly been concentrating on the tour.

'Perhaps,' she replied, hoping he hadn't asked her something that required an obvious 'yes' or 'no'. To make up for it, she pulled an attentive face as Ryan explained how he had chosen a particular type of grass specifically for its ability to thrive in sandy soil.

'It needs to be watered every day, though.'

'As I discovered,' said Charity. Ryan pulled an embarrassed face.

'Moving swiftly on,' he said.

He showed her the vegetable patch and the kitchen greenhouse.

'I'm growing three kinds of heirloom tomatoes in here,' he said, as he opened the door and ushered her inside. It smelt very green in there. Very fertile.

'Heirloom tomatoes?' Charity echoed, finding pleasure in the idea that plants, like jewels, could be handed down the generations.

Ryan pulled a small red fruit from one of his tomato plants and handed it to her.

'This variety has been around since the 1800s.'

'Can I eat it?' she asked. 'Or are you supposed to keep them, like the family jewels?'

'I don't think they gain value with age,' said Ryan, joining in with the weak joke. 'Just rub the dirt off. I don't use pesticides,' he added.

Charity popped the tomato in whole. She was impressed. The tomato Ryan had grown tasted like no tomato she had ever eaten before. That is to say, it actually tasted of *something*. Unlike the supermarket toms back home, which tasted only of the packaging they arrived in.

Charity gave Ryan the thumbs-up rather than speak with her mouth full.

'Just let me know when you're making a salad,' said Ryan. He led her back outside.

'I will,' said Charity. Though she had never yet made a salad in her life. Another thing she'd have to learn, she decided.

At the side of the house was a part of the garden that Charity and Grace hadn't yet been into. It was walled, with a green wooden door that had been locked when Linda Deuble had tried it that first afternoon.

'Ah. The secret garden,' said Charity when they arrived there, and Ryan dug a bunch of keys from his pocket.

'Oh, it's no secret,' he said. 'I just kept it locked because it's kind of a work-in-progress and I wanted to be sure that you didn't go mad with the cutters before I had a chance to explain how it works.'

'The cutters?'

'For cutting the flowers. This is what is known as a "cutting garden".'

Ryan pushed open the door. Inside was a small formal garden edged with a perfectly trimmed privet hedge. The hedge contained a veritable firework display of flowers. Even early in the morning, the scent was incredible, like walking into a perfumery.

'The flowers grown here are especially for cutting and flower-arranging about the house,' Ryan explained. 'All the big houses had them in the days before the average hostess left her floral displays to Interflora.'

Charity was open mouthed in awe at the number of blooms that had been crammed in behind that wall. Asters, delphiniums, zinnias, lilies. Snapdragons, nasturtiums, sweetpeas and stock.

'It's specially planned so that there is always something in bloom. It starts with the tulips in the spring and runs until the dahlias flower in the late fall. At least, I hope that the garden will last the whole summer. This is my first year here. I'm still working things out. Making notes. I took some cues from the plants that I found already here. The ones that had survived three decades of neglect. I propagate the seeds in the greenhouse over there.'

He pointed out a small but elegant glasshouse.

'It's all a little experimental, hence I was being kind of strange about letting you see it without me being here to explain how it works.'

'I understand.'

Charity leaned over a flower that looked like a little purple starburst.

'China aster,' said Ryan.

'They're difficult to grow,' Charity commented.

'They are! Do you know about flowers?' he asked.

'A bit,' Charity admitted. 'Not these so much, but I've grown some roses. And I'm hoping to do a degree in horticulture,' she added.

'And you've been letting me ramble on like you don't know anything? Who's looking after your garden back in England?'

Charity smiled and thought of her own flowers.

'I have a very good friend who has promised to do her best for my plants while we're away,' she said.

'I bet you'll miss it, though. I don't think I could leave this garden in anyone else's hands. Not having spent so much time on it. I guess it's my baby.'

'Thank you for letting me see it,' said Charity. 'I promise I won't go mad with the kitchen scissors.'

'But some of the flowers are ready now. Hang on.'

Ryan chose the secateurs from his tool belt and headed for a rose bush with long-stemmed apricot blooms.

'A rose for an English rose?'

He smiled straight at her as he handed her the single, perfect flower.

'Thank you.' Charity suddenly felt inexplicably shy. 'I should go,' she said. 'Leave you to it. I'm sure you're busy.'

'Any time you want to help out,' he said. 'Help with the roses. Mow the lawn. Now I know it's your vocation.'

'I'll be right over,' said Charity.

'I hope so.'

15

Next door, Marcella Hunter also had an early start. At seven o'clock she was on the tennis court with her private coach. She saw a tennis coach three times a week. Not that she would admit to it. Marcella liked her opponents to think that her ability was one hundred per cent natural. After tennis, she had breakfast at the Harbor Club with Stephanie Blank (who had spent the previous hour in the gym working on her 'just born this way' abdominal muscles). Though Marcella wouldn't have spat on Stephanie if she were on fire, and the feeling was absolutely mutual, they saw each other several times a week. It was a case of friends close and enemies closer.

Marcella ordered a two-egg white omelette.

Stephanie ordered a single-egg white omelette.

'Single-egg white? But you don't need to lose weight!' Marcella exclaimed.

'You are kidding me. Look at this.' Stephanie tugged at a non-existent spare tyre and the girls entered their usual competitive fat-finding routine. *I'm so fat. No, I'm much fatter. I am the fattest.*

'Marcella . . .' Stephanie dealt the killer blow. 'I am such a *whale* right now that I'm actually *grateful* you didn't invite me to your dinner party last night.'

Marcella flushed. She didn't know that Stephanie knew she was entertaining. Now this was embarrassing. What excuse did she have for not having invited her?

'How was it?' Stephanie continued, pleasant as you like.

'Oh, you know. It was nice,' said Marcella. 'Very low key. Just . . . twelve people.'

Marcella wasn't certain that twelve people could ever be considered low key. Even in Little Elbow.

'I would have invited you, but I thought you were out of town.'

'Even though we were meeting for breakfast this morning?'

Marcella knew she'd been rumbled.

'Oh, don't worry about it! I hear that Robin Madden came into town especially,' Stephanie added.

'He was there,' said Marcella.

'You know,' said Stephanie, 'I think Robin has a soft spot for you.'

'Really?' Marcella leaned forward over the table,

'Oh yes,' Stephanie said meaningfully. 'A very soft spot.'

'What makes you say that?'

Anything Stephanie said instantly put Marcella on red alert. Especially things that might have seemed on first examination to be positive. Clarification usually revealed a thinly veiled insult. Where was the trap in this one?

'Well, I couldn't persuade Robin to drive up from Manhattan for a silly little dinner party full of such *dull* people, that's for sure,' said Stephanie.

Silly little dinner party. Dull people. There were the insults all right. But Stephanie persisted in insisting that Robin's presence was significant and that didn't seem too bad at all.

'He must have felt there was some greater incentive to be there than a free meal.' She raised an eyebrow. 'I mean *you*, you goose,' she added.

'Oh no. He doesn't like me. He . . .'

'Drove two hours to eat your soufflés? Or should I say, Paul Bustan's soufflés?'

How did she know that?

'Don't worry. Your secret is safe with me. I simply hate cooking myself. I just wish I had the nerve to pass off a Michelin-starred chef's cuisine as my own!'

The omelettes arrived. Both girls fell upon the food, wishing the anaemic-looking things were pancakes with every boring mouthful but pronouncing them delicious all the same. Afterwards, Stephanie announced, 'I am fit to burst.'

'Me too,' said Marcella, as her stomach growled in disappointment. 'In fact, I am so stuffed, it's a good job you haven't invited me to *your* dinner party this evening.'

'Darling, I thought you were out of town.'

Marcella pondered Stephanie's words all the way back home. Robin Madden liked her? She'd never really considered him in that way, a romantic way. But perhaps she should. He hadn't been on her first-choice dinner party guest list. She'd only called him because the Mendelsohn brothers were both at that Democrat thing. But now she thought about it, Robin was good looking. He came from a good family. The Madden beach house was one of the smallest in town but Robin was actually doing rather well for himself with that hedge fund. Over dinner, he had mentioned that he might start looking for a beach house of his own this summer. Something much bigger than his parents' place.

He was going places. And he had made the trip up from Manhattan on a week night to go to her dinner party.

Robin Madden liked her.

Suddenly, the disappointments of Marcella's birthday party were forgotten. Yes, she decided, Robin Madden beat Jamie Iley or either of the Mendelsohn brothers hands down.

They were rich as stink but they hadn't made their own money. They didn't have initiative like Robin. He was a much more suitable match. After all, Marcella was a go-getting sort of person too.

Marcella had been thinking about suitable matches quite a bit lately. The past year had seen several of her former classmates become engaged; even a couple of girls she thought would have some difficulty on that front. Yes, getting engaged was suddenly the 'it' thing to do.

But the frustrating thing about tying the knot was that finding a husband couldn't quite be approached in the same way as finding the right shoes or handbag. Or even the 'it' dog. If you wanted the 'it' bag or shoes, you could always bribe a sales assistant to slip you in at the top of the waiting list. If you wanted the 'it' dog, you found the right breeder, you handed over your money and, a few months later, he handed over the puppy.

When it came to finding the 'it' man, Marcella's efforts over the years had been continually thwarted. So hearing that Stephanie Blank thought Robin Madden must have a soft spot for her was like being offered a million-dollar voucher for Barneys. How could Marcella fail to turn this opportunity into a reason for people to envy her?

'You're very upbeat this morning,' said Simon, when Marcella trotted into the garden, swinging her tennis racket.

Simon was never upbeat before noon. Nor was Marcella. Usually.

'I had some good news,' she said.

'Do share.'

'Stephanie Blank thinks that Robin Madden has a soft spot for me.'

'That's *good* news?' asked Simon.

'I don't know why you don't like him.'

'I don't know why you do like him,' Simon retorted. 'He's almost as dull as Choate. Worse, in fact, because Choate can't help himself.'

'You're just jealous.'

'Of what?'

'He makes money.'

'He makes *nothing*,' Simon corrected her. 'He pushes paper and people give him money. I make something. I make documentaries.'

'Whatever,' said Marcella.

Marcella wasn't to be put off. She spent the rest of the morning fantasizing about a future as Mrs Robin Madden. God, they would look good together. So what if he was a little bit shorter than she was? This year it was fashionable to wear flats.

But how would she start to make this fantasy merger a reality? Marcella wondered. Robin would almost certainly call to thank her for the previous evening's hospitality. When he did, she would subtly suggest that they got together again some time soon.

Her hopes were considerably bolstered when the doorbell rang at midday. It was the local florist, delivering Robin Madden's 'thank you' in flowers!

'Marcella, you're being extremely uncool,' said Simon, as she waltzed back into the house gazing at the bouquet in her arms as though it were a handsome partner.

'I'll be much cooler when I call to thank him for his thank you.'

'Thank *him* for his thank *you*?' said Simon. 'This is all getting rather Japanese.'

Marcella waved Simon's objections away.

'Anjelica!' she shouted. 'A vase.'

She would call him the following morning. She shouldn't appear too keen.

16

On the other side of the fence, Charity was arranging an identical bouquet to the one that had been delivered to Marcella.

To say that the flowers were a surprise was an understatement. Charity's first surprise was that the bouquet was not for Grace. That was the way it had usually been back in London. Her second surprise was the sender.

Charity didn't think she had made much of an impression on Robin Madden. He had barely spoken to her after she had tried to make a joke about his job. He told her he was in 'M & A', for mergers and acquisitions. Charity's riposte that it might have stood for 'murders and assassinations' seemed to go down like the *Titanic*. But clearly she had been wrong. Robin must have found her interesting. Unless, of course, he had meant the flowers to be for Grace but got their names mixed up. That had happened before . . .

'Don't be so silly,' said Grace. 'Of course the flowers were meant for you.'

That evening at dinner, Stephanie Blank agreed. 'Robin Madden likes a strong woman. And you are clearly strong,' she added, basing her pronouncement on God only knew what, Charity thought. 'Were the flowers nice?'

Charity nodded. 'Yes.'

Indeed, they were nice. Roses. Red. Long stemmed. Charity didn't bother to mention that they were nice in a very manufactured sort of way. Unlike the rose Ryan had cut for her, they didn't have any thorns. But also, unlike the rose Ryan had cut for her, they didn't have any perfume. Still, Robin Madden wasn't to know that Charity was a 'flower snob'.

Charity's own interest in roses had sombre beginnings. When her mother finally passed away, a distant cousin from the north of England came down to London to help organize the memorial service. She took over, arranging the cremation, the memorial service, the wake. Everything. The only thing she allowed Charity and Grace to do was scatter their mother's ashes over the green lawn at the crematorium. Of course, as soon as the ceremonial part of the grieving was over, the distant cousin was gone back up north.

Charity and Grace chose the rose bush together. It was the best they could find. They planted it in the memorial garden next to the shiny brass plaque that proclaimed their mother's dates on earth. It had looked pretty good on the day of the funeral, but within a couple of weeks it was starting to look pretty feeble. Charity tried everything she could to revive it, but the blossoms drooped and soon the leaves started to turn yellow. She was distraught, seeing the slow death of the rose bush as symbolic, somehow indicating that she didn't care enough about her mum.

The gardener at the crematorium took pity on Charity and offered some tips. It turned out she had simply been over-watering the poor little thing. Caring almost too much. Charity followed her new friend's prescription for recovery and, five years later, the same bush was still alive.

It was the knowledge she had gained while keeping her mother's roses alive which had made it perfectly natural for

Charity to dead-head an old flower from one of Peggy's rose bushes as she passed by one summer afternoon.

'What in the hell do you think you're doing?'

Charity jumped backwards with surprise at the force of the demand.

'Stay right there, young lady. Don't you move a muscle!'

The old woman came rushing out of the darkness of her sitting room as fast as her rheumatism and her stick would allow her. She looked frail but she was fierce. When she got close enough, she steadied herself, picked up her walking stick and waved it in Charity's face. 'You vandal!' she shouted.

'I'm sorry,' said Charity, backing away to save her nose. 'But the flower was already dead and if you don't take them off they go to seed and you won't get any more blooms this year.'

'I know what dead-heading's about,' said Peggy tetchily. 'And I can do it by myself.'

'I'm sure you can,' Charity agreed. 'I didn't mean to imply otherwise. Do you think you might . . .' Charity gestured towards the walking stick.

'All right.' Peggy put the stick down but her mouth was set in a thin line of disapproval as she checked the rose bush over, as though it were a child and Charity had just pinched it. 'Goddam messing with my babies,' Peggy muttered to prove Charity's point.

'I'm sorry,' Charity said again. More softly this time. Respectfully. 'It was rude of me. They're very beautiful. I like this one best.' She pointed towards the bush next to the one she had started to prune uninvited.

'It's called a Sunset Celebration,' said Peggy, fingering the dusty apricot petals. 'And if I hadn't caught you, you'd probably have killed it.'

'I didn't touch . . .' Charity opened her mouth to protest but stopped when she saw that Peggy was smiling at her.

'She'll be OK,' said Peggy grudgingly. 'You like roses? Not very usual to find someone your age knows anything about them.'

'I'd love to have a rose garden,' Charity admitted. 'It seems an impossible dream.'

'Nonsense.'

And after that it was as though a floodgate had been opened. Though Charity had passed by Peggy sitting in her chair every day for months and never acknowledged her – or been acknowledged in turn – from that afternoon onward she couldn't get past Peggy's door again without being invited in for a chat about the flowers. Never mind that she was meant to be somewhere else.

Charity learned that Peggy had six rose bushes and she called them all by their 'given' names. Apart from Sunset Celebration, the others she referred to as 'the ladies'. There were four more hybrid tea roses. One the colour of those cough-inducing Parma violet sweets that was named for Barbra Streisand. A pink rose for Barbara Bush, a deep orange red for Dolly Parton and a beautiful, extravagant peach-toned flower called Nancy Reagan that was completely at odds with the wizened First Lady Charity knew from the photographs.

Peggy's favourite, however, was Gertie, an English rose. Its full name was Gertrude Jekyll, for a Victorian horticulturalist whose brother was, apparently, the inspiration for the original Dr Jekyll and his Mr Hyde.

Over the next few weeks, Peggy taught Charity more than she had ever wanted to know about roses. She taught her to water them with as much care as she would have fed a human baby. She insisted that Charity talked to the roses all the while she did so.

'Nice rack, Dolly,' Charity said one morning when she was feeling particularly wicked.

'With respect,' came Peggy's voice from inside.

It was a friendship Charity hadn't expected. They were such different people: age, background, class. But as steely as Peggy seemed at first it didn't take long for Charity to realize that the older woman was lonely and was greedy for her company. Talk about roses soon moved on to talk about other things. Peggy's life story, for example.

Peggy wasn't a native Londoner. That much was obvious as soon as she opened her mouth. She was from the States, but she'd been in England for thirty-five of her seventy-nine years.

'Why did you stay here?'

'I liked it. And I had nothing to go back for.'

She'd never been married. She'd been in love just once.

'And once was enough, let me tell you. You love someone, you just hand them the power to kick you where it hurts,' she said.

It was that broken love affair which led Peggy to leave her native United States and come to London at the age of forty-four. Even though it was a love affair that had ended when she was just twenty-one. 'I never thought I'd see him again, then he damn well moved next door!' she explained. 'Last time I saw him, he was a kid just come back from a stint with the army in Germany. My father forbade me to marry him. He moved out of town. But he came back. Not for me, though. He came back with a wife and a child. So much for saving myself.' Peggy sighed.

'And you've been here ever since?'

'That's right,' said Peggy. 'I ran away. The way I see it now, I ought to have done what my Daddy told me. I ought to have forgotten all about that boy and married for money.'

'Money can't make you happy,' said Charity.

'But it can buy you a better class of woe.'

Charity laughed, though she knew she wasn't supposed to.

The spring after they first met, Peggy asked Charity to pick up a package from the post office. It looked like a bunch of twigs. Some pretty sorry-looking twigs at that.

'Someone's taking the piss,' said Charity as she handed the parcel over. 'Was this meant to be a bouquet?'

'This is exactly as it should be. You are going to learn the basics of bare-root rose-growing,' Peggy told her. 'And your first rose, as it should be, is called Charity.'

At the beginning of summer, Charity's eponymous rose bush bore its very first flower. It was yellow. To symbolize joy, said Peggy. And hope.

Charity was unexpectedly thrilled to see the delicate blossom. She felt a tightening in her chest as the emotions strained to get out. She tried to tell Peggy how much their friendship meant to her. Peggy, as always, brushed it away.

She wondered how Peggy was doing in her absence.

'What are you thinking about?' asked Stephanie Blank, as she refilled Charity's glass. 'You look a million miles away. Did you leave someone behind in England? If you're thinking about a man, I want to know all about it.'

'I'm single,' said Charity.

'We both are,' added Grace.

'In that case,' said Stephanie, 'when you call Robin to thank him for the bouquet, you should definitely agree to a date.'

17

Marcella's new conviction that Robin Madden was the man for her was strengthened the following morning when her copy of the *Wall Street Journal* arrived. Marcella subscribed to the *Journal* not for the purpose of following her business interests – she had people who did that for her, didn't she – but for keeping up with the net worth of her neighbours and potential dates. This issue didn't disappoint, for there on page seven was a picture of Robin! It was accompanied by a brief profile and a lengthy explanation of some deal he had just brokered. Marcella skim-read that, taking in only the figures. There were plenty of reassuring noughts.

She picked up her phone just as soon as she finished reading. She would thank him for the flowers and invite him to the opening of the Little Elbow Opera, which was to take place on Friday night. She had taken a box, and, in theory, every seat was filled, but Choate would understand if she withdrew his invitation. He didn't like opera anyway, did he? She couldn't remember.

Marcella dialled Robin. He picked up right away, which both surprised and delighted her. She was surprised because she would have expected a man of his standing to have someone to field his calls. She was delighted because she assumed that he had caller ID and that meant he wanted to talk to her. She forgot that her phone actually blocked her number when she was dialling out.

'Hel-lo,' he said.

'Robin,' she purred. 'You bad, bad boy.'

'Who is this?' Robin asked nervously.

'It's Marcella, silly! Those flowers were simply wonderful.'

'Oh,' said Robin. 'What did you get?'

'Roses, of course.' She was slightly disgruntled that he didn't know but decided to forgive him. He clearly had much better things to do than choose her bouquet. It was enough that he had asked his secretary to do it. He might, after all, have sent a thank-you SMS. So many people did these days.

'So?' said Robin. 'What's happening?'

'Not as much as seems to be happening for you,' said Marcella.

'Too right. You saw the picture in the *Wall Street Journal*? Sweet? At last I can buy your ex-boyfriend's ass. Not that I'd want to,' he added hastily. 'I'm no homo.'

'I guessed you were being metaphorical.'

'Huh? Yeah. Sure. What is it I can do for you, babe? Time is money. Tick, tick, tick.'

'Oh, this is just a social call. I won't keep you long. I was wondering whether you have plans for Friday evening? It's opening night of the new season at the Little Elbow Opera. I have a box. Would you care to join my party?'

'Hey, babe. I'm one step ahead of you. I already got tickets myself.'

'Oh, great. We could merge our parties,' Marcella suggested hopefully.

'Some other time. This Friday night I'm going to be on a date.'

Marcella heard her heart go 'thunk'.

'Anyone I know?' she asked, as lightly as she could, knowing as she did so that the answer almost certainly wasn't going to cheer her up.

'Yeah! As a matter of fact it is. I met her at your house.'
'You did?'
This was getting worse.
'It's Charity Grosvenor.'

'Well, that's good, isn't it?' said Simon, when she told him. 'If you don't need a ticket for Robin Madden, it means you don't have to let Choate down.'

Marcella turned on her heel, whipping Simon across the face with her ponytail as she stalked out of the room.

'That *is* a surprise,' said Stephanie, when Marcella called her and relayed the news.

'I humiliated myself.'

'You only asked him to the opera.'

'He knew what that meant.'

'Well, I don't know what he sees in Charity Grosvenor,' said Stephanie. 'Really, Marcella, you're by far the better girl. He's just been momentarily taken in by her exotic accent. Just go to the opera and have a good time. He will be fascinated. Wear that red dress.'

'The one that reflects on my skin and makes me look as though I just had a face peel?' asked Marcella.

Stephanie laughed. 'How horrible. Who said that to you?'

'You did,' Marcella replied. Though not to my face, she remembered.

'Well, obviously I was joking,' said Stephanie. 'It's my favourite outfit of yours.'

But Stephanie was right about one thing. Marcella couldn't stay away from the opera just because Robin was going to be there with the girl next door. She had three guests to think of:

one of whom was Stephanie herself. The others were Simon and Choate.

Marcella had not meant to ask Choate to the opera but he had been in the room when the tickets arrived. Simon had been the one who said, 'Opera. Oh no! Do I have to go? Choate, you don't know anyone who actually *enjoys* opera, do you?' And Choate said, 'Yes. As a matter of fact I love it.' And after that it would have been rude not to ask him. Marcella ground her teeth as she remembered the rare lapse in rudeness that had saddled her with the Friday night from hell. Opera, the man she wanted to be with there with someone else, and the man she had cast off in the box right beside her.

Her cast-off. Oh, Choate, thought Marcella. If only she could bring herself to love him. Choate was devoted to her. Never a day went by when he didn't do something to remind her of his all too constant constancy. For the last month he had been calling on a twice-daily basis to enquire about the electrics in the pool house. He flooded her e-mail inbox with articles from the *New York Times* online edition.

'Thought you would be interested in this,' he wrote each time.

'The rise of illegal logging?' Marcella mouthed in disbelief.

'Well,' said Simon, 'I can see why he thought it might have been of interest to you, you being a lumber heiress, after all.'

'You're kidding me.' On a day-to-day basis, Marcella was pretty disconnected from her fortune's origins. She liked to think of herself as entrepreneurial. She had lots of business ideas. Her own ranges of scented candles would be nice, she mused. But logging did not interest her at all.

When Choate was in Little Elbow, however, things were far worse. Then he made it his mission to make sure that Marcella *saw* him every day. His reasons for popping round were largely spurious and occasionally ridiculous. Once he even went so far as to say he had promised to drop off some Mark Twain for Anjelica. As if Anjelica were interested in American literature.

It was too sad. Marcella had broken up with Choate almost a year before.

'I wish he would find someone else to fall in love with,' She sighed each time he left. 'It's rather embarrassing the way he keeps coming round here on any old pretext.'

'You could just tell him not to,' said Simon.

'How can I? He's always looking at me with those puppy-dog eyes.'

'How is your puppy, by the way?' Simon asked. 'When are you having him sent over?'

It took a moment before Marcella remembered she'd had a dog.

'Oh,' she said eventually. 'Didn't I tell you? I'm not. I called my London concierge service and told them to get it re-homed.'

Simon's mouth dropped open.

'You asked your *concierge service* to get your dog rehomed? Marcella, that's ridiculous. They'll have taken it straight to Battersea Dogs Home!'

'Oh, don't be silly.' Marcella brushed his typically British reaction away. 'Really, I don't know what I was thinking. A Maltese terrier? That dribbly bit they get around their mouths. I'm going to get a chocolate Lab. You know, Choate is a lot like a Labrador,' she mused. 'Is it really possible that he's still in love with me after I've been so cruel?'

'You've been an absolute bitch to him,' Simon agreed.

Marcella glared at her friend. She had been thinking of herself as cruel in a rather romantic way.

Anyway, it didn't seem to have put Choate off. He arrived

in Little Elbow that Friday night and came straight to Marcella's house, even though his own place was just a few blocks away.

This time, his reason for stopping by was that he had forgotten what time the opera started.

'Eight o'clock,' said Marcella. She kept him on the doorstep.

'Well,' said Choate, 'I'll see you then. I ought to be going.'

Marcella nodded in agreement.

'I'm just going to drop next door with this leaflet.'

'What?'

'It's about postponing the fourth of July fireworks so the piping plovers nesting on the beach won't be frightened away before their eggs hatch. They're getting pretty rare.'

'Oh,' said Marcella. 'I don't think I know the birds you're talking about.'

'Well, at first glance you might mistake them for an ordinary sandpiper,' he began. 'It's a small, sandy-coloured bird. The adult has yellow-orange legs, a black band across the forehead from eye to eye, and a black ring around the base of its neck. The bird's name derives from its call notes, plaintive bell-like whistles . . .'

Marcella began to glaze. Choate noticed.

'Well, I thought that Grace might be interested . . .' His voice tailed off. He turned towards the Rose House as he heard a car crunch on to the gravel drive. Marcella's gimlet eye followed his. 'I'll see you later.'

Choate practically sprinted off to intercept the car's driver.

'What the—?' Marcella stared after him.

In the hallway behind her, Anjelica, who was carrying a sandwich through to the den for Simon, also paused.

18

Robin Madden was every inch the 'master of the universe' when he called Charity to ask for a date. There was no hint in his voice that a negative answer was even a possibility. It was lucky therefore that Charity had decided in advance not to turn him down. Marcella Hunter wasn't the only girl in Little Elbow who read the *Wall Street Journal*.

'What's the dress code?' Charity asked.

'Look hot,' were Robin's instructions. 'Like you always do.'

Charity laughed as she put down the phone. At the moment when Robin called, she had been looking far from 'hot', except in the literal sense. She had been in the garden with Ryan. They were trying to move an old tree stump from the lawn on the other side of the cutting garden.

Ryan hadn't been kidding when he said that he might ask Charity for a hand in the garden. He had even taken to calling her his 'apprentice'. Charity didn't mind. She wanted to learn as much as she could. Besides, it was a pleasure to be working in such a beautiful place. It was also, if she admitted it, a pleasure to be working alongside Ryan.

'What made you decide to be a gardener?' she asked when she came back outside after taking Robin's call that day.

'Rather than what?'

'I don't know. A banker.'

'Call that a choice?'

Charity laughed and handed Ryan one of the two beer bottles she had brought outside with her. 'It pays better.'

'Really? I don't think the deal is worth it. The way I see it, I'm much better off. Because all these guys with their beach-front houses round here . . . how many of them ever get to enjoy the fruits of all their hard work? They're stuck in Manhattan Monday through Friday. Then they have to battle their way out of town on the Long Island Expressway, breathing in other people's exhaust fumes. Every time I take a breather, I don't look up and see a screensaver of the ocean. I look up and see the actual ocean. The sky. The green grass.'

'You're preaching to the choir,' said Charity.

They clinked their beer bottles together.

'A good day's work, I think.'

'Yup,' said Charity, parodying Ryan's accent.

They admired the hole where the stump had been.

'I was wondering whether you're free on Friday night?' Ryan asked.

'Oh, I'm . . . I'm busy . . .' said Charity. 'That call just now. I agreed to . . .'

'Never mind,' said Ryan. 'Some other time.'

'Sure.'

'You've been playing in the mud with Ryan all day,' Grace commented, when Charity went back into the house. 'I didn't think that fraternizing with the staff was part of the plan.'

'It isn't,' said Charity firmly. 'I'm just trying to learn more about roses for when I have a garden like this of my own.'

'And your progress on that front?' Grace asked.

'Robin Madden has asked me on a date.'

'That horrible man from Marcella's dinner?'

'That rich horrible man,' Charity confirmed. '*Wall Street Journal* this morning. Seven-figure bonus.'

The sisters high-fived.

The doorbell rang.

'I think it's Choate,' said Grace.

'Or the best part of Idaho, as I like to call him,' said Charity, referring to the state where the first Fitzgerald had started the lumber business that became the cornerstone of the family's wealth.

It was Choate.

'I wanted to make sure you had seen this leaflet about the rare piping plover,' he told them. 'Hunted almost into extinction by the millinery trade in the nineteenth century. There are now less than fourteen hundred pairs left . . .'

'What a pity.'

Charity excused herself, leaving Grace to make small talk.

19

On Friday evening, Robin arrived to pick Charity up in a Porsche.

Charity tried not to look impressed, though the nearest she had ever come to a Porsche passenger seat before was dripping an ice cream into an open-topped car that had been left unattended outside the Royal Park Hotel back in London. Robin would never have guessed. Charity was au fait with the specifications of pretty much every luxury car you cared to mention. A subscription to *What Car?* had given her an excellent grounding. It was the kind of information every aspiring trophy wife should have at her fingertips.

Robin quickly made it clear that opera wasn't his 'bag'. But if there was one thing that Charity and Grace had quickly learned, it was important for the residents of Little Elbow to be seen in all the right places, and the opening night of the opera was definitely the right kind of place.

'The seats you get on opening night are a pretty good indicator of dick size,' Robin explained.

Little Elbow didn't seem big enough to warrant its own theatre, but it actually had two. One was a children's theatre, which was open during the summer season and the Christmas holidays. The other was the opera. A three-hundred-seater. It had been built by an eccentric millionaire (was there any other type of resident in the town? Charity wondered), who used it for private performances. When he died, leaving no heirs, the theatre became the property of the town council, supported by the taxpayers and charitable donations.

The opera didn't have its own singers or orchestra, however. Each summer, it played host to a visiting company. That year, a French company was doing the honours, performing a new opera based on the conflicts in the Balkans during the 1990s.

'Never heard of them,' said Robin, throwing the programme in Charity's direction.

Like most of the people who would be there that night, Robin was more interested in the 'before and after'. The grounds of the theatre were beautifully landscaped. Proud Little Elbow residents said that this was America's Glyndebourne, and, just as at Glyndebourne, the tradition was to bring a picnic to enjoy before the show and during the interval.

Marcella Hunter had spared no expense for her guests that evening. She'd even brought along Anjelica, dressed in her maid's outfit, to serve the chicken legs.

Stephanie accepted one listlessly.

'You know,' she said, 'maybe I *was* wrong about that red dress. It really doesn't suit you at all. I'm just telling you that as a friend,' she added.

Simon was gallant. 'I like it.'

'Me too,' said Choate.

Overhearing the exchange, Anjelica smiled her appreciation at Choate's tact. What a good man he was.

Fortunately, Marcella was distracted from her annoyance by the arrival of Robin and Charity.

'I want to know where she got that dress from,' Marcella hissed. 'If that is a McQueen, I want to know why I didn't see it during Fashion Week.'

'It's not a McQueen,' said Stephanie, studying Charity with her opera glasses. 'And it looks a little tight for her.'

'I like it,' said Simon.

'Me too,' said Choate.

This time their opinions were not appreciated. Not even by Anjelica.

'Are they coming over here?' Marcella asked.

Stephanie shook her head.

Robin had arranged for himself and Charity to picnic alone. He had reserved a table in a particularly pretty bower. It was the perfect setting for a romantic first date. Quiet, private. Not that they were without interruptions.

What Marcella and Stephanie didn't know was that from the moment Charity opened the door of the Rose House, her date had been on his cellphone. Robin had one of those headsets that look as though they were designed by the costume department for *Star Trek*, which meant that he was able to talk and drive. Which he did. All the way from the Rose House to the opera house. He was still talking as he was handing over his car keys to the valet. As he was handing his tickets to the girl on the front desk at the opera. As he and Charity were being shown to their designated picnic spot by a fresh-faced teen in an ill-fitting tuxedo.

The only good thing about the headset, thought Charity, was that if you were watching them from a very great distance, you might not notice Robin's earpiece and could instead think that he was regaling Charity with some exciting tale rather than barking figures at some poor assistant back on Wall Street.

The assistant back on Wall Street was taking a lot of flak that night. Charity and Robin had been on their date for a full forty-five minutes before Robin finished his call and had time to say, 'I like your dress' before his phone rang again and he was lost to Charity once more. Ah well, she thought. You didn't get to drive a Porsche by being a slacker. She looked at their picnic with longing. Was it rude to start while he was talking? Robin answered her thought by making a start on a chicken leg, talking to his colleague all the while.

Eventually, Charity had to get up to go to the restroom. She conveyed her intention to Robin in what she hoped was international sign language.

There was a queue. As there always is. No matter how smart the venue, it seems that planners always underestimate the number of cubicles that women need. Still, it was an opportunity for the women of Little Elbow to catch up on the gossip out of sight and sound of the men in their lives.

'I was surprised to see those two together.'

'I give them to the end of the summer. Max.'

'No! They were so much in love.'

'With themselves.'

Charity was just reapplying her lipstick at the mirror when Marcella Hunter's reflection appeared beside hers like Banquo's ghost.

'It looks as though your date isn't going so well,' said Marcella. 'Perhaps you'd care to join us instead.'

'Oh, thank you,' said Charity. 'But we're doing just fine. Robin has a couple of business calls to make and I'm more than happy to do a bit of a people-watching.'

'Robin's a nice guy. A touch too involved with his work.'

'I suppose that's the way people become successful.'

'Doesn't leave much time for them to create proper relationships, though. You've got to be very understanding. That's why most of these men end up with trophy wives who are very able to entertain themselves. Women who have fortunes of their own to manage.'

'Really?'

'Well, I guess I'll see you soon,' said Marcella. She had neither used the loo nor touched up her make-up, Charity noted.

When Charity returned from the restroom, Robin was still on his phone. He held up a finger to indicate that he would be a minute longer. Ten minutes later, he was still talking to someone in Los Angeles as people began to file into the theatre and take their places.

Chairty and Robin had seats in a box. Directly on the other side of the theatre was Marcella's box. Stephanie confirmed, using the opera glasses, that Robin was still deep in conversation and *not* with his date.

'I feel rather sorry for her,' said Simon. 'Robin Madden is quite the biggest pig I've ever met. I think you're lucky to be with us instead of him. She looks like she's having a terrible night.'

'Believe me,' said Marcella, 'it's about to get a whole lot worse.'

Robin finished his call as the house lights were dimmed. Charity smiled at him in relief. A hush fell over the audience. There was a low rumble from the timpani, as the orchestra began the overture. The curtains lifted on a scene of devastation. A schoolgirl wept over the body of her dead brother (Charity guessed that much from the programme notes). She began to sing with such a sweet, high voice, it was surprisingly easy to overlook the fact that the soprano playing the schoolgirl must have been in her late thirties.

Charity hadn't known quite what to expect. She hadn't

expected to be so enthralled so early in the piece. She leaned forward over the balcony rail to get a closer look.

On the other side of the theatre, Marcella and Stephanie were taking turns with the opera glasses.

'I think he looks bored,' Stephanie whispered.

'He does, doesn't he?' Marcella agreed.

'Ssssshh,' suggested Simon.

Unaware that he was being watched, Robin turned his mobile phone over and over in his hand as though it were a set of worry beads.

'Would you just look at that man,' said Marcella. 'He simply cannot leave his phone alone.'

'I think it's time to do it,' said Stephanie, as the opera entered a particularly quiet passage. 'You've got the number?'

Marcella nodded.

'What are you doing?' Simon asked, as Marcella disappeared beneath her seat.

He looked down to see her fishing her phone out of her handbag.

'You're not . . .'

On stage, the music was as quiet as a whisper. The heroine was at her lowest ebb. She clutched a pistol in her hand and sang of the fragility of life and the eternity of death. Charity couldn't help herself. She was swept up in the emotion of it all. She strained to hear every word.

And Robin's phone went off.

20

Everyone in the theatre immediately looked in the direction of Robin's box, including the soprano. Robin was oblivious. Alas, he had answered the call, flipping open the phone and putting his headset back on simultaneously. It was a reflex action, as automatic to him as taking a big breath when surfacing from underwater.

To make things worse – as if things could be worse – Robin stood up, with a finger in the opposite ear to that which sported the earpiece, and said, loudly, 'I can't hear you. Speak up. What are you telling me about the figures?'

On stage, the soprano continued to sing, but it was clear that she was becoming justifiably agitated.

'Goddam,' Robin said to the caller. 'Speak up! Shit. I've lost it.'

Thank God, thought Charity. Robin sat back down. But seconds later, the phone was ringing again. Robin pressed Receive.

'Hello.'

'For goodness' sake.'

The soprano gestured to the conductor. The music stopped. A spotlight was turned on the box. Charity shrank down into her seat.

'Sir, if you don't finish your call at once, I'll have to ask you to leave the theatre,' said the soprano, voice quavering.

Robin snapped his phone shut, belligerently.

'Couldn't hear a thing anyway,' he said to Charity.

The opera resumed. After a moment or two, the audience settled down again and it was as if nothing had happened. Robin certainly was acting as though nothing had happened. Charity, however, was still glowing radioactive red with embarrassment. She didn't dare look at him. He was fiddling with his phone again. She hoped he was turning it off.

He wasn't.

It rang.

This time the soprano gave the orchestra the signal to quit right away. The string section shut down like the sound of fingernails on a blackboard.

'Please leave the theatre!' the soprano shouted.

'They've hung up,' Robin protested.

'I don't care. You should have turned you phone off after the last call. You should have turned your phone off before the performance started!'

As if to give the soprano the finger, Robin's phone started ringing once more.

'Don't take that call,' the soprano warned him. 'If you take that call I will leave the stage!'

Robin couldn't help himself.

'It could be important,' he explained.

'Leave!' the soprano demanded.

'The hell I will!' said Robin. His caller had rung off. 'Just start your warbling. I'll turn the cellphone off.'

'It's too late. I will not start singing again until you're gone!'

'I'm not leaving.'

'I'm not singing until you leave.'

'And I won't leave until you've been fired. I didn't give a donation of fifty thousand dollars to the opera house to hear this crap.'

'Robin,' said Charity, tugging gently on his sleeve, 'I think I'd like to go.'

'Stay there. We're not going anywhere.' Robin sat down heavily. 'Sing, bitch.'

With a heart-wrenching sob, the singer picked up her skirts and fled to the safety of the wings. There was a murmur of indignation from the crowd. Someone booed.

Moments later, the theatre manager crept out into the spotlight.

'Mademoiselle Radanne regrets that she is unable to continue tonight's performance unless . . .' He chanced a look in Robin's direction. Robin folded his arms to underline his resolve to stay exactly where he was.

Eventually, someone down in the stalls stood up and started a slow handclap.

'Get out of here!' came a shout from the upper circle.

'Robin,' Charity whispered, 'I think this is what one calls an impasse.'

'A what?' Robin said irritably.

The clapping grew louder. When Charity poked her head over the balcony rail again, she saw that several people had joined in, including Marcella's party in the opposite box.

'Robin. Really,' said Charity. 'I know that this has become something of a matter of principle for you now but I really don't think anyone is interested in principle this evening. They just want to see the opera. And it looks as though the soprano was serious. She's not coming back out till we're gone.'

'Dickheads, the lot of you!' Robin shouted at the crowd.

'I'm going.' Charity had already gathered her jacket and handbag. She was ready to run. 'Come with me. Please.'

'OK,' said Robin to Charity. 'But I'm not going because those jerks are giving me the slow clap. We're going to leave because I can tell that *you're* getting uncomfortable. But only because of that . . .'

'Oh, thank you.' Charity was on her way.

'I could buy every single last freaking one of you,' Robin shouted as a parting shot. The slow handclap became thunderous applause upon his exit.

Charity was still hyperventilating ten minutes later, when they were safely out of the auditorium and in Robin's car. But Robin didn't seem disturbed by what had just taken place. In fact, he seemed pretty pleased with himself.

'Don't you worry,' said Robin to Charity. 'Nobody makes a fool out of Robin Madden. This time next year, that bitch will be singing on the sidewalk.' He flicked open his phone and punched in a number. 'Yeah. It's me. Robin Madden. It's about the opera house in Little Elbow. I've got a feeling they may be in breach of some safety regulations. They should be closed down. Uh-huh. Uh-huh. That sounds wonderful. Why didn't I think of that? You're a genius. I'll pay extra if you can get it done before tomorrow's matinee.'

Robin closed his telephone with a smile that verged on cartoon-baddy evil.

'You'd get the opera house closed down!' Charity exclaimed.

'Got to teach those arty-farty types a lesson.'

Robin suggested that they went on to a bar but Charity feigned a sudden headache. There were very few bars in Little Elbow and the thought that someone who had witnessed her embarrassment at the opera might see her later on really wasn't appealing. Robin didn't seem too bothered by Charity's decision to have an early night. He said that he needed to make some calls, find out which clown had called him in the middle of the performance and exactly what they had called to talk about. The caller had withheld his or her ID and spoken so softly that Robin didn't have a clue whether they were male or female, whether they had called to tell him to buy or to sell. He would get to the bottom of it, though.

No he wouldn't, thought Marcella. Stephanie's little plan had worked like a dream. She couldn't imagine that Charity's date was going all that well now. And there was the added bonus that her desirability as a guest at any other Little Elbow function might have been damaged by the incident. After all, doesn't everyone judge everyone by the company they keep?

Home much earlier than she had expected, Charity joined Grace on the sofa in the den in front of the enormous television.

'Date go well?' Grace asked, without tearing her eyes away from some late-night re-rerun of *Oprah*.

'Not exactly,' Charity admitted. 'He turned out to be every bit the pig I suspected he was. He answered his phone in the middle of the opera.'

On-screen, a woman was bemoaning the way her husband had changed when he came into some money. 'He became arrogant. It was like he could buy anyone so he didn't have to be polite any more.'

Grace nodded in sympathy. Then she turned off the television and listened while Charity described her evening in greater detail. She couldn't help laughing, especially when Charity described the Mafioso-style phone call Robin had made on the way home.

'He's not really going to do anything dodgy. He was just sounding off to one of his mates,' Grace concluded.

'Oh no,' said Charity. 'He seemed serious. After all,' she lampooned him, 'Robin Madden could buy every last man, woman and child on Long Island.'

'Shame he couldn't buy himself some manners,' said Grace.

'I don't think I can go through another night like that.'

'Maybe you should choose your dates on a different criterion. What's the saying?' Grace mused. 'If you marry for money you work for every penny.'

Charity swatted her sister with a scatter cushion.

21

Charity had hoped to put the opera incident behind her, but the first thing Ryan said to her the following morning was: 'I saw you at the opera last night.'

'I think everybody saw me,' said Charity.

'I didn't know you were friends with Robin Madden.'

'Not friends exactly . . .'

'Ah,' said Ryan.

Curses, thought Charity. That had come out wrong.

'I met him next door at Marcella Hunter's. Two days later he phoned to say he had a spare ticket for the opera and I accepted it. I was so embarrassed when his phone went off.'

'I wouldn't worry about it. It could have happened to any single person in that audience and they all knew it. They won't hold it against you. Or him.'

'Was the rest of the opera good?'

'Didn't get to see much more of it. The soprano came back on after you and Robin left but she quit the stage for good when someone's cellphone started playing Eminem five minutes later.'

'That's terrible.'

'Yep. Well, people don't have a lot of respect for anything except money in this town.'

'I didn't know you liked opera.'

'There's quite a lot you don't know about me,' he said.

It suddenly dawned on Charity that Ryan must have been

offering to take her to the opera when he had asked her whether she was busy on Friday night. Who had he taken instead? She couldn't ask him but she wished she had seen. The last person she had expected to see at the opera house was a gardener. Wasn't he supposed to be watching sports somewhere?

'Dolly Parton giving it all she's got this morning,' Ryan said suddenly.

'Dolly Parton?'

He jerked his head in the direction of a velvety red blossom.

Charity couldn't help smiling. 'I've seen one of those before.'

'Doesn't quite suit her, that name. I mean, I'm sure Dolly Parton is a lovely woman and all, but strikes me a rose that classy should have a namesake with a little more gravitas.'

Charity gently lifted the rose and took a sniff at it. The fragrance immediately transported her back to Peggy's tiny London garden.

'It's lovely.'

'It is,' said Ryan. He grinned. 'Want to help me mow the lawn?'

Charity was so relieved that the conversation about the opera was over that she almost said yes.

Meanwhile, the news that fleas had been found in the upholstery at the opera spread around Little Elbow faster than a horse with a hornet between its buttocks.

The scandal arrived at the Rose House courtesy of Marcella Hunter.

Marcella simply had to find out what became of Charity's date after the mystery phone calls. She didn't think Robin or Charity knew she had anything to do with it, though about half an hour after he left the theatre, Robin had called Marcella's cellphone, causing it to sing out the first few bars of Eminem's 'Stan'. Now that was embarrassing.

'I cannot believe you pulled that stunt,' said Simon as they filed out of the theatre with everybody else after the soprano broke down in sobs, cursed the United States in three different languages and refused ever to sing there again.

'Oh, come on,' said Marcella. 'It was an easy mistake to make. I thought I'd turned my phone off.'

'I was talking about calling Robin and pretending to be a broker.'

'Oh, where's your sense of humour?' said Stephanie. 'Marcella was brilliant.'

Stephanie tucked her arm through Marcella's and they sashayed off together across the car park, like a pair of schoolgirls. Marcella was thrilled to have Stephanie onside for once.

Choate was oblivious. He had been too absorbed in the opera and then in the action on the other side of the theatre to realize that the calls to Robin's cellphone were originating in the very box in which he was sitting. He merely thanked Marcella wholeheartedly for taking him along. It was a terrible pity the performance was cut short but perhaps, he thought to himself, he might find occasion to see it again. With a date. He had scanned the theatre for a sighting of Grace Grosvenor and had none, which could only mean that she hadn't been invited as another guy's date. The field was still wide open.

Anyway, back to the fleas.

By Saturday lunchtime, five people had called the opera to say that they had been bitten by what appeared to be cat fleas. One of the complainants subsequently dispatched a health inspector to the theatre. He arrived half an hour before the matinee and ordered that the show be cancelled and the place shut down until he had completed a thorough inspection.

Alas, his inspection found that the first three rows of the theatre were crawling with nasties.

'I don't understand it,' said the manager. 'We have no cat here. How can we have cat fleas? They must have been brought in by a theatregoer.'

In fact, they had been brought into the theatre in a pill bottle by the inspector himself, who had a chronic gambling habit and a lot of bad debts. The five bite victims were people similarly indebted to a small-time Mr Big who owed Robin Madden a favour.

The opera was suspended until further notice.

Charity grew cold as Marcella relayed the tale (though of course Marcella didn't doubt the veracity of the inspector's report).

'Can you imagine? What kind of people are they letting into this town that have *fleas*? When I heard the news I took the dress that I was wearing last night and asked Anjelica to *burn* it.'

'Wouldn't dry cleaning have done the job?'

'I don't want to take the risk. You know, there was a woman in Minnesota who actually died of a flea bite.'

'Really?'

'So, in retrospect, you must feel quite lucky that you didn't stay to the end of the opera. I'm sure the fleas would have got right up to the balconies by the end of the performance. Darling,' she added, putting her hand on Charity's arm, 'we all felt quite sorry for you. In front of everybody in town. To be associated with someone so . . . so . . .'

While Marcella was mid-flow, the telephone rang.

'You should get that,' she told Charity.

'No, really, it's OK.'

'Don't stand on ceremony for me. If my phone rings, I always take the call.'

Too late. The answer machine had already kicked in. It was set to speakerphone so that Charity and Marcella could hear the call quite clearly. It was Robin.

'Hey, baby,' he began. 'You heard about the opera house? Didn't I tell you that no one disrespects Robin Madden? Well, it seems they had an "infestation" of some kind.' The girls could hear the inverted commas around 'infestation'. 'I sent in my very own inspector. And now the fat lady has finished singing. The Department of Health is all over it and my attorney is putting in an offer for the building as we speak. I figure I'll get twenty apartments on that piece of land. Maybe thirty. And it's all thanks to you, my sweet. I would never even have considered going to the opera if I hadn't been trying to style you. Now I have a vision. I'm going to call each of the apartments after an opera. *Carmen. La Travertina. West Side Story.*'

La Travertina? Marcella raised her eyebrows.

'And every apartment will have a state-of-the-art music system so if people want to listen to that shit, they can listen to it properly. Hey, baby, how about another date in consideration of your being my inspiration?'

Marcella looked at Charity enquiringly. Charity shook her head.

'Call me back.'

Robin ended the call with a short pastiche of 'Nessun Dorma'.

'So? Are you going to be seeing him again?' Marcella asked.

'I don't think so,' said Charity. 'We're not really that compatible.'

'What a shame,' said Marcella.

22

'Well,' said Marcella triumphantly, 'that put a stop to that. Charity Grosvenor is not going to be the first Mrs Madden. Or even go on another date with that man.'

'And you're not disgusted that the opera house had to close down as a result?' Simon asked. She had told him all about the overheard phone call.

'Oh, it will reopen in a couple of years,' said Marcella blithely. 'There's no way that anyone in Little Elbow is going to see Robin Madden build condos on that site. Even if he does manage to buy it, there will be a petition as soon as he submits planning. And a campaign to keep the performing arts in the town.'

Simon looked perturbed.

'Darling, what are you so upset about? I would have thought you would say that opera is elitist. You're always telling me that television is the only truly important medium these days.'

'So, are you going to go out with Robin now that he's available again?'

'Oh no,' said Marcella. 'He's way too uncouth. How could I possibly date someone who doesn't understand the value of tradition and culture? Someone who turns out to be such a *bully* to boot. I've got my eye on someone a little more cerebral.' She smoothed open the pages of the *Wall Street Journal*. 'Like this guy.'

★   ★   ★

Marcella turned to a profile of Little Elbow's newest resident. During the course of the past month, the Mendelsohn family had sold off half their waterfront estate. A chap called Jerry Penman had bought the land. The Harbor Club had been atwitter with rumours of his arrival for weeks. Not only was he mega-rich, he was under thirty, unmarried and, as yet, unproven to be gay. He was alleged to number several supermodels among his closest friends.

Unlike many of the other eligibles in Little Elbow, he was not an East Coast native born and bred. Jerry Penman had grown up in Utah, where he had lived with his large Mormon family until he moved to California at the height of the Internet boom. And that was where he made his fortune.

As a teenager, shy and spotty, Penman had spent many long hours in his bedroom, convincing himself that he was of some importance in the world by attempting to crash his high school's database and tinker with his grades. He did that easily and quickly moved on to tougher targets. One of those targets was an Internet company, which, amazingly, when it caught up with Jerry, decided it would be better to have the teenage genius on the payroll than in prison.

And so the poacher turned gamekeeper, writing the anti-virus software that would make him a billionaire. Probably a multi-billionaire if he could have been bothered to get out there and sell himself. But the fact was Jerry Penman didn't like to get out there. He didn't need to. The glitterati all went to him.

It wasn't Penman's money but how he had spent it which attracted models and actresses into his orbit (according to the *Wall Street Journal*). There was something rock-star-like about the way that Penman had gone about spending his fortune. His yacht was one of the biggest private vessels in the world. It had taken almost three years to complete. It was so large it even had its own operating theatre, which was where some of the world's most beautiful women had their extremely discreet plastic surgery and recovered far from the prying lenses of the paparazzi.

'He seems like a suitable boy,' said Marcella.

What Marcella didn't know was that she wasn't the only woman in Little Elbow with designs on Jerry Penman. Charity Grosvenor was already one step ahead of her.

Charity tracked him down over the Net. It was simple. Among the holdings listed in an article Charity found about Penman's business interests was an Internet dating service called www.hotpeopleseekhotpeople.com, and that was where Charity looked for him. It was pleasingly easy to find him among the clients of his own dating website, who were all about as 'hot' as the Arctic Circle. Though he had created an alias – *the Penmeister* – Penman had posted the photograph that ran alongside every business article she found about him. It looked as though it was the snap he had used on his identity card when he was still a humble employee of that first Internet company rather than the proprietor of the world's largest floating cosmetic surgery business.

Anyway, Charity sent him a 'wink', as the dating parlance goes, and she was well on her way to having a date with Jerry Penman before she even arrived in the USA.

Their correspondence had been frequent, if not very interesting. It was largely peppered with anomalous sports results and reports on Penman's position in various online fantasy games. But Charity was certain that the reality would be better. There were, after all, plenty of people who found it difficult to express themselves in print. Penman was a mathematical genius who could see the patterns in computer code. Why should he be able to punctuate as well?

And the longer she stared at his photograph, like a devout teenager staring at the Madonna until she starts to cry, the more she was convinced that he might turn out to be handsome.

'I can tell just by looking at him that he won't be able to string a sentence together,' said Simon, studying Penman's photograph in the newspaper.

'You think that matters?' Marcella replied. 'Linda Deuble says he's coming into town in just two weeks' time. I'm going to send him a basket of fruit.'

'Good idea,' said Simon. 'It might help with his acne.'

Exactly two weeks later, while Marcella was calling the florists to arrange for a fruit-and-floral tribute, Penman e-mailed Charity to say that, at long last, he would be in Little Elbow that very weekend. He would be arriving by private jet (one of two. The other was in Europe, which was where he also kept his yacht: *The Game*.)

'Game on,' said Grace, when Charity told her. 'You'll be married to a millionaire before the end of the summer.'

'But what about you?' asked Charity.

'Oh, I don't know if I'm interested in dating,' said Grace.

'It was the whole point. Are you going to spend the rest of the summer sitting here like Miss Havisham?'

'Funny you should say that. Choate sent me this today.'

She showed Charity the copy of *Great Expectations* that had arrived in that morning's mail.

'A *big* hint.'

'Do I have to read it?'

'I would think that was the idea. Choate doesn't strike me as the kind of guy who would make a cheap joke based purely on the book's title.'

'It's second hand,' said Grace. 'It's got his name written in the front of it. That's a bit weird, don't you think? Sending someone one of your own books?'

Saturday morning. Two a.m. Anjelica finished reading *Huckleberry Finn*. She smiled with satisfaction as she read the last line. If only Choate were sitting beside her, so that she could turn to him and tell him what she thought. She would have to content herself with a thank-you letter. When she could find the time to write one. She had stayed up until the middle of the night to finish reading the book. She would have to be awake and in the kitchen in less than five hours.

23

When Saturday came around again, Charity couldn't help but be excited.

With such wealth at his disposal, what would her first date with Penman be like? As she prepared for the evening, she slipped her passport into her handbag. Who knew? She might find herself waking up in St Tropez. Now that would be very nice.

'What kind of car do you think he drives?' mused Grace as they waited for Penman to arrive.

'Lamborghini. Definitely,' said Charity. 'Something sleek.'

Penman arrived at the Rose House in a Hummer. Charity and Grace couldn't quite believe it. Neither of them had ever seen a Hummer outside footage of the Gulf War and rap videos. It was somewhat at odds with the white-picket-fence surroundings of Little Elbow, like the cast of *Mad Max* suddenly tearing through the middle of *It's a Wonderful Life*.

'Nice car,' said Grace disingenuously, as they waited and watched for the driver to climb out. The windows were all heavily tinted, of course. Probably bullet-proof too. 'Do you think he's got a bodyguard?'

Eventually, after what seemed like an age, the driver climbed out. Perhaps it wasn't Penman, Charity considered. It was still difficult to tell exactly who he was. He was wearing sunglasses and had a bandana wrapped low around his forehead. Also, he was looking down, transfixed by the PDA in his hand.

'It must be him,' said Grace. 'Unless he's Marcella's drug dealer come to the wrong house.'

He was tall, which was a relief, but Charity felt sure that she still could have taken him in a fight. Jerry Penman had clearly used all his energy growing up rather than out. Perhaps he was seeking to counter that by wearing the camouflage gear with all those bulging pockets. Charity caught a glimpse of herself in the bedroom mirror. She was wearing a shift dress and heels.

'I hope he isn't going to take me paint-balling,' she whispered. 'I'm going to change into my jeans,' she added, making a dash for the wardrobe. 'Will you go down and open the door to him?'

'It's OK,' said Grace. 'He hasn't made it down the drive yet. He's just standing there. He seems to be doing something on his Blackberry. Perhaps he's picking up his e-mail.'

'He's supposed to be picking me up,' said Charity in annoyance. 'Well, when he's finished doing business, do me a favour and let him in.'

Grace agreed. But Charity had time to dress and change her hair without worrying that her date was getting bored. Four minutes after he had turned off his car engine, Jerry Penman was still standing in the middle of the driveway. He looked deep in concentration. (Well, as far as you could tell from his posture. He was still wearing his sunglasses though the sun had started to go down.)

'What is he doing?' Charity asked, after the girls had watched him for a further five minutes. Finally, Penman looked up from his Blackberry and punched the air!

'Perhaps he just got news about some enormous deal,' said Grace.

'Then dinner is definitely on him,' said Charity. 'I'm going downstairs.'

'You must be Jerry Penman!' she trilled as she opened the door.

By this point, Penman had advanced a further two metres towards the house before stopping to do something on his Blackberry again. At the sound of Charity's voice, he looked up and simultaneously ducked down as though ambushed by Iraqi insurgents intent on spilling Yankee blood.

'Oh, er, hi,' he said when he realized that his assailant was in fact a girl of five feet four.

'I'll just grab my coat,' said Charity.

'Good luck,' said Grace, who was hiding behind the door.

'Oh, this will be fine,' Charity assured her. 'He's just shy. He'll warm up.'

Later, Charity would reflect that her first ride in a Hummer was every bit as nerve-racking as taking part in Operation Desert Storm. It wasn't just the fact that Penman drove as though he were avoiding landmines, swerving from one side of the road to another with alarming frequency. The noise was terrible too. Penman's MP3 player was plugged into the stereo and cranked up full blast. Charity picked up the MP3 to find out what she was listening to. It sounded like a firestorm punctuated with curses. It was called 'Dirty Ho's Like It Rough' and it was filed under a playlist entitled 'Date music'.

'Wow, romantic,' said Charity.

Penman couldn't hear her.

But even though her ears were on the point of bleeding, Charity remained determined to give Penman the benefit of the doubt. He was pretty young. He thought he was being exciting with all this fast driving and vile rap (he probably had a collection that included Charles Aznavour back at his 'crib'). And, of course, he was richer than God.

'Where are we going?'

At least the choice of restaurant was impressive. Penman pulled up outside the newest place in town. Charity had heard talk of it at Marcella's dinner party. Reservations were like gold dust. And Penman had somehow secured the best table in the house. Which was a surprise, given that he was wearing combats and a bandana in a room full of men in jackets and women with big blow-dried curls straight from the 1950s. Charity felt somewhat self-conscious in her jeans. But the waiter didn't seem to mind. He didn't bat an eyelid at the couple's strange appearance as he flicked open their napkins and laid them in their laps.

'So, we meet at last.' Charity was the first to speak.

'Er, yes,' said Penman.

'It's strange, isn't it? I feel I know you so well from the e-mailing and yet . . .'

'Yet what?'

'Well, I really don't know you at all. I didn't know what your voice was going to sound like. It's nice.' Charity was being kind. In reality she wasn't certain Penman's voice had broken.

'You have an accent,' he replied.

'No, *you* have the accent,' Charity joked.

'I don't have an accent,' said Penman. He wasn't joking.

'I suppose you're right,' Charity conceded. 'On this side of the Atlantic, I'm the one with the funny voice.'

Penman nodded. They both looked down at their menus.

'This is lovely. What do you recommend?'

'I only eat hamburgers,' said Penman.

'It doesn't look like there are any hamburgers on the menu,' Charity observed. 'Unless my French is so bad I just can't see it among all the *filet de boeuf*.'

'They'll make me one,' said Penman.

Indeed, it seemed they would. 'Your usual?' asked the waiter when he came to take Penman's order. Charity ordered chicken.

'Will they give your hamburger a special French twist?' Charity asked.

'They better not,' said Penman. 'I like it plain.'

The food arrived. Charity's chicken was arranged on the plate with artistry worthy of a place in the permanent collection at the Louvre. Penman's burger was another story.

He wasn't kidding about liking his burger plain. The components of his meal were laid around the plate as though they were parts of a hamburger-shaped puzzle. Charity noticed also that no one piece was touching any other. The ketchup was contained in a little paper cup. Still, if that was what he wanted to eat. It just seemed a shame when there was so much pleasure to be had from food.

Charity couldn't wait to tuck into her own plate. She waited eagerly for Penman to return from the men's room. The smell of the chicken mingled with the rosemary with which it had been cooked was sending her salivary glands into overdrive. She hadn't eaten since lunchtime. In such a state of hunger and anticipation two minutes passed like two hours.

And fifteen minutes passed like fifteen hours. The chicken was starting to get cold and still Penman hadn't returned from the restroom. It suddenly occurred to Charity that perhaps he had left the restaurant altogether. Had she hit upon a nerve by commenting on his choice of meal? Surely she would have heard him leave? The Hummer wasn't exactly a stealth vehicle. She had heard Penman's car a full five minutes before he actually arrived at the Rose House.

No, he hadn't left. And now another possibility crept into Charity's mind and she suddenly felt extremely guilty for having been so self-obsessed as to assume that she had to be the reason for Penman's extended bathroom visit. Perhaps he was lying on the floor in the men's room, having suffered a chronic asthma attack! Charity called the waiter over.

'Excuse me. I wonder . . .' She was so embarrassed. 'It's just that my date has been gone for rather a long time.'

'Madam, I will check for you.'

A minute later the waiter returned. 'He says that he will be right out.'

Now Charity felt really embarrassed. Perhaps Penman was having bowel issues.

But right out wasn't to be right out at all. Five minutes more and Charity could wait no longer. She surreptitiously speared a carrot, which was every bit as delicious as she had known it would be. She arranged the other carrots to close up the gap so that Penman wouldn't know she had started. The carrot hadn't just been delicious, however, it was also cold. Charity wondered whether it would be rude to ask the waiter to take the meals back to the kitchen to be reheated.

And should she say anything to Penman about his disappearance when he finally returned? What if he had been struggling with some terrible bowel explosion? In that position, Charity wouldn't have wanted to have attention drawn to the problem.

Finally, he appeared. He didn't seem to be unwell. In fact, he seemed jubilant. He was walking with an exaggerated pimp roll.

'I kicked that mo' fo's ass!' he announced when he finally sat down.

'Have you been in a fight?' Charity asked him.

'A battle to the death, sister. To the death.'

'Who with?'

'With the man who calls himself the most powerful wizard on the east coast of the United States. I guess he's not feeling quite so powerful tonight.'

Penman made a small 'victory' gesture and crammed a piece of burger into his mouth, followed by a piece of bread dipped in ketchup. It was like watching a child raised in a Romanian orphanage encountering something other than porridge for the first time. He ate as though he were afraid the plate might be snatched away at any moment. Or as though he were in a hurry to be somewhere else. Even if it was only the men's room again.

'I kicked his ass real good,' Penman mumbled through a mouthful of crumbs.

Eventually Charity cottoned on. 'You're not talking about someone who is actually in the restaurant tonight. . . .'

24

'Where is this other guy?'

'He's in Baltimore.'

'And he's a wizard in a computer game.'

'In another life!' Penman corrected her.

'And that's what you were doing. While I thought you were in the restroom having some kind of fit, you were actually playing a computer game.'

'*The* Game,' said Penman. 'Like life only better.'

'OK.'

Penman looked down at his crotch. Then he told Charity, 'I need to use the restroom again.'

She raised an eyebrow.

'No,' he said. 'I really need to go the restroom.'

'Sure,' said Charity. She could hardly stop him, could she?

She glanced around the restaurant. It was a busy night. And everyone else seemed to be enjoying themselves enormously. It was a great place. The decor was lovely – like a French country kitchen. The food was delicious. Even when cold. But Charity couldn't help wishing the floor would open up and swallow her. Sitting right in the middle as she was (suddenly she wasn't sure this was the best table), there was no doubt that everyone could see how often her date had been absent in the space of the past hour and a half.

Still, at least there was no one she knew around to witness her humiliation.

'Charity?' asked Marcella. 'Is that you? I thought it was you! What a lovely surprise!'

It was certainly a surprise, thought Charity.

She hadn't seen Simon and Marcella when she walked into the restaurant. She wondered where they had been sitting. And how good their view of Charity's table had been.

'How nice to see you! What are you doing here? Is that Jerry Penman you've been having dinner with? Well, sort of having dinner with.' Marcella raised an eyebrow. 'There isn't some kind of problem with the food, is there? Food poisoning?'

'I think he's in the middle of doing some kind of business deal,' said Charity.

'Really? I heard he didn't do much business these days. Said in his interview with *Forbes* that he was giving it all up to play computer games. Dull way to spend your life, though. Especially when there are much more interesting things to do. Like go on dates.'

Charity smiled thinly.

'Would you like a lift home? I'm assuming Jerry Penman drove you here?'

'And hopefully he'll be driving me back,' said Charity.

'You mean you're not fed up waiting?'

'He won't be much longer.'

'Ah well. We must be off. A nightcap at the Harbor Club, Simon?'

'Great idea. Good night, Charity,' said Simon.

The vile twins left. Marcella whispered something into Simon's ear that made him smirk. Charity just knew they were talking about her. She glared after them. Marcella was poisonous, but in many ways Simon was the more despicable.

Always following Marcella around as though he were her lapdog. Charity wondered whether he had bought dinner. She doubted it.

But he was the son of a clan chief. And that presumably meant that he was a worthy freeloader.

Charity caught a glimpse of herself in the mirrored wall. She was frowning. She had to stop frowning. She couldn't afford Botox. At least, not yet.

Charity had desert and drank two cups of coffee before she gave up on Jerry Penman.

'He is still in the restroom,' the waiter confirmed.

'Well, he can stay there,' said Charity. 'Will you call me a taxi and let him know that I've gone home?'

Unfortunately, the taxi company said that no car would be available for the next half an hour at the very earliest. It was a busy night in Little Elbow. But Charity simply couldn't wait that long. She couldn't go back into the restaurant and sit back down either. She'd made her stand. She called Grace, to see whether she would bring the hire car out, but Grace was nervous about driving on the wrong side of the road in the dark. Half an hour wasn't so long to wait for a taxi, was it? Grace said.

Half an hour sitting alone in a restaurant is an eternity.

Could she walk? Charity wondered. It was a nice evening. But like most American towns, Little Elbow had not been built with walking in mind. Neither had Charity's shoes.

She actually stamped her foot with frustration. But she had to go. There was no way she was going to be sitting at that table when Penman emerged from the men's room having vanquished another wizard. She set out.

*   *   *

As she tried to walk along the grass verge without breaking an ankle, Charity reflected on that evening's date. What was wrong with these people? Why did Robin Madden and Jerry Penman go on dates at all if they were going to spend the evening engaged with other people electronically?

Was that the truth about rich guys? The flip-side of the ambition that had allowed them to make a fortune was that they had other obsessive behaviours too? Perhaps it didn't matter. As Charity's mother had told her when she was just a little girl, marriages weren't the stuff of fairy tales. You were lucky if the romance lasted past the honeymoon. After that, what you needed was a good friend. Or, if your husband didn't turn out to be someone you wanted to be friends with, you needed one who would stay out of your way when he was at home and be discreet when he was playing away.

So, when Charity decided to try her luck at bagging a husband while in Little Elbow, she wasn't after hearts and flowers. But a man who spent their entire dinner date sitting in a toilet cubicle playing computer games? Was an enormous yacht worth putting up with that for?

Charity paused by the bus stop. The timetable announced that there were no buses outside the hours of nine till five. Another ploy to keep hoi polloi out of Little Elbow. If you couldn't afford to drive into town in a four-by-four they definitely didn't want you there after dark.

As she stood at the bus stop, wondering whether to push on in her Jimmy Choos or sit down on the bench and wait till dawn, Charity heard the unmistakable sound of Penman's Hummer. Its wide-set headlamps flooded the street with a klieg light glare. Charity slunk back into the hedge until he'd passed.

What a mistake she had made. She'd allowed herself to believe that he was worth dating. If he hadn't been worth a fortune, she wouldn't have replied to his first e-mail, which was both brief and illiterate. Somehow, the fact that she was now stranded at a bus stop seemed karmic.

Perhaps Grace was right. If they married for money, they would end up working for every penny.

Charity wavered on down the road. After a while, she took off her shoes and carried them. At least she knew for sure that there was never ever dog shit on the verges in Little Elbow. Dog fouling and littering carried bigger fines than homicide.

While she was thinking about that, the lights of another car illuminated the path ahead. It slowed right down. Charity turned to see the car. It was a big champagne-coloured Mercedes. Marcella's car. Or at least a car very like it. Charity waved hopefully. The car sped on by. Charity told herself that it couldn't have been her neighbour. But as the car passed, she clocked its licence plate: MHUNTER 1.

The witch. Charity knew that Marcella had seen her. Why hadn't she stopped? Had Charity really put herself so far out of favour with the girl next door? She thought Simon might have had something to do with it. Perhaps he told Marcella that they shouldn't stop for someone like her. Someone who wasn't quite from the right narrow social stratum.

She felt like sitting down on the verge and crying. In fact, she was sitting down when the next vehicle appeared.

The driver wound down his window.

'Get in.'

Charity looked up blindly. Despite herself, she had started to cry. She didn't recognize the car. But the driver was Ryan.

'Your sister is going frantic,' he said. 'She says you called to say you were leaving the restaurant nearly two hours ago. She sent me out to find you. What are you doing walking down the highway?'

'I thought it would be a nice walk,' she said as she climbed into the truck.

'Funny time to choose to go walking.'

Charity settled back into the seat. She was grateful to her sister but embarrassed too. Grace would certainly have told Ryan that Charity had been stranded by Penman, wouldn't she? And yet he didn't mention it. Perhaps Grace hadn't told him.

Ryan stopped the car outside the Rose House.

'Thanks for rescuing me,' said Charity.

'Any time,' he replied. 'Though perhaps you could do us both a favour and pick your dates more carefully in future.'

Grace had told him. Charity nodded and rushed inside.

Penman didn't call to find out what had become of her, but the following morning there was an e-mail from him in Charity's inbox, complaining that she had left without paying her half of the bill. Bizarrely, he also suggested a 'return match'. Charity deleted it and placed a block on all future e-mails. That was one experience she did not want to have to repeat. Yacht or no yacht.

Two weeks later, Marcella was still crowing about Charity's disaster date to anyone who cared to listen. And to anyone who didn't care to listen. Like Simon.

'That girl has no taste,' said Marcella. 'Either that or she doesn't care whether her dates have any social skills so long as they're loaded.'

Simon nodded. He neglected to remind Marcella that she had been interested in Penman herself. That was ancient history as far as she was concerned. Instead, Marcella continued to opine quite contentedly on the low-grade dating potential of computer nerds.

'Someone like Penman is only an accidental millionaire,' said Marcella. 'So he doesn't have the class to cope. Anyone who has money knows that class is by far the more important quality.'

She flicked through the *New York Times* until she got to the announcements page.

'Oh my God.'

'Bad news?' asked Simon, expecting to hear that Marcella had spotted a name she knew in the obituaries. But it was worse than that.

One of Marcella's former schoolmates had just become engaged to a Greek shipping magnate.

Telling Marcella that she should be happy for her friend was like telling her she should be happy for the girl who got the last pair of Jimmy Choos in her size. She was not in the least bit pleased. Especially since hearing that this particular girl had snagged a husband was like seeing that the girl who had nabbed the strappy shoes you wanted never shaved her lily-white legs and accessorized with in-growing toenails. It just was not fair. Marcella was now one of just three of her classmates to remain unattached. It was like not being invited to a sample sale.

The only thing that would make her happy was some adoration. So she called Choate. And Choate said that he would love to come over that night but unfortunately he had made a prior arrangement. He declined to elaborate.

'What on earth can he be doing that's so important he can't come and see me?' Marcella pondered out loud.

25

Marcella found out that Choate and Grace Grosvenor were on a date before they were even able to order their entrées. Not much that happened in Little Elbow escaped the notice of Marcella Hunter. Her eyes and ears were everywhere. In this case it was Stephanie Blank who called to tell Marcella that Choate had been spotted at the Harbor Club.

'You must be pleased,' said Stephanie, calling from outside the club on her cellphone. 'I mean, I guess it's a sign that Choate is over you at last.'

Marcella groaned inwardly. Out loud, she said, 'You're right. Well, I hope he has a wonderful evening. It's good to know he's getting out there again.'

'In a big way, I'd say,' Stephanie continued. 'I couldn't believe it. You know, I don't think I have *ever* seen Choate Fitzgerald look so happy.'

'And he is definitely with Grace Grosvenor?'

'Oh yes. She's the really pretty one, right?'

'Yes,' Marcella growled.

'Similar haircut to yours only blonder? You know, at first, when I saw her from behind, I actually thought it might be you, but then I thought, no, that's not Marcella. Marcella's hair is a little more brown at the roots and her body is a little more . . . well muscled.'

Well muscled. Marcella fumed. Stephanie meant 'fat', of course.

'She has on the most fantastic dress. I might have to stop by the table and ask her where she got it. I think it could be Zac Posen. Do you want me to say "hi" to her when I do?'

'I don't think so,' said Marcella.

'I suppose it isn't really appropriate. You being the girl who broke Choate's heart and all. Though it doesn't look too broken any more. Well, would you look at that, he's laughing about something. And I mean really laughing. I've never seen that before. I must be going,' said Stephanie. 'I can see my date through the window. He's looking like he's missing me. Just thought you'd want to know Choate's moving on in his life.'

'Thank you,' said Marcella. 'Bitch,' she muttered as she hung up the phone.

'Goodbye, Marcella,' came Stephanie's voice from the handset in the unfortunate delay before the connection was severed.

'Oh, fuck.'

Marcella sat down heavily on the chaise longue next to the phone. It had been a terrible mistake to invite the Grosvenor girls over for dinner. Simply stupid. Choate might never have plucked up the courage to talk to that girl again otherwise. As it was, they were on a date! A proper date.

She remembered her own first date with Choate. He had taken her to the Harbor Club too. God, how dull it had been. He'd spent the entire evening looking as if he were about to succumb to an attack of diarrhoea, his face contorting with agony while Marcella tried to keep the mood light with tales of her recent trip to Paris to see the autumn/winter collections – tales that didn't seem to interest Choate at all.

The date had been a disaster, but when Choate called to say that he wanted to repeat it, Marcella had agreed. Everyone deserved a second chance. And since her most recent ex wasn't going to be giving her a second chance, Marcella decided to give Choate one instead. And a third and a fourth.

There was no doubt that Marcella had started to see Choate in an attempt to make his immediate predecessor jealous, but looking back, she was sure that it had come to be more than that.

Marcella had tried her very best to make it work, she told herself now. After all, theirs should have been a match made in heaven. It certainly would have been a match to make the front cover of *Forbes*, the business magazine. A merging of two empires: Hunter and Fitzgerald Lumber. They could have taken over the world.

But it wasn't to be. Was it Marcella's fault that she got tired of making all the conversation and so her head had been turned when someone more interesting had come along?

She knew now she'd made a mistake, she berated herself. If only she had been more mature. If only Choate had been a little less stuffy. If only he had danced with her as he'd danced with Grace at the birthday party. If only he'd laughed with her. If she'd known that he was going to turn out to be charming less than six months after she gave him his marching orders, she would never have let him go.

Suddenly Marcella couldn't remember how much Choate's laugh had grated on her. All she could see was a shot at true love lost.

That song about paving paradise came on Anjelica's radio. Anjelica liked to listen to the radio while she did Marcella's ironing.

'For God's sake shut that off!' Marcella shouted, as Joni Mitchell expressed in her song lyrics exactly what Marcella was feeling. 'I'm developing a headache.'

★   ★   ★

'How was it?'

Charity had waited up for her sister to return from her first date with Choate.

'It was pretty difficult,' Grace admitted. 'He had this strange expression on his face the whole time. Like he was trying not to burp.'

Choate had certainly taken his time building up to asking Grace for a date. Though he had plenty of opportunity. It seemed to Charity that he was always on their doorstep for some spurious reason or another, from the day he brought round the leaflet about the piping plovers and the firework ban. It was obvious to her that he had an enormous crush on Grace. In fact, she thought Grace was being a little cruel by refusing to acknowledge it.

But eventually, Choate made his move. A bouquet arrived at the Rose House with a note asking Grace to join him for dinner.

'At last,' Charity commented. 'So, where are you going?'

'I don't know. But he's picking me up at seven o'clock.'

Choate arrived at seven o'clock on the dot.

'Somehow I guessed he would be punctual,' said Charity.

Somehow she'd also guessed that he would be dressed like a man twenty years his senior. She gave Grace a sympathetic smile as the sisters watched Choate get out of his car and they noted the roll-neck sweater beneath a very formal-looking jacket.

'Perhaps he's come straight from work,' said Charity kindly. 'Or the golf club.'

'Do you think I ought to change?' Grace asked. She was wearing a pair of jeans. While Grace changed into something a little less comfortable, Choate and Charity sat together in the sitting room.

'So, you're from London,' said Choate.

'That's right. Kensington.'

'I was in London once,' said Choate. 'I have friends in Kensington. Perhaps you know them . . .'

'Oh, we don't really know our neighbours,' Charity interrupted him. 'It's a London thing. Everyone is very unfriendly.'

Silence fell between them. They smiled at each other. More like two patients in a doctor's waiting room than potential friends.

Luckily, Grace didn't take too long to transform herself.

Grace Grosvenor never had to make much effort to look pretty. She had been christened after the Princess of Monaco. The sisters' mother was eight months pregnant when the princess died and spent her last four weeks of confinement watching old Grace Kelly films that were being run in tribute.

Grace grew up to have the beauty, elegance and style of her namesake. She was always being approached in the street by model scouts and photographers. An Arab prince once stopped her in Marks and Spencer, Marble Arch, and asked whether he could pay for her shopping. She'd never met a man who didn't fall in love with her soft face and her gentle manner.

Looking at Choate's face, glowing like that of a kid in front of a Christmas tree, as Grace walked into the room in a sunshine-yellow dress, Charity would have put money on it that Choate Fitzgerald wasn't about to be the first man to resist her younger sister's charms.

'I'll make sure she gets home safely,' he said.

Charity knew he would.

26

In the days after Marcella heard that Choate was seeing Grace Grosvenor, Simon McDonnough took his duty as a house guest seriously and tried to console her. Though he wasn't sure why she needed consoling. The words 'dog in a manger' came to mind when she talked about the 'true' feelings she had supposedly held for Choate all the time she had been telling Simon that she wished Choate would just get over her and go and bore someone else into a coma instead.

'Stephanie said Choate was looking at Grace like she's a goddess. Choate never looked at me like that.'

'Rubbish. He looked at you like that all the time,' Simon reminded her. 'You hated it. Remember? You called it the *gaze of doom*.'

'Oh, but I didn't really hate it. I was clearly suffering from low self-esteem and found it uncomfortable to be the focus of someone's devotion.'

Simon nodded.

'But now I'm ready for that kind of love. I know I am. It took me some time to realize but now I have and . . . Oh, it's just typical that someone like her should come along just at this moment when I've finally worked out what I want. He hasn't dated since I dumped him. Not at all.'

'Actually, he did go on a couple of dates with that Rabin girl.'

'Sarah Rabin? The one with the jowls?'

'That's the one.'

'He did? When?'

'The end of last summer.'

'I don't believe it! She never told me. I invited her to my party! And she came. The two-faced bitch.'

'Technically,' said Simon, 'she didn't do anything wrong. Choate was single. You'd dumped him. She wasn't stepping on your toes.'

'It's still so tacky. Didn't she stop and think for one moment how I might feel?'

'I suppose she thought you wouldn't feel anything much at all, since you were the one who ended your relationship with Choate by telling him that spending time with him was more painful and tedious than a visit to the dentist's office.'

'We all say harsh things in times of great stress,' Marcella defended herself.

'As mean things go, you have to admit that was pretty spectacular.'

'I wanted to make it clear to him that things were over. I thought it would be far more cruel to leave him with too much hope.'

Simon rolled his eyes.

Marcella paused in her self-justification and put on that steely look again. The one she had worn while comparing Choate to having wisdom teeth pulled. 'Simon, whose friend are you supposed to be? In whose house do you plan to spend the entire summer?'

Simon immediately looked contrite.

'I don't understand it,' Marcella continued. 'I thought Choate and I had something real. How could he have forgotten all about it and moved his affections to her?'

'It's almost certainly a flash in the pan,' said Simon.

*　　　*　　　*

But two weeks later, the new romance was still going strong. Choate and Grace Grosvenor were spotted together all over Little Elbow. Marcella's friends were more than happy to let her know that Choate had been seen buying two tickets for such and such a play or ball game, or that they'd spotted him coming out of the florist's with more roses than he could carry.

In the meantime, Marcella called Choate every day, but no longer did he race to pick up her call or return it the very second he had a chance to. In fact there was one terrible occasion when Choate didn't return Marcella's call for a full twenty-four hours!

Marcella performed a small ritual in her bedroom using a voodoo candle she had bought to decorate the house the previous Halloween. She wrote Choate's name next to her own on a piece of parchment and burned them together in the flame, muttering something about 'binding these people together', as she did so. Choate phoned half an hour later.

'I've been worried about you,' Marcella wheedled.

'Oh, I'm doing fine,' said Choate. 'In fact, never been better.'

The words were like little knives stabbing into Marcella's heart.

'So, you're still seeing Grace Grosvenor?'

'Yes. She's a wonderful girl.'

'He thinks she's a wonderful girl! He's setting himself up for a fall,' Marcella muttered darkly when she reported her telephone conversation with Choate to Simon.

'Don't you think you're being a dog in the manger over this?' Simon finally asked her.

'Are you calling me a dog?'

'It's just a turn of phrase. It means . . .'

'I know what it means,' Marcella interrupted. 'And whatever it means, I am not being it. I just care about Choate. I don't want him to get hurt. We don't know who those girls next door really are!'

'Not that again. I'm sure that Choate must have some idea by now. He's been round there pretty much every day since your dinner party.'

'I need to know more about them.'

'Would knowing any more stop Choate from fancying her?' Simon asked.

'It may not stop him from fancying her but it will certainly stop him from marrying her if he finds out that she's not from the right stock. Choate Fitzgerald is from a very fine family. He won't want to throw away years of careful breeding on some girl who is just one generation away from working class. I mean, for all he knows, she could have criminal blood. What man in his right mind would want to have children with a woman who has crime in her background? What if the tendency has just skipped a generation?'

'What if Choate's personality doesn't skip a generation?' Simon mused. 'By mixing his genes with her potential criminality, they could create a boring psychopath. Someone who ties his victims up and talks to them about spreadsheets until they die of ennui.'

'Simon, I'm being serious.'

Simon nodded. 'Of course you are. And you're right. It would be a terrible thing to undo the years of careful breeding that resulted in Choate Fitzgerald's overbite. But do you really think that Choate is in danger of marrying Grace Grosvenor? It won't have crossed his mind. They've only been dating for a fortnight.'

'Simon,' said Marcella, 'Choate is in danger of marrying the very next girl who smiles at him. I know. He's ripe.'

'Ripe?'

'It's the only way most men get married. They can meet the woman of their dreams the moment they come out of short trousers, but it simply won't work out. Because with men it is all about timing. Catching a man is like playing musical chairs. When the time is right, they marry the woman who finds herself sitting on their knees. No matter if she is kind or cruel, beautiful as a rose or like the back end of a jitney. Proximity and availability are the only things that really count when it comes to marriage. And Choate is ripe. I could tell by the way he squeezed my hand during the vows at his cousin's wedding last summer. He's on the hunt for a wife.'

Simon looked horrified.

'So, if I can find out the truth about the Grosvenor girls, then I can save Choate from a whole lot of heartbreak. And heaven knows the boy needs to be protected from any more heartbreak. You know, Simon, I had no idea how much I truly meant to him before we broke up. He's probably still on the rebound. I mean, if you think about it, that Grace Grosvenor could be seen as a direct replacement for me. We're about the same height. The same dress size. We're both blonde.'

'She's natural,' Simon commented dangerously.

'Or has a good hairdresser,' Marcella retorted. 'Whatever, Choate probably walks down the sidewalk a few steps behind her so that he can see her hair and not her face and pretend he's still with me. That's the kind of guy he is,' she added.

'Well, what are you going to do now?' asked Simon.

'We . . .' Marcella corrected. 'You are on my team, aren't you, Simon? While you're living under my roof?'

Simon could only nod.

'We're going to do some proper investigation. If those Grosvenor girls have a skeleton in their cupboard, I am going to take it out and dance with it.'

27

On the other side of the boundary fence, Grace and Charity had no idea how much they were upsetting Marcella Hunter. They were simply enjoying their time in Little Elbow.

Charity in particular was enjoying the garden.

The embarrassment of her first ever meeting with Ryan and her subsequent disaster dates had been completely forgotten. Now she looked forward to seeing him emerge from the guest house each morning. She liked to watch him move about the garden, inspecting and perfecting his handiwork. She took to making an extra cup of coffee and carrying it out to him for a progress discussion.

'You know,' he said one day, 'don't feel that you aren't allowed to have any real input into the garden yourself. Any time you want to help me mow the lawn or dig out a few flower beds.'

'I'm on my holidays,' Charity laughed. But she did volunteer to help with the dead-heading in the cutting garden.

'Did you grow up here?' she asked Ryan as they stood side by side, picking out the buds that weren't going to flower.

'In Little Elbow? No. Do I seem like I did?'

'I sense from the way you say that, that you're not entirely approving of the natives.'

Ryan just smiled.

'So where did you grow up? And how did you end up here?'

'I grew up in Florida,' he explained. 'And I moved here because I had family connections. My great-aunt lived in this town when she was young. It was different then, though. Just a little seaside place. Not Manhattan by the sea like it is now.'

'And how did you get this job?'

'I know the landlord,' said Ryan. 'I know exactly how he wants this garden to look and I'm the only person he can trust to deliver his vision.'

'His *vision*,' Charity echoed.

'Pretentious, eh?' Ryan smiled.

'Certainly is,' said Charity.

Ryan stood back from the plant he had been tending.

'What brought you girls here?' he asked.

'Oh, we just fancied a change. London can get very boring. I thought it would be a good idea to go somewhere completely different. Make some new friends.'

'And have you made some new friends?'

'We've been invited to a few dinner parties.'

'And to help out with mowing the lawn . . .'

'You know, that's the best offer I've had so far this week,' said Charity. 'But I've got things to do. E-mails to send.' They'd finished the dead-heading. Ryan had finished his coffee. Charity took his cup and went back inside.

When she looked out of the kitchen window, she saw that he had taken his top off to start mowing. She couldn't help watching for a while.

Charity's reverie was interrupted by the ringing of the door-bell.

'Good morning, Charity!' trilled the visitor.

It was Marcella Hunter.

'I hope you don't mind me dropping by like this. I've just been baking,' she said. She lifted the enormous basket that had been sitting at her feet and handed it over the threshold. 'I've made some extras for you.'

'Thank you,' said Charity.

'Oh, it was easy,' said Marcella. 'No effort on my part at all.'

That bit was true. When Marcella said 'baking', what she actually meant was 'calling the baker'. She'd had Anjelica pick up her order, take the twenty-five individually wrapped cookies out of their cellophane and arrange them on a gingham tea towel.

'Oh, brilliant!' Grace had heard the doorbell and come to investigate. 'I was just thinking that I needed something to eat.'

'Now, you don't look like you ever think about eating,' said Marcella. 'How do you keep your lovely figure?'

Grace was already eating a cookie.

'I'll make a cup of tea to go with these,' she said.

Charity felt a bubble of irritation. Now there really was no choice but to invite Marcella in.

'I hear that you have been stepping out with Choate Fitzgerald,' said Marcella confidentially.

Grace started to open her mouth.

'Oh, you can't keep anything a secret in this town. You only have to sneeze and someone will bring you chicken soup. You know, I am so glad to hear that Choate is getting out and about again. I'm afraid we were all quite worried about him for a while.'

Charity raised an eyebrow.

'Well, I probably shouldn't be saying this, but I haven't been entirely honest with you about my relationship with dear old Choate. You see, Choate and I used to be an item. Oh, it was quite serious for a while. But then we started to grow in different directions. Or rather, I started to grow but Choate remained exactly as he was. Fuddy-duddy.'

Grace gave a soft smile.

'But he's old fashioned in the best way,' said Marcella.

'I think so,' said Grace.

'One thing is for certain. He's consistent. You'll never have to worry that he'll spring some awkward surprise on you. Like a weekend in St Tropez. Or flowers.'

'Actually,' said Grace, 'he has sent me flowers. Lots of them.'

Marcella's face registered annoyance. But only momentarily. Grace missed it.

'Well, perhaps he's changed,' she half hissed.

'Would you like to sit down?' Charity asked.

Marcella drank her tea and continued to talk about people the sisters had never heard of. A couple of those people had bought boob jobs from the doctor who seemed determined that every woman in North America would have size 34Ds. Chelsy Cialdini had decamped to Manhattan. Complications with her plumbing.

'So she's moved out of her beach house while the repair work is done?' asked Grace.

'Not that kind of plumbing,' said Marcella.

All the while she was talking, Marcella was also scanning her surroundings. She was looking for any more clues about the Grosvenor sisters' background. Personal photographs. Greetings cards. Anything.

Eventually, Charity decided to cut the visit short. She would give Marcella the tour of the house she had come for and end it, conveniently, by the front door.

'It's such a lovely house for entertaining,' said Marcella as they moved out into the hallway. 'Don't you think it's absolutely criminal to think of all those dinner parties this house could have seen over the years when it was empty?'

'It does seem a shame,' said Charity. 'I often wonder what happened to make the family who lived here abandon the place.'

'Tax evasion is what I heard,' said Marcella. 'Gosh, they didn't spare any expense, did they, when they were redoing the decoration. I think this is Osborne and Little,' she added, fondling the edge of a curtain.

Charity led her through into the dining room.

'Oh, how lovely.' Marcella clapped her hands. 'That table is quite beautiful.' She ran her fingers over the polished mahogany. 'What a fantastic space! If I had a dining room like this one, I would be entertaining all the time!'

'Your dining room is bigger,' Charity pointed out.

'Yes, I suppose it is. But this room. The light. The window looking out on to the ocean. Can't you just imagine it? You could serve cocktails in the room with the French windows, then bring everybody in here. I'd have it lit by candles only. So much more flattering. You can fall in love with anyone by candlelight. How many people could you get in here? There are eight chairs but I imagine that table extends to seat sixteen. Sixteen is a lot of people to have for dinner, though. You could just start with eight.'

Charity got the hint.

'Look, why don't you come over for dinner on Thursday?' she asked. 'And bring a friend.'

'Will Choate be here?'

'If Grace is.'

'Then I'm sure I'd be delighted. Be wonderful to catch up with dear old Choate. I haven't seen him in ages. Which feels strange, you know. Because it used to be that I simply couldn't get rid of the man. Always mooning around my kitchen. I guess I meant much more to him than I thought.'

'Hmmm,' said Charity thoughtfully.

'Ah well. It will be good to see him. Your sister seems to be making him very happy.'

'I think she is.'

Eventually, Charity managed to manouevre Marcella back out on to the front step.

'Enjoy those cookies!' Marcella called as she headed for the gate.

'They're pretty good cookies,' said Grace. 'Do you think she baked them herself?'

'No,' said Charity, extracting a double-chocolate chip cookie from the very bottom of the pile. It was still wrapped in cellophane. Charity smiled. If you were going to dissemble, she thought, you shouldn't rely on underpaid staff to help you do it.

'That was a disaster,' said Charity. 'Now we've got to throw a dinner party for Marcella Hunter.'

'She threw one for us. It's the friendly thing to do,' said Grace.

'Marcella doesn't want to be our friend.'

'Did it work?' asked Simon.

'Like a charm,' said Marcella. 'Some people need a little prompting before they remember their social duties. But yes, we have an invitation to dinner with Grace and Charity. Choate will be there. And it will be his first chance to see how Grace shapes up as a potential wife. Let's see how Grace fares under a little light pressure, shall we?'

28

For all Marcella's worrying that Choate and Grace were on the verge of an engagement, there wasn't actually an awful lot of passion going on. In fact, three weeks after their first proper date, Choate had yet to attempt anything more than a kiss on the cheek when he returned Grace to her doorstep after a night out.

Grace didn't mind. In truth, she was grateful that Choate wasn't more forward. She didn't tell Charity, knowing that her sister would definitely think it odd, but Grace needed time and space. She hadn't expected to be spending her summer in the Hamptons. And she definitely hadn't expected to find herself in a fully fledged romance within a few weeks of arriving there.

Choate certainly seemed to think they were an item. Not a single day passed without some token of his esteem landing on the doorstep. Flowers. Chocolates. Books on how to spot a piping plover . . . It was clear he was over the moon when Grace asked him to be a guest at the first dinner party at the Rose House that summer.

Charity was well aware that the rest of the guest list would not be so easy to please. She had hoped that her suggestion that Marcella should bring someone with her would lead to a new introduction, but she chose to bring that toad Simon McDonnough. Apart from Simon and Marcella, the guest list comprised only Stephanie Blank. Charity wasn't entirely certain that she liked Stephanie any better than Marcella, but she hoped that they might be distracted from the standard of the catering by having to impress each other and thus cancel each other out in some way.

The Grosvenor girls had quickly learned that Little Elbow was the kind of town where people took their entertaining very seriously. You couldn't just shuffle people straight to the table as soon as they arrived and give them a glass of whatever they were going to be having with their food while they waited for you to finish cooking. Cocktails were in order. And canapés.

And the table itself had to be laid properly. Not just candles but floral arrangements. You couldn't just direct people to their places verbally. You had to create proper place settings.

Charity looked the whole matter up on the Internet. She went straight to the guru: Martha Stewart. Martha had an opinion on everything from the colour of the tablecloth to the size of the candles. It didn't take long before Charity found herself sympathizing with the people who had put Stewart in jail.

'Dinner party etiquette is a minefield,' Charity concluded. 'I think we should just do things English style.'

Grace was more than happy with that.

But that didn't mean Charity didn't want the table to look spectacular. And on the day of the party, Ryan obliged by appearing at the kitchen door with an armful of roses.

'My God,' said Charity. 'My sister gets more flowers than Elton John.'

'They're not for her,' said Ryan. 'Well, they're for both of you. For your dinner party. From the garden.' Then he touched his fingers to the brim of his baseball hat and excused himself.

It was nothing, of course. He was probably just doing a bit

of pruning and cut the roses because he knew that in a day or two they would be overblown and he would have to dead-head them anyway. Still, they were as beautiful as any of the hothoused flowers Choate had sent Grace. And they smelled far more lovely.

'I think he likes you,' Grace said of Ryan.

'What else would he do with those flowers?' Charity replied. 'Anyway, he's not what I came for. Remember?' She arranged the roses haphazardly in the one vase that wasn't full of tokens of Choate's esteem.

Choate was the first to arrive, of course. Followed by Ste-phanie Blank. Marcella and Simon were half an hour late.

Marcella noticed the flowers immediately.

'Those roses. How lovely!'

'From the garden,' Charity told her.

'Ugh,' said Marcella. 'Is that a greenfly?'

Charity peered at the leaves. 'I don't think so.'

'You know,' Marcella continued, 'I hate to be difficult, but I wonder if you could move the roses off the dining table. I have a thing about bugs.'

'There really are no bugs,' said Charity.

'Now I know these roses are straight from the garden,' said Marcella, 'I'm going to be thinking about it the whole time.'

Charity dutifully moved the roses to the sideboard. As at the Royal Park Hotel, in the Rose House, the guest was always right.

Unlike Marcella, Charity and Grace hadn't employed a Michelin-starred chef for that evening. They had prepared the food themselves. By London standards, they had pulled together a feast fit for a queen. Well, perhaps a pearly queen. It was a meal that would pass muster for most people back home, but would it work in Little Elbow?

Stephanie was already inspecting the silverware. She lifted up a side plate to read the mark upon its bottom.

'Arte Italica,' she noted with grudging approval.

'It came with the house,' Marcella told her. 'Isn't that right, Charity? The house was fully furnished?' Lest the Grosvenor sisters take any credit for anything Stephanie found to her taste.

'Oh, how unusual,' said Marcella when Grace brought out the first course. 'Salmon done the old-fashioned way.'

Charity and Grace had spent what seemed like a lifetime preparing the salmon on brown bread.

'What is the current way, Marcella?' asked Stephanie Blank.

'Well, since wheat is strictly off the menu for most people these days, you don't usually see it on bread any more.'

Stephanie agreed. 'Bread is an absolute no-no for anyone who cares about their health.'

Marcella picked the salmon off the top of the bread and folded it as though she were about to pop it into her mouth. 'Oh, wait! Girls, have you been really naughty?'

Grace and Charity looked at each other in utter confusion. Naughty?

'You spread butter on that bread, didn't you? Dairy *and* wheat! The two deadliest sins. I can't eat this.' She placed the salmon back on the plate and pushed it away with a barely disguised look of disgust. In fact, it wasn't disguised at all.

Stephanie followed suit. Grace was about to ask Marcella and Stephanie whether they would like a fresh piece of salmon from the fridge – untainted by butter or breadcrumbs – when Marcella barked at Choate, 'Put that down, Choate. Right now!'

Choate jumped out of his skin and dropped his mouthful as though he had just spotted a maggot.

'You know how dairy affects you.'

'How does it affect him?' Simon mouthed across the table to his landlady.

'Gas,' Marcella mouthed back. Theatrically. 'Terrible, terrible gas.'

'My God,' said Simon.

The entire table was enthralled. Blushing deeply, Choate pushed his plate away and gave Grace an apologetic smile.

'She's right,' said Choate to Grace. 'I should have let you know. Selfish of me not to.'

'But I made spaghetti carbonara for the main course,' said Grace desperately. 'That's wheat and dairy.'

'And pork,' said Stephanie Blank. 'There's ham in carbonara, isn't there? No pig for me, I'm afraid. I'm converting to Judaism.'

'You are?' Marcella was agog.

'Gideon will only marry a Jewish girl.'

'You're marrying Gideon? You've only had three dates.'

'He doesn't know yet.'

'But what will your father say?' Marcella asked.

'Oh, he won't mind. I'm not actually going to give up being a Catholic too. I'm just going to learn the Jewish songs. And I never really liked ham anyway. Or seafood . . .'

Charity raised her eyes to heaven. She'd prepared *linguine alle vongole* for anyone who wouldn't eat meat. Clams.

'Perhaps we should just call the Chinese,' Charity said, laughing.

'Oh, you are funny! But it is so difficult to host a dinner party these days,' Marcella agreed with her. 'More like a test than a pleasure. I should know. Particularly when you're not just cooking for friends.'

Marcella smiled warmly at Grace as she used the 'f' word.

'Can you imagine what it's like when you're entertaining

and there are *business* interests at stake? Such a nightmare. Choate has some terribly awkward colleagues to cook for. Choate, as you know, shouldn't touch dairy, for the comfort of everybody present.'

Everybody laughed. Except Choate and Grace and Charity.

'But that's nothing compared to one of his business associates, who not only couldn't touch dairy, he couldn't eat wheat, meat, fish or tomatoes. Tomatoes made his throat seize up. I had to become an expert in tomato-free vegan cooking overnight. And let me tell you, there is hardly a vegetarian recipe in the world that doesn't call for tomatoes. I was at my wits' end for days before that man came round, wondering what on earth I would cook. But that's all part of being in a partnership, isn't it? You take the time to learn about the other person and the people who are important to them and their careers and adjust your menu accordingly.'

She looked straight at Grace. Grace looked at the table-cloth.

'It made your life easier, didn't it, Choate?' Marcella twisted the knife one more time. 'That I knew how to make sure that everyone felt comfortable with the cuisine.'

'It did,' Choate admitted.

'It isn't much of an effort to make for love,' Marcella concluded.

'Chinese or Indian?' said Charity through clenched teeth.

In the kitchen, Grace was distraught.

'Nobody is eating anything.'

'Ungrateful sods,' said Charity.

'She's right. We should have found out what everybody couldn't eat before we started cooking.'

'It would have been just as easy for them to let us know. There's nothing on these plates that will actually kill any of them,' said Charity. 'They should have had the manners to eat it and worry about wind and bloating later. Marcella was just showing off in front of Choate. And humiliating him and us at the same time.'

'It worked, didn't it? Choate probably won't want to see me again after this.'

'I don't think so,' said Charity.

'Ahem.' They heard a cough and turned to see Choate hovering at the kitchen door with two more plates.

'I took a couple of my lactulose pills and ate mine,' he told them.

'Lactulose?' said Grace.

Charity nudged her and mouthed, 'For the gas.'

'It was delicious,' said Choate. 'The salmon, that is. Not the lactulose.'

'I'm sorry I didn't ask you what you can and can't eat,' said Grace. 'I should have thought . . .'

'No. I should have told you. But it slipped my mind. Fact is, if Marcella hadn't drawn my attention to it, I would have wolfed it down and paid the consequences. The carbonara smells good too.'

Charity was just pouring the pasta down the waste disposal unit. (In truth, the waste disposal unit was one of her new favourite things and she quite enjoyed having the opportunity to watch it make short work of her hard work.)

'Can I help with anything?' Choate asked.

'I'd ask you to help Grace with the ice cream,' said Charity. 'But obviously that's not appropriate now. Perhaps you could take these menus out to the dining room and ask people to pick whatever won't interfere with their digestions, their diets or their religious beliefs.'

'I'll do that,' said Choate. Charity handed him a couple of takeaway menus.

Moments later, Marcella's voice rang out. 'Are you serious? Chinese food? Monosodium glutamate? Are they trying to kill me?'

Charity was beginning to see how that might come to seem like a good idea.

In the end, they did order Chinese and Choate made a special effort to say, every five minutes, that he couldn't remember when he'd last had such fun at a dinner party. Simon too seemed to be enjoying himself. Meanwhile Marcella and Stephanie deconstructed their meals into their component parts.

'I can't eat nuts.'

'Bamboo shoots give me migraine.'

'Me too. And don't even get me started on sweet-and-sour sauce.'

Charity was relieved when Marcella excused herself to go to the bathroom. But the relief was momentary. After a while she began to worry that Marcella had been spending a very long time upstairs. On the pretence of needing to use the bathroom herself, Charity followed her up there. She was about halfway up the curving staircase when she saw Marcella flit across the landing, from the direction of one of the bedrooms.

Charity hovered until Marcella was safely in the bathroom. She didn't want her new adversary to know that she'd seen her come out of the bedroom, but she did want to know what Marcella had been doing in there.

Charity headed straight for the room Marcella had just exited and flicked on the light. There was no obvious sign that she'd moved anything. Neither was there anything incriminating on display. Satisfied that Marcella had seen nothing she shouldn't, Charity tiptoed into her own bedroom – the yellow room. She opened the top drawer on the right-hand side of the dresser. At the very back, behind a profusion of knickers and tangled stockings, the little black book she had brought with her from London was still safely in its hiding place. She closed the drawer again and this time she locked it. She tucked the key into a pocket.

'I thought perhaps you'd drowned in the bidet,' said Charity when Marcella emerged from the bathroom and they met on the landing.

'Oh, you know. Got carried away with the reading material,' she said. 'I haven't seen a copy of *Hello!* for a long time. It's always such fun seeing all those familiar faces in the party pages.'

'It is,' Charity agreed.

29

Despite the horrors of the menu, Grace and Charity's guests stayed into the wee small hours. Choate was the last to leave. He insisted on helping to tidy up. He rolled up his sleeves and washed everything that wouldn't go into the dishwasher. Once again he expressed his dismay at having been unable to eat Charity's carbonara sauce.

'Well, how about I cook it for you specially and you eat it out on the beach,' she suggested. 'Then it won't matter what kind of effect it has on your digestion.'

Thank goodness he laughed. Then his face settled into a shy smile for Grace's benefit. There was no danger that he wouldn't want to see her again.

Choate Fitzgerald was an unusual sort of guy, thought Grace as she watched him drying a saucepan. Though he was only a handful of years older than she was, he seemed to be from a different time altogether. His manners were absolutely impeccable. The writers of *The Rules* would have been thrilled with the way that he always called to arrange a date in plenty of time. He actually apologized for his impudence if he rang to ask Grace to do something with less than a whole day's notice. He was never, ever late. He always picked Grace up at the door of her house and returned her there at the end of the evening. Likewise, he always picked up the tab. He was aghast when Grace suggested one night that he might let her buy their tickets for the cinema.

At restaurants and bars he was polite and gracious to the staff. He filled Grace's glass before he filled his own. He never failed to compliment her on her outfit.

Contrast that with the last guy she had dated back in London. He was rarely on time. He never had any money (except for beer). He rarely noticed if she'd had her hair done or if she was wearing a new dress. And he had cultivated his ability to belch the national anthem with the pride of a pianist learning to play Rachmaninov's Concerto No. 3 in D Minor. He did, however, have a way about him that could entice a smile from any girl aged six months to sixty.

Choate didn't have that particular guy's easy charm but he had a lot else besides. Grace had been thinking about that quite a lot. When it came down to it, charm couldn't keep you warm. It couldn't put food on the table and pay school fees.

Choate spoke about duty. He spoke about a future family. He spoke about the things that he would do with his children (none of which involved teaching them how to hot-wire cars or swear in three languages). He was mature. He was dignified. After even their short acquaintance, Grace knew that Choate Fitzgerald would always put duty before his whims.

And he had stood up for her. The dinner party had been a disaster and that horrible witch from next door had made a field day of it. But Choate had been so gracious even when the insults had implicated his bowels. He had tried so hard to make Grace feel better.

He was a good man. No doubt about it.

The dinner party had been, by Grace's calculation, their eleventh date. Back in London, Grace would ordinarily have expected to be spending the night with a man on their fifth date. But not with Choate.

That night, however, as Choate went to kiss her goodnight

on both cheeks again, Grace decided it was time to seize the initiative. She moved, quite deliberately, so that when Choate went for her left cheek, he got her lips instead. And then she threw her arms around his neck so that he couldn't pull away.

For a moment, Choate was frozen, his lips squashed against Grace's, the rest of his face in an attitude of surprise.

'Kiss me properly,' Grace murmured, without taking her mouth away.

Grace told herself that she was feeling something. Deep inside her, there was definitely a sensation of warmth, as Choate finally, properly, returned her embrace. Yes, warmth. For real. She could feel it radiating from her heart.

Love at first sight was for fairy tales. The best kind of love didn't hit you like a thunderbolt but developed over time. After you'd known someone for a while and could be sure that they were someone with more lasting qualities than sex appeal or a nice car. That was what made love more real. More solid and durable. A true foundation for a future together.

Grace convinced herself that her feelings for Choate were growing, becoming romantic, evolving into something that might one day be called 'love'.

When he had finished kissing her, Choate looked down into Grace's eyes. She smiled at him, wanting him to know from that smile that she was fond of him too. And the gesture was repaid threefold. Choate beamed back as he allowed himself in turn to believe that Grace Grosvenor might think as much of him as he was coming to think of her.

Grace squeezed his hand.

'Will I see you tomorrow?' she asked. 'I know we haven't arranged anything but . . .'

Choate couldn't keep the delight from his face. Though, true to his old self, what he said in reply to Grace's question was, 'I'll have to check my Blackberry.'

'You do that,' she said. And went inside.

From the shelter of the curtains in the darkened sitting room, Grace watched Choate get back into his car and drive away. She smiled as he allowed himself a little engine-revving before he set off. It was the nearest Choate came to punching the air.

Grace had known that night that Choate loved her. Though he didn't say the words out loud, his eyes had shouted his feelings for her. She knew that she had made him happy by the simple act of being warm towards him. Her power over Choate was very real.

Reliability, solvency, decency. All these things were worth more than passion, weren't they?

All the same she checked the answer machine and felt the little let-down she always felt when she discovered that there were no messages. Definitely no message from someone back home.

30

The following morning, Marcella was in a very good mood. She felt confident that the disastrous dinner party at the Grosvenor sisters' house would have made Choate think twice about dating Grace. How on earth could he consider a future with a woman who obviously didn't know the first thing about entertaining at the kind of level a proper Little Elbow hostess needed to operate at? These things were so important. A successful businessman could be sunk by the wrong sort of consort.

She called Choate to press him for details.

'Oh, Choate. I'm so sorry about last night,' she said.

'You should be.'

Marcella didn't really hear him. 'Still, I suppose it's for the best that you know sooner rather than later that Grace Grosvenor isn't really the kind of woman who will be able to cope with your high-powered career and all its attendant social requirements—'

'Grace was very upset,' Choate interrupted. 'But I told her that it was my fault. I should have let her know about my issues with dairy. Just as you should have let her know about your wheat intolerance. The English do things differently.'

'Choate, what are you talking about?'

'I have to go. I'm picking Grace up at noon.'

★   ★   ★

'Aaaaargh!'

When he heard Marcella scream, Simon dropped his newspaper and ran to her aid at once.

'Are you hurt?'

'Right here!' she said dramatically, pointing at her heart.

'Are you having a heart attack? Lie down,' Simon barked.

Marcella shook him off. 'I am not having a heart attack, you idiot. I was being metaphorical. He's still going to continue seeing that girl!'

'I take it you mean Grace?'

'Of course I do. But how can he? She's not the right woman for him. She can't cook. She's a terrible hostess. She doesn't know the first thing about being a proper Little Elbow wife!'

Simon looked dismayed. 'What on earth is a proper Little Elbow wife? And does any man really want one?'

'It's not funny,' said Marcella.

'Darling, do you think perhaps you should just give up on Choate? There must be some other poor sod in this town who would suit you even better. There have got to be other men who you find more interesting. You had a chance to be with Choate and you chose not to be. You don't even find him attractive. You told me his hands were too soft. You hate the way he combs his hair.'

'Simon, I would have thought that you of all people would understand that this is not about who I find *attractive*. There may be many men that I could happily pass an evening with, but there are far fewer who would make suitable husbands for me. A girl like me just doesn't have the choices that a girl like Grace Grosvenor has.'

'Marcella,' said Simon soothingly, 'I think you're at least as beautiful as Grace is.'

'At least?' Marcella growled. 'Look, this is not about who I could attract either! Believe me, I could have just about any man I set my mind on. But I can't marry a man who has less money than I do. I have an empire behind me. What if I was to marry someone penniless and he divorced me? Hunter Lumber would be ruined! I've got to marry someone with more to lose than I have. That leaves just three men of my acquaintance: Jerry Penman, Robin Madden and Choate Fitzgerald.'

'You really think that?'

'Yes. I do. I have been brought up with a sense of history, Simon. You of all people must understand that. And history brings with it responsibility. My ancestors sweated to make Hunter Lumber the force it is today. I couldn't bear for my grandfather's money to be frittered away by someone who hadn't earned it. Now I can't date Robin, Jerry *or* Choate. Where am I supposed to find a suitable guy?'

'It sounds like you need a Plan B.'

The problem was that Choate Fitzgerald had been Marcella's Plan B.

Of course, prior to Grace Grosvenor's appearance in Little Elbow, Marcella had not been in the least bit interested in Choate Fitzgerald. She had, however, counted on him remaining interested in her. She had convinced herself that she would find someone before he did but if, for some unthinkable reason, she didn't find someone, then Choate would be a worthy match for her in the long term. They might not have had much passion, but they could probably have had enough sex to pop out an heir and a spare and then gone into their twilight years together. There were plenty of marriages like that in Little Elbow. The wife lived in the country, the husband lived in Manhattan, worked on Wall Street and sent home the money. At weekends, when the husbands came out to the country to relax, the wives went into Manhattan to shop.

What was she supposed to do now? Marry someone who had less money than she did???

Marcella looked at her face in the mirror. She was twenty-seven and like most twenty-seven-year-olds, she felt that time was running out. Quickly. She pulled at the corners of her eyes. Should she have an early eye-tuck? If you had one before you really needed one then it was usually a little less noticeable. Or how about Botox? Then she thought about Sarah Rabin's experience. Botox was out of the question. Perhaps the greyness that Marcella saw in her complexion was just because she had been burning the candle at both ends lately. Perhaps a facial would be good enough to fix her up for a while.

Marcella booked herself an appointment at Mimi's salon. They were fully booked, but she insisted that they cancel a few other people to fit her in. She'd pay triple. This was an emergency.

31

Mimi's salon was always busy and that day was no exception. Grace had been waiting for half an hour when she was finally invited into one of the treatment rooms and asked to sit down in a pedicure chair. The chair reminded her of the seats she had seen in the business-class section of the BA flight as she and Charity headed for their places in the back of the plane. As soon as she sat down, the pedicurist flicked a switch that made the seat vibrate. Grace couldn't help laughing.

'I should warn you I'm really ticklish,' she said. 'I might kick you.'

'You better not,' said the pedicurist.

'I'll do my very best to control myself,' said Grace, squirming the second the woman looked as though she was about to pick up her feet. It was bad enough being ticklish. But even thinking about being tickled made Grace want to bite the leather of the chair she was sitting in.

The pedicurist grabbed Grace's ankles and forced her feet down into the bubbling water.

'Too hot?'

'It's fine,' said Grace.

'Where are you from?' the pedicurist asked. 'You don't sound like you're from round here.'

'I'm not,' said Grace. 'I'm from England.'

'Ah, England. I was there once,' said the pedicurist. She grabbed Grace's left ankle and pulled her foot out of the water as though she were yanking a lobster from a tank in readiness for the pot. Grace smiled regardless.

'Which parts of England did you visit?' she asked.

'London.'

'I'm from there!'

'I went to Tooting Bec. You know it?'

'Know it? Like the back of my hand. I've lived in Tooting Bec all my life!'

'Well, my sister, she lives there with her husband.'

'Which street?'

'They have a fish-and-chip shop. On the main street near the subway station.'

'Not Wings?'

'Yes. That's the one.'

'I eat there all the time. Honestly, I'm there every other night. When I'm not on a diet,' she added ruefully.

'And where's your house?' the pedicurist asked.

'We don't have a house. I don't know if you remember much about the other shops on that street, but if you walk from Wings towards the Tube station, you'll see there's a greasy-spoon café on the right. My sister and me live in the flat right upstairs.'

'From the *greasy-spoon* café?'

'Yes. Tony's.'

'But it's a dirty place. Cockroaches, my sister told me. They had the inspectors in.'

'I know. My sister called them after we found roaches in our kitchen. Must have climbed up through the plumbing. The place has changed hands since then, though. It's still not the best restaurant in London, but the flat upstairs is cheap. And beggars can't be choosers.'

'So, why did you come here? It's not cheap in this town.'

'You can say that again.'

'No beggars in Little Elbow. How can you afford to come here? In the summer?'

'If I tell you, I don't think you'll believe it.'

'Try me,' said the pedicurist.

'OK. It happened like this . . .'

Praise the Lord for the thin walls at Mimi's!

Marcella Hunter could not believe what she was hearing. She didn't know much about London's various districts outside Bond Street and Sloane Street, but one thing she did know was that Tooting Bec was nowhere near South Kensington. And there certainly weren't many greasy-spoon cafés in those parts of London she had shopped in. Here at last was the truth. Marcella couldn't wait to get back to the house and have Simon confirm what the evidence suggested.

'There you are,' said the beautician. 'You're finished. Your face is glowing today, Miss Hunter.'

It wasn't just because of the beautician's magical lymphatic massage. Marcella hadn't felt this good in a long time. All her suspicions had been proven!

But how would she use her new information? Would she just whisper to Choate that he might want to ask Grace whether her parents were really dead or in prison? Would she confront Charity? Would she drop the bombshell in front of a dinner party? Oh yes. That would be good. Marcella would arrange a party at once. She would invite Stephanie Blank. She'd serve a full English breakfast – whatever that involved – and say, as Anjelica brought it to the table, 'I just wanted you Grosvenor girls to feel at home! Living as you do above a greasy-spoon café!'

Oh, what fun this was going to be!

32

Back at Marcella's house, Simon listened to her revelations with widening eyes. He confirmed, as she had known he would, that Tooting was nowhere near South Kensington. In fact, Simon elaborated, the average denizen of Kensington and Chelsea was more likely to have been to South Africa than trek that far south of the River Thames.

'Isn't this just fantastic!' said Marcella. 'Choate can't possibly marry a girl from that kind of background! I cannot wait to have my dinner party.'

'Are you sure you want to raise the subject of Grace and Charity's background over dinner?' asked Simon.

'Why not?'

'It could make you look rather petty. Not to mention an eavesdropper. And perhaps it doesn't matter to Choate where the Grosvenors come from.'

'Oh, it matters,' said Marcella.

'She might have already told him.'

'She hasn't told him. I'm telling you, Simon. Choate is no more likely to want Grace when he finds out that she's a chiv—'

'*Chav*,' Simon corrected.

'Than he is to fall in love with Anjelica. Talking of whom . . . where is that girl?'

'Last I saw of her, she was going to scrub the grouting in your bathroom with a toothbrush. As you requested.'

'Well, I need her down here at once. There's a party to be organized. I wonder if I can get everything together for tomorrow night? I can't wait much longer. This news is making me burst!'

Stephanie Blank was delighted to be invited to what Marcella promised would be the most memorable dinner of the year. 'Memorable as in full of *explosive* revelations,' she added salaciously. Sarah Rabin too was keen to come along.

In fact, only Simon turned down Marcella's invitation.

'I've got other plans,' he said.

'But you can't have!' said Marcella. 'You're my house guest.'

'I said I would meet up with a producer who is only going to be in New York for a couple of days. I'm going into Manhattan tomorrow morning.'

'Bring the producer to dinner,' said Marcella. 'The bigger the crowd, the more fun it will be.'

'I'm not sure that it will be so much fun,' said Simon. 'Some people don't enjoy seeing other people humiliated.'

Marcella looked at Simon as though he had just told her that some people don't enjoy a sunny day, or the smiles of their loved ones.

'Oh, Simon, you are such a prig.'

'It may backfire on you. That's all I'm saying.'

'How could it possibly backfire?' Marcella shrugged. 'I'm not the one who has been lying. Ah well, I'll give you a full blow-by-blow report when you get back from Manhattan.'

'I can't wait,' said Simon, through clenched teeth.

'Now where is Anjelica? You know, I don't think I'm going to bother with a caterer this time. Anjelica did fantastically well in the kitchen last time I threw a party. I think she rather enjoyed it so I'm going to give her the opportunity to have the kitchen entirely to herself this time.'

As you can imagine, Anjelica wasn't thrilled with the news. The party was, of course, scheduled for her evening off. Marcella sympathized and apologized but she wasn't about to let Anjelica have a choice in the matter.

'And the following morning, I will call that lawyer and let him know that you should have a green card at once. How could they refuse one to an illegal immigrant as talented as you are?'

Anjelica smiled stiffly.

Now all Marcella had to do was to make sure that the Grosvenor sisters would both be in attendance. She was aware that she wasn't the most popular visitor to the Rose House, especially since the dinner party she had made so very difficult. So perhaps a simple written note wouldn't be enough to assure that the girls took up her invitation. This was an invitation that would have to be delivered face to face.

Armed with another basket of cookies, carefully denuded of *all* their cellophane this time, Marcella clipped up the long driveway of the Rose House. That gardener was working on the borders to the front lawn. Marcella put her hand through her hair as she passed him. He was very good looking. She wondered whether he would be available to do her garden too. Marcella's own gardener, Miguel, was good at his job but at seventy years old you could hardly accuse him of being eye candy.

'Perhaps you would give me a call,' she said, throwing her card in the gardener's direction. 'I might be able to give you some extra work. I'm sure you could use the additional cash.'

The gardener looked faintly amused by the idea. Marcella ignored him and rang the front doorbell.

Charity answered.

'Oh, hello.'

Her greeting was less than effusive.

'More cookies. How nice. Thank you.'

'It really was no bother at all.'

Charity nodded. She was sure it hadn't been.

'You know, Charity, I feel like you and I have got off on the wrong foot. I feel that you might have interpreted my sense of humour for sarcasm and where I meant to raise a smile, I raised only hackles instead.'

At that moment, Charity felt goose pimples up and down her back.

'I'm so sorry for that. The thing is, I was just copying the way Simon talks. It seems to me like you British people are always being vile to each other, but Simon assures me it's a sign of affection to be so rude.'

'Yes,' said Charity. 'There is a certain class of Brit that thinks that way.'

'Anyway,' said Marcella, 'now we've got that cleared up, I'd like to invite you girls over to my house again.'

'Oh.'

'Just another small dinner. I have a couple of girlfriends in town and I'd love for them to meet you. What do you say?' Marcella smiled. She looked almost shy.

How could Charity refuse? Perhaps Marcella really did want to make amends.

'Will you be inviting Choate?' Charity asked.

'Oh no,' said Marcella. 'Simon can't make it so I've decided that this time it's girls only. Don't you think that will be fun?'

'I'll ask Grace whether she's free,' Charity promised.

'Oh good. Really, you must come.' Marcella held Charity by the tops of her arms and looked into her eyes.

'Promise me you will be there. It just won't be the same without you.'

'Since you put it like that,' said Charity.

Marcella returned to the Hunter house singing a happy tune. She sashayed out into the garden, where Simon was topping up his tan by the pool.

'It's all set,' she said. 'The trap is laid and the prey has been enticed. You are *so* going to regret missing this party, Simon. This is going to be the night that people talk about for years.'

Simon smiled thinly over the top of his gossip magazine.

'Are you sure you have to go to Manhattan?' Marcella wheedled. 'Couldn't you just tell that producer that something more important came up?'

'There is nothing more important than my meeting with this producer. I need to get my documentary off the ground. You don't want me to live at your house for ever, do you?'

Marcella pouted. 'Suit yourself. But I'm telling you, you are going to miss the most entertaining night in Little Elbow ever!'

Simon was lying about the producer, of course. Since arriving in the United States just before the Burns Night party where he had charmed Marcella and secured himself free lodging, Simon hadn't had the slightest sniff of a professional contact. But he would go to Manhattan for the night if that was what it took for him to be excused from Marcella's party.

It wasn't surprising that Marcella was amazed he would eschew gossip for work. There was no one who liked a good 'scene' more than Simon. But he had a bad feeling about this one. He was extremely uncomfortable with the idea. Did money really matter so much to his charming hostess?

* * *

Simon left for Manhattan first thing the following morning. He'd booked himself the cheapest hotel room he could find and took food from Marcella's fridge to save him from having to buy any while he was in New York.

Marcella wouldn't notice that there were a few things missing from her refrigerator. She was catering on a grand scale. The guest list for her intimate soirée had grown like Topsy. Practically every woman in Little Elbow had accepted Marcella's invitation for an evening of 'girlish treats, including', she added *sotto voce*, 'some absolutely priceless gossip'.

Well, how could anyone refuse? The denizens of Little Elbow needed gossip as much as they needed oxygen.

33

When Grace and Charity walked into Marcella's house that night, the first impression was that it was going to be a very fluffy sort of evening indeed. While issuing her invitations, Marcella had decreed that everybody in attendance should wear pink. Marcella herself was wearing a little pink cashmere sweater over a pair of pink Capri pants. On her feet were a pair of pink sequinned ballet shoes and she wore a pink Alice band in her hair. She had never looked more friendly and harmless.

When Anjelica had welcomed the last of the guests and relieved them of their coats, she re-emerged from the kitchen as a cocktail waitress, serving, of course, pink-coloured cocktails. The choice was a cranberry-pink Sea Breeze or a strawberry Bellini.

'Made with strawberries from the farmers' market,' Anjelica added, as she had been instructed. Nothing less than the finest organic produce for the ladies of Little Elbow.

The sisters recognized quite a few women from their very first social engagement in Little Elbow – Marcella's birthday party. There was the girl who'd had Botox. The two girls with matching breasts. And, of course, Stephanie Blank, the potato-chip heiress whose smile seemed to contain twice as many teeth as the average mouth.

'Well, you can say one thing about Marcella,' said Stephanie as she sipped her first cocktail. 'She likes to make sure that

her guests aren't in danger of getting a DUI on the drive home.'
She accosted Anjelica. 'Darling, will you go back into the
kitchen and put some actual *alcohol* in this.'

As they drank their cocktails, the guests munched pink-
coloured macaroons and caught up with each other's latest
news. Engagements, marriages, births and separations.

'No! They're not getting a divorce?!'

'You're right. He won't give her one. Way too expensive for
him.'

'She's having a baby at *her age*? IVF?'

'Either that or a miracle.'

Stephanie Blank broke off from spreading scandal to
corner the Grosvenor sisters. 'You enjoying your summer?
You really have fitted right in.'

Charity smiled, gratified at the comment.

'And you, Grace, you're now officially seeing Choate
Fitzgerald, right? Quite a catch. We local girls didn't know
who would be good enough for him. Until you turned up. An
English upper-class girl is the perfect match for someone who
values lineage as much as Choate does.'

Marcella's mouth twitched upwards at the corners as she
drifted by with the macaroons and caught Stephanie's eye.

'Girls!' After a while, Marcella silenced the chat by clapping her hands. 'We're going to be totally casual tonight.
Supper is a buffet.'

Everything on the buffet was pink. From the smoked
salmon to start (done the 'modern' way, of course) to the
low-calorie mousse to finish. Anjelica felt that the goat's
cheese mixed with beetroot had been a mistake, however.

'That looks as though it's been pre-digested,' said Stephanie, voicing Anjelica's concerns.

Sarah Rabin joined the sisters.

'You know, I have been meaning to introduce myself to you

properly for weeks now. You're from London, right? I was wondering if you might know my cousin, Brian. He's been working in London for a hedge fund.'

'Oh, these girls don't get their hands dirty with money,' said Stephanie. 'They have people who deal with that sort of thing for them, I'm sure.'

She smiled her crocodile smile and left the sisters alone.

'What do you think?' Charity asked Grace.

'It's all right. Some of the girls here are quite nice.'

'It all seems very low key for Marcella. I can't help thinking that she's going to spring a surprise on us all.'

'Like a male stripper?' Grace suggested.

'Now, that kind of surprise I could handle. But it's not Marcella's style.'

'Perhaps you're being a little bit paranoid, Charity. Perhaps she really is all right underneath it all.'

'Ladies!' Marcella clapped her hands together again. 'I hope you've all enjoyed your supper.'

There were polite murmurs of agreement as Anjelica gathered fifteen plates still loaded with goat's cheese and beetroot.

Marcella grinned. 'Because now, it's time to play some games. We're going to play "truth or dare". Except, since dares are tedious when there are no boys in the room, this game is just going to be called "truth".' She walked over to the sideboard, whereupon there lay a pretty straw hat. 'OK, ladies. I have taken every single one of your names and written them on slips of paper, which I have put inside this hat. If your name is pulled out of the hat, then you have to answer a question. As I am the hostess, I am going to be both the picker and the questioner.'

There was a murmur of dissent.

'Marcella's house. Marcella's rules,' she said to silence them. 'You are welcome to leave if you don't like it. But you know you want to stay,' she added wickedly. 'Because you know that I will ask only the most probing questions!'

That prompted some very nervous laughter.

'So, have Anjelica recharge your glasses, then follow me into the lounge room. Make yourselves comfortable and prepare for some shocking revelations!'

Charity and Grace followed behind the other guests.

'What on earth is she going to ask us?'

'She'll probably ask you whether you've had sex with Choate yet,' said Charity. 'It's driving her nuts.'

'Suddenly I feel like going home,' said Grace.

'Oh, it's not going to be too bad,' said Charity. 'She's got no dirt on us. Just think yourself lucky you're not Ms Half and Half.' The sisters had been chatting to Chelsy Cialdini.

'She wouldn't bring that up, surely!'

'It wouldn't surprise me if that's precisely why she's holding the party,' said Charity.

When they got into the lounge room, the sisters found that they had been allocated the last of the seats, on opposite sides of the room.

'Sit next to me, Grace,' said Marcella.

Grace obliged.

'Isn't this cosy? Is everybody ready? Now, remember, girls, no cheating. We're playing *truth*. And if I don't think you're telling the truth in response to my question, then there may well be a forfeit.'

Stephanie Blank groaned.

'Come on, Stephanie. You know you're going to enjoy this game.'

'It's the build-up I can't stand. Get on with it,' she responded.

Marcella dipped her hand into the hat and pulled out a piece of paper. 'Well, would you look at that? Wait no longer for your moment in the spotlight. The very first name out of the hat is . . . Stephanie Blank.'

'This should be exciting,' said Stephanie facetiously. 'Ask me a difficult one.'

'Stephanie,' Marcella persisted, 'have you ever slept with either of the Mendelsohn brothers?'

'Oh, that's too easy.'

'What's your answer?'

'Yes. Of course. But he was only fourteen at the time, so it really doesn't count.'

'Fourteen!'

'And I was thirteen,' said Stephanie. 'It was Bradley. He was a virgin. He cried.'

There was a little ripple of laughter at that.

'Come on, Marcella. That was old news.'

'But I thought you lost your virginity to Eddy Kitsantonis when you were sixteen,' said Marcella.

'So did he.' Stephanie smiled.

Chelsy Cialdini, who had been dating Eddy for a week, shot Stephanie a daggered look.

'OK, next out of the hat is Sarah Rabin.'

The girls all turned to look at the new victim. Sarah looked at her knees.

'Sarah,' Marcella asked her, 'have you ever had Botox?'

Sarah opened her mouth to protest, but decided against it. Her lawyer's daughter was in the room. 'Yes,' she muttered.

'What's that?' asked Marcella. 'I didn't hear you.'

'Yes, I had Botox. But it was for my migraines. They got so bad, I could barely see sometimes.'

'Sweetheart . . .' Stephanie Blank squeezed her hand. 'You don't have to explain. We're all going to go there some time.'

'But it's true! I never would have . . .'

The other girls weren't interested in continuing this conversation.

Marcella held up the hat.

'Sarah,' she said, 'why don't you choose the next victim? . . . I mean, subject.'

Grateful for the chance to deflect the spotlight, Sarah stuck her hand into the hat and fluttered her fingers through the name-slips that remained. Eventually she chose one. She lifted it out with some ceremony, unfolded it and read out the name thereon.

'It's Grace Grosvenor,' she said. 'Do I get to ask the question too?'

'Oh no,' said Marcella. 'That would be a terrible waste.'

Grace glanced across the room at Charity. Charity gave her a little 'thumbs up' for courage.

'Grace, now, there are all sorts of things I've wanted to ask you since you got here. Like how do you get your hair to look so pretty and is it your natural colour?'

'It is . . .' Grace started to say. Marcella silenced her.

'I thought so. But since the rules of the game are that each person can only come under the spotlight once, I'm not going to ask you about your hair. I'm going to make your question a real good one.'

From across the room, Charity watched with concern as Grace gripped the edges of the chair she was sitting on.

'Grace Grosvenor . . .' Marcella paused for dramatic effect. 'Are you really an English heiress from South Kensington, who went to boarding school in India and is indirectly related to the Queen? Or are you in fact a common-or-garden secretary at a building yard, living in Tooting, in South

London, masquerading as someone of worth in order to snag yourself a rich husband and escape your miserable poverty-stricken life? Are you really the daughter of wealthy parents who made their fortune in tea or are you a cold-hearted gold-digger who intends to part Choate Fitzgerald from what is rightfully mine? . . . I mean, his,' she added pretty quickly.

34

'A gold-digger!'

Mouths fell open around the room.

Grace opened and closed her mouth like a fish, suddenly out of water, trying desperately to get some oxygen. She looked at Charity.

'Don't help her, Charity,' Marcella warned. 'Don't even think about it. Because I shall know if you're lying too.'

Grace did the only thing she could possibly do. She got to her feet and with a loud and dramatic sob of despair, she fled from the room.

'I'll take that as a yes,' said Marcella.

Charity had no choice but to follow her sister.

The room she left behind was silent for a second, then the murmuring started.

'No. It can't be true. A gold-digger? Where on earth did Marcella get that idea from?'

'Ladies,' said Marcella, 'I got it right from the horse's mouth.'

The room grew quiet again.

'Now, we Little Elbow girls know that if there's anything worth hearing you'll hear it at Mimi's. Well, it seems that Grace Grosvenor didn't know just how thin the walls are between those treatment rooms. So she felt quite free to be candid about the true facts of her life. Which were somewhat different from the "facts" she's been telling us at the dinner parties we invited her to out of the kindness of our hearts. We've been duped. Choate has been duped. I had to unmask her.'

'So what did you hear?' Stephanie asked. 'Tell us everything.'

'Well, for a start, those girls have never set foot in South Kensington, except in their capacity as cleaning ladies. Charity worked as a hotel maid! Grace Grosvenor worked in a lumber yard! They got the money to come here by winning a lottery!'

'So, they are real millionaires?' said Sarah Rabin.

'Far from it. They won just enough to rent the Rose House for the summer. And when I tell you how little the Rose House is renting for, girls, I swear you will throw up.'

'Tell us! Tell us!' the girls cried like hungry chicks.

'Marcella,' said Stephanie, 'I take my hat off to you. The truth-or-dare thing was genius! You must have been bursting, waiting for her name to come up.'

'It was worth the wait.'

'Oh yes,' several of the girls chorused.

'So, who is going to tell Choate?' someone asked.

'I don't think it will be long before he hears!' said Stephanie gleefully.

That was true. The entire Little Elbow coven was there. Grace's humiliation would be in Montauk and East Hampton by midnight. It might even make the gossip columns in the late edition of the next day's *New York Times*.

'How long will they stick around, do you think?' asked somebody else.

'I don't think it will be too long before the Rose House is back on the rental market,' said Marcella.

There was a murmur of delight. Almost everyone in the

room knew someone who wanted to rent the Rose House. Especially since it was so cheap! What kind of idiot must the owner be?

'Marcella, you ought to call Linda Deuble right now,' said Stephanie. 'She should know the truth in case their rent cheque bounces.'

'Our cheques won't bounce.'

The women turned to see Charity at the door to the sitting room. She looked furious but strangely centred. Like a mother tiger who'd had her tail pulled, planning to eviscerate her tormentor. But Marcella didn't see any reason to be afraid.

'Come back to collect a doggy bag?' asked Marcella.

A titter rippled around the room.

'I've come back to have a word with you,' said Charity.

'Really? Are you ready to tell us the truth at last?'

'Oh yes,' said Charity. 'If you're ready to hear it.'

'Try us. We love to hear a good story about poverty in the Third World! Perhaps we can have a fund-raiser for you girls. Ladies, put your hands in your pockets for Charity and Grace! We'll raise your plane fare to go back to where you came from. Tooting, isn't it?'

'That's where they had the riots,' said Stephanie knowledgeably.

'The London riots were in Brixton,' said Charity.

'Another place I would never go,' said Stephanie.

The assembled ladies agreed.

But Charity ignored Stephanie and concentrated on Marcella. 'Grace has gone back home. You'll be pleased to know she is absolutely distraught. That was quite some stunt you pulled. I assume that you organized this entire party in our honour? Well, I hope you're proud of yourself. And all of you,' Charity looked around the room at the other girls, 'I hope my sister's distress has enriched your evening too.'

Most of the women had the manners to look slightly ashamed.

'Because it's all very funny, isn't it, to "unmask" someone in a party game? To make them look like a fool in front of a room of people they hardly know.'

'It's a taste of your own medicine. You've been playing us all for fools since you got here!' Marcella interrupted. 'You lied about your background from the very beginning.'

'If you'd come to me first, then you would know that isn't true. Marcella,' said Charity, 'would you step outside with me for a moment?'

A gasp went up. The word 'catfight' was whispered.

Marcella got to her feet. 'What do you need to say to me that can't be said in front of my friends?'

'We're witnesses, Marcella!' Stephanie Blank shouted. 'We'll testify in court.' But she didn't try very hard to stop Marcella from going outside. And as soon as the door closed behind Marcella and Charity, Stephanie was the first to press her glass against it to hear what was going on.

Marcella and Charity stood in the hallway beneath a painting of Marcella's grandfather Edgar.

'If you're going to hit me,' said Marcella, 'you better make the first punch a good one. I am trained in ju-jitsu.'

'I'm not going to hit you,' said Charity.

'Don't try kicking me either. I can kick like a mule.' She did a demonstration roundhouse that almost knocked a vase off an antique credenza.

'I don't want to hurt you. In fact, I have brought you outside to spare your blushes.'

'You're the one who should be blushing!'

'I don't feel any kind of shame. I've no need to. Only sadness. For you.'

'Honey,' said Marcella, planting her hands on her hips, 'I'm not crying. I'm just looking forward to the day when you freeloaders pack up and move off my patch. I don't need any protection.'

Charity sighed. 'What I am about to tell you, I thought you would rather hear in private first, since it's a very delicate matter and it will put your little stunt back there in a very bad light. You've left me no choice but to tell you the one secret I have been keeping. It's about Grace . . .'

A secret! Marcella was like a little girl coming downstairs at Christmas time and seeing a doll's-house-shaped gift beneath the tree. She could have clapped her hands with delight. Instead she struggled to maintain the illusion that she wasn't impressed. Meanwhile, Charity lifted her eyes to the ceiling and hoped that, if there was a God, he would forgive her for what she was about to do.

'Marcella,' Charity began, 'I can quite believe that you heard all those things you repeated to your guests during that game of truth or dare. All that stuff about the grotty flat in South London, the builder fiancé, coming to the States to find a rich husband. All of it sounds quite feasible. I've heard stranger things from Grace myself. And I can't blame you for being shocked by what you thought you had discovered as a result. Choate is your friend. You care about him and the last thing you want is for him to fall into the clutches of a gold-digger. He's a very wealthy man and somewhat naive about love, I think.'

'I'll say,' said Marcella.

'Well, it's good that he has dear friends who look out for his interests.'

'So? What's the big secret?' Marcella interrupted. 'Get on with it. I have other dear friends through that door.'

'I'll make it brief,' said Charity,

'It all happened last year,' she began. 'Grace has always been mad about horses. Every since we were little girls. As soon as she was old enough to hold a pair of reins, she was out there on a pony every moment she got the chance. She became quite accomplished. She was always bringing home cups and rosettes. Anyway, last year she was out riding on a friend's estate. She hadn't been riding for quite some time. Not since she started modelling. So it's possible that she wasn't quite up to her usual fabulous standard.

'She didn't know the horse she had been given terribly well. Turned out he was the temperamental sort. Quite unsuitable for someone who wasn't riding every day. Grace and her friend were trotting along the bridle path when some farmer in a nearby field let off a shot at a rabbit. Grace's horse bolted. She managed to cling on for a while but she was knocked off his back by a low-hanging branch when the horse made a dash for some trees. Her riding hat came off during the fall. She always was blasé about that kind of thing. I don't think it was properly fastened. She hit her head hard when she landed. It took a while for the ambulance to get there. And when she came round from her coma, she had completely forgotten who she was.'

'She was in a coma?'

'That's right. For three whole months. We thought we'd lost her.'

'Three months? She didn't tell me that,' said Marcella.

'Well, of course not. Why would she? The thing is, Marcella, most days Grace doesn't even remember that she had an accident at all. She has amnesia.'

Marcella's eyes widened as far as they could go.

In the other room, where Stephanie was relaying what she heard to the rest of Marcella's guests, there were gasps of surprise. This was better than a soap opera.

'My God,' said Marcella. 'How much memory has she lost?'

'Everything before the ninth of March 2004. The day of the fall.'

'Will her memory ever come back?'

'The doctors don't think so.'

'But what about that comment she made about eating fish and chips as a child? And living in the flat above the café?'

'A complete fiction,' said Charity. 'Needless to say, we were all horrified when Grace finally opened her mouth and came out with that terrible cockney accent you heard her speaking in at Mimi's. There's certainly no cockney in our family.'

'Then where did she get it from?'

'Apparently it's quite common for head trauma victims to assume aspects of a different personality altogether when they finally come round. The brain searches around for snippets of information that seem like memories. Sometimes they are real memories. But sometimes, they are just things you might have learned at school or seen on television. The nurses at the hospital where Grace lay in her coma would quite often watch *EastEnders* on the ward television.'

'That soap opera about East London?'

'Exactly. We think, and the neurologists agree, that since she came round from her coma, Grace's brain has been trying to piece her personality back together using scenes from the *EastEnders* omnibus.'

'That is simply *tragic*,' breathed Marcella.

'I quite agree. It's desperately distressing to have to point it out to her. Just the other day Grace asked me if I remembered when we lived in the flat over the greasy spoon . . . that's a downmarket café,' she explained for Marcella's benefit. 'And I had to tell her that wasn't really her memory at all. She was getting herself mixed up with Sonia from *EastEnders* again.'

Marcella shook her head and pursed her lips in a gesture of sympathy. But Charity knew she wasn't really feeling sympathetic. She could almost see Marcella's brain whirring as it ran through the possibilities for making mileage out of Grace's little problem. It was going to be round Little Elbow like pubic lice in a nudist camp cafeteria by nightfall.

'Well, you were absolutely right,' said Marcella. 'I feel such a fool. If only I'd known . . . I would never have been so cruel. How can you ever forgive me?'

'It's OK,' said Charity. 'How on earth were you supposed to guess that Grace has a brain injury that sometimes makes her talk like Eliza Doolittle before her transformation? It's absolutely incredible, I realize. I never would have believed it until it happened to my own sister. Of course, you jumped to the conclusion that Grace had been lying to your dear friend Choate in order to part him from his fortune. In your position, I would have done exactly the same. Though perhaps I wouldn't have gone so far as to arrange a party to reveal her lies in public,' Charity added, twisting the knife.

'I feel terrible,' said Marcella.

On the other side of the door, Marcella's guests agreed that she should, indeed, feel bad about the whole affair.

'And you're certain there's absolutely nothing that can be done?' Marcella asked. 'About the amnesia?'

'Well, of course, that was one of the reasons why I decided to bring Grace here to spend the summer in the Hamptons. The doctors in Britain have done all they can. I'm hoping to get Grace some better treatment here in the

States. The United States is always at the cutting edge of these things.'

Marcella seemed pleased with that. 'I'll ask around and find out if anybody has a good recommendation.'

'Thank you,' said Charity. 'We're hoping to see Dr Edward Sherwin at St Elizabeth's.'

'Oh, he's very good.' Marcella nodded at the familiar name. Hadn't she just read a profile on him in the *New York Times*? He'd removed some supermodel's brain tumour.

'But you know,' Charity continued, 'I would really be grateful if you could keep the precise details of our conversation to yourself. If you could just tell your guests that you were mistaken about what you heard in the salon . . . I don't want people to start treating Grace differently. You know what it can be like. People will hear about the accident and start to show that they feel sorry for her. Worse still, they might start to treat her as though she's retarded. She may not remember much before 2004 but she definitely knows when she's being patronized.'

'Of course,' said Marcella. 'You can rely on my absolute discretion. And may I just say that I actually feel quite honoured that you would share this information with me at all. In your shoes, I might never have bothered to talk to me again. I think it says something about the bond that you and I have established these past few weeks.'

'Absolutely,' said Charity.

'What a tragic life you girls have had. First your parents dying and then Grace's accident. So many awful burdens. You must be due something wonderful any day now.'

'I think something wonderful may already have turned up for Grace,' said Charity. 'In the shape of your friend Choate.'

'Yes,' said Marcella. Through lightly gritted teeth.

'Well, I had better go next door and check that Grace is

feeling better. I'm sorry that our family skeletons have caused you embarrassment.'

'No, *I'm* the one who should be sorry,' said Marcella.

'And you won't tell anybody else?'

'Of course I won't.'

Marcella walked Charity to the front door and opened her arms for a hug before she bid her goodbye.

'Just you tell Grace that she has two sisters in this town,' were her parting words.

'I will,' said Charity. 'I'm glad you understand.'

Seconds later, Marcella was back in the dining room and bursting with the news.

'So?' asked Stephanie. 'Did you get the truth out of her? Are they as poor as church mice? Are they *chavs*?'

'Ohmigod,' said Marcella. 'It's even better than that. Turns out that Grace Grosvenor is a *retard*.'

35

Anjelica tidied away the party mess, of course. She picked up the straw hat that Marcella had used for the 'truth game' and emptied out the pieces of paper. As she had suspected, every single one of them had the name 'Grace Grosvenor' written inside.

She had heard about the accident, of course. Not from the dining room with Marcella's honoured guests but from behind the kitchen door. It was hard not to listen to the conversation when it was about the woman who had taken up residence in Choate Fitzgerald's heart. Anjelica admitted to herself that when Grace fled from the house, accused of having inflated her social position, Anjelica felt a little thrill at the thought that Choate might find such dissembling a deal-breaker. But then it struck her that if he decided that a girl who, despite her background, still had the wherewithal to rent the Rose House was not good enough for him, then Anjelica had no chance of capturing his heart. None at all. So, instead, she really had to hope that class really wasn't an issue for the man she adored.

But this accident. This brain damage. How would Choate receive that news?

From her tiny room at the top of the house, Anjelica had a partial view of the Rose House driveway. That night, she watched the driveway like a mother on a vigil for a child. But

Choate's car didn't appear. Anjelica thought perhaps Grace might have called him, to pre-empt the gossip, and if she had called him, Anjelica assumed Choate would want to go over to the Rose House and talk the issues through face to face. Perhaps Grace had told him over the phone and he'd decided he didn't need to see her/didn't *want* to see her any more. Anjelica felt her heart swell at the thought. Then she crossed herself against the evil of wishing such bad luck on others and settled down to read another chapter of Huck Finn. She was reading it for the second time. She read the inscription about a dozen times first.

As it happened, Choate did not find out about Grace's accident until the following morning. Marcella spent a frustrated night. As soon as the girls left the house, she tried to call Simon to let him know how the evening had gone. He would simply not believe what had transpired! But he didn't pick up his cellphone. Which meant she couldn't ask him how best to broach the subject with Choate. In the end, she decided that a straightforward phone call was best.

'Marcella.'

For the first time in a long time, Choate picked up the telephone right away.

'Oh, darling,' said Marcella. 'I'm so glad I got hold of you.'

'What can I do for you?'

'Are you at the Rose House?'

'No. I'm in Manhattan. It's a weekday. I'm in the office, of course. Working. You called me at work.'

'Then I won't keep you long. It's just that I wanted to know how Grace is and I'm reluctant to call the girls directly because I think I made a bit of a faux pas last night.'

'Oh yes?'

'It was really awful. We were just playing a party game.

You know it, I'm sure. Truth or dare? Anyway, Grace's name came out of the hat and, because we were on truth rather than dare? I, quite jokingly, of course, asked her whether she really grew up in Kensington or whether she was in fact the daughter of a cleaning lady, come to the Hamptons to seek her fortune by marrying a wealthy man.'

'You did what?'

'I know. It was just a silly joke. I don't know why it popped into my head. I realize now how rude it must have sounded. Anyway, I thought she'd just laugh it off but her reaction was so strange! She totally freaked out and ran from the room. Charity, quite rightly, bawled me out for being so rude, but then she told me about the accident and the head injury.'

'What head injury?'

'You mean she hasn't told you?'

Marcella allowed a pregnant pause that made it sound as though she were considering a terrible moral dilemma.

'Oh gosh. I don't know if I should say . . .'

'Please do,' said Choate.

'Well, I suppose this call isn't really going to make sense if I don't tell you the whole story. Choate, Grace had a terrible fall from her horse in 2004 and it has left her profoundly brain damaged.'

Choate blinked in surprise. 'Brain damaged?'

'Terribly. She can remember nothing at all from her life before the accident. In fact, she can't even remember the accident! She's a complete vegetable as far as her memory is concerned.'

'I don't understand. She seems OK to me.'

'Trust me, Choate. The girl is absolutely *ga-ga*. It's the reason why she keeps swapping between accents and always seems so vague when you ask her about her past. She has no past. The doctors say that in all probability she will never get her memory back. She doesn't recognize her favourite child-hood friends. From time to time, she even gets confused about her own sister.'

'She's never seemed confused to me.'

'She is. I overheard her at the beauty salon talking about her "childhood". She was telling the pedicurist that she grew up above a shop in one of the roughest parts of London. I was going to tell you that she had been pulling the wool over your eyes about her apparent noble background. Stephanie per-suaded me not to. She doesn't think it's politically correct to bother about class. But apparently, the fact that Grace keeps talking about life in the East End of London doesn't even stem from her childhood at all. While she was in hospital, the nurses in the intensive care unit had the television in her ward tuned to some British soap opera and Grace's poor damaged brain adopted the storylines from that show as her own.'

'But that's terrible! Poor Grace.'

'Poor Grace indeed,' said Marcella. Another pause. 'You know, Choate, I lay awake all night just thinking this situation over and wondering what should be done. The point is, I know how much you like this girl. In fact, if I know anything about you at all, dear friend, I would go so far as to say that you are already a little bit in love with her. And I also know that one day you would very much like to be married and perhaps you're even thinking that Grace might make the perfect wife and mother. But love can sometimes blind us to the practicalities of the situation. And there are some things that love simply can't overcome. Like retardation. Grace's brain injury is a terrible liability,' Marcella added. 'I mean, who knows whether the rest of her brain might be affected in years to come. She might have a child and forget all about it. She could leave it in a supermarket.'

'That would not be good at all,' Choate had to agree.

'I need to know that you'll think about what I've said. Do you promise?'

Choate promised.

'I'm sorry to be the bearer of such bad news,' Marcella concluded. 'But obviously, Grace wouldn't have remembered to tell you herself.'

'How was your party?' Simon asked.

He'd had a very dull evening in New York. The hotel room he'd booked himself into didn't even have a private bathroom, let alone satellite TV. Instead he had eaten the sandwiches he made before leaving Marcella's house and forced himself to read one of the books on Warhol he had been promising himself he would read for months. It was as boring as he had expected.

'We had a wonderful time.' Marcella reprised the story, right up to and including the part where she told Choate. 'Poor Choate. I'm sure he's devastated.'

'I'm sure he is. Was it really necessary for you to tell him?'

'Of course it was! She wouldn't have done. Like me, he has to consider not just his own future but that of an empire. He can't risk marrying someone who can't even remember where she grew up. Brain injuries are curious things,' Marcella added knowledgeably. 'Who knows what the long-term effects might be. I said, and Choate agreed, that it would be an absolute disaster if he were for any reason unable to run their affairs and Grace couldn't remember how to.'

'How very thoughtful of you,' said Simon.

Marcella beamed. 'And how about you? How was your big important meeting? Worth missing the party of the year for, I hope.'

'It was very productive,' Simon lied. He was helping himself to the contents of the refrigerator again.

'Wow,' said Marcella. 'You're hungry. Didn't that producer take you somewhere good last night?'

'I can't believe you told them I had a head injury!' Grace wailed at her sister.

'What else was I supposed to do? Let them think that you're a gold-digging liar?'

'Well, how am I supposed to act now? Like this?' Grace pulled a face and loped around the room like Quasimodo.

'Stop it. You don't have to change anything at all. I've told them that the effects are intermittent. Most of the time you're OK.'

'Thanks for that,' said Grace. Sarcastically.

'Look, everything will be fine. I think the embarrassment of having called you a liar when it turns out that you're actually brain damaged will keep Marcella off your case for a bit. But you have to tell Choate.'

'Tell him what?'

'Oh, don't get amnesiac on me now, Grace. You have to tell him about the accident. Because if you don't tell him, Marcella will. And it's far better it comes from you.'

Ryan was spiking the lawn in preparation for some fertilizer.

'I heard about your sister. I'm sorry. That must be really tough.'

'We manage,' said Charity.

'Well, clearly,' said Ryan. 'I would never have guessed. I hope you don't mind me saying something. It's just that I heard when I was in the grocery store this morning and I wondered if there was anything I could do to make life easier. Have you contacted a doctor out here?'

'Not yet,' said Charity. 'You know, I really don't want to talk about it right now.'

'OK.'

As she stepped down into the garden, Ryan held out his hand towards her. Charity put her hand in his. It was warm. She was sure that he hesitated for a moment before letting go.

'You know, even before I heard about the accident, I noticed how you are around your sister. You really care for her, don't you? It's good to see.'

'Thank you.'

'You seem like you have the weight of the world on your shoulders today.'

'It feels like that every day,' said Charity. 'Sometimes I'm better at carrying it than others.'

'Family obligations can be tough,' said Ryan. 'My grandmother had a sister who needed a lot of attention.'

Charity nodded but she didn't really want to know. She directed her attention to the roses instead. Over the past few days, many more buds had begun to unfurl. There was one bush in particular that caught Charity's attention. It had blooms as big as a man's curled fist. Charity cupped one of the blooms in her hand and brought it closer to her face. The bouquet was perfect.

'Beautiful, isn't it?'

Charity started.

'You were miles away,' said Ryan. 'What do you think? Starting to look pretty good, eh?'

'I think you have a magic touch. What's your secret?'

'I talk to them. Like your Prince Charles. Doesn't he talk to his flowers?'

'So the story goes,' said Charity. 'Some people think it's a sign of madness.'

'Could be. Apparently, my great-aunt used to talk to her flowers too. She had the best garden I've ever seen.'

'Better than this?'

'Oh yes. At least, as far as I could tell from the photographs. She even bred some roses of her own. In fact, this is one of hers.' Ryan led Charity to a bush that sported delicate peach-coloured blooms.

'That is beautiful. I wish I could create something like that.'

'It's easy.'

'No it isn't.'

'You know, I've got to go to the nursery this morning. I wonder if you'd like to come with me and choose some plants for the bed in front of the kitchen window?'

'I'd like that,' said Charity.

'We'll go in half an hour.'

36

'Does the owner of the house have a particular colour scheme we should be sticking to?' Charity asked.

'Choose what you like.'

'But I don't want you to get into trouble.'

'I won't get into trouble,' said Ryan.

Charity picked out a yellow rose.

'I think that's completely beautiful,' said Ryan. 'And very you.'

'What do you mean?'

'It's understated. Elegant. Smells like heaven.'

Charity found herself blushing. When he noticed, Ryan looked down.

'I mean, not that I know what you smell like,' he blustered.

'How about this one for Grace?' said Charity, quickly changing the subject. Grace's rose was a pink one, of course. 'I think she would choose this if she were here.'

'That's lovely too. Well, look at that. Two English roses.'

By the time they had dug the roses in, it was almost seven o'clock.

'I'm sorry,' said Charity. 'I'm sure you were probably meant to get off work hours ago. Do you get paid overtime?'

Ryan laughed.

'I didn't think so. Well, maybe I . . .'

'Don't worry about it. Sometimes I stay late. Sometimes I

get off early. But I'll be going now and let you get on with your evening, unless . . .' He paused. He shook his head minutely then said, 'No. I'm going to plunge right in.'

Charity found herself biting her lip as she waited for what was to come next.

'Charity, would you like to come for dinner with me? Tonight? If you don't already have plans, that is? And assuming that you'd like to.'

Like to? Charity would have liked nothing better. But how could she say yes?

The reasons why not ran through Charity's mind like the soundtrack to a public information film. It was impossible. To accept a dinner invitation from Ryan would be too much like accepting a date. And Charity couldn't date the gardener. The whole point of coming to America was to find a rich husband. How could she possibly accept a date with one of the staff? What if someone found out? In Charity's mind's eye, the public information film flipped forward to the possible fallout. Charity living in a trailer, while her gardener husband drank whisky from a bottle in a paper bag in the front of his pick-up truck on his way to plant roses for a rich man's wife.

'I've . . . I've already got plans for tonight,' Charity stammered. 'I'm sorry.'

Ryan nodded. 'Of course.' There was a pause. Thankfully, Ryan didn't fill it with an invitation to join him some other evening instead. 'Well, I'll be round at some point tomorrow to see how these are doing. Give them a bit more water.'

'Maybe see you then,' said Charity.

'Maybe,' said Ryan.

He started to load his tools into the wheelbarrow.

'I should go and get ready.'

Charity gave a strange little wave and headed back to the house. She'd handled that OK, hadn't she? She hadn't caused any offence.

But Ryan seemed to be taking for ever to gather his tools together and leave. Dreading the moment when he walked past the house on his way to the guest house and saw that she was still very much at home, Charity decided that she had better go through the motions of getting ready for a big night out.

She got into the shower. She dressed in one of her favourite dresses. A red one. Monsoon, though it looked far more expensive. She blow-dried her hair and slipped on her favourite shoes. She came downstairs. Ryan was still outside. He was adjusting one of the sprinklers. It had jammed in one direction and was soaking a delicate plant that preferred its soil a little dry.

Damn, thought Charity. Now she would have to leave the house and get in her car and drive off and sit God only knew where until she could be sure Ryan had gone out or gone to bed. But how long would that take? How long would it take to fix a sprinkler? What if it took him four hours and he really did have nothing better to do?

While Charity was busy worrying about all this, Ryan came up to the house. He knocked on the kitchen door.

'Hey.'

'Hey,' said Charity.

'I hate to bother you, but . . .' He paused and actually took off his hat like a man in a 1950s movie. 'Wow, you look amazing.'

Charity muttered 'Thank you' and looked straight at her shoes.

'I need something long and thin to make an adjustment to

the sprinkler out there. I was wondering whether one of you girls has a safety pin?'

'I'll have a look.' Charity opened her handbag and rootled around inside.

'That's a beautiful dress. I hope someone's taking you somewhere special.'

'Just the Harbor Club,' said Charity. Then she panicked that Ryan might actually be planning to go to the Harbor Club himself that night. It seemed that anyone could get in there. They had a bar in the front of the building that played twenty-four-hour sports. 'But actually, my date just called to say that he won't make it. Family bereavement,' she added quickly.

'Oh, that's terrible.'

'It was no one close,' said Charity, crossing her fingers behind her back and praying that she wasn't going to bring the wrath of the gods down for lying. 'Some elderly aunt he hardly knew. But, well, his mother is obviously very upset, having lost her big sister, and he feels that he should stay at home and make sure she's all right.'

'Of course.'

'So, I'm not going to the Harbor Club after all,' Charity concluded.

'All dressed up and nowhere to go,' said Ryan. 'Unless . . .'

What harm would it do to spend just one evening with Ryan? If anyone in town thought it odd that she was fraternizing with the help, then Charity would just explain that was the English way. Every now and then you had to socialize with your servants to keep them onside. And now that she had got herself all dressed up – albeit to prolong a lie – Charity did feel it would be a shame not to go out somewhere. It wasn't often that her frankly difficult hair went so 'right'. She admired the wave in the darkening window on to the garden.

'What are you suggesting?' she said.

'Well, with you in a dress like that, we'd have to go somewhere nice. But with me in my work clothes like this, I'm afraid we're pretty much limited to Rowdy Hall.'

'Rowdy Hall?'

'It's an English pub. In East Hampton. They serve fish and chips.'

At the sound of the word 'chips', Charity realized just how hungry she was. Her stomach growled. 'That sounds incredibly good,' she said, quite honestly.

'Give me two more minutes with this sprinkler, then I'll wash my hands and we'll hit the road.'

'OK,' said Charity. 'Maybe I'll change.'

'Don't change,' said Ryan.

In the end, Ryan worked on the sprinkler for just another forty-five seconds, ensuring that Charity didn't have time to change her mind. In three minutes, they were climbing into Ryan's truck.

Though Rowdy Hall wasn't the kind of venue that got written up in glossy magazines, the faux English pub was absolutely heaving with people when Ryan and Charity arrived. They had to wait to be seated. The smells drifting from the kitchen made Charity's stomach grumble ever louder. The temptation to lean over to their neighbours' table and steal a chip was unbearable.

The food may not have been sophisticated by East Hampton standards, but to Charity, fish and chips had never tasted so good. And after fifteen minutes, she forgot she was the most overdressed girl in the house and began to concentrate only on the food and the fun they were having. They moved from the subject of gardens to the people of Little Elbow. Ryan had worked for quite a few. He did an impression of Stephanie Blank finding a slug which had Charity squealing.

Wasn't it always the way? The interesting guys were inevitably the unsuitable ones. She thought about her date with Robin Madden. It had been more like a job interview than the beginning of a beautiful friendship. She had the sense that Robin's first dates always went the same way. More a swapping of information than an evening of flirtation. How do our backgrounds match up? Our educational attainment? Our connections? Our bank accounts? Robin might as well have sent his CV in advance.

And Jerry Penman? Oh my God. Men like him shouldn't be allowed to go out at all.

With Ryan it was different. This was more like the dates she had enjoyed back in London. So much laughing . . .

Charity brought herself up short. This wasn't a 'date'. Just two people eating at the same table. Friends. That's all.

Ryan's hand snaked across the table towards hers.

'It's getting late,' said Charity suddenly. She summoned their waitress with a little wave. The girl came straight over and put the bill on Ryan's side of the table. Charity grabbed for it.

'I should get this,' she said.

'Are you kidding?' Ryan snatched the bill back.

'Then let's go halves.'

'No way. I can afford to buy you fish and chips if that's what you're worried about.'

'Look, we need to go halves because if we don't then it's a date and . . . Ryan, please. You're just the . . .'

Charity's voice trailed away.

'Just the gardener?' He finished the sentence for her. 'Here.'

He threw down a twenty-dollar note. 'We'll go halves. I'll meet you in the truck.'

Charity closed her eyes and wished she could travel back in time just thirty seconds.

Ryan hardly spoke on the way home.

It was a terrible ending to what otherwise would have been a wonderful night.

37

Grace's evening had gone rather differently. She had another date with Choate.

He arrived absolutely on time, of course. And bearing yet another enormous bunch of flowers. Grace was honest enough with herself to know that if Choate broke up with her that night she would definitely miss those flowers.

'We need to have a talk,' said Choate as soon as he walked into the house. 'A proper one. Can we go down to the beach?'

That was it, thought Grace. He knew about the accident and the amnesia and he wanted nothing more to do with her. She agreed to his suggestion to walk on the beach. Best to get the embarrassment over and done with.

'I've been talking to Marcella about you,' was the first thing he said.

Of course, it had to be Marcella who told him.

'You know, I value Marcella's opinion very highly,' he continued.

'I know what that's like,' said Grace. 'It's great to have a friend you can rely on to tell you what to do in the most difficult circumstances.'

'Absolutely. She's always been very honest with me, even if some of the things she has said haven't exactly been what I wanted to hear.'

'Sometimes the truth hurts,' Grace agreed.

'I think Marcella has a sisterly kind of concern for me,' Choate went on. 'She thinks she knows what kind of woman I should end up with, for example.'

And that woman definitely isn't me, thought Grace.

But then it happened.

'Grace.' Choate darted in front of her and suddenly dropped to one knee. Right there on the sand. Then he bobbed back up to check that he hadn't inadvertently knelt in any dog mess. There was no dog mess. He knelt back down.

'Before I met you I was living a half-life. I had no real purpose. No direction. Sure, I was building my business and putting lots of effort into that. But my spiritual side was sadly stagnant. Since I met you, Grace, there are whole hours when I don't look at my Palm Pilot. I look at the view instead. At the sunset. At your beautiful face. Even Manhattan looks somehow less grey. Grace, it's as though I couldn't see before I met you. I don't ever want to go back to being that man. I want you by my side for always.'

Suddenly Grace knew exactly what was coming.

'Grace Grosvenor. Will you marry me?'

'I can't,' Grace sobbed.

'Why not?'

'I'm not the woman you think I am.'

'Grace,' said Choate, 'I know everything about you. You don't have any secrets from me. Marcella told me about the accident.'

'But Choate,' said Grace, 'how can you possibly want to marry a woman who doesn't remember anything that happened to her before the age of twenty-four? I'm damaged goods,' she added dramatically.

'On the contrary. I like the fact that you can't remember anything about your past,' said Choate.

Grace stared at him. 'How on earth could you find it a plus point?'

'Because . . .' Choate cleared his throat and got to his feet. His knees were killing him. 'Because if you can't remember your past, then in some strange way, it's as though you don't have one. And then I can imagine that I'm the first man ever to make love to you.'

Grace blushed at the thought.

'Perhaps I will be,' said Choate. 'Unless your memory comes back, we'll never know for certain and that's perfectly all right by me. Say yes to me, darling. I won't take no for an answer.'

Because it was clear that he wasn't kidding, Grace really did say 'yes'. Or, more precisely, 'OK.'

Choate didn't seem too worried by her muted response. It wasn't a 'no' and that was all that mattered to him.

'I hope this fits,' he said, swiftly producing a small velvet-covered box from his pocket.

'Oh my God.' Grace's first thought was that the ring reminded her of a paste knuckleduster an old boyfriend had worn as part of his 'pimp' outfit to a fancy dress party. But this sparkler was real. It had been hewn out of rock by a sweating South African. It was worth more than the average car. It was worth more than the above-average car with sunroof, DVD player and air-conditioning.

Choate pulled the ring from the velvet lining and took Grace's left hand. She stretched her fingers out automatically. In actual fact, the reflex owed more to the muscle tension of pulling away from something but Choate interpreted it as permission to stick the sparkler on her ring finger.

'Oh!'

Grace immediately burst into tears.

'There, there, my darling.' Choate wrapped her in his arms.

'I know this is emotional. It's the moment every girl dreams of. You probably can't quite believe that this is finally happening to you. But rest assured it really is. You're going to be Mrs Choate Fitzgerald.'

Grace cried all the way back to the house. Choate seemed perversely happy with the state of affairs. It clearly didn't cross his mind that she might be sobbing for any reason other than pure joy.

'I'm feeling very emotional,' she told her new fiancé. 'If it's OK with you, I think I'd like to lie down for a while. On my own.'

Choate, ever the gentleman, agreed.

At eleven o'clock, Charity returned from her disaster at Rowdy Hall to find her sister sitting on the sofa in the dark, staring into the distance in the manner of someone shell shocked.

'Grace?' she said. 'Are you OK? What happened? Did you talk to Choate?'

Grace nodded.

'And was he upset? Did he break up with you?'

Grace shook her head. And stretched out her left hand in Charity's direction. When the feeble light from the hallway caught the diamond, it was as though someone had flicked on another switch.

'What is *that*?' Charity gasped.

Grace told her the whole story, how far from being put off by the news of Grace's amnesia, Choate had seen it as a bonus, rendering her a psychological virgin if nothing else.

'That's one way of looking at it,' Charity said.

'I don't know if I'm entirely flattered,' said Grace.

'Oh, come on. Give him a break. Is there a single man out

there who wouldn't wish "former boyfriend amnesia" upon the woman he loves? Let me see the ring again.'

Grace duly stuck out her hand.

Charity examined Choate's ring with the cold eye of a professional gem dealer.

'It's enormous,' she said. 'And the colour and clarity are amazing. I can't see a single flaw. Either this is cubic zirconia or you have just been presented with an engagement ring worth six figures! Sterling!' she added. 'Now, we need to get you a good lawyer, pronto.'

'A lawyer?'

'Yes. For the prenuptial agreement, of course. Choate will almost certainly insist on having one – or rather his family lawyers will – so you need to find a good one who can ensure that this marriage is worth your while. You don't want to be divorced and back in London in five years' time without a penny to your name. Or maybe you should marry in London, which means that we don't have to worry about the prenup so much. If you marry under British law then everything is split fifty-fifty. But hang on. That's no good. We've got nowhere to stay back in London.'

Grace looked uncomfortable. 'It's all so fast.'

'Grace . . .' Charity shook her hand. 'This is a moment for action. Choate won't mind. He wants to marry you as quickly as he can in case you change your mind. Oh, well done, Grace. I knew that you could do it. Mum would be so proud of you. If only she could have known before she died that one day you would be living in an enormous house in the Hamptons with everything you could ever wish for at your fingertips! All those worries she had about what would become of us after she died. I told her not to worry about you. I knew your face would be your fortune.'

Grace put her hands to her face as though trying to put a physical weight to its value.

'Choate is going to want to make love when we're married!'

'You mean you haven't already . . .'

'We've barely even kissed.'

'You're joking.'

'He isn't pushy. And I was quite happy about it.'

'Well, yes,' said Charity.

'But I don't think I . . .'

'Perhaps you'll have incredible chemistry,' said Charity.

'How likely is that? It makes my stomach flip when he kisses me.'

'That's a good sign.'

'It flips as though I've eaten something that disagrees with me. And sometimes he keeps his eyes open.'

'That's just because he can't believe how beautiful you are,' Charity tried to reassure her.

Grace shuddered.

'Grace,' Charity insisted, 'all these worries you're having, all these nightmare thoughts, are perfectly natural. You've just accepted a marriage proposal. It's a big deal. Think of how nervous you were when we got on to the plane to come out here. It should have been something to look forward to. But of course you're looking on the dark side. What intelligent person wouldn't consider the possible downside to the very best of prospects? When the initial shock is over, you'll be really happy, I swear.'

'But what are you going to do when I get married? Will you go back to London and leave me all alone?'

'No fear. You'll invite me to live in the guest house at Choate's until I can get myself sorted out. He won't refuse you the comfort of having your sister around.'

'OK,' said Grace.

'That guest house is pretty big,' Charity continued. 'I'd be quite happy to live there for the rest of my life. If my new brother-in-law allows it! Oh, Grace, this is the best news. This is what I call hitting the jackpot.'

Grace let Charity get all excited about her wedding to Choate but as she lay in bed that night she knew that she was going to have to tell Choate the truth and fast. Things had spiralled out of control.

She had let Charity persuade her to start dating him only because she thought that it would help her to get over the situation she had left behind in London. And at the beginning she'd had no intention of starting something serious. Grace wasn't sure she was ready for a new attachment. Then, when she realized that Choate was that rare creature – a truly nice guy – she had done her very best to fall for him. And she had certainly succeeded in liking Choate. She liked him very much. But could she ever *love* him? And even if she could love him, could she ever love the life of a wealthy Hamptons wife?

For every bit as lovely as Little Elbow was, Grace didn't believe that she could ever be truly happy there. She just didn't quite fit in. She found it so tiring to spend every day having to be someone that she really wasn't. The pressure to have to look good all the time. Always having to remember which fork to use, what to say, what not to say and how to say it.

Ridiculous as it was, Grace longed to be back in London. Her life there was distinctly Third World compared to the life she could have as Mrs Fitzgerald, but at least she knew the rules of living in London. She'd liked her job. She liked the people she worked with. There was always time to have a laugh. She missed her girlfriends. She really missed her girlfriends. Grace had met no other women she felt she could connect with in the months they'd spent in the States – there was only Charity, who didn't count because she was her sister. The women here were so competitive with each other. They made her feel small. All their conversations involved slagging off the other women, who were supposed to be their friends. They couldn't trust each other at all. Not like the girls back home, who could tell each other secrets and know for certain that they wouldn't hear those secrets turned into a cheap anecdote for the crowd down the pub.

Grace looked at her diary. Charity didn't know it, but she had been counting down the days till they boarded the plane back to London and got back to living their real lives. They had to do that – go back to their real lives. This time in the States had been an adventure. They'd have some tales to tell and some fabulous clothes to wear. But all Grace really wanted was to be back at their kitchen table in London with a nice cup of tea and a Jaffa Cake . . .

38

The following day, the entire population of Little Elbow was
to attend a big charity polo match in aid of children orphaned
by an earthquake somewhere nobody had ever visited on
vacation. Charity and Grace had received their invitations the
previous week and RSVPed in the positive. Charity was
excited – polo seemed the very height of sophistication.
She had spent hours, even days, wondering what to wear.

Grace was altogether less ramped up about the day ahead.
Of course, Choate would be there – he would be making the
trip from Manhattan especially – and Grace knew she had no
choice but to break his heart the minute she saw him. It was
the only way to limit the damage. Perhaps, if luck was on her
side, he wouldn't have told anyone else about the engagement
yet. She had to make sure. She phoned him.

'Ah, the future Mrs Choate Fitzgerald!' She could hear the
smile in his voice.

'Choate.' There was no corresponding smile in her voice.
'You and I need to have a conversation about something.'

'About what?'

'About getting married.'

'Of course,' said Choate. 'We need to start making wedding plans right away if we're going to do it in the fall.'

Grace detected no hint of fear. No hint that Choate understood that when people in a relationship have to have a
'conversation about something', it is usually a bad sign.

'When can I see you?' Grace continued.

'Well, I'm going to put in another hour at the office then drive straight from Manhattan into Little Elbow for the polo match. I'll meet you there.'

'Fine. But you have to promise me that you won't mention our engagement to anybody in the meantime,' Grace warned him. 'Nobody at all. Not even your mother.'

'I get it.' Choate laughed. 'You want to be the one to tell them. I perfectly understand, my dear. Getting a marriage proposal is the most important moment in a woman's life. You want to make the most of it. Savour it. Enjoy your triumph.'

Grace winced. 'I'll see you later.'

The polo match was being held at a horse farm on the outskirts of town. A number of white tents had been erected around the field for the spectators, who were, to be honest, far more interested in seeing each other than seeing the men on horses thundering up and down the field in pursuit of the tiny ball. Inside the tents, tables had been laid with a buffet that would have seemed like heaven to any of the orphaned children they were raising money for. To the denizens of Little Elbow, however, it didn't seem *all that*.

'Who did the catering?' Marcella asked, picking up a vol au vent and studying it as though it were a rare beetle.

'I'll give you their number,' said the waitress.

'I don't need their number. Just their name so I know to avoid them.'

The waitress blushed. Marcella smirked at Simon. He shook his head.

'God, this is dull,' said Marcella, glancing in the direction of the polo field oh so briefly.

'Then why are we here?' Simon asked.

'Because everybody else is here. Duh! Plus Choate is always at the polo. He wouldn't miss it for the world. And I want to be here to console him over his heartbreak upon discovering that his girlfriend is a head case.'

'If he's heartbroken, surely he won't be here?' said Simon.

'Simon, you don't know Choate at all. He wouldn't break an appointment if his mother died. How do I look?'

'Fabulous. As usual.'

'Thank you. This was Choate's favourite dress. It's a bit of a disaster to have to wear something so very last year but needs must. The worst of it is, I had to take it back from Anjelica. I gave it to her to wear for her meeting with the immigration lawyer.'

'Have you set that meeting up yet?'

'Do I look as though I've had the time?'

The first person the sisters saw as they entered the main marquee was Marcella. She made a beeline for them and kissed Grace again with the tenderness that made her very suspicious.

'How are you?' she asked, extra slow.

Grace resisted the urge to talk very slowly in reply.

'I've sent Simon in search of a table. Will you join us for a glass of champagne?'

'I want to see some of the polo,' said Grace.

'You do? Really, it's a terrible bore,' said Marcella. 'No one actually comes to the polo to watch the polo.'

'I would like to watch the horses. I like horses.'

Marcella took Charity by the arm. 'Are you sure that's wise? Letting her stand near the horses? What if she has a flashback to the accident?'

Grace, who heard every syllable of Marcella's concerned 'whisper', just grabbed Charity by the other arm and dragged her in the direction of the field.

'I'll be fine,' she snapped.

'We'll see you later,' said Charity.

'What is wrong with you?' Charity asked when they were well away from the tent and Marcella's earshot. 'Can't you see she was just trying to be nice after having been so mean to you at her party?'

'She's one person I will be very glad not to have to see ever again.'

'What do you mean? You're going to live right across the bay from her. You might as well try to be friends. Or friendly acquaintants at least.'

'No point.'

'No, really,' said Charity. 'You should try to make amends. She is one of Choate's oldest friends and . . .'

Grace interrupted her. 'Charity, I don't need to make amends with Marcella Hunter because as of next week I'm going to start pretending she never existed. I've made my decision. As soon as Choate arrives, I'm going to take him somewhere quiet and tell him that the wedding's off.'

'What?'

'I was awake all night thinking about it. It's the only thing to do. I've got the ring in my pocket and I'm going to give it back. Hopefully he'll be able to get a refund.'

'Are you nuts?'

'No.'

'That ring is worth a fortune.'

'But it's an engagement ring and I can't keep it if I can't marry him. And I can't marry him because I don't love him.'

'You told me you did love him.'

'I was just trying to convince myself. I don't even really fancy him.'

'That doesn't matter,' said Charity.

'You're joking.'

'I'm not. Marriage isn't all about love, Grace.'

Grace just stared.

'In any case, what exactly is your idea of love in the first place?' Charity continued. 'A sudden flash of recognition? Just knowing that someone is *the One*?' She pulled a soppy face. 'It's immature to think that you can't make a marriage work without this ridiculous thunderbolt thing. In twenty years' time, none of the people standing in this field today will be bothered whether or not they fancy the people they married because they'll all prefer a nice cup of tea to a night of passion. Other things become much more important. Steadiness and decency. Choate's got those by the bucket-load.'

'I'm not saying that he hasn't, but . . .'

'Along with the cash,' Charity ploughed on.

'Cash doesn't matter to me half as much as it matters to you,' Grace snapped back.

'That's because you've never had to give up anything that really mattered to you because you didn't have enough money.'

Grace looked stung. She knew at once what her sister was referring to. And if that was about to form the backbone of Charity's argument, then Grace really couldn't see how she was going to be able to argue back.

Fortunately Charity decided to appeal to Choate's less obviously material qualities. 'Well, how about respect, then? He respects you. And you could respect him, couldn't you?'

'I do respect him. Which is exactly why this charade has to end. He's in love with a woman who doesn't exist!'

'You exist for him.'

'I just don't love him!' Grace shouted.

Though she was at least fifty feet away from them, Charity

was sure she saw Marcella prick up her ears. 'Keep it down, Grace.'

'I will not. I don't want to lie any more. I want to go home. And when I say home I do not mean the house here, I mean proper home. London. I want you to give me my air ticket. I'm going to fly back as soon as I can.'

'You can't.'

'You told me the ticket was exchangeable.'

'I lied.'

'Oh, well, there's a surprise! Charity Grosvenor doesn't tell the truth! It's just another example of the way you've always been. You're so controlling. You just keep taking decisions for me. You don't ever give me a chance to work things out for myself. You think I'm some kind of moron who can't be trusted to run my own life.'

'I've only ever tried to protect you.'

'From what? I was happy, Charity. Really happy. Now I'm in a town I don't know, surrounded by people I don't like, engaged to be married to a man I don't love.'

Grace was so busy ranting, she had completely forgotten about the game, as had quite a few other people within earshot. Charity was grateful for the thunder of the horses' hoofs, which drowned out most of Grace's tirade. If only there were a way to get her to shut up. Milliseconds later, Charity's prayer was answered, as a freak shot sent the polo ball sailing high into the air and straight into the side of Grace's head.

39

Grace was instantly silenced, her face registering shock in true silent-movie-heroine style. She remained on her feet for just a few more seconds before falling sideways like a tree being felled. And as she fell, she whacked the other side of her head on the hard sun-baked ground.

The game stopped at once. Someone screamed. It wasn't Charity – she was too surprised. A crowd quickly gathered around Grace's prone body. She was out cold. The first-aiders were by her side within seconds, but when she didn't respond to their ministrations, it was decided that Grace had to go to hospital. An air ambulance was duly summoned.

'Is she going to be OK?' Charity asked.

Nobody could be sure.

In the meantime, Choate Fitzgerald arrived at the polo ground. He was in exceptionally high spirits. In fact, he had been singing all the way from Manhattan. Who cared if the traffic on the I-495 was so bad it would have been quicker to jump from car roof to roof like an Australian sheepdog than drive? Choate's smile would not be budged. He could endure any hardship as long as Grace was at the end of it. He was the happiest man in the Hamptons. Until he realized that the girl at the centre of the crowd was his fiancée . . .

'Let me through!'

Even people who had known Choate his entire life had

never seen him respond to a situation with such passion. He shoved people aside, causing Marcella Hunter's left ankle to turn in its Manolo Blahnik sandal. Her heel snapped. Her instant response of 'I'll sue' was thankfully cut short by Simon McDonnough.

'Grace Grosvenor might be dead,' he reminded her.

Marcella instantly forgot about her shoe and brightened.

Choate threw himself down on to the ground beside his beloved. 'Grace! Grace! Don't leave me!' he wailed.

He picked up her floppy body and covered her face with kisses.

'Choate,' Charity screamed. 'Don't move her! She might have a fractured skull!'

'My darling, my darling! I love you! Don't go.'

Choate sobbed, rocking Grace's limp frame back and forth.

'It's like that scene in the opera,' murmured Marcella. 'The one with the dead brother.'

Charity and the first-aiders tried to prise Choate from her sister's body. On the polo field, the air ambulance was landing. Another first-aider was trying to get the crowd – none of whom had ever seen a dead body and all of whom were hoping that their luck was about to change – out of the way. And then, as though she were waking from a lovely afternoon nap, Grace opened her eyes.

A gasp went up around the crowd.

'Choate!' she said in surprise. The warmth in her voice as she said his name was palpable. 'What on earth is the matter? What are you crying about? I don't think I shall ever have reason to cry again now that we're engaged.'

Another gasp went up around the crowd. This time it was Marcella Hunter's turn to pass out (though thankfully, she managed to stay on her feet).

'You're engaged?' she half snarled at her former boyfriend.

'That's right, everybody,' said Choate. 'Grace and I. We're engaged to be married. I proposed just the other night. On the beach.'

Grace had struggled upright into a sitting position. She touched the tender spot on her head and winced.

'Did I fall over?' she asked.

'You were hit by a polo ball,' someone explained. 'You got knocked out.'

'Oh, how silly,' said Grace. 'I can't have been paying attention.'

'I'm sure you were, my dear.' Choate helped her to her feet. 'I'll find the clown who hit that ball and have him strung up next to the highway.'

Grace laughed. 'There's really no need.'

The assembled crowd laughed too. Nervously. Lawsuits were uncomfortably common in Little Elbow.

'Oh, I am glad to see you,' she said, planting a kiss on Choate's cheek. 'You arrived at exactly the right time. My knight in shining armour.'

'You're not wearing your ring,' Choate observed.

'Oh!' Grace exclaimed. 'Where is it?'

'It's in your pocket,' said Charity flatly. 'In its box.'

'Now I remember,' said Grace. 'I put in it my pocket because I wanted you to put it on my finger all over again. In front of everybody!'

'Well, my darling, if that's what you want . . .'

Choate Fitzgerald obliged. The crowd, who moments before thought they might be attending a death, gave a polite ripple of applause (to be honest, some of them were slightly less excited by the prospect of a happy ending than they should have been).

'Everyone's invited to the wedding!' Choate exclaimed.

Somebody gave up three cheers.

Marcella ran from the scene with Simon in pursuit.

'I think it would be a good idea to get Grace to the hospital now,' said Charity.

'But I'm fine,' Grace insisted. 'I want to stay here and enjoy my first polo match as Choate Fitzgerald's wife-to-be.'

And that, thought Charity, was exactly why Grace needed to be taken for a brain scan.

40

So, Grace and Charity got their first helicopter ride, even if it was not quite the pleasure trip they had expected. Choate came too, holding Grace's hand all the way. He continued to hold her hand right up until the staff at the hospital inserted her head first into the big white scary scan machine. Then he held Charity's hand as they waited for Grace to come back out again, at which point he detached himself from Charity and reattached himself to Grace like some sort of sucker.

'Well,' said Dr Maria Sigaloff half an hour later, 'everything seems to be OK. Just a little bit of a bump on her forehead to show for her adventures. Her reflexes seem fine. There's no evidence of any internal damage. But given the fact that Miss Grosvenor was out cold for a while, I think we should keep her in here overnight. As a precaution.'

'Good idea,' said Charity.

'I don't see why,' said Choate. 'I can look after her perfectly well at my house. I think you're being over-cautious, Doctor. Grace is exactly the same as she always is.'

Grace, who was reclining on the hospital bed between Charity and her new fiancé, gave Choate's hand a squeeze.

'I know Choate will look after me,' she agreed.

'I'm sure he can,' said Dr Sigaloff. 'But I'm not going to discharge you until tomorrow. We don't want you to sue.'

'Oh, I won't sue. I'm English!' Grace joked.

Choate laughed along. Then he and Grace fell into looking

into each other's eyes again. Like a pair of love-struck teen-agers.

'I'll leave you to get some rest,' said the doctor. 'Mr Fitzgerald, if you can bear to let your lovely fiancée have a break, it would probably do her some good to get some sleep.'

Choate promised that he would. Just not yet. He told the doctor that the thought that he might have lost Grace to the second horse-related accident in her life was still giving him the shivers.

'She's had a head injury before?' Dr Sigaloff looked concerned.

'I'll tell you about it,' said Charity. 'Outside.'

'Please do.'

Outside in the corridor, Charity explained. 'Choate's being overly dramatic about Grace's previous accident. She fell off a horse a couple of years ago but she was wearing a helmet when it happened and everything was fine. No time in hospital. Nothing. Hardly a scratch. Really, it was nothing to speak of at all.'

'Then we won't worry about it,' said Dr Sigaloff.

The doctor's bleeper beeped.

'Oh, excuse me. A woman's work . . .'

Charity nodded. Dr Sigaloff started to walk away. But then Charity suddenly started after her and caught her sleeve.

'Doctor, I need to ask you a question.'

'Yes?'

'I know that the scans didn't show anything of concern, but is it possible that Grace still might have some sort of amnesia?'

'What makes you ask that?'

'Er . . . nothing,' Charity mumbled. 'It's just that I want to know the worst-case scenario.'

'Well,' said the doctor, 'it's certainly possible, given she received quite a blow to the head. But Miss Grosvenor doesn't seem to have any trouble remembering anything. She recognizes you, doesn't she? And her fiancé. She certainly remembers their engagement on the beach the other night.'

'But what about farther back?' Charity asked. 'Our childhood, for example? Does she remember that?'

'Oh yes. She's fine. While you were on the phone to your insurance people back in the UK, I asked Grace lots of questions about that and Choate corroborated her answers. She talked about boarding school in Pondicherry, your house in South Kensington. She even remembered the dog you guys shared when you were small.'

'Not Woofy?' said Charity.

'That's right. Good name for a dog. I really wouldn't worry, Ms Grosvenor. The human skull is remarkably tough. It's built to withstand the odd knock without too much lasting damage to the brain inside. By my estimation, your sister should be ready to go home first thing tomorrow. You should get back home and change for the polo ball. It's one of the highlights of the summer. Have fun!'

She dismissed Charity with a smile.

But Charity didn't feel like dancing. Her brief conversation with Dr Sigaloff had been anything but reassuring. The answers that Grace had given to those questions about her childhood were worrying her. Charity needed to ask more questions. But they weren't the kind of questions she could ask in front of Choate. Unfortunately, Choate was in no hurry to leave his injured beloved alone. Charity had to ply him with coffee until he had no choice but to leave the room for a pee break.

'I'll be thirty seconds,' he promised Grace.

'At least take the time to do your trousers back up on the way out,' said Charity.

With Choate gone and not knowing how long she would be alone with Grace, Charity launched straight into her questioning.

'Grace,' she said, 'I need some straight answers and I need them now. Do you remember what we were talking about before you got hit on the head?'

'Of course I do. We were talking about me marrying Choate.'

'Sort of,' said Charity. 'But do you remember exactly what aspect of marrying Choate you were talking about?'

'Isn't he great?' Grace meandered off-topic. 'Thank God he came along when he did. I'm sure it's his kiss that woke me up when I was unconscious.'

'So you're pleased to be marrying him?'

'What a stupid question. Of course I am!'

'So you're telling me that you're completely over the break-up of your first engagement? You're completely over Danny?'

Grace's brow wrinkled.

This is it, thought Charity. This is when she remembers.

'My first engagement? To Danny? I'm afraid I don't know what you're talking about,' said Grace.

41

Two months earlier

While Marcella Hunter was packing her bags (or rather having someone pack them for her) in preparation to leave her smart Park Lane hotel and return to the States, Charity Grosvenor was on the top floor of a double-decker bus from central London to Tooting with a P45 in her hand.

'I realize Ms Hunter can be a difficult guest,' Charity's boss Ronnie had acknowledged. 'But this time, Charity, you went too far.'

Charity had given up pretending that the dog relieved itself directly into the shoe.

'Did she actually put her foot in it?' was the only thing she wanted to know now.

Her boss responded by pushing the P45 across his desk towards her.

Charity wouldn't miss the job – who would miss cleaning up other people's mess? – but she would definitely miss the money. Hotel work was one of the few occupations with the flexible hours Charity needed in order to be able to finish her A-levels, ten years after she first started them. Now she was even hoping to go to university, with a view to studying horticulture. Thanks to Peggy, Charity's interest in roses was blossoming into a vocation.

'Can I just go up and say goodbye to Peggy?' Charity asked as she folded her last pay slip into her wallet.

Ronnie sighed. 'I don't see why not.'

'Who's going to look after her if I'm not around?'

'I don't know. The management wants her gone too.'

'She pays her bills.'

'They think the hotel is losing out because it can't offer a penthouse suite. The rock stars and the movie stars go elsewhere instead.'

Charity knew what the management were getting at. A reclusive seventy-something American who had made her fortune in sawdust (as she put it) didn't garner many valuable column inches in *OK!* or *Hello!*

Peggy had lived in the penthouse at the Royal Park Hotel for the past twenty years. She didn't like to talk about how she came to be there, but someone who remembered someone who was working at the hotel when Peggy first arrived said she had originally checked in for just a week.

A little later, some people who claimed to be Peggy's business associates flew in from New York. A couple of them held a meeting with the hotel management and negotiated a rate for a very long stay. But even after that, no one expected Peggy to be in the penthouse for *twenty years* . . .

Charity stepped out of the lift into Peggy's sitting room. While the rest of the hotel had been stripped back to the plaster and refurbished in the bland coffee-and-cream colours of just about every 'boutique' hotel, the penthouse suite was exactly as it had been in 1985. Chintzy. Lots of gold detailing on the faux antique furniture. It was as though time had stood still. Which was exactly how Peggy liked it.

'What happened to you today?' Peggy barked in greeting.

'They sent some other girl up. Stupid moron tried to water my flowers without asking first.'

'Sorry,' said Charity. 'I've been given the sack.'

'What did you do?' asked Peggy. 'I know you're not so good at dusting but . . .'

'I put dog shit in a guest's shoe,' said Charity simply.

'And that's a sacking offence?'

'If they didn't specifically request it.'

'Well . . .' Peggy sighed. 'I suppose that might be a problem. Come out here.'

The penthouse suite at the Royal Park Hotel had its own private roof terrace. Peggy had been growing roses out there for years. The first bushes arrived with the associates from New York. As Charity got to know Peggy better, she learned that they had come from Peggy's house on Long Island. Now Charity joined Peggy on the roof terrace for what might be the last time.

There was a clear view out across Hyde Park towards the very westernmost reaches of the city. The terrace was so high up that the noise of the traffic below was just a little background susurration, like the sound of a calm sea. Peggy said she liked it. Before she came to London, she'd lived near the ocean, after all.

Charity often wanted to ask Peggy whether she missed her garden, but never quite plucked up the courage. It seemed a touchy subject. She also often wanted to shake her and tell her to leave the hotel and go back home, but she knew something of grief and loss. She knew how it could keep you in limbo.

'I feel like I'm deserting you,' said Charity. 'But Ronnie says that if I get caught on the premises again after today, then his job is on the line. I don't want to do that to him.'

'No,' said Peggy. 'You've got to go. There are better things in store for you than cleaning up after crazy old coots like me.

You're the kind of person who needs a kick up the ass to get going. Well, here's your kick. Get going.'

Peggy handed her a freshly cut rose.

'I'll see you again,' she said.

Charity nodded. 'Of course. I'll wear a disguise to get past the door guys.' But she very much doubted that she would ever see Peggy again. What would become of her? she wondered. She supposed that Peggy must have people who would ensure that she didn't come to any harm. She was obviously wealthy beyond Charity's imagination to have been able to persuade the Royal Park to let her occupy their best suite for twenty years.

'Peggy . . .' Charity began.

'No. No more. Just go. Go,' said Peggy. 'I do not want a scene.'

Charity took the service lift back down to the ground floor, pressing the rose to her face the whole way.

Charity left the hotel by the front door that day. As an employee, she'd had to slink in and out round the back. Outside the shiny front door, the door guys were busy loading bags into a waiting taxi. Big cardboard bags tied shut with extravagant ribbons. Charity clocked the labels – Prada, Versace, Christian Louboutin – and wished that she could have the cash this particular hotel guest had spent on one trip to the shops as ready money in her hand. What difference would another pair of shoes make to this person, who almost certainly had too many anyway? Three hundred pounds for a pair of stilettos that would be worn for just one night could keep Charity going for three weeks. It was so unfair.

'Doesn't it make you want to spit?' Charity asked Greg, a doorman she had been friendly with.

'All the time,' said Greg. 'Especially 'cos I know that the

number of bags I find myself loading is always inversely proportionate to the tip. Shall I hail you a cab?' Greg asked.

'On my budget?' Charity laughed.

As the bus chugged on through Balham, Charity glanced at her old Casio watch. It was almost half past four. Her sister Grace would be knocking off for the weekend in another half an hour. The bus back to the flat they shared went right past Grace's office. Charity cut her journey short.

42

Grace Grosvenor worked full time as a receptionist and office manager for a timber merchant. She'd been there since she left school at sixteen. Charity didn't know how Grace could stand it. The yard was always full of leering builders. But Grace didn't mind. The lads were very respectful to her. They didn't cat-call when she was looking good or bark at her when she wasn't. Probably because Danny Dennis, Grace's fiancé, was a builder too.

Danny came into the yard every day for three months before he plucked up the courage to ask Grace out.

'I thought you were too good for me,' he admitted when she asked what took him so long. Grace certainly looked as though she belonged in an entirely different world. She was as well groomed as any receptionist at a Mayfair hedge fund.

Danny proposed after just two months. Of course, he wanted to stake his claim as soon as he could, but it was another six months before he could afford to buy a ring. And two years after he went down on one knee in the kitchen of the flat above a café where the sisters lived, Danny and Grace still hadn't married.

It wasn't that he was stalling, Grace insisted. It was simply that Grace had carried a dream of her ideal wedding since she was old enough to say 'bride and groom' and Danny didn't think she should compromise. They were saving to make her dream come true.

*   *   *

As Charity entered her sister's office that afternoon, Grace was drooling over a bridal magazine, cutting out a Vera Wang diffusion-line gown to slip into her 'wedding file'. She was always drooling over wedding dresses.

'What do you think?' she asked Charity.

'Two thousand pounds for a dress you'll only wear for half a day?'

Grace sighed. 'I'm only going to do this once. I want to make sure than when Danny sees me walk up the aisle he knows he's made the right decision.'

'He's certainly had enough time to ponder that decision since you said "yes" to his proposal. Are you planning to get married this millennium? Only I'm not keen to be the oldest bridesmaid in history.'

'What are you doing here anyway?' Grace asked. 'I thought you were working the late shift.'

'So did I. But one of the guests made a complaint.'

'What did the guest say?'

'That I put a dog turd in one of her Manolo Blahniks.'

'No! That's disgusting!' Grace gasped. 'Did you?'

'Yes.'

'Oh.' Grace backed away as though the dirt were still on Charity's hands.

'But it was her dog that laid the turd right in the middle of the carpet!'

'And you got sacked? That's so unfair.'

'Exactly what I said.'

Grace squeezed her sister's hand.

'It's OK. I just need a drink,' said Charity. 'Take me out?'

'I can't take you out. I'm saving for my wedding.'

'And if you buy me half a pint of lager shandy, that

will set you back so much that you'll have to get married in five years and 364 days instead of five years and 363 . . .'

'All right. I'll buy you a shandy. I'll just give Danny a call and see if he wants to come too.'

Charity rolled her eyes. 'You're not Siamese twins, Grace. You can come out without him.'

'I know,' said Grace. 'But I don't want to.'

Charity told Grace the full story of the dog mess on their way to the Old Duck. Grace agreed that it was bad enough that people failed to control their animals in public places, but the pound coin on the Post-it note definitely added insult to injury.

'I've still got the pound.'

'What are you going to do with it?' Grace asked.

'I should have left it on the floor with a Post-it note of my own explaining how she could stick it up her arse,' Charity replied.

'No, treat yourself to something nice to sweeten the pain,' said Grace. 'Something extravagant. Like three Mars Bars.'

Charity laughed. 'You can't even get three Mars Bars for a pound.'

But you could get a lottery ticket. While Grace bought yet another bridal magazine in the newsagent's next to the pub, Charity filled out a form. The six numbers she chose were the dates of her own birthday, her sister's birthday and their mother's.

'Oh, that's just a waste of money,' said Grace when Charity handed the filled-in slip to the shopkeeper.

'And that isn't,' said Charity, nodding towards the mag. 'Checking to make sure that white is still fashionable?'

'As a matter of fact, metallics are the only choice for the truly fashionable bride this year.'

'I wish I hadn't asked.'

Charity took her lottery ticket and tucked it into her otherwise empty wallet.

43

Still Charity wasn't feeling lucky.

The following day, the cashpoint ate her card. The loose-change tin on the windowsill in the kitchen contained nothing but an old ten-franc piece and a button. There really was nothing to do but stay in and watch the National Lottery show.

While Grace got ready for a night with the girls, Charity sat down in front of the TV with a mug of Heinz tomato soup and a pile of books she was supposed to be studying as part of her garden design project for her A-level coursework. Right then, however, it was just too depressing to flick through *Hamptons Gardens*. Stuck in a flat above a greasy café in Tooting, she was three thousand miles in literal terms and a million miles metaphorically from the people who lived in those beautiful houses in one of the smartest parts of the US. Charity closed the book and turned it over so that she didn't have to look at yet another fabulous rose garden with the Atlantic Ocean as a backdrop.

Instead, she rolled her eyes all the way through the lottery *Jet Set* quiz show, as punters got even the simplest questions wrong.

'Canberra is the capital city of which country?'

'Sydney?'

'A kid is the name given to the young of which animal?'

'Human beings?' Grace offered her own answer as she popped her head round the door before going out.

'See you later, Einstein,' said Charity.

Then it was eight o'clock. The lottery show presenter tried to whip up some enthusiasm for the big draw ahead . . . but Charity wasn't excited. Fancy restaurants weren't grinding to a halt as well-dressed guests insisted on knowing the lottery numbers before they had their carpaccio. No, by watching the lottery Charity felt she had become part of a vast mass of deeply unhappy people, spending a last quid for a last chance. She imagined them in their sitting rooms all over the nation. No light except that which came from the TV. Maybe a takeaway on the table in front of them. Perhaps they were eating beans from a can (as she was now that she had finished her soup). The drum-roll introduction to the lottery was just a brief moment of hope before the numbers fell and reality hit back hard.

Ah well. Charity smoothed the lottery ticket out on her knee and prepared to tick the numbers off. Or rather the *number* off. On the very few occasions when Charity had bothered to play, she typically got one number.

'Thirty-one . . .'

First number out of the barrel and she had it.

There we go, she thought. That'll be my one and only number this time.

But that night was to be different. In the sky above Tooting, a celestial finger was pointing at the roof of 145B High Street while a godlike voice boomed, 'It could be you.'

'In fact,' boomed the voice, 'it *is* you.'

'That's just not possible,' Charity breathed. 'It can't be.'

It could and it was.

Not six numbers but five. Charity looked at the five crosses she had made on her ticket with astonishment. That meant something, didn't it? If you got a tenner for three numbers then you definitely got something for five, right? Fifty quid? Maybe even a hundred. Five hundred perhaps?

Twelve and a half thousand pounds.

Half an hour later, Charity was finally able to start believing her luck. Twelve and a half grand was news worthy of a half pint of lager at least. Grace would be at the pub. Charity pulled on her jacket. She'd go and surprise her sister there. Champagne all round.

She was almost out of the door when she had a better idea . . .

With her jacket still on, Charity sat back down at the kitchen table. She took out a pen and a piece of paper and started to make a few notes.

Twelve and a half thousand pounds was nowhere near enough to make a long-term difference to her life, she knew that, especially if she went to the pub to celebrate her winnings. It wasn't just that she would have to share her luck with Grace – of course she would happily split anything with Grace – she was bound to meet someone else there who thought they needed a share too. Almost everyone who frequented the Duck had some sort of sob story: from hip operations for which they'd been waiting too long to gambling debts they needed to pay off so that the bailiffs didn't take the kiddies' PlayStation. If Charity let her guard down, the money would be divided up and gone in an instant. Just a fleeting moment of happiness. Unless . . .

Charity looked at the hardback book she had been leaning on while she did her sums. *Beautiful Houses of the Hamptons*, it was called. The rose garden by the sea beckoned. Sunshine. Clean sea air.

Maybe it was time to take a real gamble.

44

Rent a house in the Hamptons and pass themselves off as
heiresses to snag a couple of rich husbands? Grace thought
her sister's plan was both ridiculous *and* immoral. In any case,
Grace already had a fiancé, and there was no way she was
giving him up for the chance of a 'better life' in the USA.

'Danny *is* my life,' she insisted.

So Charity went ahead with her get-rich scheme alone.

It quickly became clear, however, that six and a quarter
thousand pounds, even with the favourable sterling-to-dollar
exchange rate, wasn't going to rent a whole lot of house by the
seaside in the chi-chi Hamptons resorts. One real-estate agent
actually laughed out loud when Charity revealed her budget
over the telephone.

It was Peggy who suggested she call Deuble Associates.
Though she wasn't allowed to visit the hotel since her sacking,
Charity had called Peggy often since their last meeting.

'Stop calling to check up on me!' Peggy complained. 'I'm
OK and the new girl is far more thorough with a vacuum than
you ever were.'

Still, Charity knew that despite her gruffness Peggy was
secretly very happy to hear from her. And Peggy was thrilled
to hear about Charity's windfall. She thought that Charity's
idea of a summer in the Hamptons was an excellent one.
Charity was careful to leave out the 'marrying a rich man' bit
of the plan, however.

'The only problem is,' said Charity, 'I don't think I can afford to rent a place for the whole summer.'

'You must be talking to the wrong people. When I was on Long Island, the best real-estate agency was Deuble Associates. They won't rip you off. Though of course,' said Peggy matter-of-factly, 'chances are that Mal Deuble is dead by now.'

Charity agreed. Peggy hadn't been in the States for twenty years. It was unlikely that she would have any good leads. But as it happened . . .

Mal Deuble hadn't quite popped his clogs but he had handed most of his business over to his daughter. And though the Hamptons rental industry was very busy, Charity had one big advantage over her East Coast rivals: she was up before they were. Charity was the first person to call Deuble Associates that day and that is how she came to be the first person to hear about the newly renovated Rose House in the charming hamlet of Little Elbow.

'We didn't expect this place to come on to the rental market this year. The garden is still a work-in-progress,' said Linda Deuble apologetically. 'And it doesn't have a pool yet. Which is why the owner has put it on at such a low monthly rate.'

Charity found it hard to imagine that a pool was such an issue. Particularly when the property the agent was describing had direct access to the beach.

'You understand that there is going to be a lot of work going on while the garden is completed? Some of it noisy. And the gardener will be living on-site.'

'I understand,' said Charity. In any case, she thought, the noise of a rotavator couldn't be half as frustrating as the constant noise of traffic on the road outside the flat. 'How much is it?'

Charity crossed her fingers while she waited for Linda Deuble to tell her the price.

'Two thousand dollars a month . . . Hang on. That can't be right. Can I put you on hold for a moment?'

Charity felt her optimism ebbing away as she waited for Linda Deuble to come back on the phone having added an extra zero to the monthly rate.

'Well,' said Linda when she finally came back, 'if you want it, you got yourself a *gift* . . .'

Charity had the deposit wired across to the States straight away. Once Linda Deuble confirmed receipt of the cash, Charity made plans to move in that very weekend, right after her last A-level exam (she'd already booked her flight, thinking she might have to stay in a hotel in the first instance). Linda duly sent back digital photographs of the house.

'I hope you'll be very pleased,' she said in the accompanying e-mail.

Considering the other listings she had received, for the money Charity was able to pay she expected something quite tiny. When she opened the first picture of the house – a front view that looked like the opening shot of a Jimmy Stewart movie – Charity's first thought was that she had been sent the wrong file. She gazed with wonder at a picture of the back porch, complete with swinging love seat.

Oh, but it would have been nice to sit on that porch with Grace – just swinging backwards and forwards on the seat and drinking cold white wine and talking and laughing about the holidays they went on as kids, when Littlehampton in Sussex, with its Mickey Mouse rollercoaster, had seemed the very height of holiday bliss. It didn't seem right to be going without her.

Perhaps, thought Charity, she should let Grace come out for a couple of weeks. And bring that big lug of a fiancé if she absolutely had to. After all, there must be something good about him. Grace loved him. And Charity loved Grace. She resolved to try much harder to love Danny too.

The day of Charity's departure soon arrived. She celebrated her last night in Tooting with Grace at their favourite Indian restaurant. Danny didn't come. Charity could tell that Grace was disappointed, though she said that it was better with just the two of them. Two sisters sharing quality time. They hadn't done that for a while. Hardly ever since Danny came on to the scene.

'You'll be all right on your own in the flat?' Charity asked several times.

'I'm not going to be on my own. Danny will be round there every night.'

'You're going to let him move in as soon as I've gone.'

'Not move in properly,' Grace insisted. 'Anyway, I don't know why you're worried about me. You're the one who's really going to be on her own.'

'I'm going to have a fabulous time. Seven bedrooms. Sea views. A swing on the porch.'

'Don't rub it in,' said Grace.

'You could still change your mind,' said Charity.

'I could never change my mind.' She bowed her head and poked at her chicken korma. 'My life is here with Danny. I wish that you could see your life here as well but . . .' Grace sniffed. 'I understand you want something more.'

'You're not going to cry, are you, Grace? I'll only be gone three months.'

'You'll be gone for ever if your plan succeeds. Unless you're planning on bringing your American millionaire back to live in South London! I can't see that happening. You'll want to keep your background quiet.'

'I'm not ashamed of you, Grace, if that's what you're

thinking. I just wanted something different. And I wanted it for both of us.'

'I know.'

Grace suddenly sat up straight as though finishing moping were as easy as clicking her fingers. 'Have you worked out who you're going to be yet?' she asked.

Charity was surprised. It was the first time Grace had asked for any further details about her sister's plan. Previously, she had registered her disapproval through lack of interest. 'Have you got a new name? Or a title? Dame Gladys Chequebook? Lady Mucky-muck?' She laughed.

Charity laughed too. 'I don't think I'm going to have a title.'

'You've got to have a title! I'd have a title if I was reinventing myself.'

'Too easy to find out it's not the real thing.'

'Boring.'

'I'm not really going to have a very different persona from the one I've got now,' Charity explained. 'I'm just going to smarten it up a bit. So, as far as my new friends are concerned, I'm going to be from Kensington instead of Tooting. And I'm going to have been to a slightly better school than our old comp.'

'What? Like Lady Margaret's?' Grace named the local grammar school. 'Those girls were really posh.'

'Relatively speaking. I was thinking about somewhere with hats in the uniform. Maybe even a boarding school.'

'Like Harry Potter!'

'Perhaps I'll say I went to Hogwarts,' Charity joked.

'You could say Cheltenham Ladies',' said Grace. 'Danny did a job for someone who went there. She was really posh.'

'Too much risk of bumping into someone who really went to Cheltenham Ladies'. I'm going to make my boarding school in India, like the one Hina went to.'

Hina, Mrs Patel, had been their mother's best friend.

'Are you still going to have a sister?' Grace asked next.

'Of course I am.'

'And will she still be called Grace?'

'Yes! It's a perfectly posh name. No need to change that.'

'Good. Well, you'd better have a new persona for me too.' Grace pursed her lips and put on a ridiculous plummy accent. 'You can tell your new friends I also live in South Kensington in a very nice four-bedroom house. I went to boarding school, where I was very good at playing lacrosse and riding ponies. I won gymkhanas up and down the country. I could have represented Britain at the Olympics but I was too busy doing a degree in French and Forestry at Oxford University.'

'French and Forestry?'

'Original, eh? No one would be able to prove I hadn't done that.'

'Hmmm. Apart from the fact that Oxford probably doesn't offer that curious degree. I'll give you a degree in English Lit instead.'

Grace approved. 'As long as you tell everyone I'm brainy. There's just one other thing I want you to say about our childhood.'

'What's that?'

'I want you to tell people that we had a dog. A great big golden retriever called . . .'

'Woofy.' Charity smiled.

'You remembered!'

'How could I forget? I was almost as sad to see your imaginary dog go as you were.'

Woofy had been Grace's constant companion from the ages of four to seven.

'I was gutted when Mum told me that Woofy had to go. It

was really hard to ignore him so he would find another little girl to live with.'

'I'm sure he found a good home,' Charity consoled her.

'Do you think so?'

'Definitely. Yes.'

'Only, I know he wasn't real or anything, but he was the only dog we had.'

Charity nodded.

Now Grace really did start crying.

'You're not crying about Woofy, are you?'

'Of course I'm not. Honestly, sometimes you act like I'm soft in the head. I'm crying about you. I can't believe you're flying to the States tomorrow morning. You're going to be so far away. I'm going to miss you.'

'You won't miss me. You'll be busy with work and your wedding plans and the time will pass in a flash.'

'Promise you'll call me every day.'

'I promise.'

'And promise that you will come back. If only to pick up your things?'

'I swear.'

'I love you, Charity.'

'I love you back.'

They held hands across the table. Charity tried hard not to think about the fact that this was the first time they would properly spend time apart in their lives. Eventually, she broke away and offered Grace some more naan bread. She had to be the strong one.

The following morning, the day of Charity's departure, the sisters said a final goodbye over breakfast. Charity's taxi to the airport wasn't due until the afternoon, but she couldn't stand the idea of Grace mooning about the flat while she tried to pack. So, she sent Grace off to the shops. Insisted. Charity hated a big fuss over goodbyes. More fuss equalled more finality as far as she was concerned.

All the same, Charity's toughness with Grace didn't stop her from shedding a little tear as she leaned on the kitchen window-sill and watched Grace head off towards the Tube station.

Charity knew she was unusually protective of her little sister. And probably, as Grace occasionally complained, unusually interfering in her adult life as well. But there was a good reason why Charity was so involved with Grace's day-to-day existence. She wasn't just her sister. She was her surrogate mother too.

Their real mother had died ten years earlier. Lung cancer. At forty, she seemed much too young to have it. But Marion Grosvenor had been smoking at least twenty a day since the age of fifteen, and before that she had been breathing in her parents' cigarette smoke. Both her mum and dad were heavy smokers. They'd started before anyone wondered whether it was such a good habit to pick up.

It took a long time for Marion to die, but the first time she had to go into hospital overnight, Grace was just ten. Charity was fourteen. Their father hadn't been seen or heard of for six years – since he ran off with a woman from Leicester – so, when their mother went into hospital, Grace and Charity stayed with a variety of different people: friends of her mothers, mostly women who worked in the same super-market. It was amazing how many people rallied round. At Helen's house they had spaghetti hoops on toast. Gillian gave them money to stop at the chippie on the way home from school. At Mrs Patel's it was always a three-course meal with home-made kulf ice-cream to finish. Mrs Patel's quickly became the preferred option for a night away from home.

It was hard to keep going while Marion was so ill, but Charity found that school offered some distraction. Her mother was proud of her academic success.

'One day you might find a cure for cancer,' she'd told Charity as she lay dying.

'Get yourself a job with better pay and longer holidays,' said the doctor who was reading her mother's chart.

'I'll definitely go to university,' Charity told her mother. 'I promise you that.'

But Marion died just as Charity entered the upper sixth. And Charity's dream of going to university became just that. A dream. She didn't finish her A-levels. She left school and started work. She knew her mother would have been disappointed. But the alternative was to turn to the local council for help, and that meant going into foster care. There was no way Charity would do that. What if they couldn't house her and Grace in the same place? Far better for Charity, who had just turned eighteen, to go to work, so that she and Grace could stay together, because the most important thing was to keep her little sister close. They were all the family they had.

That's why Charity knew the importance of money. Things could have been very different if their mother had left any money behind. It would have made life before then different too. She could have gone private. Even if it hadn't saved her life, it would have made her last few months more comfortable.

More often than she wanted to, Charity remembered the cancer ward and shivered. She had known as soon as she first visited her mother in that dingy, windowless room that she wasn't going to come home again. The staff did their best with jolly artwork in the corridors, but to Charity it was as bad as any nineteenth-century poorhouse.

* * *

So, Grace became Charity's responsibility. And as far as she was concerned, even though Grace was turning twenty-four in a couple of months' time, she was still Charity's responsibility. And as such, Charity had the right to question the life her sister was choosing to lead, didn't she? She had the duty to point out that Grace could have so much more if she wanted. And she should want so much more.

If only she could get Grace away from her hopeless fiancé, she might start to see more clearly how her future could be. She might start to realize that there was more to life than Danny Dennis could offer her. Danny was proud of himself when he promised Grace a house on an estate outside the M25 and a Volkswagen Golf (second-hand). After a couple of months in the Hamptons, that wouldn't seem such a hot prospect. Grace would swap her TV-listing-magazine aspirations for the kind of life lived by the inhabitants of the pages of *Vogue* and the *Tatler*. Grace had model looks. She was a diamond. She deserved the right setting.

Alas, it wasn't going to happen . . .

An hour later, however, while Charity pondered caving in and telling Grace that she and dozy Danny were welcome to spend as much time as they wanted with her in the States, she heard her sister's key in the lock. Grace stepped inside and slammed the front door shut behind her.

Charity's sister never slammed doors. Charity popped her head around the kitchen door to see Grace standing on the grubby welcome mat with her face buried in her hands. Her shoulders were shaking. It was obvious that she was in tears.

'Stop crying! I haven't gone yet,' said Charity.

'It's not that.'

'What happened?'

A woman who lived down their street had been mugged in

broad daylight a couple of weeks before. Charity immediately assumed the worst. But Grace's handbag was still safely tucked under her arm. She was still wearing the fake Gucci watch Danny had bought in the market. It very rarely told the correct time but Grace would not be parted from the first gift Danny ever gave her.

'Grace, what is wrong with you?'

It was quite a while before Grace stopped crying for long enough to answer her sister's question.

'It's Danny,' she said.

'Has he been in an accident? Did he fall off some scaffolding?'

'It's worse than that! Much worse!'

45

Eventually, Charity managed to manoeuvre her little sister from the hall into the kitchen. While Charity made another cup of tea – the cure for just about everything – Grace, sitting at the table, continued to snort loudly all over her folded arms. She still couldn't speak properly. Every time she tried to open her mouth, a big gulping sob drowned out what she wanted to say. The suspense was making Charity crazy. If Grace didn't manage to get her story out in the next twenty minutes, Charity was going to have to either miss the news or miss her plane.

'What has he done?' she begged for an answer. 'Have you had an argument? Has he called off the wedding? Have *you*?'

Grace actually wailed at the word 'wedding'. Then she opened her handbag and pulled out a piece of paper.

A 'Dear John' letter? Charity wondered.

It was a statement printout from a cash machine.

'What's this?' asked Charity, noting the zero balance at once.

'It was our wedding account. Danny has cleared it out.'

Charity stared at the bank statement as if the row of zeros might suddenly form a clue. 'How much was in there?'

'Almost three thousand pounds.'

'Did he tell you he was going to take the money out?'

'Of course he didn't! Why do you think I'm so upset!'

Grace slumped down on to her folded arms again.

'What do you think he's done with it?' Charity asked.

'I've got a bloody good idea. I tried to call him as soon as I saw the statement, but he wouldn't pick up his phone. So I went to the Duck thinking he might have gone over there to watch the match. And as I got there, I saw him in the car park, getting into a car. With the barmaid!'

'Did you talk to him?'

'They drove off before I could.'

'Didn't he stop when he saw you?'

'He didn't see me. I ducked back behind the fence. They're running away together. With my money!'

'Grace, that's quite a conclusion,' said Charity. 'Maybe she was just giving him a lift.'

'Oh no,' said Grace grimly. 'She was always all over him. And last weekend, when he claimed he was out with the boys, she wasn't at work either. It's obvious. She must have been with him. They've been having an affair for weeks!

'I should have listened to what you said,' Grace continued. 'All these years I've been kidding myself that he kept putting the wedding off because he wanted me to have the day of my dreams. I thought he really cared that I wanted a proper white wedding with all the trimmings. How likely is that? It's much more likely that he's been putting the wedding off because he doesn't really want to commit to me at all. The longer he waits, the more chance he gives himself that someone better will come along. And now someone better has come along.'

'Grace, there is no one better than you! Definitely not behind the bar at the Duck.'

'Stop it. There's no need to protect me. You always told me that the simplest explanation is usually the right one. And here's the simple explanation. He's taken my money to run away with that slut. Well, I'm going to run away too. I want to come with you,' Grace said suddenly. 'I want to go to America.'

And she did.

So there you have it. The truth. Marcella had been right all along.

After leaving Grace with Choate at the hospital, Charity did not go to the polo club ball. Instead, she went back to the Rose House and sat alone on the love seat, worrying.

Grace was not herself. That much was obvious to her sister. But would she become herself again, over time, as the bump on her head got smaller? Or were the changes wrought by the polo accident irrevocable?

As the night grew colder, Charity pondered the unthinkable. If the damage to Grace's memory was permanent, then she need never worry that Grace would blow their cover by an ill-timed remark about Tooting. But it also meant that Charity had lost her sister.

46

Grace returned from the hospital the following day. Dr Sigaloff pronounced her one hundred per cent fit apart from the sore spot on the side of her head. Choate drove Grace home. She held his hand all the way. Fortunately, he drove an automatic and didn't need that hand to change gear.

After a couple of days spent recuperating, Grace was suddenly very busy. While she had been in the hospital, she and Choate had talked a great deal about their forthcoming wedding and had decided to marry at the very end of September – just four weeks away. They might still be lucky with the weather, but there were contingency plans to be made. The Fitzgerald House had a dining room big enough to accommodate forty people seated and twice that number for cocktails, but though Charity would be Grace's only guest, Choate's side of the gathering numbered hundreds. He had many business associates who would be put out if they didn't receive an invitation.

A week after Grace was released from hospital, she and Charity travelled into Manhattan for her first wedding-dress fitting. Choate's mother met them there, saying that, since the Grosvenor girls' mother wasn't able to be there for her baby daughter, she would appoint herself as mother of both the groom *and* the bride. The sisters met up with Julia Fitzgerald at her suite at the Four Seasons. She had already assembled a pile of catalogues from New York's foremost wedding dress designers for Grace to peruse over tea.

'I like these best,' said Grace, passing one particular catalogue to her future mother-in-law. Before Charity even saw the book she knew who the designer would be. Vera Wang.

'I'll have Elizabeth call her right away,' said Julia, clicking her fingers. Her personal assistant snapped to attention and Grace had an appointment with Ms Wang that very afternoon.

While Grace was measured for the dress of her dreams, Charity sat in the salon and looked out at the people of New York going about their business. How long it seemed since she and Grace had arrived in town. A real pair of small-town girls they'd seemed back then, despite having lived in South London all their lives. Charity remembered how Grace had baulked at the idea of spending a couple of hundred dollars on a handbag. Now she was spending thousands on a dress. Or rather, her fiancé was.

Money was, however, still an issue for Charity. The problem was, since her accident, Grace didn't know they didn't have any of their own. The lottery money was almost gone, since, of course, the girls had run over budget.

Charity had explained to Choate that she and Grace were momentarily embarrassed financially. They had expected to be back in London by the end of September and thus their dollar account had run dry and Charity's British bank refused to transfer any more money without seeing her in person.

'Ridiculous,' said Choate. Which it probably was. Charity was pretty sure that in the age of the Internet, transferring money internationally didn't require a personal appearance in front of the bank manager any more. But Choate seemed happy enough to accept the situation and loaned Charity enough money for another month's rent on the Rose House.

Grace should, of course, charge any wedding-related expenses directly to him. That included her outfit.

Grace emerged from the changing room in a floor-length column of white silk.

'Mummy would have liked this, don't you think?'

Charity nodded.

'You know,' said Grace, 'I've been wondering if I should have some sort of Indian embroidery to represent the time we spent there. My sister and I spent a lot of our childhood in Pondicherry in south-east India,' Grace explained to Ms Wang's assistant. As her sister told the lie in a way that made it thoroughly clear that it was her truth, Charity noticed that Grace's upper-middle-class accent was perfect now. Never a waver in the direction of her old strained vowels. She pronounced the 'th' in 'south-east' as the Queen would. The old Grace would have pronounced it 'ff'.

Charity grew cold as she listened to her little sister chatter away in that unfamiliar voice.

That evening, Julia Fitzgerald invited Charity and Grace to join her for a small intimate dinner in her rooms. There were, as in all these small intimate dinners, twelve people in attendance. Grace and Choate were the guests of honour. The others present were friends of Choate's mother. A couple of older women discretely discussed surgery, though Charity wondered how much more lifting their faces could possibly take. They didn't look younger for the work they'd had done. They just looked like women of a certain age who had had work done. Perhaps that was the point. The obvious face lift, like the obvious suntan in the 1930s when it first became fashionable, said, 'I can *afford* to do this to myself.'

Charity answered the usual questions and murmured the usual platitudes about her sister's forthcoming nuptials.

'Yes. They are so well suited. I thought that from the start. Grace was instantly enraptured. I don't know what she would have done if he hadn't asked her to marry him!'

And Grace did seem every bit the happy bride-to-be.

'What about you, Charity? No lucky man waiting in the wings?' a fellow guest asked.

Charity shook her head. In truth, throughout her time in the States, no man except Ryan had interested her at all. But since their disastrous night at the pub in East Hampton, their relationship had definitely cooled. Ryan had expressed his concern for Grace, following her brief hospital stay, but he hadn't invited Charity to help him in the garden again. Not even to see how the roses they had bought together were faring. She considered asking him about flowers for Grace's wedding, but decided against it. In any case, Choate's mother had already made arrangements with the most expensive florist on the east coast of the United States.

The guest who had been asking Charity about the wedding turned to talk to Grace herself. Charity was left picking at her food, wondering how soon she could politely slip away. The seat to her left had not been occupied.

'Sorry I'm late,' called a booming voice from the door.

Choate's mother stood up to greet the grey-haired man who had just arrived.

'Robert Tiller! Sit here. Sit next to Charity. Entertain her.'

'My pleasure.'

Charity smiled pleasantly, but there was nothing much to get excited about.

'I hear you girls are renting the Rose House in Little Elbow. I have a place in Little Elbow myself. You like it there?'

'Oh yes.' Charity was ready to make small talk. But at the

end of the evening, Robert Tiller said something that really surprised her.

'I'd love to take you to dinner, young lady,' said Robert Tiller.

Charity gulped imperceptibly. It was not an invitation she was prepared for.

Robert Tiller had not made Charity's dossier of eligible bachelors but she certainly knew all about him. He was extremely wealthy. So wealthy, in fact, that he had tried to hide some of his funds from the IRS by opening bank accounts in the names of his wife's dogs. His wife was the reason Tiller hadn't made the list. But she had recently – very recently, as it happened – passed away in the middle of a tennis match. At least, her tennis coach said they had been playing tennis when she had a heart attack. It was subsequently discovered she had been paying her coach's rent.

If Robert Tiller missed his wife, it certainly looked as though he had been doing his best to get over the loss. After an acceptable period of mourning – three weeks, to be precise – he re-emerged into society.

Apart from the fact that he had been married, there was one big reason why Robert Tiller hadn't made the dossier. He was seventy-nine years old.

'So, whaddya say?' he pressed. 'Tomorrow night.'

'Well, I don't see why not,' said Charity hurriedly. Before she changed her mind. After all, a billionaire was a billionaire and maybe he just wanted company. Not every invitation to dinner had an ulterior motive behind it. There was nothing wrong with having dinner with a billionaire of a certain age. Perhaps they would become great friends and he would introduce Charity to one of his sons. Robert and Mindy Tiller had two sons during the course of their fifty-year marriage. According to the gossip column in the *New York Times*, the youngest was just going through a divorce.

'The car will come to collect you at seven o'clock tomorrow night,' Robert announced. 'Can't wait.'

He licked his lips.

This was not a date that Charity was looking forward to. But the fact was, she was absolutely skint. The lottery money was all gone, as was Choate's top-up, and Linda Deuble would expect another rent cheque in a couple of weeks' time. Not to mention that Charity now had to pay Choate back. Charity had heard that Robert Tiller was an extremely generous tipper. A few weeks previously, he had left a Manhattan waitress a thousand-dollar tip for a twenty-dollar sandwich. If that was the kind of money he threw around, then it wasn't unreasonable to expect that he might send a few expensive presents in Charity's direction. Presents she could exchange for cash to pay her rent.

But what would she have to do for them?

Charity looked at her reflection in the mirror. While her sister seemed to have been getting lovelier by the day since donning her engagement ring, Charity was starting to look tired. It should have been the end of the mission: one of the sisters marrying well. But of course, since the polo accident, Grace didn't know that she wasn't an heiress any more and couldn't be relied upon to spread Choate's wealth.

Tiller's car did come at seven. Driven by a liveried driver. It was enormous. There was room for a double bed in the back. As that thought crossed Charity's mind, she swiftly moved it out of the way. Double beds and Robert Tiller were not two items that did well in juxtaposition.

47

Robert Tiller was waiting for Charity in a distinctly 'comfortable' outfit. It was the kind of silk smoking jacket she had hitherto seen only in Bond movies.

'Welcome to my humble home,' he said, sweeping an arm in the direction of the far end of the hallway. He meant 'humble' in the Little Elbow sense of the word, of course. This was a long hallway, with about ten doors leading from it. And the paintings that lined it were as beautiful as anything Charity had ever seen in a gallery.

'Is that . . .?' Charity began.

'Monet,' said Tiller dismissively. 'Never really liked it. My dear departed wife chose that. Picasso, ditto. I just don't get that modern art. Now this I really like. We're going to be eating in here tonight. I just had this room redone and I decided to go for something a little different. Behind this door is my idea of art. I think you'll be impressed.'

Charity nodded. She probably would be. If Robert Tiller had Monet and Picasso in the hallway, then he probably had the original Mona Lisa in his dining room.

He pushed open the door. And Charity could only gasp. She'd seen some incredible examples of money badly spent since arriving in the US, but never in a million years did she expect to see what lay on the other side of the polished mahogany panelled door.

'Mindy always did the decorating. With her passing, I

decided it was time I put my own stamp on the place. Do you like it?'

Charity could only hope that he would interpret her silence as awe.

It was shock and awe, to be precise. Robert Tiller had transformed what Charity imagined (given the rest of the house) had once been a genteel, tasteful dining room into a room straight out of Saddam Hussein's palace.

In the middle was an enormous marble-topped dining table on a gilt-covered pedestal carved with naked beauties, surrounded by ten chairs supported by more golden nymphs. But it was the walls which really took Charity's breath away. They had been covered by an incredible fresco, painted in the style of an enormous sci-fi book cover. In an Arcadian landscape, men in uniform clung on to their guns, while scantily clad women clung on to their legs. In the background, other men, presumably the foreground characters' enemies, writhed in agony, spurting blood from truncated limbs or being consumed by flames shot from the gun-towers of tanks.

'So, what do you think?' Robert persisted.

'There's quite a narrative going on here,' Charity said.

'Narrative, eh? You're right. You are a very clever girl. This is my life story as art. I was in Korea,' Robert explained. 'These are all my buddies from my platoon. That's Chuck, that's Eddy and that's Elton. None of them made it back. And this is them in heaven.'

'Heaven,' Charity echoed in a murmur.

Tiller's idea of heaven was definitely not Charity's. She took a closer look at a vignette in the far right corner. A soldier, presumably a good one, was receiving oral sex from a Barbarella-type blonde bombshell. Glancing around the room, Charity soon realized that the oral sex was actually a recurring motif. The fresco was incredible.

'Sometimes I just like to sit in here on my own and talk to my buddies. I know they can hear me,' Tiller mused. 'You know, apart from me, the artist and my housekeeper, you're the first person to see this room.'

'I'm honoured,' Charity stuttered.

'I'm glad to hear you think that. I can tell you know a lot about art.'

'I know what I like,' said Charity tactfully.

'Exactly,' Tiller agreed. 'So do I. And I know that the guy who painted this room has more talent in his little finger than Picasso and Monet put together. I mean, at least you can tell what's going on here.'

'Mmmm. Yes.'

Charity cocked her head to one side as she tried to ascertain whether the Korean soldier closest to the sideboard was really having a sensitive part of his anatomy eaten by a dog.

'Shall we sit down?' Tiller pulled out a chair for his guest. Charity sat down and was somewhat disturbed to find that the hapless Korean and the hungry Alsatian were right in her line of sight.

'I hope you like steak,' said Tiller, as he pressed a buzzer to summon his staff. Steak? Of course.

Charity learned a great deal about the Korean War that evening. Specifically, she learned about Robert Tiller's part in it. It didn't take long for Charity to realize that his time in the army had been the most exciting time in Tiller's life. The killings he had made in big business simply didn't compete with the high he got from getting a direct head-shot at some hapless chap on the other side of the front line. His eyes glittered as he talked about blood spilt and bodies maimed.

Charity felt increasingly uncomfortable (psychologically and physically – the naked-lady chairs were not very well designed at all).

By half past nine, Charity couldn't stand it any longer.

'I should go,' she said, seizing her first possible opportunity to interrupt Tiller's memoirs. 'It's getting late.'

'It's not even ten.'

'I need my beauty sleep.'

'Then I will escort you home.'

'I'll be fine with your driver.'

'That's not how we do things where I come from, little lady.'

Tiller climbed into the back seat of the car beside her. Charity scooted over as far as she could and fastened her seat belt. Tiller didn't fasten his but instead remained loose so that every corner the car took caused him to slide along the seat in Charity's direction. Charity retained a tight-lipped smile as he squashed her against the door. It was a short ride, after all. But . . .

'Aren't you going to invite me in?' Tiller asked when they got there.

'Well, I . . .' Charity began. 'It's late and . . .'

She hoped to appeal to his gentlemanliness. But he continued, 'I would really appreciate the chance to look at the main rooms. I'd like to see if they restored it to its former glory. I used to come to this house when I was a kid,' he finished wistfully, and cocked his head on one side.

For a moment, Robert Tiller looked like a sweet old guy. The manic gleam of the Korean vet who found life never quite lived up to that early excitement was gone. Besides, what possible harm could come of it? Tiller was a seventy-nine-year-old man with a pacemaker. Charity could definitely outrun him.

'Of course,' said Charity. She opened the door and stepped aside to let him in. She felt as though she were the chatelaine of a stately home. The Rose House was an important part of local history. What right did she have to prevent Tiller from seeing how the house was faring in the twenty-first century?

'I don't have any idea what the house was like originally,' said Charity as she led Tiller into the main reception room. 'The furniture is all new.'

'It looks good,' said Tiller.

'But not quite to your taste,' said Charity, a reference to Tiller's more adventurous interior design. 'And here is the den . . .'

'I remember this room. This very spot is where I had my first kiss.'

'It is?' Charity laughed. 'That must bring back some happy memories.'

'It does. The Rose House girls had the best breasts in Little Elbow and they weren't afraid to share the joy.'

Charity's smile wavered. That manic look was back and Tiller seemed to be sketching a pair of breasts in the air with his cupped hands.

'Great big titties.'

'Oh no.'

Charity suddenly found herself back up against a sofa in the face of Tiller's relentless advance. There was nothing she could do. The edge of the sofa hit the back of her knees, which immediately folded, depositing her on the cushions.

'Robert, I really don't think that . . .'

'Come on, little lady. We've been building up to this all night. I saw the way you looked at me when I was telling my war stories. And I can assure you there's lead in the one pistol I'm still packing.'

A scream was the only appropriate response. But somehow

Charity managed to keep her cool. As Tiller lunged towards her, she deftly moved out of the way so that he ended up with his face in the cushions and not in her cleavage. Tiller wasn't to be put off. He dived in her direction again. Charity rolled from the sofa to the floor and to safety.

'I like a girl who puts up a bit of a fight!' said Tiller.

'I'm not putting up a fight,' said Charity. 'I'm telling you I'm not interested.'

'If there's one thing I've learned in business, it's never take no for an answer.'

'Please don't make me karate-chop you,' Charity begged him. 'I'm very good. I took a lot of lessons.'

'Just give in to your desires!' said Tiller, leaping from the sofa.

'I don't have any desires. At least, not for you!'

What happened next, when Charity replayed it in her mind later that night, would always remind her of a painting she had seen of a tiger leaping on a great white hunter. The expression on the tiger's face was not of aggression but shock, as, mid-air, he felt the sting of the hunter's bullet in his chest and the terrifying leap became a plummet.

Robert Tiller suffered his first heart attack two seconds after leaving the sofa.

He would have broken Charity's ribcage if he had landed on her, but he missed because she rolled out of the way one more time. He landed chin first on the delicate Chinese rug.

He was out cold.

Charity tried to roll him into the recovery position but he was just too well fed. Instead she scrambled to her feet and raced out to the driveway to fetch Tiller's chauffeur. But the car was gone. Clearly the chauffeur had assumed that his boss would not be requiring his services again that night.

'Shit.'

Charity stabbed the number 911 into her mobile phone and they promised to send paramedics pronto. But she knew that she needed to do something before the ambulance arrived. What were the correct first-aid procedures in this situation?

'Shit. Shit.' She walked around Tiller's prone body. He was still breathing, wasn't he? She stared at his chest, praying that it would heave upwards with a breath. She picked up Grace's powder compact, which was lying on the coffee table, and held the mirror over his mouth to see if any breath frosted up the glass.

Then, much more quickly than Charity had dared to hope, the den was lit by the glare of headlights. Someone had pulled into the driveway. Charity dashed from Tiller's side again to let the paramedics in. But there was no ambulance in the drive. Just Ryan's old pick-up.

'Hey,' he said, when he saw Charity, 'I left my wallet in the pocket of my old jacket. It's in the greenhouse. I just got to grab it and get back to Joe's to pay my bill.'

Charity grabbed his arm.

'Are you OK?' Ryan asked, properly taking in the way Charity was looking. Hair all over the place. Eyes wide and wild.

'I'm fine, but . . . do you know first aid?'

'Some,' said Ryan. 'Have you hurt yourself?'

'Not me.' Charity dragged him into the house. 'I think he's had a heart attack,' she said, pointing to Tiller's prone body.

'Is that . . .?'

'It's Robert Tiller.'

'You're kidding. What was he doing?'

'He jumped off the sofa.'

Ryan looked to her for an explanation.

'There's no time to explain.'

Ryan agreed. He managed to haul Tiller's body into the recovery position. He was breathing, but erratically. Ryan assured Charity that he knew some basic resuscitation techniques but he wasn't sure he wanted to use them on the man.

Fortunately, the paramedics arrived before Ryan had to give the kiss of life.

Soon they had Tiller in the back of the ambulance.

'Hop in,' the paramedic told Charity.

'Why?' she asked.

'You are his girlfriend, right?'

'I am not,' said Charity. She tried not to look at Ryan. She felt besmirched by the very idea.

'We need to call his next of kin,' said the paramedic.

'He lives just a few houses down,' said Ryan. 'I'll swing by and let his housekeeper know you're taking him to the hospital.'

The ambulance tore off into the night, leaving Charity and Ryan standing alone on the front step.

'Thank you,' said Charity. 'I'm sure you saved his life.'

'I'm glad I could be here.'

'Would you . . . would you like to come inside the house for a drink?'

'I should just get my wallet and head on back to Joe's. I've got a bill to settle.'

'Of course.'

Ryan headed off into the darkness of the garden. Charity slunk back into the house. The sitting room was still in a state of chaos. She replaced the sofa cushions and pulled the rug straight. Her stomach churned at the memory of Tiller's heart attack and the moments that had preceded it. Not just through fear that he might have died but embarrassment that he had been there in the first place. The whole evening, from dinner in the 'war room' to the arrival of the paramedics, had been a masterclass in embarrassment.

Charity knew how it must have looked. Robert Tiller, half undressed and half dead on the floor next to her sofa. No wonder Ryan didn't want to come in for a drink. Then an even sadder thought struck her. In all probability he was heading back to Joe's to settle up the bill for a date. She imagined a girl sitting there in one of the booths, twirling a hank of blonde hair around her finger as she watched the door for the return of her beau.

She imagined Ryan racing in from the car park.

'What took you so long?' his date would ask.

'You are never going to believe this . . .' he would tell her before launching into the story of Charity's sugar daddy.

'He had a heart attack while they were making love! Euww. That's so gross!'

And then Ryan and his girlfriend would climb into his car and he would drive her back to her apartment where they would make love, with no danger that one of them would pass away in the process.

'Nnnnngh.' Charity bit a cushion to stop herself from screaming out loud.

48

With the den straightened up again, it at least looked as though nothing had happened. Charity went upstairs to her bedroom. That night Grace was staying in Manhattan with Choate and his mother. Choate had promised to take her up the Empire State Building. Charity could only hope that Grace wouldn't choose that exact moment to remember Danny and the fact that she had once told Charity that if she and Danny were ever in New York, they would visit the Empire State and she would make him propose all over again.

Charity dressed for bed. She sat at the dressing table and brushed out her hair. The expensive highlights she had splashed out on during their first day in NYC needed redoing, she noticed. Perhaps Grace would be able to get that item on to the wedding budget. The thought reminded Charity that she was still a long way from being safe on this side of the Atlantic.

Feeling her eyes glaze with tears, Charity unlocked the top drawer, pulled it open and thrust her hand inside. She pulled out the little black book she had been so scared of Marcella finding.

From the exterior, it looked like a boring black notebook, the kind accountants use to keep their records. But this book was far more interesting than that. Inside Charity's notebook was the kind of information that social diary editors would kill to get their hands on. Dynamite stuff. Not that they needed to kill for it. Most of it was freely available on the Internet. But how they would have appreciated it if Charity had published this particular oeuvre. It could have saved them so much time. For this book contained the names and vital statistics of fifty of the most eligible men in the world. It was Charity and Grace's hunting guide.

It had been quite easy to assemble the information. Charity just booked herself a slot on one of the computers in her college library and got Googling. She plugged in the name of the town where she and her sister would be staying. The very first hit was incredibly useful. Some community-minded soul had set up a website specifically for residents of Little Elbow.

Charity wasn't particularly interested in reading about local council elections or the plight of the piping plovers found nesting on East Hampton's beaches, but one of the pages contained photographs from a fund-raising ball held the previous summer. Charity duly copied down the names of every single man pictured, then painstakingly Googled each chap, combing personal websites, business profiles and news items in an attempt to work out who was married, separated, divorced or single. And in possession of a good fortune, of course . . .

For each of the men she was able to find online, Charity prepared a dossier. She printed out whatever photographs she could gather and pasted them into her notebook, and beneath them she copied out the subjects' intimate details in her small but neat handwriting. It wasn't long before she had twenty single guys on file, then thirty, forty and finally fifty. She stopped there. Fifty seemed like a very reasonable number of potential dates to get through in three months.

After researching her prey, Charity ranked them in order of desirability, awarding points according to marital status:

single got the full five points, widowed a four, divorced a three, separated two and married nothing. Number of children: a minus point for each one. Children meant exes *and* alimony. Age: a tricky one to calibrate. Under thirty-five was good. But over fifty could be better if the chap in question was a widower with no heirs, who might be eager to marry and pop out kids quickly – before it was too late.

Of course, when she first hit upon the idea of preparing her little black book, Charity hadn't known for certain that she would have her sister in tow. Grace's presence called for a bit more work on the plan. Now Charity had to give consideration as to how she and her sister might divide the quarry between them. On their first night in Manhattan, she had done exactly that.

She decided that Grace had a better chance with the younger men and apportioned most of those under thirty to her sister. She also marked with a 'G' all those men who had been previously linked with models or worked in industries where they might be expected to meet hundred of beautiful girls. Grace definitely had the advantage there. Charity also picked out a couple of men that she knew Grace would simply like the look of. There was a Wall Street guy who looked a bit like Owen Wilson. And a property developer who looked a bit like Danny, only intelligent, Charity thought with a smile.

The following morning, they took the train to Little Elbow. And just a few weeks later, Grace snagged Choate Fitzgerald. Only son and heir of Julia and Randy Fitzgerald of Fitzgerald Lumber. Holder of a degree from Yale University and an MBA from Harvard. Member of the Young Investors* Club. Keen on skiing, sailing, collecting wine and ornithology.

Choate was twenty-nine. Unmarried. Never even a sniff of an engagement. He was eligible bachelor number four in Charity Grosvenor's dossier.

Opening the book up for the first time in a couple of weeks, Charity remembered how easy her plan had once seemed. She flicked through a few of the guys. There was Choate. There were the Mendelsohn brothers – both crossed off on that first night at Marcella's party. Robin Madden also had a line through his name. As did Jerry Penman. No yacht was worth that kind of pain. Charity paused for a moment on the guy who came in at number two, behind Jerry. His name was Bryan Young. Charity didn't have much information on Bryan beyond his net worth, which had been published in *Forbes* Rich List. He kept himself to himself. He wasn't a party animal. Charity hadn't been able to find a single picture of him. She hadn't heard anyone speak of him. Not even Marcella.

Ah well. Perhaps he had better things to do than spend the summer partying.

In any case, Charity hadn't dug out her dossier in order to work out who to target in the dying days of her campaign to marry for money. She wanted the photographs that were tucked into the back of the book.

Forget about the shoes and bags she had picked up in New York. These photos were Charity's most precious possessions. The first showed her and Grace in their junior school uniforms. Grace must have been five. Charity was nine. Then there was a picture of Grace and Charity sitting on the wall outside the house where they grew up (a modest modern semi). Going by the outfit she was wearing, Charity guessed herself to be thirteen in that picture. Grace must have been nine. Finally, there was a picture of the two sisters with their mother, taken the same year, in Littlehampton. The last holiday they took before she died.

Charity touched her finger to her mother's face. Would Grace even recognize the woman in this photograph?

Charity's thoughts were interrupted by the sound of a car in the driveway. She peeped out of the window, praying that it wasn't the police, wanting to interview her about Tiller's heart attack. It was Ryan, back from his date. Charity exhaled in relief and stepped back behind the curtains so that he couldn't see her as he headed for the guest house. Except that he didn't head for the guest house. He went straight to the front door of the main house instead.

As he rang the bell, Charity remembered that she was in her pyjamas. Should she change? She decided against it. After all, Ryan wasn't going to be coming in. He probably just wanted to let her know what Tiller's housekeeper had said.

Ryan rang more urgently.

Once downstairs, she opened the door just a crack so that he couldn't see her in the cotton PJs that were printed with kittens sitting on clouds (a birthday present from Grace).

'Hi,' she said as lightly as she could.

'I just wanted you to know that I dropped in on Tiller's housekeeper on my way back to Joe's. She went straight to the hospital and she just called to let me know that he's fine. They'll probably keep him in for a while but he'll live to fight another day.'

'Thank you.'

Ryan nodded and started to turn away. 'Goodnight.'

'Ryan,' Charity called him back. He stopped but didn't come closer. 'It wasn't . . . It wasn't what you think it was. You do know that, don't you?'

'What do you think I thought it was?' Ryan asked.

Charity felt her chest tighten. He'd asked that question in a sarcastic tone of voice she didn't recognize. But he had obliged her to carry on.

'You know. Me and Tiller. We weren't . . . we weren't actually doing anything when he . . .'

'It's none of my business,' he said. Curtly. 'You can entertain whoever you like.'

'But I wasn't . . . I mean . . .'

'What?' asked Ryan.

'I just had dinner with him because I met him at a party in Manhattan and he seemed really lonely. His wife has just died and . . . I didn't think there would be any harm in accepting an invitation to dinner.'

'I understand,' said Ryan.

'Do you?'

'What does it matter if I don't?'

Which is when Charity found herself blurting out, 'It does matter.'

Ryan, who had been half turning to go again, stopped turning.

'It does matter,' Charity repeated. 'To me. For some stupid reason, I don't want you to think badly of me. And I think that you do.'

Ryan didn't say 'yes' but he didn't say 'no' either. Which was a 'yes' in anybody's book.

'It's not just about tonight,' she continued. 'There was the time you had to pick me up after that stupid date with Jerry Penman. And that awful evening at the opera, when the guy I was with ruined the night for everyone. You must think I have terrible taste in men . . . I mean, friends. And I feel like you've been avoiding me altogether since that night at Rowdy Hall.'

'Perhaps,' said Ryan. 'But I know I overreacted. I was being proud. Fact is, it was a nice gesture, offering to pay your share.'

'It's what we do in England.'

'But I don't think it was about cultural differences, was it? It's understandable. I'm the gardener. You're renting the house I work in. You were being kind.'

'I didn't mean to patronize you. I don't think you need patronizing.'

'You're right there.' He sounded irritated.

'That came out wrong,' said Charity. 'Oh . . .'

Her eyes were glittering with tears. But Ryan didn't seem to be softening. His mouth remained set in a straight line.

'It's been a terrible few weeks,' she blurted. 'Grace's accident . . .'

'She's OK, isn't she?'

'Yes. Well, no. I can't explain.' Charity wiped away the first tear that managed to escape. 'I don't know what's going on. She just doesn't seem entirely herself. I think this wedding might be a mistake. This whole thing with Choate . . .'

'They seemed happy enough when I saw them before you left for Manhattan.'

'But . . .' Charity realized she couldn't even begin to tell him the real reason she was afraid. So she burst into tears properly.

'Hey. Hey. Don't cry.'

Ryan was there at once. He put his arms around her and she buried her face in his shoulder.

'It's all right,' he said. 'You're just stressed out. First your sister having her accident then Robert Tiller choosing your couch as the place to have his first heart attack. You must think you're jinxed. But they're both fine. They're both survivors. Come on. Let's go inside. I'll make you some tea. Isn't that the English cure for everything?'

Charity tried to laugh but it came out as a much bigger sob instead.

Ryan made tea, but it definitely wasn't the English way. He added coffee creamer instead of milk and left the tea bag in way too long. The result was disgusting, but Charity didn't tell him. It was nice to have something warm to wrap her hands around.

'You have to understand that I feel very responsible for my sister,' Charity began. 'Since our mother died, I've sort of been the mother figure in her life. I feel responsible for her happiness.'

'She's very happy now.'

'But is she? I watch the way she is with Choate since the accident and it doesn't seem quite real. I wonder if she's suffering after-effects from the knock on her head.'

Ryan nodded. 'You're probably extra-cautious because of the accident when she fell off that horse back in England.'

Charity closed her eyes tightly. This was her opportunity to come clean about all the lies. Could she? Should she?

Ryan carried on. 'The way I see it, if the doctor tells you not to worry, then you shouldn't worry. You getting yourself tied up in knots like this isn't helping anybody, least of all Grace. Just take things for what they are. Maybe Grace is rushing into getting married. But maybe she isn't. A near-death experience can have a galvanizing effect on people. It can make us realize how much someone means to us. When faced with how close he had come to losing her, Choate realized that he wanted to start the rest of his life with Grace as soon as possible. And she obviously agreed.'

Charity nodded. 'Maybe you're right.'

'People spend a lot of time trying to convince themselves that they shouldn't take a chance on love. If you look at anybody closely enough you can find a reason not to be with them. The way they laugh. The fact that they put too much pepper on their food. The fact that they don't fit the cookie-cutter image of the person you thought you should be with.'

Charity thought about her own cookie-cutter man. The very outline of him was based on the fact that he would be able to take care of her. And that meant he had to be rich. Or did it? Right then, being taken care of meant something very different to having someone to help pay the rent.

'You're not going to drink that, are you?' said Ryan, nodding towards the cooling cup Charity still held in her hands. He reached over and took it from her, putting it on the table. Then he took Charity's hands in his.

'You're a good person,' he said.

Charity accepted the compliment uncomfortably.

'Let your sister be happy and concentrate on your own happiness for a while.' He paused before he added, 'Allow yourself to be loved for a change.'

They both knew what was coming next. Ryan leaned towards Charity and she found herself leaning in turn towards him. Their lips brushed for the first time.

After that initial gentle kiss, it was as though a dam had been broken. Ryan and Charity both stood up from the kitchen table and stumbled, still kissing, into the den. Where Charity had struggled to avoid any kind of contact with Tiller, now she pulled Ryan down on top of her as she collapsed backwards on to the couch.

She sighed with pleasure as she felt Ryan's hands slide beneath her pyjama top. At the same time, she unbuttoned his check shirt, pushing it off his shoulders, revealing his perfect chest.

When they were both naked, Ryan lifted Charity in his arms.

'Let's go to your bedroom,' he said.

He carried her all the way up the stairs.

Afterwards, they held each other close. Charity's head rested on Ryan's shoulder. His arms encircled her. She had never felt so safe. Or so wanted.

But then he said, 'Charity, there's something you need to know.' And the tone of his voice told her that this was something he considered very serious.

Charity held her breath as she waited to hear what he had to tell her. It could only be a disappointment. She wished she could wind back time. After the exhilaration of finally giving in and allowing herself to get close to him, she didn't think she could bear to hear him tell her that this was as close as they would ever get. He was about to tell her about the date he had taken to Joe's, she was sure. Somewhere there was someone that he really felt something for . . . This was just a moment of weakness. A mistake.

'I haven't always been entirely honest with you,' he began.

'Tell me,' said Charity, as he hesitated. 'Get it over with.'

'My name isn't Ryan Oldman,' he said. 'It's *Bryan*. Bryan Young.'

49

If Ryan hadn't been holding her so tightly that her nose was literally pressed into his shoulder, he might have caught the flicker of recognition in Charity's eyes. But he didn't. Instead he carried on talking.

'Pretty geeky name, huh? Bryan?'

'It's not so bad,' said Charity. Was it was just coincidence, she wondered, that Ryan's real name matched that of the number-one bachelor in her book? 'But why change your surname too? Young is a perfectly nice name.'

'It's complicated,' Ryan replied. 'Fact is, if people knew my real name, they'd treat me somewhat differently. You remember how I told you that I'm the only gardener the owner of this house would trust? That's because I *am* the owner. I inherited this house when I turned twenty-one. Along with more money than you should ever give someone who's only just legally allowed to drink and a bunch of business interests that, to be frank, I'm just not interested in.'

'No,' said Charity, as all the pieces fell into place. She felt a bubble of excitement rising in her chest. It was all she could do not to laugh out loud. She tried to contain herself by asking more questions. 'And you let the house get derelict?'

'My aunt let the house get derelict. This was her place. She disappeared off to Europe in 1970. Never came back.'

'Did something happen to her?'

'Oh no. Perhaps I should have said "escaped" rather than

disappeared. But it was pretty unexpected. She left everything. Including her roses. When I turned twenty-one, I got a
letter from her lawyers saying it was mine. By which time it
just looked like a big pain in the ass. What does a twenty-one-
year-old guy want with a derelict house?'

Charity sympathized.

'I wish she could see this place as it is now.'

'I think she'd be proud,' said Charity. 'You've made it
fantastic.'

'Thanks. So there you have it. My name is Bryan Young
and I've been hiding my true identity from you ever since you
arrived. Do you hate me for lying to you?'

Charity shook her head. 'It's a perfectly understandable
thing to do,' she told him. 'You wanted to make your own
way. Not be judged by what you have. Make sure that people
liked you for you rather than your inheritance. I understand
that.'

'I knew you would. Especially since you and your sister
come from the UK. I bet you get judged on your posh accent
all the time.'

'Oh yes,' said Charity.

'You're still within your rights to refuse to speak to me.'
Ryan held her gaze steadily. 'Or kiss me.'

Charity didn't have to be asked twice.

The following morning, Charity awoke to find the pillow on
which Ryan had lain empty. Well, not quite empty. Where his
head had been, Charity found a single perfect rose and a note.

'Gone to garden store. Call me when you wake up.'

He'd signed the note Bryan with the 'B' in brackets.

Charity picked up the rose and sighed contentedly. Then
she sprang from bed like a child on Christmas morning and
flung open the bedroom window.

The garden of the Rose House looked better than ever before, now that she thought she might have found the way to stay there.

For the first time since her mother had died, it seemed to Charity as though things might work out. Who would have believed that Ryan Oldman would turn out to be the elusive *Bryan* Young? And that Charity would be head over heels for him. And that it would be proper love, definitely, because she'd felt it before she found out he was rich. It was like a fairy story. This was her reward for going through all the shittiness – her mother's death, giving up her education to look after Grace, the menial jobs, the stinking little flat in Tooting. She'd found someone she wanted to be with and discovered that he was someone *worth being with* to boot. In every sense. Nothing could flatten her mood.

Charity danced around the kitchen while she waited for her coffee to brew. She'd hit the jackpot. Love *and* money in one glorious, sandy-haired package.

She called Ryan on his cellphone to thank him for the rose.

'I can't wait to see you,' he told her.

The feeling was absolutely mutual.

Charity couldn't wait to tell Grace what had happened that night, but Grace had left a message on the answer machine to say that she would not be back until mid-afternoon at the earliest, though she was already in Little Elbow. She was going to be spending the morning with her future mother-in-law, interviewing potential wedding caterers, before having lunch at the Harbor Club.

So Charity breakfasted alone in the garden. She wrote a long-overdue postcard to Peggy, then spent the rest of the morning sketching out the ideal wedding present for Grace. She had been to Choate's house and had been thoroughly unimpressed by the use he made of the land surrounding it. There was a line of mature trees that made a perfect wind-break. She could plant roses behind them. She decided that she would find a way to bring a clipping of the rose bush that decorated their mother's final resting place out here too, so that Grace could feel close to their mother despite being so far away from the South London crematorium. Together with Ryan, she would create for Grace the perfect rose garden.

While Charity was thus absorbed, the doorbell rang. She got up and smoothed down her skirt. She headed into the house at quite a leisurely pace. But the doorbell rang again. And again. The caller was impatient.

When Charity saw the enormous bunch of flowers obscuring the visitor through the glass panel in the front door, she assumed it must be yet another bouquet from Choate. He had stepped up his flower-sending since Grace had accepted his ring. If that were possible. Charity wondered whether there were any flowers left at all for the other women of Little Elbow.

'For Grace, I assume?' Charity said as she opened the door.

'Is she here?' asked a familiar voice. A British accent.

Charity stiffened in anticipation of the awful shock before the visitor lowered his flowers to reveal his face.

50

'Danny!' Charity exclaimed. 'What the hell are you doing here?'

'Don't look so pleased to see me,' said Danny, stepping forward as though to step into the house. Charity moved forward herself to prevent him.

'I'm not pleased to see you. What are you doing here?'

'I've come to take Grace home.'

'Well, you can't. She's not here,' said Charity, already starting to close the door in Danny's face.

'No you don't.' He put his foot in the gap. He was wearing an enormous pair of boots with reinforced toecaps. Charity had forgotten that this was a man who dropped iron girders on his feet on a weekly basis. He had no fear of getting his foot stuck in the door.

'Get your foot out of the door, Danny,' Charity barked.

'Not until you tell me where Grace is. She's in there, isn't she? You're lying.'

'I'm telling you the truth. She is not in the house.'

'Then tell me where she is!' Danny raised his voice. 'I'll go and find her.'

'No.'

'Tell me!'

'No. Why should I? You lost the right to know where Grace is when you deserted her for that slag!'

'What are you talking about? What slag?'

'Oh? Has there been more than one?' Charity asked sarcastically. 'The one you spent all the money Grace had saved for the wedding on. Does that jog your memory? Did you have a good dirty weekend at Grace's expense?'

'I haven't had a dirty weekend with anybody! And I didn't steal the money. I borrowed it. Which Grace would have found out if you hadn't dragged her out here with you before she had a chance.'

'I didn't drag her anywhere. She wanted to come. I couldn't stop her. And if you were only intending to "borrow" the money, why didn't you ask Grace before you took it out?'

'There wasn't time. I was offered a business opportunity. I had to take it right then or miss out.'

'I can't wait to hear about this business opportunity. Did someone offer to sell you some magic beans?'

'I don't have to tell you anything,' said Danny. 'It was Grace's money. She's the only person I need to answer to. And I know that she'll be understanding. Let me in.'

'I told you, she isn't in here.'

'And I told you I don't believe you. Grace! Grace!' Danny pushed against the door that Charity was still desperately trying to shut in his face and tried to shout past her and into the house.

'Go back to Tooting, you loser. And take your pathetic flowers with you.'

'I'm not going anywhere without Grace!'

'And she's not going anywhere *with* you. Get out of my house!' Charity pushed ever harder.

'I want to see my fiancée!'

'She's not your fiancée any more. She threw your poxy little ring in the Atlantic the day we got here. And if you don't fuck off right now, I'm going to call the police.'

'You're a bitch, Charity Grosvenor.'

'You're a tosser.'

'I knew you had it in for me from the minute we met.'

'I just wanted what's good for Grace.'

'I *am* good for Grace.'

'I see things quite differently.'

'You think you're too good for anybody.'

'Well, my sister and I are definitely too good to associate with the likes of you.'

'It's not up to you to make decisions for your sister. Open the door.'

'Fuck off out the way. Don't make me start screaming.'

'Don't want to cause a scene in front of your smart new neighbours, eh? Let me in.'

Danny gave one last shove.

Which prompted Charity to push the panic button hidden behind the front door.

The police station in Little Elbow was generally as quiet as a public library. Very few strangers passed through the tiny town, making it difficult for burglars to even think about casing the rich joints that lined the beachfront. Every new face was noticed and subtly apprehended with a polite 'Do I know you?' Which is why, when Charity's panic-button push flashed up on the computer screen, a squad car was mustered in less than thirty seconds. Such was his surprise at being summoned by a panic button, Officer Lewinsky even left a half-eaten doughnut to answer the call.

He was running up Charity's drive in less than five minutes, during which time Charity had held the door firm against her sister's former fiancé (in truth, Danny stopped pushing almost immediately and was just sitting on the step, refusing to move until he'd seen Grace, when the squad car arrived).

'Bloody hell!' said Danny as Officer Lewinsky relieved him of the flowers and placed him in an armlock in one simple move.

'This man tried to assault me,' said Charity.

'She won't let me see Grace. Grace Grosvenor is my fiancée!'

'Do you know this man?' Officer Lewinsky asked.

'I've got no idea who he is. I've never seen him before in my life.'

Officer Lewinsky, who was patting Danny down, pulled his passport out of his pocket.

'Danny Dennis,' he read. 'He's British.'

'And I've never heard of him,' Charity insisted.

'But he knows your sister?'

'Not really he doesn't. Perhaps he saw Grace in London. He's a stalker.'

'I'm Grace Grosvenor's fiancé,' Danny protested.

'No you're not,' said Officer Lewinsky. 'Grace Grosvenor is engaged to Choate Fitzgerald.'

Danny stared at the police officer uncomprehendingly. 'She's engaged to me. Are you telling me she's got someone else?'

'It's none of your business,' Charity snapped at him. 'He's clearly nuts,' she told the police officer. 'Would you please just take him away? Look!' She pointed at a scuff mark on the bottom of the door. 'I think you'll find that's criminal damage.'

'I'll take him to the station,' said Lewinsky. 'Don't worry, ma'am. He won't be allowed to bother you again. In fact, he'll probably be on the next plane out of here. The United States doesn't need this kind of man within its borders. Not when we're already fighting the hidden terror of, er . . . terrorism.'

'Quite right. Thank you, Officer,' said Charity.

Lewinsky pushed Danny's arm a little farther up behind his back. Danny unleashed a torrent of four-letter words.

'I wouldn't use that kind of language in front of an officer of the law if I were you,' Charity observed.

'Charity Grosvenor, you'll rot in hell for this.'

'At least my sister won't be rotting in Tooting!' she couldn't resist shouting back.

It was a narrow escape. As the squad car sped away, Charity leaned heavily against the door as though she were still trying to stop someone from pushing his way in. Still, there was no reason at all why Grace should find out about this. Office Lewinsky was almost certainly right. Danny would be on the next plane back to London. There was no reason to keep him hanging around in Little Elbow police station. And once he had been deported, there was very little chance that he would ever be allowed back into the country. Not with American immigration policy being what it was.

In the kitchen, Charity poured herself a large medicinal glass of Chardonnay and tried to calm her breathing. Grace would never know. She would never know. And hadn't Charity been acting in her best interests anyway?

But the shock of finding Danny on the doorstep had rattled Charity more than she had expected. It reminded her that even if Grace couldn't remember her life back in London, links to that world still existed. Hopefully, Danny had been put off by the knowledge that Grace had become engaged to Choate. There was little chance that he would continue a campaign to win her back if he wasn't able to do it in person. If he got deported, as Lewinsky had said he would be, Danny wouldn't be allowed back into the States. He wasn't the kind of guy who wrote letters. He didn't have the sisters' ex-directory phone number and that would be easy enough to keep from him.

But now Charity wondered who else might come in search of the girls if they didn't return to London at the end of the summer. Grace's boss? Probably not. Charity had written a letter on Grace's behalf handing in her notice. Mrs Patel? Could she be kept away? Did she need to be kept away? Mrs Patel would be thrilled that Grace was marrying well. But no, Charity decided, she would not be happy to find out how Grace had managed such a social coup. Not to mention the fact that Mrs Patel would probably insist on a brain scan when she found out that Grace didn't remember Tooting . . . She would have to be cut off. Charity felt her throat constrict painfully at the thought.

But it was decided. Grace Grosvenor as Charity had known her for the past twenty-four years was never coming back. She was about to marry a man with enough money to buy the whole of South London and, fingers crossed, Charity no longer needed to worry about her future either. Ryan had been so passionate. He'd told her that he'd never met anyone like her, that he'd felt certain they would have a future together from the first moment he saw her. Well, Charity was happy to agree with him on that.

All she had to do now was destroy any evidence that tied her or her sister to their unedifying past.

Now Charity walked upstairs purposefully and took the little black book and the very last of the family photographs from their hiding place in the dresser. She took one last look at the pictures and felt tears pricking her eyes. Still, they showed a past that definitely wasn't the one Charity would admit to. They had to go. As did that ridiculous dossier. If that were to fall into the wrong hands . . . particularly now Charity was entangled with her number-one target.

But how to dispose of these links with the past safely?

Charity didn't dare put them in the trash can. The rubbish at the Rose House was carefully divided into recyclables and compost. Charity considered feeding the pictures to the In-sink-erator, but soon decided that was a terrible idea. It would probably get blocked up. Burning the little black book wasn't an option. The Rose House had many magnificent fireplaces but they had all been converted for gas. Unless . . .

Next door, Marcella Hunter's gardener, Miguel, had been clearing the scrub around her tennis court and piling the dried-up branches and bushes he cut away down on the sand to create a bonfire for the Labor Day celebrations. Marcella had been planning her party for weeks. It promised to be a big night. There had been no fireworks in Little Elbow on 4 July that year, as per Choate's leaflet on behalf of the piping plovers nesting in the vicinity. The fireworks were cancelled so that the rare birds could raise their chicks in peace. Marcella was more than a little irritated to miss putting on her annual Independence Day display and had promised to send the birds away with some really big bangs for the start of September instead.

When Charity was sure that the coast was clear (quite literally), she headed down to the beach to add her own tinder to Marcella's bonfire. Marcella's gardener had made a big pile, maybe five feet high and carefully stacked so that it would burn safely without collapsing. Wearing a pair of old gardening gloves that Ryan had left draped across the handle of a wheelbarrow, Charity created a small tunnel through the driftwood and garden rubbish and placed her dossier and the photographs right in the middle.

She closed her eyes against the tears that pricked them when she said goodbye to the photographs. It was almost as hard as that last visit to the hospital where her mother lay dying. But it had to be done. That very evening, the bonfire would be set alight for the late Independence Day/Labor Day hurrah and the Grosvenor sisters would finally be free of their past.

51

Marcella Hunter was preparing for her Labor Day barbecue. The guest list, which had started out at more than a hundred people, was shrinking steadily. The reason was simple: Stephanie Blank had sent her invitations out first.

'Darling,' she'd said, 'I had no idea you were planning a party.'

'But I *always* have a Labor Day party,' said Marcella.

'Do you?' said Stephanie. And Marcella remembered that she hadn't invited Stephanie to her Labor Day party for the past two years.

As the day dawned, Marcella's guest list had shrunk to thirty people.

'It'll be a disaster,' she told Simon.

'That sounds like an enormous party to me,' he said.

'Ugh!' Marcella sobbed. 'You don't understand anything!'

The telephone rang. It was Linda Deuble, the real-estate agent, responding to her invitation, issued just the previous day. 'I would love to come,' she told Marcella. Marcella said she was delighted with that news, but she struggled to hide her opinion that anyone who could attend a party at such short notice probably wasn't what you might call 'A list'. Even more irritatingly, Linda seemed to have decided that her invitation was a sign that she and Marcella were now on intimate terms. She asked a lot of distinctly personal questions. Marcella tried to get off the phone several times. But then Linda said: 'And you'll never guess what's going on over at the Rose House.'

Marcella pricked up her ears.

'Well, as you know, the Grosvenor sisters' lease was due for renewal at the end of next week, which is when they were supposed to be going back to London. Of course, everything has changed now that the younger sister is marrying Choate Fitzgerald. I assumed they would be extending their lease so I dropped by with some new paperwork. Charity wasn't there, but Ryan the gardener was. I asked him if he would pass the new contract on, to which he replied, "I don't think so." "What do you mean, I don't think so?" I asked. He said, "I don't think I'll be renting the house out any more." And then he introduced himself as the landlord!'

'The what?'

'He's the landlord! The guy I'd been thinking was the gardener turns out to be the guy who owns the house. His real name is Bryan Young. Of the . . .'

'Breakfast cereal Youngs of Michigan!' the women chimed together.

'Exactly,' said Linda. 'Now isn't that a turn-up for the books?'

It certainly was. Marcella would never in a million years have imagined that Linda would come up with such a useful piece of gossip. Now all she wanted to do was get off the phone and get round to the house next door with an invitation to her party! As a gardener, the incredibly good-looking guy next door had looked worth a fling. As owner of the house, he was worth a marriage proposal.

Marcella slicked on some lipstick.

'Where are you going?' Simon asked.

'I'm inviting next-door's gardener to the party.'

'Are you that desperate to bump up the numbers?'

*   *   *

Ryan was most amused to receive his invitation to Marcella's Labor Day party.

'It's a bit short notice, I know,' she said. 'But I assumed you'd be doing something else. And then I thought, that's just silly. There's a one per cent chance that he isn't busy and if I missed that one per cent chance to express a bit of neighbourly hospitality then I could never forgive myself. It's Bryan, isn't it?' she added.

'Ryan,' he corrected. But a smile spread over his lips. Someone had been talking.

'So, do you think you'll come?' Marcella asked. 'Do you think your boss might let you finish work early?'

She was fishing. Ryan knew it.

'Well, I'd love to,' he said. Marcella's eyes glittered at the thought of the social coup in the offing. 'But I can't. I have a date.'

'A date?'

'Yes,' said Ryan. 'With Charity.'

Marcella felt the blood in her veins start to crystallize. Charity? Again?

'By the way,' said Ryan, 'I hope you're not planning on lighting a bonfire tonight. The piping plover protection order is still in place. Still no fireworks allowed.'

Piping plovers be damned. As Marcella swept back into her house, she was ready to torch the entire Rose House in her rage. She stormed into the kitchen, where Anjelica was preparing canapés, and threw around a few choice insults.

'Can't you even make a proper blini, you stupid bitch!'

Anjelica reeled.

Simon heard Marcella and stopped her as she flounced by him in the hall.

'Marcella, you can't say that kind of thing.'

'I can say whatever the hell I like.'

'No. No, you can't,' Simon insisted. He grasped Marcella by the wrist. 'I don't know what's wrong with you, Marcella. You've got everything and yet you're always so unhappy.'

'I don't have everything, can't you see that?!'

In the kitchen, a fat tear rolled off the end of Anjelica's nose and fell into the blini mix. What was she doing there? Taking abuse from that horrible woman. And still no sign that she would ever help Anjelica get the visa she needed to remain in the States and start studying. When telling Anjelica that her services would be required on Labor Day, Marcella hadn't even bothered to dangle the carrot.

Was there anything worth staying for anyway?

It wasn't just Marcella who had been shocked by the news of Choate's engagement. Marcella had ranted about it to all her girlfriends. And that was how Anjelica heard the news: by eavesdropping on one of Marcella's conversations. It wasn't difficult. Marcella wasn't given to lowering her voice. Besides, as far as she was concerned, there was no need. Anjelica's feeble grasp of English didn't pose a threat.

Anjelica was distraught. On the afternoon that she heard, she locked herself in the laundry room and sobbed into a pile of guest towels. She didn't even come out when she heard Marcella shouting that she wanted a sandwich.

'Dammit, where is that girl?' Marcella muttered. 'I'll call Immigration and have her taken away this afternoon.'

But Anjelica didn't come out. She stayed in the laundry room and went back over the past two years as Marcella's housekeeper. From the first time she saw Choate she had loved him. His was the kindest face she had ever seen. But it had been a fantasy, she knew now, that Choate would ever notice her. They might have been compatible in their interests, but their lives were just too different. How could she ever have hoped that he, heir to millions, might stoop to date the girl who took his coat or cleaned the windscreen of his car while he was visiting her mistress? She had been crazy to think that he even differentiated her from the dozen other uniformed maids he saw in the course of a day.

But there had been something, hadn't there? That afternoon when she saw him reading Mark Twain in the garden and asked him which book he thought she should start with. He had taken her seriously when he answered her. And he had seemed pleased when she told him that she had taken his advice.

She could only hope that the English girl would make him happy. Anjelica hadn't been sure that it was a good match. Whenever she had seen Choate and his new fiancée together, the girl had seemed distracted. She had been slow to laugh at Choate's jokes. Her smiles seemed to contain more pity than love. So much pity that Anjelica had been certain that the English girl would get bored and call the relationship off.

But why would pity be reason enough? Choate had many qualities that some women would be prepared to suffer a little boredom for. Prestige and wealth meant much more to those people than love.

It was too much, the thought that Choate might marry someone who didn't love him! Anjelica sobbed loudly. She wiped her running nose with the back of her hand and carried on cooking through her tears.

52

By the time Ryan came back from the garden store, Charity had almost recovered from her close shave with Danny. Thank goodness no one else had been in the house when that lowlife rocked up. As it was, there was no need for Ryan to know that anyone had been round except Marcella, who had collared him on the driveway.

'We've been invited next door for a Labor Day barbeque,' Ryan told Charity. 'At least, I was.'

'I don't think I'm top of her invitation list,' said Charity. 'But don't let me stop you.'

'Well,' said Ryan, 'it's tempting. After all, this is my first invitation to the hallowed Hunter estate. Except for the time she invited me to mow her lawn . . .'

'So go,' said Charity, not meaning it at all.

'I have other plans,' she was gratified to hear Ryan tell her.

Ryan's other plans included a very private barbeque at the Rose House. Grace had left a message to say that she would be dining with her mother-in-law-to-be at the Fitzgerald mansion that night. Choate was in Manhattan. In order to carve two weeks out of his busy schedule to take Grace on honeymoon to Hawaii, he would have to spend every spare moment in the office between now and the wedding. Still, Grace rather liked spending time with Julia. She was very kind and seemed delighted at the prospect of a daughter-in-law, having had no daughters of her own.

So, Grace ate fish at the Fitzgerald house, while Ryan and Charity barbequed chicken marinated in a secret recipe that he promised he would let Charity have when they were married and not before. The reference to a shared future – however light hearted – made Charity shiver with happiness.

It was the perfect way to spend a late summer evening. Though it wasn't quite as peaceful as they had hoped. At seven o'clock precisely, a screech of feedback announced that Marcella was turning on the sound system for her Labor Day party. She had cancelled her live band – a guest list of thirty didn't warrant such attention to detail – and had hired a DJ instead. He was, alas, a fan of drum and bass.

The beat of Marcella's sound system all but drowned out the gentle piano music drifting out of the Rose House. But Charity didn't care. She would have happily sat right on top of one of Marcella's speakers so long as Ryan was sitting opposite her, smiling at her and making her smile goofily back.

'So, I told Linda Deuble that I didn't want to rent the house out any more but I hope that won't stop you from staying here just as long as you want to. After all, I've got seven bedrooms and just one girl I'm interested in having sleep in them.'

'I'll stay,' said Charity. 'As long as you can put up with me.'

'I think that could be a very long time,' said Ryan, taking Charity's fingers and licking off the butter that covered them. They'd been eating corn on the cob.

'These people are the dregs,' said Marcella, surveying her party. 'I can't believe that both the Mendelsohn brothers went to that Blank girl's party instead.'

'You should at least try and pretend you're pleased to see

these people,' said Simon. 'They may be your "B list" but at least they've made an effort.'

Marcella sneered at that and grabbed another drink as Anjelica drifted by with a tray full of cocktails.

'I don't think I can stand another hour of this. I need to get rid of them. Tell Miguel I want to light the bonfire now. And do the fireworks. That should let them know the night is over.'

'It's not properly dark,' said Simon. 'It'd be a waste to do the fireworks now.'

'It's my party,' Marcella replied. She had downed her cocktail and was already reaching for another. Anjelica, who was holding the tray Marcella was aiming at, had her back to her. She didn't know that Marcella had her fingertips on the edge of a mojito, so that when Anjelica started to walk off, the tray tipped, soaking Marcella with rum, mint leaves and lime juice.

'You goddam stupid slut!' Marcella screamed.

Anjelica cringed. 'I'm sorry. I'm sorry.'

Marcella's hands were clenched into fists. Simon immediately put his arm around her as a preventive measure, but he couldn't stop her ranting.

'You've ruined my dress. I'm taking the money out of your wages, you stupid bitch. You should look where you're fucking going.'

'I didn't see you,' Anjelica explained. 'Because I had my back to you.'

'You should have eyes in the back of your head when you're carrying a drinks tray. This dress cost twelve hundred dollars!'

'That's more than I earn in a month,' Anjelica exclaimed.

'Then I guess you're working for nothing next month.'

'But you already owe me from last month,' Anjelica pointed out. 'You haven't paid me since July.'

Marcella's guests grew quiet as the row grew louder.

'What the fuck am I supposed to pay you for? You break more shit than any stupid maid I've ever had. If I added up what you broke and charged you for it, you'd be working for me for nothing until you're ninety-four.'

'That's not true,' said Anjelica.

'What about those whisky tumblers? They were crystal.'

'Er, I broke those,' Simon interrupted. 'Look, sweetheart, it's just a dress. I'm sure it will clean up.'

'Don't fucking interrupt me,' Marcella snarled at him. She turned back to Anjelica. 'Clean this shit up, you stupid bitch, and try to stay out of my way for the rest of the night.'

'Marcella,' Simon tried again. 'I really think you're over-reacting. You can't talk to people like that.'

'I'll talk to people however the fuck I want.'

Anjelica stood open mouthed as Marcella lurched away.

Anjelica didn't clear the mess up. She left the broken glass on the patio and raced back into the tiny room she shared with Marcella's discarded exercise bike and elliptical machine.

This was no kind of life. Sleeping in a single bed with only a home gym for company. It wasn't even as though she had time to use the bloody things, what with getting up at six to make Marcella's breakfast and being on call till Marcella had her cocoa. Well, Anjelica had finally had enough. She was going to leave Little Elbow that very night. She didn't have enough money for a flight, but if she turned up at the airport and admitted her dodgy legal status, then she had no doubt that someone would soon find her a seat on a plane heading south. Even if it meant that she could never come back to the States again.

Anjelica gathered together her belongings. Her clothes fitted into the kind of case that Marcella typically needed for her toiletries. Apart from her clothes and two pairs of shoes, Anjelica had nothing but a crucifix, two photographs of her family and her books.

She picked up *Huckleberry Finn* and opened it to the title page. There it was, in his childish handwriting: 'Choate Fitzgerald, aged ten and a half'. Anjelica held her breath as she put the book down again. Once upon a time, she had taken the fact that Choate had lent her his own copy of *Huckleberry Finn* as a sign of his affection for her. How stupid.

With all her worldly goods in one suitcase and a carrier bag, Anjelica headed out to the ancient station wagon Marcella let her use to run errands. She put on the sole audio tape she had brought with her from home. It was a tape of traditional songs: love songs. These were tunes that her mother had sung to her, back when a happy-ever-after still seemed possible.

Blinded by tears, Anjelica pulled the station wagon out of the driveway and on to the road. Then she put her foot down.

The first of Marcella's fireworks seared across the sky at just before ten o'clock.

'That moronic woman,' said Ryan.

Charity looked at him quizzically.

'She's letting off fireworks. I told her she shouldn't. The second batch of chicks still haven't fledged. The endangered-species order is still in place.'

'The piping plovers?' asked Charity.

'That's right.'

'Do people really take birds so seriously around here?'

People certainly did.

Ryan was already calling the Little Elbow police. They duly promised to investigate. Like most Little Elbow residents, Officer Lewinsky had been a little less than sympathetic when it was ordered that the 4 July celebrations be toned down so that the rather drab little birds could nest and fledge, but that night he was on duty and Marcella Hunter's party was in direct contradiction of the Endangered Species Act.

In the meantime, Lewinsky had given Ryan permission to try to reason with his neighbour. Ryan had every intention of doing so. With a hosepipe.

'Coming?' he asked Charity.

She opted out. But she heard the shouts as Ryan directed a super-powered jet of water at Marcella's bonfire. They almost distracted her from the ringing of the phone.

It was Officer Lewinsky again.

'Miss Grosvenor. There's been an automobile accident. I'm afraid your sister was involved.'

53

Charity didn't wait to tell Ryan about the call. Her mothering instinct took over and she went straight out to the car. Never mind that she was quite possibly over the limit. Lewinsky had told her that her sister was fine but Charity hadn't liked the sound of his voice. Grace wasn't in the hospital, sure. But should she be?

Grace wasn't very good at driving on the 'wrong' side of the road. The result of which was that she continually found herself driving on the wrong side of the road. Leaving the Fitzgerald mansion after a jolly evening with her future mother-in-law, Grace had turned out of the smart gravelled driveway straight into the oncoming traffic.

Ordinarily, it wouldn't have mattered. The Fitzgerald house was on a private road and there was very rarely any traffic after the gardeners had gone home. But that night, there was one other car and it was travelling at speed.

Anjelica was singing along to her favourite love song at the top of her voice. She was crying so hard she might as well have had her eyes shut. She wasn't quite sure what she was going to do when she got there, but she was going to Choate's house. His copy of *Huckleberry Finn* was on the dashboard. Maybe she would throw it at him, challenge him to be a man and tell her how he really felt about her. And if he claimed he didn't feel anything, she was damn well going to kick him in the balls for having led her on.

'Oh, Cho-oo-oate,' Anjelica choked out his name. And, thank God, at the very same moment her foot slipped from the accelerator to the brake, so she was almost at an emergency stop when Grace, coming in the opposite direction and on the wrong side of the road, drove straight into her and ricocheted off into a fire hydrant. It erupted in a geyser twenty feet high.

No one was hurt, thank goodness, but naturally the police and the fire service were called and, when it was established that Grace could be safely moved from the wreck that had been the sisters' hire car, she was gently loaded into the back of a squad car – an entirely different squad car from Anjelica – and driven to the station to make a report.

'Don't you worry,' said Officer Lewinsky, when Grace arrived at the station, wide eyed and shaking. 'It was clearly the other woman's fault.'

'But I was on the wrong side of the road.'

Charmed by Grace's beauty and her accent, everyone agreed that it was an easy mistake to make. If any of the police officers had ever been outside the United States, they were sure that they would have made exactly the same mistake themselves. Grace was given a cup of tea – 'We keep some specially for British felons,' Lewinsky joked – and someone was sent out to get her some cookies. 'Got to keep your blood sugar up at times like these.'

'What's happened to the other woman?' Grace asked. 'Where is she?'

'She's in a cell, ma'am. You've got nothing to fear.'

Grace wasn't sure she had anything to *fear* in the first place. She'd just wanted to know that the other woman wasn't injured.

'She's in the cells,' was all Lewinsky would say.

The cells. It seemed so odd that there would be any need for cells in somewhere as genteel as Little Elbow.

While she waited for her sister to arrive, Grace was allowed to sit in the police superintendent's office. He had the comfiest chair. He also had a CCTV screen that allowed him to see exactly what was going on with the real criminals, down in the cells.

Grace tried not to look. She was sure it wasn't ethical. Those prisoners must have some rights to privacy, even if they were scumbags, as one officer on the desk had referred to them. But in the end she couldn't resist. She was desperate to know who'd run into her.

For now, the screen was showing the men's detainment area. In the first cell, a down-and-out paced like a polar bear in a zoo. Grace felt sorry for him. She'd seen him in the centre of Little Elbow a few times. He'd asked for a smile – politely – and she gave him a dollar. She wondered what he'd done. Probably just looked too untidy on one of the busiest tourist weekends of the year.

In the second cell was a dog. She recognized the dog too. He belonged to one of Choate's neighbours. He was half husky, half escapologist. Called Berkley (pronounced 'Barkley' in the English way). Berkley must have been found sniffing around someone's pedigree bitch again. He'd been brought in to prevent an unwanted litter. The dog too was pacing like a zoo animal.

Grace sipped her tea. By now she was feeling quite recovered from her adventure and was fascinated by the goings-on downstairs. The CCTV cameras flipped from Berkley the dog to the next cell. And Grace saw something that made her splutter tea all over a pile of important documents.

'Danny?'

★　　　★　　　★

Grace rushed out into the lobby and grabbed the first officer she could find.

'You've got to take me down to the cells,' she said urgently.

The officer smiled at her gently. 'Now, Ms Grosvenor, I don't think there's any need for such chest-beating. It's quite clear what happened here. We don't need to take you to the cells. On the contrary, you have been the *victim* of a terrible crime. An illegal immigrant in a stolen car drove straight at you. You're just a little confused.'

'No,' said Grace. 'I'm not in the slightest bit confused. You have to take me down to the cells because I think you're holding my fiancé.'

When he saw her, Danny fell to his knees and reached for Grace's ankles through the bars.

'Grace, is it really you?'

'Oh, Danny!' she cried.

'Get out of here, Ms Grosvenor,' shouted Officer Lewinsky, as he bustled into the corridor. 'That man is behind bars on suspicion of trying to assault you. He turned up at your house this afternoon and tried to kill your sister.'

'Danny?'

'I arrested him myself.'

'Charity told him I was a stalker. She had me arrested. Tell him, Grace. Tell him you know me.'

'I do know this man,' Grace confirmed. 'We were going to get married.'

'As that woman can confirm,' said Danny, pointing beyond Grace to her sister.

Charity had arrived.

There was much paperwork to be done as a result of Grace's revelation. Officer Lewinsky had already set the wheels in motion for Danny to be deported. The immigration services would be picking him up first thing in the morning. Charity knew that Lewinsky wasn't going to be happy to have to explain her 'silly mistake'.

'I thought he was someone else,' she said unconvincingly. 'There's a man that looks very much like Danny who has been impersonating him around London.'

'I see,' said Lewinsky.

Fortunately, at that moment he was called away, giving Charity time to work on her story.

When Lewinsky came back into the room a few moments later, he was smiling.

'Well,' he said, 'I've talked to my colleagues and they've convinced me that the best thing to do is pretend that I never laid eyes on your friend Danny.'

'But what about the immigration people?' Charity asked.

'Oh, there's still plenty to keep them happy here.'

Lewinsky looked towards a CCTV screen that showed a view of the women's cells, where Anjelica sat on a bench with her head in her hands.

In the cells, Grace and Danny had yet to hear Lewinsky's verdict. They continued to hold hands through the bars. Every few seconds, Danny brought Grace's hand up to his mouth and kissed her fingers. There was so much to catch up on.

First and foremost: what had happened to the wedding fund?

'I took a risk,' said Danny. 'I decided to invest in that pyramid scheme selling mops and stuff I told you about.'

'Why didn't you ask me first?'

'I thought you'd say no. Well, more to the point, I thought Charity would say no and you always listen to Charity.'

'Charity isn't always right.'

'Well, she was right about the pyramid scheme. I lost everything we had. Handed the money over in cash and never saw the guy again.'

'You were trying to make more money,' said Grace sympathetically.

'I was an idiot. Charity is definitely right about one thing,' said Danny. 'You were engaged to a loser.'

'Don't say that.'

'It's true.'

'You always did your best.'

'Did I? I'm not so sure. I wanted to marry you the minute I first saw you, Grace. Seeing you sitting in that office, I realized that home for me would always be a place with you in it. I thought I'd died and gone to heaven when you said you would be my wife. And what have I been doing for the last two years? Just fannying around. Making you wait for your big day. I should have been working every hour that God sent. I should have been trying to better myself, getting as much money together as I could so that you could be my wife as soon as possible.'

'Oh, Danny.'

'When I realized that I stood to lose you, I knew I had to come after you. But obviously, I didn't have any money after the homewares scheme failed.'

'You didn't take out a loan, did you?' Grace gasped.

'I sold my signed programme from the 1966 World Cup.'

'But your dad gave you that. You loved that programme.'

'I love you more. I should have sold that bloody programme the day I proposed to you. Not waited until I had to buy a plane ticket to come and find you. Stupid thing is, even after buying the ticket, I've now got enough money for the wedding you always wanted. Except that I don't suppose you want the wedding that you wanted any more. Charity told me all about your fiancé. How he's the richest man in New York and all that. She said that Vera *Wong* woman you were always on about is going to actually come round to the house to measure you up for three dresses to wear on the day.'

Grace looked at her shoes. She decided it probably wasn't appropriate to tell Danny that she had been thinking of using three different dress designers. A different outfit for the wedding morning, afternoon and night.

'So I totally understand that my coming here is too little too late. I didn't chase after you at once because I didn't feel like I was good enough for you. I thought you'd made the best decision. And now I know that my instincts were right.'

'No,' Grace protested. 'That's not true.'

'But you're engaged to that other bloke now. And he sounds like a good one. I can't take you away from the life you could have out here and drag you back to Tooting.'

'This place might as well be Tooting if you're not here with me. I've been so lonely without you, Danny.'

'He's got enough money to give you everything you need.'

'Except love.'

They were interrupted by Officer Lewinsky.

'Ms Grosvenor, your fiancé is here. Your *other* fiancé.'

54

Lewinsky had Choate wait on the bench outside the station. As soon as he saw Grace, he leapt up and wrapped her tightly in his arms.

'Thank goodness you're all right. I got here as soon as I could. I was asleep when I got the call . . .'

'Thank you,' Grace mumbled into his shirt.

'Oh, my darling. Whatever happened?'

'Choate, do you think you could loosen your hold just a little bit?'

He let her go. Grace staggered backwards. 'Wow. That was quite some hug.'

'I just wanted to feel you in my arms. I've been so worried. I thought I might lose you.'

'Well, as you can see, there's hardly a scratch on me.'

'But you've got a bruise on your forehead,' said Choate, touching her with a tenderness that brought tears to Grace's eyes, and not just because it was a sore spot.

'Knocked some sense into me,' said Grace.

'We've got to get you to the hospital right away. Grace, it's no time at all since you last got hit on the head. Who knows what's going on inside your brain? There could be permanent damage.'

'I don't think this new knock is going to leave me any more stupid than I've already been,' said Grace. 'Sit down. I've got to tell you something.'

Choate did as he was told. He plonked himself back on the bench. Grace sat down beside him.

'Choate, I can't marry you. I'm in love with someone else.'

'How did he take it?' Danny asked when Grace came back inside.

'He was . . .' Grace paused. 'He was surprisingly calm about the whole thing.'

Danny nodded. 'It probably hasn't hit him yet.'

Outside, Choate was thinking exactly the same thing. After Grace left, he remained on the bench with his head in his hands for quite some time, waiting for it to hit him. He knew he wasn't going to get off lightly – so far he'd felt strangely unaffected by Grace's departure but there had to be a moment of crisis around the corner. Tears, wailing, recriminations. He would probably run after Grace and humiliate himself by begging her to change her mind. She was the woman of his dreams, after all. He couldn't live without her. And yet . . . It didn't matter to him, did it, that she never picked up a book? Or read a newspaper? There were a hundred other reasons to love her. And he did love her, didn't he?

Whatever love means.

As Choate sat with his head in his hands, he suddenly, strangely, found himself thinking of Prince Charles and Lady Diana Spencer announcing their engagement back in the 1980s. He was slightly too young to have cared all that much when the engagement took place, but he'd watched the footage of that moment a thousand times in news reports surrounding Diana's death and Charles's subsequent remarriage.

Right then he saw them clearly in his mind's eye. Charles and Diana at what was supposed to be one of the happiest moments of their lives. Diana was radiant. But Charles . . . well, he'd just looked trapped, hadn't he?

Now Choate realized why he didn't feel as though the sky was caving in. He wasn't devastated. He was actually *relieved*. He realized in that moment that he had become engaged to Grace Grosvenor in the way that Charles must have ended up with Diana. Grace had seemed a 'suitable' match. She had ticked all the right boxes. She was beautiful. She was charming. And she had no dodgy past that might cause embarrassment. At least none that she could remember. Grace was the modern equivalent of a virgin princess. Well, now she was telling him that wasn't the case at all. Choate wasn't even her first fiancé!

Choate mused on how different Charles and Diana's lives might have been had she announced that she wasn't squeaky clean and Charles found himself free to marry Camilla instead. The differences between the two women were stark. Diana may have been more beautiful, more 'suitable', but it was Camilla who actually understood Charles. They had shared interests. A shared sense of humour. Those things were more important than a pretty face in the long run. Choate remembered a little sadly how unimpressed Grace had been by his jokes and his poetry. She'd had nothing to say about them other than, 'That was nice.' There was no debate when he talked about politics. Choate wanted debate. People thought he was boring because they didn't know how to engage him intellectually. Well, he thought they were boring in return.

It suddenly struck him that the only person who had ever tried to talk about literature or current affairs with Choate Fitzgerald was his ex-girlfriend's *maid*.

Was it really possible that Anjelica Solorzano was the only woman in Little Elbow who read anything other than *Vogue*?

That was a far more depressing thought than losing Grace Grosvenor to Danny Dennis. Whoever he might be. Choate briefly wondered whether he was supposed to track this Dennis man down and punch him. He didn't feel like it.

Officer Lewinsky emerged from the police station.

'Mr Fitzgerald,' he said, 'I feel I should offer you my condolences for the unsettling events of this morning and last night . . .'

'No, really.' Choate held up his hand to stop any further toadying. 'It's quite all right.'

'Well, I'll leave you to it, sir. I have to go down into the cells to interview Ms Solorzano.'

'Solorzano?' Choate automatically corrected the police officer's pronunciation of Anjelica's beautiful surname. 'Anjelica Solorzano is in the cells?'

'She was in the other car.'

'Is she all right?'

'I hope so. She's in big trouble either way. Ms Solorzano shouldn't be here. It seems that her paperwork isn't exactly in order.'

Choate got to his feet immediately. 'I'm coming with you. You're not to start talking to her until she has a lawyer. I'll call my lawyer right now.'

Suddenly, Choate Fitzgerald knew exactly what love meant.

55

Marcella and Simon were up bright and early. Well, not so much bright as just plain early. The Labor Day party had descended into disaster. That prick Ryan or *Bryan* from next door had completely drenched the bonfire and half Marcella's guests at the same time. And yet Marcella was the one who could be facing charges for disturbing the nesting site of some silly little bird that she'd never ever seen. Ridiculous.

It was Simon's idea to tidy up.

'The police are bound to come by first thing,' he told her. 'We had better try and make it look as though we only had a little fire. Minimize the damage.'

So, at the crack of dawn they headed down to the beach to start clearing up.

'Where's that stupid girl Anjelica?' Marcella moaned as they crossed the lawn.

Simon didn't comment. Later, they would have to have a conversation about Marcella's outburst.

'I haven't seen her all morning. This is a complete waste of time,' she added as Simon handed her a bin liner. 'I don't need to minimize my chances of being charged. If the idiots want to arrest me for upsetting a stupid bird, my lawyer will get me off.'

Simon started loading empty beer cans into his black bin liner. 'What about the littering?' he asked.

'It was Labor Day. It's just a few cans.'

Within three minutes, Simon had picked up twenty-seven.

'I can think of better things to do with my life,' Marcella continued to moan, 'than clean up a beach I pay thousands of dollars in taxes to have someone else clean. I hope you know how unhappy I am about this . . .'

Simon nodded. It seemed to him that Marcella spent an awful lot of time being unhappy these days.

'I am going to sue that stupid man next door! Now I know he's got the money to pay damages, I am going for the jugular! Trust me, this time next year his house will be my annexe!'

Simon was prepared for a very long rant. But suddenly Marcella was struck dumb. She was staring at something in the remains of her fire. It was curled at the edges and blackened with soot, but instantly recognizable. A photograph of the Grosvenor sisters.

Marcella reached into the long-cold ashes and pulled the picture out. The fire had been doused before it could completely destroy the sisters' smiling faces. Or Charity's dossier. The little notebook was barely burned at all.

'What have you found?' Simon asked.

'Well, well, well.' Marcella was flicking through the pages of Charity's secret black book. 'I think I have just found gold.'

56

By the time the paperwork to release Danny from the police station had finally been completed, it was almost eight o'clock in the morning. Charity had called Ryan to let him know that there was no need for him to come to the station. Grace was fine. She hadn't, however, let him know that Grace was so fine she had remembered that she was really from Tooting and had subsequently reunited with the working-class-builder fiancé Charity had had arrested. How was she going to explain that?

While Grace's dream was coming true – Danny had finally put himself out for her and proved his love (selling his World Cup programme! It was the equivalent of donating a kidney) – Charity saw her own dream rapidly slipping through her fingers. The pretence was over. It had to be. And how was that going to look?

Ryan may have lied about his own identity and background, but lying to protect yourself from being judged on your wealth was somewhat different from lying with a view to getting your hands on someone else's money. It wasn't going to look good.

The best that Charity could hope for was enough time to prepare a decent case for her subterfuge.

Grace and Danny emerged from the station arm in arm. When she saw Charity, Grace scowled. Danny scowled. And the likelihood that either of them would want to help Charity out by keeping quiet about Tooting seemed very small indeed. Still, Charity had to give it her best shot.

'There's absolutely no reason why either of you should want to help me out,' she began. 'But something happened yesterday afternoon, with Ryan.'

'The gardener,' Grace explained to Danny.

'Something that makes it essential that we don't mention Tooting for a little while longer.'

'Oh no . . .'

'Just do this for me, Grace. You're going back to London tomorrow afternoon. It's not long to keep quiet. Can't you and Danny just say you met while he was doing work on our flat?'

Danny snorted. 'I don't think I owe you anything at all.'

Grace too just shook her head sadly. 'You can't build anything on lies, Charity,' she reminded her sister. 'Sooner or later the real story will come out.'

'I know. Just not yet. Please. Give me a chance to figure out how to do this to give me the best chance to make things between me and Ryan work out.'

Grace looked at Danny, hoping to read a solution in his face. Danny shrugged.

'I'm not going to tell any more lies,' Grace decided.

'Me neither,' said Danny.

Charity's eyes filled with tears.

'Grace,' she pleaded. 'I really think I'm in love with him. I loved him even when I thought he was poor.'

'Then hopefully he'll feel the same way about you,' said Grace.

Ryan was at the front of the house. He put down the rake he was using to spike the lawn and approached the car with a huge grin on his face. Charity looked at her sister one more time.

'Please,' she said. 'I'll never ask you to lie for me again.'

Grace looked straight ahead.

Ryan opened the car door for Grace and was solicitous about her accident.

'It was nothing,' said Grace. 'Lucky I was driving so slowly. And lucky I got to the police station when I did. Ryan, this is my fiancé Danny.'

Danny climbed out from the back of the car. Ryan looked at him in confusion.

'But I thought . . .'

'That I was going to marry Choate. So did I. But the one thing that did happen when I had my little accident was that it brought back my memory. Danny flew out here to see me a couple of days ago and somehow,' she added, with a sidelong look at Charity, 'he ended up in Officer Lewinsky's cells before he could track me down.'

'Well, welcome to America,' said Ryan.

'Awright,' said Danny, shaking his hand.

Charity inwardly winced.

'I'm a builder,' Danny went on to explain.

Charity held her breath.

'I met Grace and Charity when I was doing some work on their house in South Kensington.'

Grace goggled. Charity spluttered. Ryan just listened politely.

'I didn't think she'd ever fall for me,' Danny continued. 'What with her being such a posh bird.'

Grace's face softened. 'Danny . . .' she whispered.

'It's true,' said Danny, touching her face. 'Grace and Charity lived in a completely different world from me. That's why I got frightened about committing to her. And that's why, when she came out to the Hamptons, I thought she was lost to me for ever.'

'Oh, Danny.' Grace cuffed him. 'You're going to make me cry.'

'Don't start,' Danny told her. 'You going to invite me into this house you've been renting or what?'

'I owe you one,' Charity whispered to Danny as he passed her on the way to the front door.

He shrugged it off. But Charity knew it was no small thing that he had done for her. She'd had him thrown in a cell and he'd still found it in himself to be generous towards her. Maybe he was the right man for her sister after all.

Needless to say, having spent three months apart, Grace and Danny weren't particularly interested in socializing with Charity and Ryan that afternoon. So Charity and Ryan had lunch alone on the terrace. It was the perfect opportunity to explain what had really happened – the lottery ticket, their real lives.

'Ryan,' began Charity. 'You know how you felt compelled to hide your real background so that people wouldn't judge you . . .'

He looked at her in anticipation. His face was so kind it seemed perfectly possible that he would hear what she had to say and take it in his stride.

'Well, supposing you found out that . . .'

The doorbell rang.

'I'll get it,' Ryan said. 'Stay there.'

'*Bryan*,' said Marcella. 'How good to see you.'

'Everyone calls me Ryan these days,' Ryan pointed out.

'Sure. Listen, Bryan, I'm so sorry about last night's misunderstanding with the fireworks and the bonfire.'

'It was nothing personal,' said Ryan. 'I hope you'll send me your friends' dry-cleaning bills.'

'Oh, that's quite all right. We were all quite ashamed at the thought of having upset those poor little plovers!' she trilled.

'I saw them first thing,' said Ryan. 'They looked happy enough.'

'They did, didn't they? I saw them too while I was cleaning up around my silly bonfire. Talking of which, you'll never believe what I found. It's the strangest thing.'

Marcella handed over the first of Charity's photographs.

'I can't believe she meant to burn this, can you? What with her mother being dead and all? I mean, it's a Polaroid. It's irreplaceable.'

Ryan took the charred snap and looked at it curiously.

'There are a couple of others,' she said, handing those over too. 'Doesn't that look like they're standing in front of a . . . what does Simon call them . . . a council house? And this. I have no idea how this came to be on my bonfire.'

She reached into her Chloé handbag and brought out a Ziploc bag.

'I'm afraid it got a bit wet when you hosed my party. But I think this must also belong to Charity. It certainly looks like her handwriting.'

Marcella opened up the dossier to its very first page, which was headed, in blurred but very distinguishable handwriting, 'Top bachelor: Bryan Young'.

57

So Charity did end up going back to London the following day after all.

After Marcella's bombshell visit, she had tried to pass the dossier off as a joke, but Ryan wasn't laughing.

'Everything they said about you was true,' Ryan spat. 'You really are a gold-digger. You must have thought you'd hit the mother lode when I told you who I really was.'

'Ryan, I can explain.'

'I don't think you need to. It's all pretty self-explanatory. The names. The pictures. The *scoring system*. You had quite a game plan worked out. Penman. Robin Madden. Choate. I'm surprised I can't find Robert Tiller on your list.'

'It was just a bit of fun,' Charity protested. 'No one was ever meant to see it. Or take it seriously.'

But Charity could see it was hopeless. Ryan was already slipping away from her. The look she had seen in his eyes when he walked in to find Robert Tiller on the floor in the sitting room had returned. Incomprehension. Dismay. Disgust.

'You know, there are still a lot of guys on this list that you haven't crossed off,' he snarled at her. 'I'm sure you'll find a couple of them at the Harbor Club if you hurry. Labor Day weekend is when everybody who's anybody comes into town.'

'Ryan, I don't want to . . . It was all a game. Just a silly game.'

'I think you should fly back to England with your sister.'

'But Ryan, what about the things you said?'

'I thought I was saying them to a different kind of girl. Goodbye.'

He slammed his way out of the house and raced away in his truck. He was gone.

Charity snatched up the book and tried to rip it apart with her bare hands. But just as the flames had hardly touched it, her efforts to rip the book in half were in vain. The stiff leather-look cover hardly yielded at all.

In the end she threw it down on to the bed and threw herself after it. Her careful planning had cost her the ultimate prize.

It would have been no consolation to Charity to know that Marcella Hunter's morning wasn't turning out very much better. When she returned from her mission to blow Charity's life apart, Simon did not want to share in her joy. Instead he called her 'petty'.

'Marcella,' he continued, 'you have been, in your own special way, a very good friend to me. When I didn't have anywhere to stay, you generously offered me your home, but the idea that you've only been so generous because you thought that it might in some way be your entrée into British society is repulsive to me. I am not just a man with fancy ancestors. I'm a man who has emotions and feelings like any other. Quality isn't conferred by birth. What's important is how you use your privileges. In my opinion, Marcella, you've abused your privileges and it makes me feel sick that I in some way encouraged you.'

Marcella was looking green.

'It doesn't matter who was born where and of whom. We're not dogs. We're not worth more just because we have a pedigree. A cat can look at a queen. A cat can marry a queen if he feels like it!'

'Don't get carried away,' said Marcella.

'I'm not going to be held back by who I am or am not a moment longer. Marcella, I have nothing. Nothing at all. But I have been in love with you since the minute I met you.'

'Why haven't you told me this before?'

'Because I didn't think you would be interested. It's become clear that all you worry about is what people have and where they come from. I may come from the right place but I certainly don't have the right amount of money.'

'You don't?'

'No, I don't. I have nothing. Marcella, if I want to visit my family seat, I have to pay seven pounds fifty to the National Trust like everybody else . . .'

Marcella sat down heavily.

'Anyway, I know now that wishing that you and I could be together is still hopeless, but for a totally different reason. The way you treated Anjelica last night was hideous. Watching you try to break up Grace Grosvenor and Choate Fitzgerald chilled me to the bone. And now Charity and that gardening chap. The idea that you could be so jealous of another woman's happiness . . . Your behaviour cured me of my pathetic, hopeless crush.'

Marcella's mouth dropped open.

'So, I'm leaving. Tonight I'm staying with Stephanie Blank. Tomorrow afternoon I'm catching a plane back to Edinburgh. I'm going to get myself a job. Hopefully I'll be able to make myself a life I can be proud of.'

'Simon . . .' Marcella choked out his name. 'How can you go?'

'How can I stay?'

With that, Simon turned and walked from the room, leaving Marcella looking stunned on the sofa. She sat there, mouth slightly open, eyes glazed for a good five minutes as she ran over the conversation that had just passed in her head. Had Simon really just told her that he loved her? She'd always assumed that he thought of her as nothing more than a friend. His flirtatiousness had never been directed at her. Had she wanted it to be? Or had she just pushed the notion that she might have feelings from him out of her head because it just seemed so . . . ridiculous?

Was it ridiculous?

Marcella walked into the kitchen to pour herself a glass of water. Stuck to the fridge door with a smiley-face magnet was a picture taken at her birthday party, right back at the beginning of the summer. She and Simon were standing side by side in the gazebo. They looked very happy. The picture had been taken about half an hour before the Grosvenor sisters arrived.

Unconsciously, Marcella reached for the photograph and traced Simon's jawline with her finger.

It had been so wonderful to have Simon around. Marcella remembered him serenading her that night at the Gatsby party. She hadn't really heard it properly because she was too busy stalking the Grosvenor girls, watching everyone's reaction, wondering whether she was still the fairest of them all. And totally missing the point that to Simon she would always be the fairest.

'Simon!' Marcella hollered up the stairs.

'Don't worry,' he hollered back. 'I'm not taking any of your silver.'

Marcella climbed the stairs two at a time to arrive slightly breathless in the doorway of Simon's room.

'I don't want you to go,' she said.

'I won't bitch about you to Stephanie, if that's what you're worried about.'

Marcella swallowed her hurt. 'That's not what I'm worried

about,' she said. 'I'm worried that I don't want you to go at all. I don't want you to leave my house tonight and I certainly don't want you to go back to Scotland tomorrow. Simon, I'm worried I'll never see you again!'

And with that she started sobbing.

'Hey.' Simon took both of Marcella's hands and kissed them.

'You don't want to stay here with me, do you? You probably don't even want to be my friend any more.'

'I've never wanted to be your friend. Only your lover.'

'Then let's give in to our urges.'

'Do you have them too?'

'Definitely.'

Simon stood up so that they were nose to nose. He was going to kiss her.

Then the doorbell rang.

It was Officer Lewinsky.

'I need you to come to the station, Miss Hunter.'

'Great. Can I have my maid back now?'

'No,' said Officer Lewinsky. 'Miss Marcella Hunter, I'm afraid I have no choice but to charge you under Section Eight of the Federal Immigration and Nationality Act. You have been knowingly employing an illegal immigrant.'

58

October, London

October in England and already it seemed as though winter was kicking in. A nondescript summer was drifting greyly into another damp, dull autumn. Charity leaned her head against the cool glass of the bus window and watched South London pass by like a black-and-white film. She was on her way home from work. The one small piece of luck she'd had since returning to London was that her old boss had called to say that the Royal Park Hotel was hiring again. Except that it wasn't like the Royal Park used to be. Charity was back but Peggy was gone.

'She went at the beginning of September,' said Ronnie. 'It was funny how it happened. One afternoon she just appeared in reception surrounding by all her cases and asked for someone to find her a cab to Heathrow.'

'She went home,' said Charity.

'Thank God,' said Ronnie. The penthouse was redecorated and modernized within a week.

The summer seemed so long ago. For Grace, it was as if the three months in America hadn't happened at all. Within days of getting back to London, it was as though she had never been away. She and Danny quickly resolved their differences. For a couple of weeks, he even stayed away from the pub unless Grace was going to be there too.

Then Grace was back at her wedding albums, adding new pictures every day. But they were different pictures from the ones she'd chosen before. The extravagant Vera Wang dresses were replaced by gowns by less expensive designers. Grace wanted to be married more quickly now.

In fact, she couldn't wait a moment longer. That October evening, Charity got home from work to hear Grace say, 'We're getting married this Saturday. We're doing it at the register office and I'm going to wear this.'

She produced a bag from Oasis.

'It's not the wedding that counts. It's the marriage.'

Danny grinned.

'We'll have your dream day when we renew our vows after twenty-five years,' he assured Grace. 'You'll be there, won't you, Charity? To be one of our witnesses?'

How could she refuse? She was still painfully aware that it was a miracle that Danny was even speaking to her after his spell in the Little Elbow police station.

'I'll be there,' she promised.

The following Saturday, the weather managed to cheer up for just long enough for the bridal party to drive to the register office with the top on the Golf down.

Grace looked simply beautiful in the dress that cost eighty rather than eight hundred pounds. Danny's face shone with his love for her.

Afterwards, they drove to their mother's grave. Grace placed her bridal bouquet upon the headstone.

'I may not have married a millionaire, Charity, but I feel as if I have done.'

Charity nodded.

Then Grace and Danny left for their honeymoon. Seven

nights in his granddad's static caravan in Norfolk. It rained all week.

After their honeymoon, Grace and Danny got themselves a new flat, leaving Charity alone in the hovel above the greasy spoon – the only thing to look forward to was resitting the biology A-level that had kept her out of university that year.

A couple of weeks later, on a Saturday morning. Charity was sleeping in. She'd worked a late shift at the hotel the previous night and it had been a tough one. With Peggy gone and the penthouse available for hire, the clientele at the Royal Park had been getting more glitzy. That week, it was home to a couple of Premiership footballers. They needed a lot of room service. And they wanted the sheets changed after every new fan.

So Charity wasn't too happy when the doorbell rang at eight o'clock in the morning. She wasn't expecting anybody, so she didn't even bother getting up the first time. Anyone trying to flog her a new cable package would soon give up and move on. But then the doorbell rang again.

Charity poked her head out of her bedroom window to see whether it was worth walking down the stairs. The button on the entryphone that let you buzz someone in from upstairs was long since broken.

'Who is it?' she called down. She could see nothing.

Except for an enormous bouquet of roses.

59

Ryan had just caught a cab in from Heathrow, having taken the red-eye from New York, with the beautiful flowers grown in the Rose House greenhouse as his hand luggage.

'Surprise,' he said. But there was more to come.

'You brought me roses,' breathed Charity.

'I'm just the courier,' Ryan explained. 'These are from your friend from the Royal Park Hotel penthouse.'

'Peggy?'

'My *Great-auntie* Peggy,' he said. 'Peggy Young.'

The Rose House had a new resident. Peggy Young arrived in Little Elbow less than a week after the Grosvenor sisters' departure. Ryan had been writing to his great-aunt for months, begging her to come and see what he had made of the garden she had once cared so much for. He hadn't expected his entreaties to work and in truth they hadn't. After all, Peggy had never met her great-nephew. It was Charity's sea-view postcard which finally persuaded Peggy to go home.

'I found myself looking out over Hyde Park one morning, with a postcard of Long Island in my hand, and suddenly my hotel room just wasn't enough any more.'

So Peggy moved out of the hotel and flew back to the States. Within forty-eight hours of making her mind up, she was standing in Ryan's rose garden.

'Bryan,' she said. 'What is this rose called?'

'I'm Ryan,' he reminded her. 'And that rose is a hybrid tea rose called Charity.'

Peggy smiled. 'Let's talk about Charity, shall we?' she began.

Ryan took a lot of persuading that he shouldn't just forget about Charity and move on. The idea that Charity and her sister had come out to the Hamptons armed with a plan to track him down repulsed him. Peggy agreed it didn't look good. But the Charity she knew wasn't that calculating. She remembered a girl who had worked hard, who was kind and who was devoted to her younger sister. That's why, when Charity came up with the idea of a summer abroad, Peggy had secretly asked Mal Deuble to persuade Ryan to put the Rose House on the rental market. Ryan had no idea that eight thousand of the ten thousand dollars' rent per month he received came from his great-aunt and not from his tenants.

'Charity didn't have the advantages we had. I don't think you can blame her for using what she does have to try to make it in life. She is a very pretty girl, isn't she?' Peggy cast a sidelong glance at her great-nephew. His brow wrinkled in thought. Peggy knew what he was thinking and smiled.

And now here he was, in London.

'You were right to be angry,' said Charity as they talked over the end of Charity's time in Little Elbow. 'I did hold back from you when I thought you were just the gardener. I was looking for a meal ticket, not love. I didn't think love was so important.

'I guess I was just tired of scraping by, having to wait on people like Marcella Hunter. Acting like she's better than me because she was born into a different family. It just didn't seem fair, so lying to get a piece of her life didn't seem such a moral problem. But to think what I was prepared to do . . . I nearly screwed things up for Grace too.'

'But she's happy now. With Danny.'

'She is. I've gone over and over that last day in Little Elbow,' Charity told Ryan then. 'Wondering if there was anything I could have said to stop you turning away from me. Your face – so closed towards me. I felt like the sun would never shine again. I thought I'd blown it for ever. I never thought I'd see you again. I'm so sorry.'

'I'm sorry too. I was so judgemental. You didn't know me when you wrote that list. You fell for the real me. You did fall for the real me, didn't you?'

'Right down to your green fingers,' said Charity. 'I wasn't lying to you about that.'

'Will you come back to the States with me?' Ryan asked.

'Do you really want me to?'

He smiled. 'I need an under-gardener. Plus, you're invited to a wedding.'

EPILOGUE

For the residents of Little Elbow, the following summer truly was a summer of love. Marcella and Charity had been exactly right about Choate Fitzgerald. The man *was* ripe. He followed Anjelica back to her home town in Guatemala and married her there. It was quick and quiet. They were blissful.

Marcella Hunter didn't throw one of her legendary birthday parties that year. Not that she missed the 'event of the season'. She spent her birthday in Scotland. At Gretna Green. With Simon.

The bride and groom honeymooned in the Highlands, where, in her new capacity as Marcella Hunter McDonnough, Marcella presented the trophy for caber-tossing at a Highland Games meeting in the grounds of Simon's former family home. The caretaker waived their seven pounds fifty fee to look at the portraits of Simon's ancestors.

Marcella could not have been luckier than to have married Simon. All through the hell of her facing charges for employing an illegal immigrant, Simon had stuck by her. He had continued to stick by her when her grandfather flew in from his golf-course home in Florida and disinherited her on the spot for being a disgrace to the Hunter name.

Marcella's grandfather Edgar was deeply disappointed to find that his granddaughter was facing jail on such awful charges. Especially since he himself had campaigned so hard for the rights of immigrant workers. By flaunting the law,

Marcella was adding to the problem. If so many people continued to work under the radar, then the government would never admit that the United States needed a different kind of immigration policy to cope with employment demand and protect the people who filled it.

'What do you expect me to do?' Marcella asked when Edgar announced that from now on she would have nothing she hadn't earned.

'You can do Anjelica's job.'

'What? Clean up after myself?'

'No,' he said. 'You can clean up after me. I think I'm going to stay in Little Elbow for a while.'

The disinheritance wasn't the only bombshell that Edgar dropped on Marcella's world. While she ranted about being too highly born to do her own housework, Edgar finally told Marcella who her father was. And he wasn't, as Marcella's mother had told her, the dashing young heir who died in a plane accident before he knew Marcella had been conceived.

'He was an itinerant farm worker from Tennessee. He took a thousand dollars to get out of your mother's life before you were born.'

Luckily, breeding didn't matter to Simon at all.

It was while persuading Ryan to give Charity a second chance that Peggy was given a second chance of her own. When she first saw him walking along the beach, she thought she was hallucinating. It wasn't possible. It couldn't be him. Surely he must be dead by now.

But it was him. Edgar Hunter. The man she had first come to know when he was just the gardener at the house next door, the son of the couple who lived in what was now Marcella's guest house but was at that time the staff quarters.

'Marcella's grandfather was just the gardener?' asked Ryan.

'Yes. Back then the house was owned by the Stein family. The Hunters were just the help. Fresh off the boat. But I didn't care about that. I was in love with him. It was just around the end of the Second World War. You have to understand that terrible as it was, that war ushered in plenty of positive change for women of my generation. I was the only daughter of an extremely wealthy family. I had everything I ever wanted except my independence. But when the war came, even my father could not stop me from doing my bit. I got myself a job. And I got out of the house. Meanwhile Edgar was in France and, after that, on peacekeeping duties in Germany.

'When he returned, I thought that things had changed in his absence. I still loved him but he was no longer the gardening boy and I was no longer the cloistered heiress. I'd been out in the world. I'd tasted freedom and I was going to hang on to it. I told my parents about our secret affair. Edgar came to ask for my hand. My father chased him out of the house with a rifle.

'And the very next day Daddy arranged for my mother and me to take an extended vacation in California. Only it wasn't presented to me as a vacation. He told me that my mother was ill and I had to go with her to Los Angeles where the only doctor who might cure her was based.

'Edgar didn't know where I was. He didn't write letters. I didn't hear anything from any of my old friends. Until a month later, when my father wrote to tell me that Edgar had taken up with another girl. She was pregnant, they were getting married and moving down to Florida.'

'That must have been hard.'

'Not half so hard as waking up in Little Elbow one morning

nearly thirty years later to find that Edgar had made his fortune and bought the house he used to work in. The house next door to ours. I couldn't stand to see him so happy there with his family, while I was all alone, so I left town for Europe before he moved in. But I never forgot him.'

And neither had Edgar forgotten her.

Just sixty years after they had first planned to marry, Edgar Hunter and Peggy Young finally walked up the aisle. Charity was there to see it happen. And when Peggy threw the bouquet of roses grown by her great-nephew from the plant that Charity had chosen, Charity was the girl who caught it.